HAIL TO THE CHIEF

"Make way for the president!"

The crowd stopped their conversations as President Mitchell Lawrence entered the tent, his hand raised in a jovial greeting, the sweet-faced First Lady on his other arm. I held my breath, trying not to be star-struck and only partially succeeding. They were shorter in person, but wasn't that what everybody said about celebrities? It was like watching wax figures walk into the room. They beelined for Senator Tauber, and I spun around to gape at their son.

"You're . . ."

He extended a hand and I shook numbly. "Andy Lawrence. Nice to finally meet you, *Kate Quinn*." Before I could close my slack jaw, he shot me a wink and leaned in to whisper. "We'd better not talk too long. They're already staring."

He was right. As he strolled off whistling something that sounded suspiciously like "Hail to the Chief," I saw eyes all over the room travel between us. Us—the children of the two men competing for the office of President of the United States, chatting away. At a *bar*.

I feverishly scanned the crowd for Meg and the senator. They were deep in conversation with two couples I didn't know, backs turned to the president.

When I brought the sodas back to our table, Gracie grinned. "That boy likes you."

"I don't think so," I muttered, hesitating by my chair.

OTHER BOOKS YOU MAY ENJOY

THE
WRONG SIDE
OF RIGHT

Jenn Marie Thorne

speak

SPEAK
An imprint of Penguin Random House LLC
375 Hudson Street
New York, New York 10014

First published in the United States of America by Dial Books,
an imprint of Penguin Group (USA) LLC, 2015
Published by Speak, an imprint of Penguin Random House LLC, 2016

THE LIBRARY OF CONGRESS HAS CATALOGED THE DIAL BOOKS EDITION AS FOLLOWS:
Thorne, Jenn Marie.
The wrong side of right / by Jenn Marie Thorne.
pages cm
Summary: After her mother dies, sixteen-year-old Kate Quinn meets the father she did not
know she had, joins his presidential campaign, falls for a rebellious boy, and when what she
truly believes flies in the face of the campaign's talking points, Kate must decide what is best.
ISBN 978-0-8037-4057-0 (hardcover)
[1. Politics, Practical—Fiction. 2. Presidential candidates—Fiction. 3. Elections—Fiction.
4. Fathers and daughters—Fiction. 5. Love—Fiction.] I. Title.
PZ7.1.T48Wr 2015
[Fic}—dc23   2014028077

Speak ISBN 9780147509840

Printed in the United States of America

1 3 5 7 9 10 8 6 4 2

To all of my parents

1

Tuesday, June 10

The Day the News Broke

147 DAYS UNTIL THE GENERAL ELECTION

The moment my horrible yearbook photo first appeared on millions of televisions, sending jaws dropping, phones ringing, and joggers tumbling off their treadmills across America, I was in the middle of my AP US history final.

The test room was silent, apart from the incessant *click click click* of the overhead clock, until the buzzer sounded and we rushed to hand off our best efforts and flee the building in relief. It was the last scheduled exam of the year, nothing waiting for us outside these halls but summer. Two seniors skipped past me along the linoleum. Even I felt myself smiling, really smiling, not just faking it.

"What did you think?" Lily Hornsby caught up behind me, more dazed than giddy. She'd been my assigned study partner in US history, which was a lucky break—she'd turned out to be one of the friendliest people in my new school.

"Mostly okay." At her wince, I backtracked. "What was with that Grover Cleveland question? We didn't go over that stuff at all!"

"I know, right?" She sighed. "At least it's done. So what are you up to this summer?"

Good question. I'd been so focused on schoolwork all year

that I hadn't thought ahead to the break. I should have been applying for summer jobs, pre-college programs, whatever it was that normal people did between junior and senior year. But until today, I'd been at my mental limit just studying for tests, thinking forward one day and then the next. Any further than that and the haze set in again, heavy and thick with sadness.

"I'm not sure yet," I admitted.

We swung through the front doors, met by a blinding blue sky and a solid wall of Low Country humidity, plus the now familiar marsh smell that hugged my school on hot days. It was summer, all right. I needed to find a way to fill it.

"Whoa." Lily pointed at the parking lot. "What's up with that?"

Some sort of news event had sprung up in front of the school—three vans with satellite dishes on top, parked in a lazy triangle next to what looked like live reports being filmed.

Even in daylight, even on the opposite coast, the scene felt familiar. I wrapped my arms around myself, my skin prickling with dread.

"You all right?" Lily touched my shoulder.

"Yeah." I forced myself to turn, glad that I'd parked on a side street and wouldn't have to walk through that mess. "I just hope nobody's hurt."

"It's probably a teachers' strike." Lily shrugged, but I felt her glance at me a second later. She knew about my mom, everyone did, which made her careful, sometimes painfully so. I forced a smile, embarrassed that I'd let myself get spooked.

A group of Lily's friends was waiting for her on the corner. I gave an awkward wave and started to duck away, but Lily stopped me.

"A bunch of us are gonna go celebrate at Mario's tonight," she said, nodding in the direction of the James Island pizza place that was a magnet for most of my high school. "Like eight o'clock? You should totally come."

She grinned and hurried away before I could conjure one of my usual excuses. One of her friends, a tall kid from my physics class, raised his hand in greeting and I called out to the back of Lily's head, "Okay!"

This is fine, I pep-talked myself, stepping into the shade of ivy-strung trees. *I'll go out. Be normal.* Or at least learn to imitate it better.

Just as I got to my old Buick, my cell phone buzzed.

My uncle Barry cut me off mid-greeting.

"Kate, honey, you need to get home right away."

His voice was fake calm. Panicked. My feet planted themselves into the ground, my hand starting to tremble. "What's going on?"

"I'll tell you when you get here, but you gotta come straight home, and listen, honey, this is important. Don't talk to any of the reporters. Okay?"

I glanced behind me, barely able to make out the crowd in the parking lot from here. "Okay. I'm on my way."

I drove with both clammy hands clutching the wheel. The music on the radio sounded harsh, like the soundtrack to a horror movie, so I shut it off and listened to my short, sharp breaths and thudding heart.

Almost a year ago, I'd gotten a call just like this one. I was coming out of a movie theater with a bunch of friends, turning my phone on, laughing about how bad the movie was. I answered, even though I didn't recognize the number. It was Marta, my mom's best friend. Her voice was controlled too, like Barry's, like she was fighting to keep a scream at bay.

"You need to come home, Kate," she'd said. "Something's happened."

It wasn't until I'd gotten to my house that fear set in, icy and creeping, frost on a field. Our LA bungalow was surrounded by local news crews, there to report my mother's death.

Community hero, founder of the Cocina de Los Angeles Food Bank, dead at age thirty-five.

"It was instant," Marta had told me, safe inside the living room and wrapped in a blanket like I was the one who'd been pulled from a car wreck. "She didn't feel any pain."

As if anybody could know that.

Marta had a quiet word with the news crews and they packed up and left. She stayed the night and I half slept for seventeen hours and when I woke up, my mom was still dead, but her brother, Barry, and his wife, Tess, had arrived.

They were nice people whom I'd met a few times before. They had a grown son and a landscaping business in James Island, South Carolina. They were all I had in the way of family—no grandparents, no father, not even his name, and suddenly no mother. They were willing to take me.

And now, nearly a year later, they were calling me, telling me to come home, to my new home, where this couldn't be happening, couldn't possibly be happening to us again.

I pulled around our corner to find a gridlocked freeway where our house should be. My foot hit the brake. There were news vans in neighboring driveways and rows of cars penning in the tidy hedges all along the usually sleepy street. I recognized only a couple of the bumper stickers and window decals—parents, here to pick up their kids from the day care center Tess operated from our house.

An agitated blonde came down the sidewalk, balancing her toddler on one hip while struggling to shove his cluttered bag over her shoulder. I rolled down my window and drifted closer to her SUV.

"Mrs. Hanby!"

Her taut face dropped when she saw me. She let her son into the car, glaring at the news vans. "You need to get in there fast, hon. They just keep coming—I barely managed to get Jonah out!"

Behind the glass of the backseat, Jonah blinked at me, saucer-eyed. I probably looked just like him. I swallowed, had to ask.

"Is it my aunt? Is Tess okay?"

"Oh sweetie. You haven't seen the news." Mrs. Hanby came around to give my arm a squeeze, her eyes squinting with pity. "She's fine, but you need to go on home now and find out for yourself."

She tapped my car twice, like she was spurring a horse and weirdly, it worked. I drove, holding my breath, past two gleaming black Town Cars, past my uncle's truck with the big sign on it advertising "Quinn Yards," past the first news van, dimly registering the letters *CNN* emblazoned on it. There weren't any cars in the driveway. But there were people—hordes of them, masses, carrying cell phones, microphones, cameras.

I turned in slowly, hoping they'd move out of the way, praying I wouldn't have to call attention to myself by laying on the horn.

I didn't need to. They parted, all right. They practically ran, flanking my car like the waves of the Red Sea before falling in behind me. I shut off the engine and heard an unnatural hush settle around the Buick. A camera was pressed against the passenger window. Its red light was on.

I opened my door and the tide rushed in. They were a crash of voices, a wall of faces, something out of a zombie movie.

"Excuse me," I cried, trying to politely shove a cameraman so I could shut my car door. The crowd pressed closer, howling. I couldn't make out words until a petite brunette with a peacock-branded microphone scrambled into my path and asked:

"When did you first learn that Senator Cooper was your father?"

"What?"

The words weren't connecting. They were nonsense words. Magnetic poetry.

I tried to push forward, but there were hands, microphones blocking me at every angle. Then there came a ripple in the wall and a large bald black man walked through, wrapped one arm around me, and ushered me past the crowd, onto the porch, and through my front door, saying, "You're all right, kid, you're all right."

Aunt Tess was first to greet me. I coughed a sob and rushed to hug her, but she gently held me back.

"Kate," she said, in an unnaturally singsong tone. "You have a visitor."

And then, through the door to the living room, I saw him.

He was slowly rising from my uncle's battered armchair, his hand shaking as he loosened a red silk tie. He stared at me, eyes wide, like I was a ghost, like I was covered in blood or wielding a gun, like I was terrifying.

I knew exactly who he was. Everybody in the country did, especially juniors who'd just finished their AP US history exams.

Senator Mark Cooper. Republican, Massachusetts.

Candidate—President of the United States of America.

2

He took two steps and stopped, and as he froze, everyone else did too, watching the space between us. And by everyone, I mean the everyone-in-the-world who was in my tiny living room.

Two men in suits flanked the senator from a deferential distance. The shorter man beamed at me like a happy leprechaun, eyes crinkling and bald head shining. The other scowled down at his phone, his dark hair and heavy brow giving him the hooded look of a bird of prey. A sharply dressed redhead was leaning against the love seat, lips parted as though she was dying to say something but didn't dare. I glanced over my shoulder, spotting my huge rescuer blocking the front door. His stance was familiar from action movies. Security. *Secret Service?* My aunt stared up at him in polite terror, as if it might be against the rules to walk away. And just as I was wondering where my uncle was, he swung through the kitchen door with a glass of iced tea.

"Here you go, sir." Uncle Barry held out the drink with his eyes fixed on the carpet. He looked like a servant in his own home, but who could blame him? He was offering a beverage to the man in line for the most powerful position in the world. For his part, Senator Cooper looked less and less terrified, more and more weary the longer he stood there. Then he broke, taking the glass from my uncle with a thank-you, and the words I'd heard outside echoed faintly in my head, finally forming a coherent sentence. *Him. Father. He is my . . .*

His eyes returned to mine, freezing me to the spot. He extended his hand with a smile that didn't reach them. "I'm Mark Cooper," he said, sounding exactly, freakishly like his campaign ad.

"I'm Kate." I shook. "Kate Quinn." He looked so lost that I said what he was supposed to say. "It's very nice to meet you."

It was as though I'd put down a loaded gun. The whole room let out its breath in one big huff.

But then Senator Cooper opened his mouth—and closed it. Downed the tea and handed the glass to my uncle, who was sweating through his Gamecocks T-shirt. The room was too quiet. I didn't know how to fill the silence.

The red-haired woman pulled away from the love seat, smoothed her sweater set, and peered at me with something like sympathy. "Kate, I'm sure you've got a lot of questions, and the truth is—we do too."

The senator turned away, his suit wrinkling as his shoulders collapsed. "There's no question, Nancy. I mean, come on. *Look* at her."

Redhead Nancy's smile faltered, her eyes flicking back to him. "Sir, we need to be sure. This is too big a—"

"I know what this is." He stopped moving. Just stood there, staring at the ground.

Bird of Prey peered down at Leprechaun, and by some

silent agreement, Leprechaun stepped forward. "Should we go ahead?"

Go ahead with what?

At the senator's weary nod, he disappeared through the swinging door.

Bird of Prey scanned the room. When his eyes met mine, they stayed there. There was something clinical in his stare, like he was adding up my face, my clothes, my expression. His phone buzzed. He lifted it without breaking eye contact, then barked a greeting, *"Webb,"* and turned to follow the small man into the kitchen.

I had to stop myself from racing after them, dragging them back. Instead of this tableau settling into place, I felt it spinning off, disintegrating like I was on a carnival ride. I glanced, desperate, at my aunt and uncle, but they were united in paralysis.

"I'm sorry—" I had to say something. "What is this? What's going on?"

The men's voices in the back room got louder, one-sided conversations into cell phones. Yelling about me? About this famous man, settling into my uncle's chair with his head in his hands?

I drew in a breath, but my voice still came out shaky. "Are you my father?"

His head shot up, eyes alert and very blue. Blue like mine. "I think I am."

The defeat in his voice muffled any thrill I might have felt from those words.

Nancy let out a cocktail-party laugh and started rubbing

my back like she was trying to get dirt off of it. "Let's just make sure, sir."

As if on cue, a woman in scrubs came in from the kitchen, looking at least as dazed as me, holding a medical bag, rubber gloves, a syringe.

Nancy pressed past me. "Did you sign?"

The woman nodded.

"And you understand that means you cannot speak to *anyone*, not your husband . . ."

"I understand." The woman turned to me and visibly softened. "Kate, is it?"

I nodded, numb.

"We're gonna draw some blood. Not a whole lot."

I perched on the sofa and let her tie a band around my arm, trying not to wince at the pinch of the needle in front of all these strangers.

"For a paternity test?" I asked, and everyone ignored me.

The senator waved one hand in my general direction, the other raking through his thick hair. "This is a foregone conclusion. We need an action plan. Where's Elliott?"

Nancy motioned to the kitchen with a dramatic sigh and the senator rose from the armchair and strode from the room. As soon as he was out of sight, my body went pins and needles in one big rush, and not just from the blood that the nurse, doctor, whoever she was, was tamping down with a cotton ball.

"This isn't possible," I said. My aunt and uncle shook their heads, mouths agape in helpless agreement. "I don't understand how this is possible."

Nancy crouched in front of me, her skirt stretching across her knees.

"Seventeen years ago, your mom worked on a state senate campaign for Senator Cooper. That's how they met . . . ?"

She paused, head cocked, as though she were hoping I'd continue the story myself.

"A . . . campaign?" I shook my head, starting to squirm with pretty, red-haired Nancy squinting at me, with the voices of the press roaring low outside the front windows. "I'm sorry—that's not right. My mom *hated* politics. It's not her, there's some confusion, or . . ."

Nancy pressed her lips together, rocking onto her heels. "So you didn't know. She never told you who your dad was."

I opened my mouth but no sound came out, just this hiss like white noise. I swallowed hard. "No."

"There might have been a reason for that, Kate." Her voice was bedtime-story soft. "You see . . ." She glanced at the door to the kitchen before continuing. "Senator Cooper was married at the time."

Married. For one hazy second, I thought she meant to my mother. But why would she keep that from . . . ?

Oh.

"No." I clamped my hand over my mouth, shocked by the sound I'd made, the sound my brain was making, and stood up, away from her, away from this. "That's not my mom. It isn't possible—there's been some misunderstanding."

My uncle had his head bowed.

"That is not my mother." I let out a shrill laugh. "Barry, tell—"

Tess sighed. "Tell her. Or I will."

My uncle stepped forward, hands clenched in his pockets and shoulders stuck in a shrug. "Your mom did work on that campaign, Kate, when she was in college, in Massachusetts. I remember our folks were so glad she was helping the Republicans. And then one day she quit, just like that. Said she was going out to California, didn't tell us a thing else. We lost touch with her for a couple months and then she told us she was pregnant with you. We asked and asked, but we never could get out of her who the daddy was."

Neither could I. She'd told me so much about her childhood in the South, about going off to college. How she fell in love with California. But never why she'd moved there. And never, ever, would she speak a word about my father. Deep down, I'd always assumed he was dead, that one day she'd admit it to me. She was so moral, so focused on how she treated others, on the impact she made in the world. The thought had never for a second crossed my mind that my father might be out there. That my mother would have ever been "the other woman." She'd always said she'd tell me one day, when she felt I was ready. But that day never came.

I don't know what happened around me or how much time passed, but the next thing I noticed was Nancy taking a call and the senator and his entourage heading for the front door.

"We'll have a statement for you tomorrow, Tom . . ." Nancy followed the group as if pulled by the tide, phone still pressed to her ear. "That's all I can tell you, and you're lucky I even answered on a day like this. My first call tomorrow. Yes."

Bird of Prey was murmuring into the senator's ear, just

loud enough for me to make out. "Don't say a thing. Look confident. This is *great* news. *Non*-news. A wave, a smile, nothing guilty, and don't engage."

The nice bodyguard had his hand on the front doorknob.

"Wait!" Everyone turned to look at me. "You're leaving?"

And then, it cracked. All the numbness, the strangeness, the sheer lunacy of this day shattered like a frozen pipe, and out came the waterworks.

I covered my face with my hands. I was not supposed to be bawling. Not in front of these strangers, not rocking back and forth, saying, "I don't understand this, I don't . . ."

And then an arm was around me, a silk tie brushing against my cheek. *Not Uncle*, went my brain. I blinked up into the senator's face. He wasn't looking at me, just holding me up, patting me like I was a baby, saying, "Shhh . . . there, there. We'll be back tomorrow, and we'll figure this thing out."

He smelled like cedar. Was this what fathers smelled like?

Across the room, Leprechaun shot me a cheery thumbs-up, and I was so confused by the gesture that I stopped crying long enough for all of them to get out the door.

"Well!" Barry clapped his hands. "Pasta for dinner?"

3

Wednesday, June 11
This Is Actually Happening
146 DAYS UNTIL THE GENERAL ELECTION

I woke with the usual litany of realizations.

I'm awake.

I'm in South Carolina.

My mom is dead.

But now, a new one—an *oh yeah* that made me bolt upright, nearly capsizing my twin mattress into the frame.

My father. I have a father. Maybe. Probably. Oh my God.

Outside my window, I could hear voices, the whirring of generators. And something else—a piped-in announcement, muffled by bad speakers.

I pulled back the yellowed lace curtains. The police were here. They'd put a partial blockade around our house, but the press still lined the block, waiting. For me.

I closed the curtain with a sigh. At least with the cops here, no one could climb the oak tree in the side yard to get a shot of me in the bathroom.

The light was faint outside. Streetlamps still lit. I turned on my ancient flip phone. 6:07 A.M. and wow—twenty-seven missed calls and texts. Spotting Lily's number, I flinched, remembering that I'd blown off last night's invitation, but her text didn't even mention it. "Saw the news! Call me if you need ANYTHING."

Most of the other texts were from my best friend Penny back in California, increasing in freakedoutedness from "Kate? Anything you care to tell me?" to "Turn your phone on I'm DYYYYYING" to a simple, elegant "ARGGGGGHHH-DEADcallme."

My fingers ached to push that call button and wake her up immediately, if only to hear her reassuringly brassy voice on the other end of the line. But no—not now. Later. When I knew what on earth to say.

In the dingy light of the bathroom, I brushed my teeth, trying to conjure the senator's face while analyzing my own. His eyes—those were probably the closest match. My mother's were hazel, long and narrow like a cat's, while mine were blue and round. I'd inherited Mom's tiny stature, that was for sure, what nice people called "petite," my doctor called five-two, and Penny called "at least a quarter hobbit."

My mouth wasn't quite Mom's, though. My hair was dirt brown where hers was sunset auburn. My nose was smaller, stubbier. Mom used to call it a ski-jump nose. When I was little, she would slide her finger down its bridge, and when it hit air, she'd let out a yodel, like an out-of-control skier.

My vision blurred. I swiped at my eyes and blinked hard to refocus, on the faucet, the cracked grout, anything but Mom. Thinking about her sent my brain along the wrong track, the down track, the track that pulled like quicksand, stronger and stronger the deeper I sank.

I didn't have time for quicksand. It was 6:22 A.M. I had to hurry.

I dug through my closet for something nice, something I'd wear to a college interview maybe. Everyone was so dressed up yesterday, the men in suits, Nancy in her silk sweater set and skirt. The best I could find was a plain blue cotton dress that my mom had bought me last year and I'd never worn. I slipped it on, yanked off the tag, and hurried downstairs to my uncle's office, where I curled up in his swivel chair and clicked the computer to life.

Barry's homepage was a news feed. My name was in the headlines.

My cursor hovered—and dashed away. Not yet. Focus.

Google. Senator Cooper. I started with the Wiki.

Age forty-seven. Born and raised in Massachusetts. Harvard undergrad, Yale Law. Worked as a public defender, then switched to the district attorney's office in Newton. He left to pursue a seat in state government.

His campaign was based in Boston's Kenmore Square neighborhood, near the Boston University campus.

That was where my mom went to college.

An image floated up: Mom as a young woman, auburn hair pulled into a ponytail, a backpack across one shoulder as she strolled the campus, spotted a sign for campaign volunteers, stopped to take a look.

But then another image drove that one out—the real one on the screen. There was a woman standing next to Senator Cooper in most of his campaign pictures.

Her name was Margaret Abbott Cooper. They'd been married for nineteen years. The photos showed a tall and elegant woman, her hair a smooth, ash-blond helmet that just grazed her shoulders. There was a chilliness to everything about her—except for her eyes. In every photo, I saw a spark of humor in them, like someone had told a good joke just before the click.

I read on quickly, reeling from each new tidbit. Especially this one:

They had two children. Twins. Eight years old. Their names were Grace and Gabriel.

A brother and sister? It was possible. Suddenly the world had cracked open and *everything* was possible. I couldn't tell whether they looked like me. I stared at their pictures until a ray of sunlight on the computer screen reminded me to hurry up.

Today would not be like yesterday. Today, I would be prepared.

Click. Google: Cooper for America.

The official campaign website was so crammed with slogans, it was impossible to find actual information. I gave up and found a blog with a list of political staff members.

The friendly redhead was Nancy Oneida, Senator Cooper's communications chief, in charge of "crafting his message," whatever that meant.

The Chief Strategist for the campaign was that tall, groomed guy—Bird of Prey—the one who'd glared at me. Elliott Webb. The blog called him a *"Machiavellian wunderkind."* It sounded appropriately pretentious to me.

Louis Mankowitz was the crinkly-eyed leprechaun. He and Senator Cooper had been roommates at Harvard. He'd worked on all of the senator's campaigns, starting with his run for state congress.

That was the one my mom worked on. He must have known her. He might even have known about . . . whatever there was to know. I still wasn't ready to think about that.

The blog highlighted other staff members, but I didn't recognize them from yesterday. Those three must have been the senator's core team, then. Nancy, Louis, Elliott. The ones he trusted most—or as the blog put it, his "inner circle."

The doorbell rang. Voices filled the house. The invasion had begun.

In the kitchen, Barry was overloading a tray with coffee mugs, putting sugar in some, milk in others. I heard the front door opening and shutting, more people spilling into the living room, others back in the den where the TV was blasting. This was a bigger group than yesterday. Barry winced at the just-emptied coffeemaker.

"They have such specific orders," he muttered. "This one's *two-thirds* a Splenda packet?"

"Let me help," I said, hoisting the tray. As I ducked into the hall, I glanced back. "I'm sorry about all this."

He looked too confused to reply.

There were ten people in the TV room. The senator wasn't one of them. I spotted Nancy, though, casually gorgeous in khakis, pointing to something on the TV screen as she chattered into her phone. Then I followed her finger—and nearly dropped the tray.

I was on TV. My picture was, anyway. And not just any picture—my most recent yearbook photo. They'd taken that shot a few weeks into the school year, only two months after Mom died. I'd barely been able to get out of bed that day, hadn't remembered to primp for a photo shoot, and wouldn't have cared anyway.

I should have cared. Because there I was, looking half homeless, dirty hair thrown into a ponytail, dead eyes, splotchy skin, strained smile.

On national television.

"How did they get that photo?"

Everyone in the room stopped talking.

Nancy leaped from the sofa. "She should not be doing that!"

At first, I thought she meant I wasn't allowed to come in, but then I saw her waving wildly to staff members and felt hands gently prying the tray from my fingers. Leprechaun winked over the coffee mugs at me. "I got this, kiddo." *Louis,* I remembered. *Campaign Manager.*

As he circled the room distributing drinks, Nancy hurried over with an indulgent smile.

"Early riser!" She put her hands on her hips. "I'm impressed—my kids don't get out of bed at this hour for anything less than a trip to Disney World."

It surprised me somehow that Nancy had kids. She seemed to exist in a different sphere, free from such messy things as families and theme parks. She pinched the fabric of my sleeve appraisingly.

"And don't you look *nice*? Elliott!" Her voice hardened, and I glanced behind me to see Bird of Prey in the doorway, surveying the room as if searching for a mouse to pick off. "Doesn't Kate look *nice*?"

She seemed to be proving some kind of point, like they'd made a bet and she'd just won.

Instead of answering, Elliott blinked once and said, "Leave." Instantly, most of the room hurried out the door, still chattering, jotting notes, until only Nancy, Louis, and Elliott remained. The inner circle.

It was a neat trick. Elliott must have learned it at Evil Political Power-Player School, along with "Grooming for Maximum Intimidation."

"She does look nice," Elliott said, shutting the door. "Better than yesterday, anyway. And a hell of a lot better than that photo they keep showing."

I felt my cheeks flush. It wasn't like I'd planned to look like crap in my yearbook shot—and yesterday I'd been dressed to take a test, not to meet a firing squad of reporters.

"I'm on that," Nancy said. "We've got a couple of family shots leaking to the press right now."

"Did Mark approve them?"

"Are you joking?"

I followed their conversation like a Ping-Pong match. There was a strange energy between them, like if one wrong word was said, somebody might start chucking ninja stars.

Nancy smiled, eyes narrowed. "I'm keeping him above the fray."

"And where is he now?"

Louis the Leprechaun blinked, startled, as both of his colleagues turned to him. "Talking to Meg! He'll be here soon."

Meg. His wife.

My skin prickling, I turned away from their conversation. On TV, thankfully, my photo had vanished, replaced by footage of President Mitchell Lawrence and his family at an event for his reelection campaign. The president's blond son was waving from the center of the screen. He was probably about my age, with a lopsided smile and a funny look in his eye, like he was searching the crowd for an escape route.

Good-looking, if you were into that golden boy sort of thing. Lily Hornsby had a photo of him in her locker.

I felt a chill, and sure enough, Elliott was staring at me.

"We need to decide what to advise," he said.

"*I've* decided." Nancy laughed mirthlessly. "I'm just waiting for you to agree with me. As usual."

"Can't hear myself think . . ." Elliott grabbed the remote and muted the TV. I glanced over to see my photo back up, and now stats scrolling on the screen: my age, my mom's name, my . . . GPA?

I collapsed onto the sofa. "How do they know so much about me?"

Louis shrugged affably. "Most of it was in the *New York Times* article."

I stood up again. "There was a *New York TIMES* article?"

"That's what started all this." Nancy sighed. "We got an early tip-off, but they rushed to publication. We beat the press here by less than twenty minutes."

"So . . ." I held on to the sofa. "Is that how he found out? The article?"

Louis patted my back. "If you're asking whether your dad

knew about you before the article, the answer is no. He had no clue, kiddo. I can promise you that."

Your dad, he said. *Just like that. So it must be true.*

"And he was *dying* to meet you!"

The two men stared at Nancy until her grin dropped away.

Elliott cleared his throat and motioned to the sofa. "Have a seat, Kate. I want to ask you a couple of questions."

He sat opposite me in Uncle Barry's La-Z-Boy. I felt suddenly defensive of this room, glad that Barry and Tess weren't in here to see Elliott perched on the edge of the recliner like he didn't want his suit to touch it.

"Do you follow politics?"

I hesitated. Did I know about the Electoral College, the executive branch, the names, political parties, and dates of office for every US president? Yep.

Did I know the first thing about anyone running for office right now? Um . . .

"Not much," I admitted. Elliott's face seemed to brighten.

"What do you think of the president? You a fan?"

"Elliott," Nancy groaned. He shushed her and she stomped away.

"I . . ." I wasn't sure what he was looking for. "I don't really know enough to form an opinion."

To my shock, he smiled. "Are you pro-choice? Pro-life?"

"Elliott!" Both Nancy and Louis cried out this time. I most certainly did have an opinion about this one, but by now I'd caught on to what he wanted. I gave him my blankest expression.

"I haven't really thought about it."

Elliott nodded and rose from the chair. "Okay, Nancy. But this is *your* play. I want to make that crystal clear. If she gets out of line, you rein her in. If she crashes and burns—"

"I've got it," Nancy snapped.

Me. Crashing and burning?

Outside, there was a roar of voices.

The TV switched to live footage. A mob of reporters, an overcast sky, a house with white siding, the big bodyguard from yesterday, and right behind him, the senator, making his way to my front door.

The sky had become heavy, threatening to unload at any moment. I warily scanned the senator's suit, hoping it wasn't some kind of rare material that would disintegrate at a drop of rain.

He looked stiffly around the backyard, opting finally to lean-sit on the plastic slide of the jungle gym. I stood gripping the swing chain, bracing myself.

I had a working theory, developed during the maddening eons that the senator and his advisors had just spent speaking privately behind the closed doors of the TV room.

He's going to tell you to deny it. He's going to explain that he can't possibly ever see you again. This is an election year. I could ruin his life. I really don't blame him.

He took a deep breath and began.

"I want you on my side, Kate." He smiled, palms in the air, a practiced pose.

I nodded. "Of course."

24

Here's where he says "after the election," or whatever he's going to say. Keep your mouth shut and do. Not. Cry.

I watched him, trying to soak in details while I could, his thick salt-and-pepper hair with my shade of brown underneath, the way he swirled his hand into the air when he was talking.

"The cat's out of the bag, as Elliott so eloquently put it."

He was struggling, blinking a lot, smiling like his cheeks were frozen in that position. A raindrop hit the top of my head.

"We . . . My . . ." He started over. "Seventeen years ago, your mother and I made a mistake."

The chain of the swing held me up.

Here goes. I knew this wouldn't be pretty, but . . . don't cry.

"No, Kate, I'm . . ." He stood upright, stumbling over the bottom of the slide. "I'm trying to say that it *wasn't* a mistake. Not all of it. I mean—here you are!"

"I am indeed." Stupid response, but all I could muster.

A flicker of amusement crossed his face, but it was short-lived. He flinched from the rain and glanced at his watch.

"Let me get right to the point. I'd like you to come up to Maryland, to my home there outside DC. I'd like you to meet Meg. Gracie and Gabe."

The jungle gym started spinning.

"Now, I'm going to leave today—go up and explain things to the twins. They know a little, but if you could come up tomorrow, I think it would be good. It would . . . it would be the right thing."

He looked like he was trying to convince himself. His eyes were focused past me, scanning some mental horizon.

"I'll leave it to you to decide." He pushed off from the play set and started quickly away.

"Are you happy?" My hand closed tight around the chain.

He turned back, confused by my question. It was an important one, so I asked again, louder.

"Are you happy to find out about me? Is this good news?"

I knew how desperate my face must look, but I couldn't wipe it clear.

He grinned. It slumped at the corners and then fell off his face until he was blinking down at his shoes. "It is good news. Of course." He spoke like he was searching for words out of a grab bag. "But it's . . . a difficult time to find out such good news."

Suddenly, I saw him. He looked exhausted and sad, and just for one second, when he glanced up at me, hopeful. But then the smile came back, and it was like he was in 2-D on my TV screen, saying "A New Day for America!"

I recognized that smile, and not just from campaign ads. It was *my* stock smile. The one I'd worn all year.

"Take your time," he said.

Once he was inside, I sat on the swing, immune to the drizzle. It was a pleasant feeling and a strange one to be alone but not, like when I was little, in bed while Mom's dinner guests stayed on laughing and clinking glasses. I could see no one but hear them everywhere, surrounding this house. All of them here because of me. And my father.

And he *was* my father. I didn't need the mirror or even the blood test for confirmation. There were ways he moved that seemed familiar, from life, not television. By now I felt like an idiot for never having recognized him on the news, for not hitting PAUSE and saying, "Wait a minute—it's *him!*"

And if he was my father, then there was a whole family out there that I'd never known about. Sitting on the swing, I felt the same pang of longing I'd had when I first clicked on the photo with the twins in it.

And on the heels of longing came a pang of guilt. What about Uncle Barry and Aunt Tess? They'd taken me in, given me love. Wasn't that enough?

They were wonderful people, and they did their very best for me. Even so, they had to be counting the days until my graduation. Their teen-parenting days had ended eight years ago when my cousin went off to college. The last thing they'd expected was to be saddled with me.

Of course, the same thing could be said of the senator—and then some. But here he was, inviting me to meet the family, risking political fallout.

I stared at the house. A curtain moved in the back window. Someone in the TV room was watching. One of the staffers. And as the curtain shifted back into place, it all became clear.

I planted my feet. Steadied the swing.

This wasn't a risk. It was a campaign strategy. Invite her home, bring her on board. That's what they'd been talking about all morning behind closed doors. Damage control.

They were trying to use me, salvage some bit of his reputation, make a last-ditch effort to rescue his campaign, to quiet those newscasters who had been droning on all day long, asking, "Will he quit?"

This isn't about me at all.

But did it matter?

I didn't know the senator well enough to trust him—that was a fact. But if I said no now, would I ever get the chance again?

Past the fence, the press chattered to their cameras, and inside, the masses of staffers placed calls, made plans. But out here, all I could hear was the quiet tapping of rain on plastic. I closed my eyes and listened.

4

Thursday, June 12
Visiting My Long-Lost Family
145 DAYS UNTIL THE GENERAL ELECTION

If the flight attendant recognized me, she did a good job of pretending not to.

"Beverage before takeoff?" she offered.

"Thank you!" I reached across my seatmate for a cup of orange juice. Tim, the aide that the campaign had assigned me, held his newspaper way back like he was terrified I'd spill something on it. I hazarded a smile. "I've never flown first class before."

Sighing, Tim crammed away the newspaper and pulled out an e-reader. He was probably mid-twenties, awkwardly skinny, with a giant Adam's apple bobbing above the collar of his boxy suit.

"Do you live in DC too?" I asked, by way of, you know, *friendly conversation.*

"Yeah." He stuck on a giant pair of noise-canceling headphones. I snuck a look at his screen, spotting something about "jellybeans" and the "INF Treaty." My AP brain whirred. A biography of Ronald Reagan? Okey dokey.

Tim and I were clearly not going to be pals. He hadn't for one second warmed to me since he'd piloted me out of the house, through the backyard, over the fence, past my neighbors' houses, and down the block to a waiting Town Car in the 4:00 A.M. darkness to keep the press from noticing. At first I'd interpreted his silence as grogginess, but after the fourth "Thank you!/*grunt*" exchange, it occurred to me that Tim was sulking.

He probably blamed me for derailing the senator's campaign, like I was some dastardly mastermind, plotting to destroy his beloved Republican Party. Step One of Evil Plan: Birth.

If only I *were* plotting all this. Then I'd know what to do now, exactly what to say when I met Margaret Cooper—the one person who had a legitimate reason to despise me.

My stepmother. Officially.

Nancy had called late last night as I was packing for the weekend.

"The tests came back." I held my breath, in some weird way clinging to that last moment of ambiguity. "Congrats, Kate. He's your dad!"

I wasn't sure congrats was the right sentiment, but I appreciated her attempt, and kind of wished that she were waiting for me in Maryland instead of the senator and three strangers.

Not strangers, I reminded myself. *My family.*

The Coopers' Maryland home was sprawling and grand, surrounded by a high iron fence and acres of green lawn, old oaks dotting the property as if they were keeping guard. It was built in a style that I guessed was Colonial—the wooden exterior was painted a clean, crisp white, but you got the sense that this house had been here for hundreds of years.

When we pulled into the circular front drive, I saw the senator waiting on the porch, a huge oak door ajar behind him. Beside me, Tim perked up like he'd been poked with a cattle prod. He smoothed his suit, and as soon as the car stopped, leaped out to open the door for me and carry my little bag to the house. I shot him a sidelong glare, remembering what little help he'd been this morning as I'd clambered over wooden fences with it slung across my shoulder.

As I reached the top of the brick stairs, the senator gave my arm an awkward pat, then turned brightly to Tim, hand extended. "Thank you for your help today, son."

"It was my pleasure, sir. Your daughter is delightful." Tim shot me what I'm sure he thought was a million-dollar grin as he trotted back to the car.

Delightful. Whatever, Tim.

The senator coughed. "Come on in."

Stock smile in place, I stepped into the house and prepared to greet the family, but the only person in the gleaming front foyer was the security guy from back in South Carolina, the one who'd pulled me from the mob of reporters.

"Oh, hi again!" I grinned. "I'm Kate, by the way."

"I know." He winked. "James."

"Nice to meet you."

The senator hesitated at the far end of the room, apparently perplexed by the exchange. "Meg's out back. Come say hello."

We passed room after lovely room, a bright parlor, a dining area, a wood-paneled library, plodding along in heavy silence. It was fine with me, despite the awkwardness. I had too many questions to know where to start, and besides, I'd have the whole weekend to get to know him. At the thought of it, I glanced over, but the senator was frowning into his phone.

Past a set of tinted glass doors, the garden erupted into light, and there at the bottom was Margaret Cooper. At least, I assumed it was. She looked nothing like the woman from the campaign photos. This woman wore rolled-up jeans and a stained T-shirt, a pair of gardening gloves next to her on an iron patio table. Her blond hair was knotted in a spiky bun on top of her head.

My steps faltered. I'd mentally prepared to meet the campaign wife—not this new person I knew absolutely nothing about.

She stood quickly from her patio chair when she saw us, then sat again, as if thinking better of it—and with that gesture, her outfit transformed before my eyes. She'd dressed down on purpose. I wasn't sure why, but I could see it, just as I could now pick out moving figures along the edges of the property—security guards silently patrolling the perimeter.

The senator hung back as we approached, until I was reluctantly walking ahead of him. His wife smiled at us, a pinched, almost ironic expression. As I reached her, my brain scrambled for what I'd mentally rehearsed on the plane.

"Hello, Mrs. Cooper. It's very nice to meet you." I'd hoped it would sound respectful. It came out petrified.

Her eyes softened, crinkling with momentary pity. Then she stood. "Call me Meg."

And she walked past, dusting her gardening gloves off against her hip as she glided into the house. Behind me, the senator looked like somebody had hit him with a freeze ray. He didn't know what to do either.

Meg shouted from one of the back windows, "Come on then, Kate, let me show you your room."

As soon as we got into the house, the senator ducked down the hall and into a study, shutting the door behind him. I hovered alone in what had to be a family room—although it was way too clean to actually be used as one—not sure where to walk, what to do, what to say, if anything, fighting the twitching in my fingers and toes, the trembling in my jaw, the sudden urge to hide under the sofa.

This is okay. It's exciting. Not scary. This is your family.

"This way." Meg squinted at me from the hall.

She led me to a room on the second floor, across a broad corridor from two kids' rooms that to my relief were complete pigsties.

My room was a guest room. Of course it was, what else would it be? It had some pretty oil paintings, antique furniture, and a window that overlooked the front lawn.

"Do you need to rest?"

"No, I'm fine." As I turned, I saw disappointment flash across Meg's face.

She nodded, burying it. "The kids will be home soon. They're really . . . anxious to meet you."

"Oh good! Me too."

Meg leaned against the door frame. I hesitated, not sure how to word my next question without bursting the dam of politeness holding this conversation in check.

"Um . . ."

She raised her eyebrows.

"What did you tell the kids? Do they know—?"

"That you're their sister?" She crossed her arms. "Yes. We told them the truth. It was not a *pleasant* conversation, but we got through it and the upshot was . . ." She smiled wryly, as if at some private joke. "They are very excited to have a big sister."

With that, she blinked hard and started down the hall, calling behind her, "Make yourself at home!"

A woman in a ball gown glared at me from an oil painting above the bed.

"Wait! Mrs. . . . um, Meg?"

She turned with such obvious reluctance that I almost mumbled "Never mind," but planted my feet instead. This needed to come out now.

"I want you to know . . ." My breath came shaky. "That I'm really sorry about this. I know it can't be easy for you, and I appreciate—"

"I knew about your mother, you know," she cut in, so softly that I had to strain to hear. "I knew it was happening at the time. I confronted him. We worked through it. Got *past* it."

She made a sharp sound, an empty laugh.

"Oh."

In the silence, I heard a car door slam.

Meg straightened. "Come meet the twins."

The two of them were waiting in the foyer when we got there, lined up side by side wearing school uniforms. If there had been five more, they would have looked like the Von Trapp children. Grace was a shade taller than her brother, with bright blond hair and a confident tilt to her chin. As soon as her eyes caught mine, they locked in place with open curiosity. Gabriel, on the other hand, made a show of staring at the ground, stealing furtive glances until he caught me looking and blanched. He had brown hair, like the senator. Like me.

"I'm Gracie and this is Gabe," Grace said. "And you're our sister. We already know." She raised her eyebrows, expecting me to be impressed.

"I'm really excited to meet you." I grinned and came closer. "I've always wanted a brother and sister, so this is great."

"We're excited too," said Gracie.

Gabe muttered something that I couldn't hear.

"Hey." Their mom snapped her fingers and crouched. "What was that? Apologize to Kate."

He scowled, but when he finally peered up at me, he looked genuinely abashed. "Sorry."

"It's okay." Whatever he'd said, it *was* okay. If I could do cartwheels, I might have. They were shoulder-height to me. Gracie had my blue eyes, and Gabe the same slouch. My little brother and sister. This was amazing.

The front door opened, Elliott Webb walked in, and it was like a cold wind blew in behind him.

"Oh good," he said, passing us with barely a nod to Meg.

"I need to have a word with you," she said, trailing him angrily down the hall.

"I've been hearing that a lot lately. Hey Mark, you ready?"

The door to the study swung open and Gabe's face lit up. As the senator strode through the foyer, the twins sprinted to give him a hug. He stooped to embrace them, setting something down on the floor.

A bag. A big one. I glanced outside. A car was idling in the front drive, James poised by the back door.

The senator stood and I asked as lightly as I could, "Are you heading out?"

"Campaign visits." He ruffled Gabe's hair. "Ohio and Michigan."

"When are you back?" Gracie asked, hands on her hips.

The senator mimicked her pose, down to the indignant squint. "Sunday."

Sunday? But today was Thursday. I was only here for the weekend. Why invite me up and then leave? Before I could form words, let alone questions, Elliott was leading him out the door, and he was calling playfully to the twins:

"Be nice to your sister!"

When he turned to wave at me the light went out of his eyes.

"The campaign never stops," Meg said softly. I barely noticed her shutting and locking the door, barely even remembered where I was, until Gracie grabbed my arm and said, in a voice that brooked no argument, "Let's go play."

We ate a dinner that one of the campaign staffers brought us from an Italian restaurant in DC. The senator had arranged for it in advance, the staffer said, so Meg wouldn't feel like she needed to cook. I had a hunch that cooking was the least of Meg's worries this weekend.

The twins did most of the talking, Gracie asking me a million questions, like "What's your favorite color?" and "Did you read *Divergent*?" that were easy enough to respond to. Gabe's questions were more direct, harder to answer, like "Why didn't we ever *know* about you?" Meg shushed him for most of the meal. He kept trying.

"When did your mom die?" he asked, and I almost choked on my eggplant Parmesan.

"Gabe—" Meg cut in.

"It's okay." I put down my fork. He was watching me with his jaw set, daring me to answer. "She died last August." Predicting his next question, I added, "She was in a car accident."

His big eyes sunk down to his plate. "I'm sorry." He said it so sincerely and sadly that I wanted to comfort him rather than the other way around.

Meg poured herself more wine and cheerily changed the subject. "*I've* got a question. What is . . . your favorite class in school? Everybody can answer this one."

Gracie sat up straighter, liking this game.

"English," Gabe said.

"Um . . ." Gracie thought. "English too."

"No fair!" Gabe was obviously not into the whole twins-do-everything-alike concept.

"Fine, science. Kate's turn."

"I think . . . history's my favorite."

Meg leaned forward, slid her wineglass away. "Really."

"Yeah. I mean, it's a lot of memorization." I smiled, remembering the AP prep I'd been embroiled in just a week back. "But in between all the facts and dates . . . there are lives. I feel like that's what history really is, a collection of decisions, things people did because of . . . I don't know. What they were *afraid* of or what they *hoped* for. I like the human side of it. It's amazing how much one person can change the world, even if they don't know they're doing it."

All three of them stared at me, and I realized that that must have been the most I'd said in one go since I met them.

Gabe broke the silence. "History's Mom's favorite too."

"Really?"

Meg didn't answer, just kept squinting like she was trying to think where she remembered me from.

"Yep, she was a history perfessor."

"PROfessor," Gracie corrected.

"In a college."

"At *Harvard*," Grace corrected again, rolling her eyes.

Meg got up to clear the table and I rose to help her, half expecting her to wave me off. She didn't. I met her in the kitchen, where she hand-washed and I dried while the twins wiped the table clean. It was nice the way everybody pitched in. It was . . . normal.

"I think I read somewhere that you're a straight-A student?" Meg asked.

I didn't know what she meant at first, and then I remembered—the *New York Times* profile.

"I got a B in pre-calc," I admitted.

"And two APs this past semester?" She dried her hands and turned to face me.

"Three," I said.

"Good."

She smiled. And in that moment, she looked so much like my mom that I had to pretend to find a spot on the counter and scour it with a paper towel until my eyes dried up again.

5

I awoke to the shriek of a whistle.

"Up and at 'em!"

I blinked to find an elfin girl glaring down at me from the end of my mattress. An eerie giggle sounded from the doorway, but by the time I'd sat up, Gabe's head was already disappearing around the corner.

Gracie fell cross-legged onto the blankets. "Mom went to the store, but she said we should help you get accamated." She scrambled from the bed. "Let's go."

"Where are we going?" I asked, rubbing my eyes as Gracie pulled me into the hallway by my elbow.

"Downstairs first," Gabe mumbled, racing around the corner.

Gracie started the tour once we reached the foyer. "This is the pantry where we have snacks and things like that . . . that's Daddy's study . . . that's the dining room, but Mom said we can move the table to fit a piano when I learn to play, so it'll be the dining *and* music room then."

I could already picture a piano in the sunny corner by the window. "Are you taking lessons?"

"No, I'm taking ballet now, but I'm really clumsy. Like I'm

the worst in my whole class." She didn't look particularly upset about it.

"I'm not a very good dancer either," I admitted.

She gripped my arm. "It probably *runs in the family!*"

"Maybe." I smiled at Gabe. "Are you a good dancer?"

His eyes widened, but before he could answer, Gracie said, "He's bad too. But he's really good at drawing."

"Ah." I caught his eye for a split second. "What kind of stuff do you do?"

Again, Gracie answered. "Plants and birds and things. They look really real."

Gabe muttered something too quiet to hear, so I lowered my head, and he repeated it. "My favorite are blue jays."

And then, apparently mortified, he darted down the hallway and straight outside. Gracie, unfazed, took me up to their playroom to show me the sketches littering his desk. They really were good—even in penciled black-and-white, I could tell the pigeons from the cardinals. When the grand tour finally took us to the backyard, I looked for Gabe to compliment him, but he was hiding behind an oak tree, engrossed in a sketch of a squirrel perched on the bird feeder.

I had the sudden sense that if I interrupted this moment, the whole scene around me would crumble—trees, sky, family, all of it.

Holding my breath, I turned away.

The Coopers usually went on a two-week trip to Martha's Vineyard this time each summer, but they were skipping it this year because, as Gracie put it, "Daddy's got to meet lots of people and tell them he's running for president."

That statement rolled out of Gracie's mouth the way it would if she were talking about any parent—how her dentist mother cleaned teeth or her accountant father did taxes.

"She's a natural," Meg told me over lunch on Friday, watching as Gracie and Gabe splashed in the pristinely tiled pool. "She'd be out there giving stump speeches right now if we'd let her."

"And Gabe?" I asked.

"No." She winced. "Gabriel hates the cameras. And the crowds. All of it, really, poor thing. I let him stay home as much as I can, but it's a battle. They want the twins front and center."

That "They" struck me. Them—the team, the campaign aides. Not "we want" or "Mark wants" but "They want." It wasn't the first time I'd heard Meg refer to the campaign that way, always with a sourness to her voice, as if she were talking about an ant infestation.

"I don't let Them set up shop here," she'd replied when I complimented how clean the house was. "This is a campaign-free zone."

Meg's attitude surprised me. She seemed ambivalent, resigned to the campaign as an unavoidable condition of her marriage. I guess I'd expected her to be a modern-day Lady Macbeth, as ambitious for her husband as he was for himself—especially given how vague an impression I'd gotten of the senator so far. He seemed like he'd woken up on a parade float, waving and smiling, letting it take him where it would. On TV, he was passionate, optimistic, charismatic. In real life, he was . . . well, right now he was absent. I had to remind myself that I didn't know him. Not yet.

Despite our staged introduction, it turned out Meg really did enjoy gardening.

"She's got a green thumb," Gracie said, watching her mom from the back deck the next morning, wearing the appraising squint of an expert. "But not as green a thumb as Grandma."

My pulse jumped so fast I had to steady myself against a patio chair. "Grandma?"

"She lives in Massachusetts. We don't see her a lot."

"Oh." I tried to make my voice sound normal. "Do you have . . . other grandparents?"

"They died a long time ago, before me and Gabe were born." She sounded sad, but in a singsong way, like she knew that was how she was meant to feel. "So now there's just my grandma."

She shot me a blink I couldn't decipher. "*My* grandma," I could read, though. As in "Not yours." Meg's mom, then.

Before disappointment had time to strike, Meg waved me over.

"You bored?" she asked. "I could use a hand."

After a half hour of companionable digging, I finally got up the nerve to ask the question that had been stirring in my mind since the senator left on Thursday.

"I'm really glad I've gotten to meet you guys," I started, my gloved hand cupping a bulb while she dug a spade into the ground like it had done something to annoy her. "This has been amazing. But . . ."

She glanced up.

"Am I . . . in hiding?"

She set down the spade, pivoting on her knee to listen. I swiped a trickle of sweat with my wrist and went on.

"I mean, it kind of feels like I was invited here so They'd know where I was." There I went, using the capital-T They, like everybody else. "So They could make sure I wouldn't give any interviews or say something that would ruin . . . whatever they're planning."

"Astute." She took the bulb from me, stifling or forcing a smile—I couldn't tell which. "You have a political mind."

I almost said thank you, but coming from Meg, I wasn't sure it was a compliment.

She covered the bulb with soil and stood, offering me a hand up. "They don't want me to jump the gun with this, Kate, but I think you can handle it."

I swallowed, waited. There was dirt tickling my nose, but I didn't dare smear it while she was watching me.

She gazed past me at one of the guards patrolling the edge of the lawn.

"The whole team will be back from Michigan tomorrow morning," she said, slipping off her gloves. "Mark's going to take you to lunch and ask you to join us for the summer." My heart started to thud. "To campaign with us. That's what this weekend was about—to see whether we could all get along. Whether the idea had any shot at working."

The sun came out from the corner of a cloud and suddenly the yard was so glitteringly bright that I felt my knees giving way.

The whole summer. Campaign. "With us." I'd be part of the Us. Meg peered at the sky like she was waiting for something to drop out of it.

"And what do *you* think?" I asked her.

She sighed. "This is not an easy situation."

I nodded through my disappointment. Of course it wasn't easy. She'd put up a good front this weekend, but I could see the effort behind it. Every smile was strained, like she was sick and pretending to be healthy. Except she wasn't sick. Just sad. Embarrassed.

Her name was on the news now too. She was being called a victim all across America. Something told me that was not a role this woman relished.

"But," she went on. "If you're asking me whether this weekend's social experiment is sound, then . . ." She frowned thoughtfully. "Yes. I think we'll get along fine."

Her expression didn't change after she said it. Even so, I felt a little frisson of joy. Meg got along with me. She didn't hate me. She was willing to give this a shot.

"There's another tactic behind this weekend," she went on, nodding for me to stroll with her to the back porch. "They want to lull you into thinking it'll be this easy. It won't. You won't be able to hole up like this, forget who you are. You'll be a part of the campaign like the rest of us. Do you think you're strong enough for that?"

I opened my mouth, ready to swear any oath, but before I could, she turned away, laughing, her hand in her messy hair.

"What am I saying? You have no idea whether you're strong enough. You have no *idea* what this will be." I winced, but maybe realizing she'd sounded patronizing, Meg looked me in the eye. "The primaries were brutal. *Brutal.* We were hoping it would be smooth sailing until the general election, but . . ."

She bit back her words.

I finished them for her. "But me."

"Yep."

My head drooped heavy. I pulled off my gardening gloves, finger by finger. My nails were caked with brown underneath, and I wondered how I'd managed to let that happen.

"I wanted to give you a heads-up. He'll ask you himself tomorrow." Meg opened the door for me, echoing the senator's words. "It's entirely your choice."

The guest room had a window bench lined with plush cushions. I braced myself against the bright corner, my old flip phone pressed against my ear.

"But do you think it's a good idea?"

My uncle's voice kept rising in pitch. "If you think it's a good idea, I think it's a good idea. And I'm right here if you need me. I'm not going anywhere, that's for sure."

He was all for it. He'd asked the right questions—whether they were treating me well, whether I felt safe, if there were enough security guards, if they were asking me to do anything I didn't want to do—but he still sounded like a cheerleader the whole phone call.

So why was I gripping the phone more and more tightly?

"I mean . . ." My mouth went dry. "Do you think Tess will

mind? I sort of offered to help her with the day care over the summer . . ."

"Oh." Barry paused. "Honestly, hon, I'm not sure she'd be able to keep that going if you were home. I mean—if you wanna come back, we'll make it work. But if the reporters found out and we needed to have police here . . ."

"No." I let my head fall against the windowpane. "I get it."

As usual, Penny was more direct.

"Are you kidding me? If you don't do this, you're complete chicken shit and I disown you."

I laughed. "It's a *bit* more complicated than you're making it out to be, Pen."

"Is it, though?" I could hear her twirling an imaginary mustache over the phone. *"Is it?"*

"Well . . . yeah. There are things involved. Feelings. And . . . reporters. And campaigning . . ."

"And travel," Penny cooed. "You know the Republican convention's *in LA*, right?"

I didn't, actually. Everything I knew about politics came from history textbooks and overheard diatribes from my mom's friends. There might have been a time when a presidential campaign would have interested me. But in the past year, the nightly news had become a dull drone, a meaningless stream of bulletins about people I didn't know.

Until now.

"This is an obvious choice, Kate," she went on, and in a flash, I pictured myself inviting her along to keep me company here—to lend me some of her bravado. But it was a fleeting, impossible wish, so instead of blurting it, I recited:

"Is that your two cents, Penny?"

Penny groaned, our usual routine. Then she sighed. "I know this is a big deal. I don't mean to bully you about it. But this is how I see it—it's crazy, and amazing, and surreal—and you have to do it. You just do."

He took me to Mr. Chen's, a Chinese restaurant tucked into an unassuming strip mall a few minutes from their house. It was surprisingly nice inside, dark and quiet, with carved booths, ornate vases, and, most noticeably, huge painted panels where the windows should be.

At lunch, the senator's eyes darted everywhere but at me. He glanced, smiled, and panicked when I looked up at him, suddenly fascinated with the plastic dragon calendar covering the door to the kitchens. He downed four ice waters and his entire meal before he finally got up the nerve to ask.

He said "good experience," "see the country," and then, at last, "chance to get to know each other."

I said, "Of course," "This is great," "I'd be happy to do anything I can for the campaign for as long as you need me to."

He got the check and we left, both of us taking greedy gulps of air as soon as we hit the parking lot.

The triumvirate was waiting for us in a clown-car of a Mercedes just outside the restaurant, where James had dropped us off. Elliott Webb opened the passenger door and the senator shot him a quick nod.

Elliott winced a smile. "Great. Now we can get to work."

6

Monday, June 16
Officially Joining the Campaign
141 DAYS UNTIL THE GENERAL ELECTION

I knew that as of Monday morning, everything was going to change. What I didn't expect were headlights blazing through my bedroom window at 6:00 A.M., and an army of campaign aides clustered on the senator's front drive.

Peeking out, I watched light spill over the porch, the front door opening wide. Everyone in the crowd fell silent. But it was Meg who stepped onto the driveway, hands on hips.

"Despite any *new developments*," she announced wryly, "this house will remain a no-work zone for the rest of the campaign. Got it? Thanks! Now go."

As the sun came up, the grumbling staff left in a slow procession for the campaign office, and when the senator got in the last car, an opaque brick of an SUV, I scrambled downstairs just in time to get in with him.

Nancy was waiting in the front seat next to James. She leaned past her chair to pat me on the knee. "So glad you said yes, sweetie," she said.

The senator gave me a playful nudge with his elbow like I'd seen him do with Gracie. He was trying. But there was something about the effort of it that made me feel both thrilled and embarrassed.

As the iron gates glided open, Nancy rapped on the window.

"Photo op?" Her finger paused on the window controller, bottom right—the one that opened *my* window. Outside the dark glass, the press mob was shouting, cameras ready. I tucked my hair behind my ears and held my breath, bracing for the onslaught of flashes that I'd been protected from all weekend.

The senator hesitated. "Not yet. Let's wait to see what Elliott's thinking."

Nancy nodded and I exhaled, watching the press recede behind us. She passed back a mussed copy of this morning's *Washington Post.*

"What're they saying today?" The senator scanned the front page. I tried not to gape, but there it was, that same awful picture of me. Hadn't Nancy mentioned leaking another one? *Any* other one?

Nancy pulled out her notes.

"Munson on Fox News is with us on this—the word *heroic* is out there." She looked over her shoulder, gauging the senator's reaction.

"But that's Fox."

"That's Fox," she repeated, riffling through the pages of a legal pad. "*Wall Street Journal* published poll results—total rush job, we need to call them out on that . . ."

"And?" The senator looked up from the newspaper.

She cleared her throat. "Sixty-two percent disapprove. Values. But like I said . . ."

"Not a viable poll—make sure we get that out there."

"Ferris was on *Meet the Press.*"

"How'd he do?"

"He was okay. Lots of generalities, but that's all we can do right now." She turned to a new page. "We actually got a good quote out of Tom Bellamy."

The senator leaned forward. "They cornered a Supreme Court Justice over this?" He sat back as if disgusted. Then he raised an eyebrow. "What's the sound bite?"

She read. "'I've known Mark Cooper since he was a law student of mine at Yale. He's a stand-up guy and Kate is one lucky girl to have him as her dad.'"

I snuck a peek at the senator, curious to see his reaction to that word, *dad*—for me so loaded. But his mind was elsewhere.

"*Lucky*'s good. We can use that. Remind me to call and thank him."

Nancy scribbled.

"*New York Times?*"

She glanced up. "Mixed. One article on sinking approval, but they're not calling for you to step down yet."

He chuckled. "How refreshing."

"CNN had . . ."

They continued like that as the drive went on, more and more rapid-fire, like a debate team warm-up exercise. I could probably have climbed onto the roof to get a better view and they wouldn't have noticed. Instead, I watched the horizon as we zipped down the Capital Beltway and crossed a forest-lined river that had to be the Potomac. I felt a twinge of disappointment not to see any obelisks or domed buildings or white houses whatsoever. But the day was bright, and this place was new to me, so I kept my eyes open, lulled by the surprising greenness of the road. Then a word snapped me back to attention. Or rather, a name.

"Anything from Lawrence?"

Lawrence. As in Mitchell Lawrence. *President Mitchell Lawrence.*

Nancy smirked. "Nada. They don't know how to spin this any more than we do."

"Nancy?" The senator sighed musically. "That does not inspire confidence."

She spun in her seat to face the road. "I apologize, sir."

Campaign headquarters was a two-story building in an industrial park just across the Virginian border. There were signs and banners everywhere, a parking lot crammed with cars, from Porsches to beaters in worse shape than my hand-me-down Buick back in South Carolina, many of them bearing *Cooper for President* bumper stickers.

I held my breath as we crossed to the brightly bannered entrance, picturing the entire building full of Tim the Sullen Campaign Aide—Tim in suits, Tim in dresses, Tim in puffy campaign sweatshirts.

A middle-aged woman in an actual puffy campaign sweatshirt held the door for us. Her eyes widened when they reached mine, but she smiled anyway. So far so good.

The first room we entered looked like the inside of a piñata, red-and-blue banners everywhere printed with "The America We Know!" I wasn't quite sure what America they were all in agreement about, but this probably wasn't the best time to ask. I spotted a wide room with long tables, more than a dozen people gathered stuffing campaign bags. Each of them wore an oversized button bearing a more straightforward slogan: "Cooper for America."

As curious eyes started to dart upward, Nancy quickly ushered us into the noisy hall. Every room we passed crackled with its own charge of activity. In the space of thirty seconds, I spotted four agitated phone calls, one closed-door meeting, two heated arguments, and a clutch of young staffers leaning over a computer screen laughing nervously. And that was before we reached the main room, a wide space packed with occupied desks, no one pausing their phone dialogue or frenzied typing even as the senator walked through. It was busy here. An active campaign.

And an anxious one.

The air was thick with it. It sunk into me like cement, not helpful given how uncomfortable I felt already. I drew a silent breath as we reached the back of the command center and slid into a huge conference room—

Where approximately *forty* staffers were waiting for us.

Oh. God.

The long table in the center was full to bursting, the edges of the room jammed with aides forced to stand while taking copious notes on laptops, tablets, or notepads. Who *were* all these people?

"Kate!" Elliott rose from the table with a Cheshire Cat grin. "We were *just* talking about you!"

The table laughed and the standers shot each other tepid smiles. I didn't get the joke until my eyes landed on the mounted TV and took in the paused news report showing, once more, dear God, that horrible, painful—*how did my forehead get even shinier?*—yearbook shot.

I clutched Nancy's arm. "Do you think we could take another photo? I'm ready when you are!"

Nancy started to reply, but Elliott cut her off. "We'll take a lot more photos. Have a seat."

Who was he talking to? This seemed like a strategy meeting. Two people at the table stood and shuffled to the edges of the room, where the standers shifted to accommodate them. Two seats. For the senator and . . .

"I'll leave you guys to it." The senator patted my back. *Oh no.* "Lou?"

Louis got up from the far side of the table, gathering his laptop and notes. He winked so mischievously as he passed that I half expected him to hand me a four-leaf clover. Instead, he followed the senator out of the room, shutting the door behind him with a dull thud.

Feeling forty sets of eyes boring into my back, I turned. Nancy was relaxing into one of the empty leather swivel chairs. She patted the table encouragingly. I took the seat next to her—and nearly slid right off as it rolled backward.

Elliott blinked. Recovered. I tried to do the same.

Someone in the back coughed. I spotted Tim standing awkwardly in the corner, even grumpier than the last time I saw him, and felt a petty twinge of gratitude that he wasn't important enough to sit at the conference table.

Elliott tapped one of a long row of whiteboards with a capped marker.

"As your *dad* told you, Kate . . ." He smirked, like there

54

were air-quotes around the word *dad*. "Your big debut is in a few days. *Four* days and three hours from now, to be exact."

Actually, my "dad" *hadn't* told me. Meg had. This Friday, I would be introduced to the world via live press conference, my first official public appearance alongside Meg, Gracie, Gabe, and the senator himself. Cameras, reporters, smiling, waving. Fielding questions. I felt my heartbeat ratchet up to jackhammer mode and shoved the thought away.

"So we're gonna take today to get to know you. And *brand* you."

Everyone on the edges of the room started scribbling.

"Brand me?" *Like a cow?*

"We've already got a lot to work with." Nancy beamed. "You're a good student, well-liked by your peers. You've stayed out of trouble."

"Of course she has!" An African American staffer down the table snorted through an impressive mustache. "She's sixteen. The scandals don't start till they hit college."

"Not true," another table guy piped up. He looked like he was in college himself, with his tousled hair and Ivy League outfit, rolled sleeves and loosened stripy tie. He pointed at Elliott. "Andy Lawrence."

Elliott pointed back, turned eagerly to the whiteboard, and scrawled the name while the room murmured.

Andy Lawrence. The president's son.

I tried to picture him, recalling that image from the news the other day, but what popped up more vividly was the inside of Lily Hornsby's locker door, a magazine cut-out taped neatly to its top right corner. Lily had a crush on Andy Lawrence.

That tall kid—I still couldn't remember his name—teased her about it over lunch one day and I remembered suspecting he was jealous of a photo from *US News and World Report*.

I'd peeked one morning as we were getting our books out, taking in blond hair, a flash of teeth, a raised hand. Honestly, I wasn't all that impressed.

"That's good, Cal." Nancy leaned forward, grinning. "We juxtapose Kate and Andy, we'll win every time."

"Wait," I interrupted. "What's wrong with the president's son?"

"Good," Elliott barked, marker raised. "Go."

I opened my mouth and shut it. Was he talking to me?

"The cow prank at Farnwell Prep," the mustached aide said.

"Too long ago," Elliott countered.

Ivy League lazily raised his hand. "Sexy Ronald Reagan."

Elliott wrote it down like the marker was on fire and several people along the edges started to laugh. Catching my bemused expression, Nancy leaned closer.

"Halloween party last year, Andy Lawrence wore Baywatch trunks and a Ronald Reagan mask. It went viral within hours—*very* poor judgment."

She seemed to smirk and sniff at the same time. It didn't seem like that big a deal to me, but I knew better than to say so out loud, especially given the obsession these guys seemed to have with Reagan.

A skinny Asian staffer in a gray suit raised his hand. "He was shit-faced at the Correspondents' Dinner."

"Whoa," I blurted.

I knew the Correspondents' Dinner from clips online. It was a press event, part dinner party, part political roast, so not exactly the most serious occasion. But to show up drunk would be pretty shocking, especially if you were the son of the president, *especially* especially if you were the *underage* son of the president. It wasn't as though alcohol had never passed my lips. Mom used to let me have a glass of wine at Christmastime, and I'd sampled the occasional warm beer at a party or two (blech)—but not with the entire country's press corps watching. It couldn't possibly have been true.

Nancy shook her head. "And nobody reported on it. A room full of press . . ."

"Can't go after the president's kids until they're eighteen. That's the rule." Elliott pointed to the whiteboard. "It's *still* the rule, but if they strike first? *We strike back harder!*"

A laugh bubbled out of me.

Elliott's face stiffened, his hand clenching the marker like he was trying to snap it in two.

He was embarrassed. This wasn't good.

"Sorry," I mumbled, trying and failing to maintain a smile. "*'We strike back harder.'* It's from that movie, right?" My voice fell mouse quiet. "The . . . one with Bruce Willis?"

My brain scrambled for the title, as if that could clear the air, but with everyone staring, I couldn't remember. Wasn't it the movie I'd gone to see the night of my mom's accident? Before that realization had time to sink in, I heard a chuckle across the table. The Ivy League guy was grinning.

"*Max Drive!* Yes! I love that movie!"

The room loosened at that, everyone daring to let out a

laugh or two. Everyone but Elliott, anyway. He was staring at me like I'd accused him of something way worse than plagiarizing a line from a subpar movie.

He leaned way over the conference table and everyone fell abruptly silent. I felt my chair roll back of its own volition.

"So now we know she loves bad action movies."

Nope, I thought, but clamped my mouth shut. Elliott's eyes flared with such maliciousness that I half expected him to order me out of the room. Instead, with painful effort, he smiled.

"Let's see what else we can learn about Kate."

⌒7⌒

"Do you have a boyfriend?"

"No." My hands were clammy against my knees. Questions had flown at me for seventy minutes, steady and relentless. Some were about public speaking I'd done, how much I knew about the Republican Party. But just as I'd settle into the rhythm of what they were after, someone else would launch a prying question, slapping me back into squirminess.

"Have you ever had one?"

The assistants lining the room peered up, pens poised. Was there a right answer to this?

"No, I . . . no." *Scribble, scribble.*

"Girlfriend?" From Elliott. Everyone held their breath.

"No. I'm straight." And everyone exhaled.

I made a mental note to thank Gabe and Gracie for the practice grilling they'd given me over the weekend.

"Have you ever taken part in a protest?"

"Any food allergies?"

"Did you attend church with your mother? With your aunt and uncle? What denomination? Every Sunday or just on holidays?"

"What was your SAT score?"

It wasn't until the door was flung open and I spilled into the hall with the others that I realized the oddest thing about that introductory meeting. There had *been* no introductions, no "Hi, I'm Kate, what's *your* name?" with any of the people in that room. None looked likely to follow either, with everyone walking past, talking into phones, talking to be heard over the sound of talking.

"No polls today," the mustached aide muttered as he passed. "Elliott's orders."

"You'll survive, Chuck," said Ivy League.

Chuck, I thought. *Got it.* As I made a mental note to gather more names for later Googling, Nancy linked her arm through mine, steering me into the hall.

"We've cleared a space for you." She waved off two young staffers who looked desperate to ask her a question. "And we've assigned you an aide."

"I'm Libby!" A girl appeared from nowhere and kept pace with us. "Short for Liberty!"

Short for Liberty was probably in her early twenties, but dressed like she was fifty. She had pink cheeks and long brown hair knotted in a tight bun. I resisted the urge to hug her for not being Tim.

Nancy swept the door open to a small office with a window overlooking the parking lot. On a desk inside, there was a stack of binders, to which Libby added the few she was carrying.

"For you to study," Nancy said. "Our approved talking points are in here, along with the campaign's policy positions. If you have a difference of opinion . . . kindly keep it to yourself!" She laughed and I laughed along, but before I could say "Wait—seriously?" she was already out the door, calling behind her, "Libby can answer any questions you might have!"

Libby bounced as she sat. I smiled warily and opened the top binder, noticing tabs for all the major policy issues: *Economy, Foreign Policy, Environment, Social Issues*.

Flipping to the last one, I blinked in surprise. "He's pro-choice?" That wasn't popular among Republicans.

"We're not supposed to talk about it. And if we get cornered . . ." She leaned over the desk and pointed to the approved talking point.

I recited it aloud. "*Senator Cooper believes that all life is sacred, including the lives of women.*"

"Perfect!" Libby chirped, with no discernable trace of irony.

A tab toward the back read "*Immigration.*" I hesitated for a second before flipping to it. On the top of the page, in bold, was written, "HARD LINE ON IMMIGRATION—no deviation."

A huge binder slammed down on the desk next to me. I jumped.

Libby smiled. "This book's got all of our immigration policy statements. It's what won us the nomination!"

I stared at the binder, dread pooling in my stomach at the prospect of finding out exactly what "hard line" meant. My finger traced the word *Immigration*, and suddenly, I was back in my LA high school, surrounded by familiar faces. I was in a sun-bleached, fenced backyard, being teased by Penny Diaz's older brother and tugged at by her tiny little sister . . .

"I'll look at this later," I said, pushing the binder away and piling a few others on top.

Libby stared at me with veiled concern. It was an expression I'd seen on more than one face today—including the senator's.

I forced a smile. "I do have a question, though."

Libby straightened.

"Who is everybody around here? I've only met Nancy, Louis, and Elliott so far . . ."

Relieved, Libby launched into a giddy rundown, starting with Mr. Ivy League. His name was Calvin Montgomery. He'd been the Communications Director for a dark horse ("fat chance") Libertarian candidate early in the primaries.

All I'd ever heard about Libertarians was a joke my uncle made while watching the news: "Republicans who smoke pot." But judging by the crisp press of Cal's button-down shirt, I was guessing he didn't quite fit the mold.

"Nancy recruited Cal after his candidate dropped out," Libby said. "He's our speechwriter. He's *very* talented." Her eyes went dreamy.

"Cute too."

"Kate!" Libby giggled, swatting my arm.

For all her blushes, Libby sat us down right next to Cal at lunch—and proceeded to say absolutely nothing, leaving me to fill the awkward silence.

"So . . . you're a Libertarian?" I tried, reaching over Cal to grab a turkey sandwich from the platter.

"Have you read *The Fountainhead*?" He squeezed my shoulder, lit by sudden fervor. "I'll loan you my copy!"

It was only after Cal ducked back upstairs that Libby found her voice again. "Is there anything I can do for you?"

I was about to dutifully answer "no" for about the fiftieth time, but spying the desperation in her eyes, I thought of something.

"Do you think we could get my uncle to send me my clothes from home? I only packed for the weekend . . ."

"Oh." Libby's face dropped. "I have to check with Nancy and Elliott. I think . . . they're picking your clothes."

"Picking my clothes?" *As in . . . new clothes?* "I'm not sure Elliott and I have the same taste in shoes."

"Oh." Libby didn't seem to get the joke. Jokes in general, actually. "Well, they're bringing in some consultants too."

"Fashion consultants?" My mouth fell open.

"Political stylists," she corrected, as if it were a completely normal job title. "They styled Carolee McReady before the primaries."

Her voice was hushed with awe.

"Oh. Wow." I had no idea who Carolee McReady was.

As I was stuffing my face with the last bite of my turkey sub, I glanced up to see Nancy motioning into the room and an impossibly tan trio staring at me with open disappointment.

"That's them," Libby stage-whispered.

Awesome.

A half hour later, I was called into the conference room, just long enough for the trio to silently sling a tape measure around me here, there, and everywhere, the dozen strategists at the table doing their noble best to avert their eyes. I wasn't sure what was more embarrassing, seeing campaign staff taking notes on my SAT score or my bra size.

When I was released back to my cubby, I let my shoulders slump, praying that the embarrassing portion of the day was over. Luckily, the office was quiet. Libby had ducked out for a team "regroup" meeting, leaving me with only the binders and laptop for company.

As soon as I sat at the desk, it hit me—this was the first time I'd had both privacy and access to the Internet. I could go on the news sites and find out if they'd changed my photo yet.

I could read that New York Times *article.*

I let my fingers hover over the keyboard. After a five-count, when no one had walked past, I started to type, hot shame sweeping up my cheeks: "Kate . . . Quinn . . . New . . . York . . . T . . ."

But then . . . If I was going to Google embarrassing things, why not start with the other tidbit that had been burning a curious hole in my brain all afternoon?

I typed it.

"Sexy Ronald Reagan."

And there he was, on *US Weekly*'s website, a post from last November, wearing a rubber Ronald Reagan mask over . . . pretty much nothing. A bare torso and a pair of bright red swim trunks. Not even any shoes.

Judging by this photo, Andy Lawrence was lightly tanned. Not ripped exactly, but lean, athletic.

The blurb underneath said: *"Naughty Andy caught shirtless: Lacrosse sure does a body good!"*

I found myself leaning against the desk to look closer. There were two girls to the left of Sexy Ronald Reagan in matching Tinker Bell costumes. I scrolled the image so they weren't in it.

Voices rose in the hallway. The meeting must have gotten out.

Okay, you've seen it, I thought. *Close the window.*

Seriously, close it.

"Caught ya!" Louis pointed at me from the doorway.

I slammed the laptop shut.

"Am I too late?" He shrugged. "I was heading over here to tell you not to read it. Hard to resist, I know."

"Oh!" I nearly laughed with relief that he was only half right. "The article? I wasn't—"

"Not *tell* you," Louis corrected himself, settling into Libby's chair. "You're gonna do what you're gonna do. But I'm a campaign advisor. So I wanted to strongly *advise* you to hold off on reading that profile—at least until the press conference is done."

He leaned back, hands clasped on top of his bald head, waiting for my rebuttal.

"That's four days away," I said. He motioned for me to go on. "It's just weird, having all this information out there about me, and I haven't seen a word of it."

"You seeing it isn't going to change the fact that it's out there," he said. "What it changes is this." He tapped his head and sat up. "Listen, back in one of our first campaigns, the *Boston Globe* wrote a piece on me—the Man Behind the Man, that kind of thing. I couldn't wait to get a copy of this thing. Went out to the newsstand at the crack of dawn. Read it probably thirty times. This reporter must have had a crush on me, because I couldn't believe what was in this article. Lou Mankowitz!" He pointed to himself, eyes wide. "He came from nothing, but now? He was a political mover and a shaker. Destined for greatness! I was shocked. I had *no idea* I was so important."

Louis leaned on the desk. I grinned in reply.

"The next day, your dad comes into the campaign office. I'm walking past him to the watercooler. I give him a wave. He stares at me like I'm a stranger and says, 'Goddamn it, Lou! You read that article, didn't you?' Apparently, I wasn't walking. I was strutting. And an informal poll of our staff indicated that I'd been a total—excuse my French—*asshole* for the past thirty hours. I swore that day that I would no longer read my own press. And if I did accidentally happen to see my name in the paper, I wouldn't believe a word that came after it."

A freckly guy from the phone bank walked by.

"Sam!" Louis shouted, and he reappeared. "What do I always say about the press?"

Sam's brow furrowed. "Don't talk to them?"

"Your *own* press."

"Don't read it?"

Louis pointed at him. "Don't read your own press! I owe you a Coke."

As I laughed, Louis turned back to me, his face serious again.

"You want to know what's in that article, I'll tell you. It says you're a great kid. A good student. It talks an awful lot about your mom."

I nodded, my smile sinking into nothing.

"You can read it all later. But for now, you've got enough to deal with. Leave it alone." He winked as he stood to go. "Otherwise, I'm telling you. You'll be squirming up there in front of those cameras on Friday."

I raised my eyebrows. "Pretty sure I'll be squirming no matter what."

Louis watched me with a thoughtful squint. "I don't think so. I've known you for five days, Kate Quinn, but I can tell you right now—you're a lot less of a squirmer than you think you are."

I smiled at the desk. "Thanks, Mr. Mankowitz."

"Mr. Mankowitz? Psh. That's the guy from the article." He grinned. "I'm just Lou."

"Lou!" a guy down the hall shouted, as if cued. "I need your signature."

I waited until he'd gone before I opened the laptop. One last look at Andy Lawrence's abs, then I cleared the search history, shut it down, and shoved it in a drawer.

The campaign left me alone for the next few hours—or so I thought.

Around three, as I was flipping through binders, learning a series of sound bites that impressively avoided expressing any opinion at all, I heard Nancy's muffled voice in the office next door. The sound filtering through was like what dogs must hear: "Hmfm, hmf, hmm, KATE! Hrm KATE! . . ."

Lou's advice rang in my ears—but this wasn't listening to my own press. This was the campaign itself. I rolled my chair over and leaned my head against the wall. The staffers' conversation became instantly clear—and really unpleasant.

Apparently the fact that I was orphaned was "polling" well. They were brainstorming what demographics would respond best to hearing about it. Even without me in the room, Nancy was careful in the way she brought up my mom, using her full name with a respectfully lowered voice. But I couldn't mistake the casual, almost cheerful tone with which everyone talked about her accident.

"Tragic," one of them said. "We can work with that." Nancy herself noted that the fact that Mom had run a food bank and soup kitchen for ten years and that I'd volunteered at the Cocina almost every day after school made for a "great backstory."

There was something so hollow about hearing Mom described as a backstory that my breath caught cold in my throat.

Elliott was the only one who sounded dubious.

"Soup kitchen, huh?" Even through the wall I could hear him snort. "How did *she* vote?"

I mouthed "Democrat" just as a staffer chuckled, "What do *you* think?"

"Look into it," Elliott said, and the room fell silent.

I rolled my eyes. If they were worried about my mom being some kind of left-wing activist, I could've told them right then not to bother digging for problems. Beyond impressing upon me the importance of voting, my mother was probably the least political person I knew. For years, her friend Marta would try to engage her in debates or get her fired up about whatever issue had sent Marta's lefty flag flying, but my mother always smiled and said, "I can see both sides of it."

I wondered what Mom would think if she could see me here, in the middle of a presidential campaign office, memorizing Do's and Don'ts for Interactions With the Press. And then, of course, I tried to imagine her, not much older than me, working for a campaign. His campaign.

It was strange. I'd tried for months to keep the thought of my mom at bay, and now it wouldn't come. The harder I tried, the more she seemed to blur.

As for the senator, he was even blurrier. I heard his voice in the corridor late in the afternoon, but he was gone before I could even get up from my roller chair. Peeking out the office window, I watched as he got into James's waiting car and drove away.

Libby poked her head over my shoulder.

"He's got meetings with donors and RNC officials all week," she divulged in a giddy whisper. "*Closed-door* meetings."

No public events. Not until our press conference. The family press conference. The "Hey Everybody, Meet My Love Child!" press conference.

Four days away.

The thought was paralyzing, so I decided to pretend it wasn't actually happening—that it was all for the girl on the long row of whiteboards, the hypothetical Kate Quinn, all her best qualities shined up and imperfections removed. Lou was half right. I was most definitely squirmy. But Whiteboard Kate wasn't.

"Kate's a great kid," mustached Chuck said into his cell phone, passing my cubby without so much as a glance as he left for the day. "Whip-smart, solid—you'll see." White-board Kate *was* solid—an A-student, a volunteer, a sad orphan.

None of those things were wrong, exactly. Still . . . I wasn't quite sure how I saw myself, but this wasn't it. If you'd asked Penny to describe me, she'd say, "She's got a weird obsession with songs about wolves, and if there were a competitive staring circuit, she'd at least make regionals." Or maybe, "She's loyal. She cares about other people. She rescued a baby squirrel from the on-ramp of the 101 when we were ten."

But my limited understanding of politics was enough to make me realize that none of those things would interest voters. They didn't want to hear about how weird I was. They wanted me to be just like them.

I couldn't help but wonder whether the Coopers felt the same way.

8

"Dinner!" Meg called from the house, and my pulse jumped.

As Gracie and I got up from our Monopoly game, I whirred with anticipation. The senator had worked late last night at the campaign office. But tonight he was right in front of me, jacket off and sleeves rolled up over tanned arms, settling into a seat at the head of the table.

Back in California, my mom and I used to eat on trays in front of the TV, or huddled silently over textbooks and Cocina paperwork. I imagined that tonight would be more like the family dinners I'd had at Penny's house, the Diazes laughing together around a messy table—and, I hoped, a special meal too, an acknowledgment that I was part of the Cooper family, if only for the summer.

But as soon as our plates were down, the senator pulled a printout from his briefcase and scowled over it in concentration, a stubby pencil in his hand.

"Daddy," Gracie called. "Is that a speech? Can I hear it?"

"Let your dad work." Meg scooted her chair so that it faced away from her husband. "Now, today was a big day, wasn't it?"

I put down my fork, beginning to glow.

71

"What was special about today?"

My smile wavered. Something about Meg's singsong tone told me that this was not a new topic of conversation.

"I dove into the deep end," Gabe said.

"That's excellent," Meg said.

"I dove like seven times," Gracie countered. "And I did a flip in the water."

I took another bite of Brussels sprouts, feeling smaller and smaller the more they talked. I watched them and waited—for a look, a nod, a question. Anything. But when the plates were empty, the family meal complete, it was official. Nobody had said a thing about me—or even to me—at all.

When I went to bed, I told myself that the Coopers were comfortable enough around me to revert to their usual dinner routine. And wasn't that a good thing? That they didn't see me as an outsider who needed to be entertained? But the sensation of being a ghost in that dining room had sunk in so deeply that at 2:00 A.M., I got up and splashed cold water on my face just to make sure I could feel it.

On Tuesday, two days and twenty hours until the press conference, Elliott poked his head into my office, squinted past me at the stack of binders, and stormed away bellowing for Nancy.

Out in the hall, they had what looked to me like the start of a massive blowout fight, daggers shooting from their eyes, their whispers like whip cracks.

"Get rid of that shit," Elliott said. "She doesn't need talking points. She's not gonna be talking."

"She needs to be prepared," Nancy said. "They'll be coming at her from every angle."

"It's your job to *keep that from happening.*"

And then, just as I expected one of them to lunge, they slid past each other and kept marching in opposite directions.

Elliott had gotten the last word. Did that mean he'd won? Was he going to have a gag order placed on me?

Part of me relaxed at the idea. A small part. The rest of me seethed. I kept studying, feverishly now, waiting for somebody to take my binders away.

It turned out I wasn't being paranoid. When I came in Wednesday morning, my workspace had been transformed into a lounge, the desk, office chair, laptop, and binders removed, replaced by an Ikea sofa and coffee table, with a new flat screen mounted on the bare wall. As I hesitated in the doorway wondering if I'd been relocated, Libby ducked in behind me with a shopping bag full of DVDs.

"You can relax today! Mr. Webb said!"

I popped in the first episode of some show called *Triplecross*. But as soon as I heard the team start a meeting next door, I left the TV playing and silently snuck down the hall to help the volunteers stuff letters into envelopes.

An hour later, the senator made an appearance. I froze, wondering what his reaction would be—angry that I'd disobeyed or proud to see me helping? I grabbed the next envelope and started to stuff.

He patted an older gentleman on the back and crouched to share a joke with a couple of college-aged helpers, his cheeks crinkling as he smiled wide. He stood, his round blue eyes traveling across all of us. Then he raised his hand in a wave, turned, and left the room.

I couldn't get the paper into the envelope. I held it in front of me until my arms began to droop.

Louis appeared in the doorway, forehead creasing as he watched the senator walk down the hall. His eyes darted to me.

My face felt heavier than usual, but with great effort I forced it up until my mouth clicked into Stock Smile Mode. When I trusted my prickling eyes enough to lift them from the table, Louis was motioning me over.

Outside the volunteer room, the hall was empty. Lou gave my shoulder a squeeze. "You doin' all right?"

"Of course!" I swallowed. "Everyone's really nice and . . ." I couldn't think what else. The lunch selection was good. The building was well lit.

Lou just nodded. "Good."

He looked like he wanted to say more but hadn't found the right words to start, and just as his mouth was opening, mine blurted:

"Did you know my mom?"

"Yeah, I did." His shoulders shrunk in on themselves. "Not well. Just for those few weeks, but—she was a nice kid. I was really sorry to hear about what happened to her."

Just as I was mentally cursing myself for making both of us so uncomfortable, he squinted at me.

"You've got a lot of Emily in you, if I'm remembering her right." I flushed at her name, realizing that he was picturing her as a college kid, just as he'd last seen her. "But you've got a *lot* of your dad, too. I can tell already."

I glanced up, surprised. He raised his chin, daring me to contradict him.

"Not just looks. Personality too. You've got more in common with him than you know."

Something about the phrasing struck a raw nerve. Complimenting my poise was one thing. But how on *earth* would I know whether I had anything in common with that man, besides our eerily similar styles of shooting a thumbs-up? Several snarky retorts came to mind, but Lou didn't deserve them. Instead, I said, "Okay."

"Listen." He lowered his voice. "Your dad is a tough guy to get to know in the best of times. Always has been. Believe me, I've known him since we were both young and stupid." He laughed. "We're still stupid, but you know what I'm saying."

I nodded, trying desperately to brighten, but Lou's face was serious.

"Stick it out." He patted my arm kindly as he walked away. "He's worth it."

Libby drove me to the Coopers' house on Wednesday, singing softly along with a Christian rock station, while I thought back to Monday night's family dinner—and what I could have done differently. By the time we'd pulled past the camped-out reporters and through the front gates, I'd come to a decision.

Tonight, I would participate. Even if the conversation had

nothing to do with me, I would butt in, ask questions. Maybe they were just waiting for me to get over my politeness. Well, tonight I would.

Especially where Gabe was concerned.

From day one, Gracie had embraced me as a long-lost sister, latching on to my arm and chattering away whenever I walked into the room. But Gabe still watched me from oblique angles, like I was one of his backyard birds—and watched Meg too, gauging her reaction to me before he dared one of his own.

Meg met me at the door wearing a classic Chanel tweed suit, her hair elegantly styled.

"You look nice," I said, eyeing her curiously. Seemed a little much for a Wednesday night.

She groaned. "Long story."

Before she could tell it, a knock sounded on the door and she hurried past me to answer. A pretty twenty-something girl wearing a Georgetown hoodie stood grinning on the doorstep.

"Hiiiiii," she cooed. I heard the kids scrambling out of their rooms upstairs. "Where are my favorite twinsies?"

"Sarah!" Gracie barreled down the stairs and clung to the girl's arm. "I have so much to tell you!"

Okay, I realized, sinking. *Maybe she's like this with everyone.*

Gabe didn't even give me his usual sidelong glower, too busy grinning at Georgetown Sarah to notice I was there.

"Donor dinner tonight," Meg said to Sarah over Gracie's chattering. Sarah sighed sympathetically, as if she'd been to a million donor dinners herself. "We won't be too late."

I caught Meg alone in the kitchen. "You didn't have to hire a babysitter. I've taken care of kids before—I'd be happy to watch them."

Meg looked uncomfortable.

"They've known Sarah since they were four. She's great with them." She must have seen the wind knock out of me, because she forced a smile and clapped me on the shoulder. "But good point. I'll take you up on that next time."

Sarah was indeed great with the twins. Me? Not so much. She spent a few awkward minutes trying to figure out how to interact with me before deciding that the best approach was to pretend I wasn't there. After our pizza was delivered, she and the twins set up a board game with only three players. I crept up to my room and tried calling Penny.

"Kate? Kate! Wffmm . . . !" There was so much noise, I could hardly hear her—a bass beat, people whooping. She must have been at a party. I finally gave up shouting *"What?"* and texted her that I'd try her tomorrow.

I flopped back on my bed. If I were in California, I'd be at that party with her. She'd be forcing me to dance, mussing my hair, complimenting my outfit, even though she looked a million times better in her thrift store finds. I'd be relaxed, distracted, maybe even confident if I were at that party with Penny.

But if I were at that party, it would mean that I was in California—and that would mean Mom was still alive. When I got home tonight, she'd be in the front room watching some old movie with her feet on the coffee table, pretending that she wasn't waiting up. And she'd share her popcorn as I curled up next to her—

I felt my limbs aching heavy, my eyes burning shut. With a deep breath, I forced myself upright and grabbed the dog-eared copy of *The Fountainhead* that Cal had loaned me.

So far, it was sort of a romance novel, the story of a fiercely independent architect and the woman he loved. They were matched in their disregard for the opinions of others, their complete self-reliance.

It got into my brain. That night I dreamed that I was knocking down the Coopers' house and building a new one where I would live all by myself. In my dream, I was proud and alone. But the feeling of independence evaporated when I woke up.

I just felt alone.

9

Thursday, June 19
The Day Before the Press Conference
Aka: Makeover Day
138 DAYS UNTIL THE GENERAL ELECTION

Makeover Day had been scheduled on the whiteboard since Tuesday, so at least I was braced for it. I thought I was, anyway—

Until I saw the new wardrobe the consultants had assembled.

It was hanging in a ring around the upstairs conference room. Dresses. Endless dresses, in pastels, in bold colors, in solids and floral prints. That was it. Well—no. There were skirts. And sweater sets. With *flowers*. It was basically the closet five-year-old me would have chosen for sixteen-year-old me.

"So! Cute!" Libby put her hand to her heart as she took it in.

I tried to muster enthusiasm as Nancy joined us, but she shot me a wry grin.

"I know," she said. "Not my top choice either, but America likes girls in skirts."

Taking my arm, she strolled with me to the volunteer room, where the others had saved me a yard-sign-assembling seat. I glanced enviously at Nancy's outfit, a midnight blue suit that made her complexion look milky white and glowing. It was impossible to tell how old this woman was. All I knew was that at whatever that age was, I wanted to look just like her—warm, poised, and elegant.

"I'm taking you for a haircut at lunchtime," she announced. "And after that—fashion show! They're doing a little polling."

"Polling?" I blinked. "On what?"

"Which outfits prospective voters like you best in." She winced an apology. "I know, it's ridiculous."

Libby brought me an un-asked-for coffee and left me in my usual post between Gary, an ex-marine in his seventies, and Pepper, a plump homemaker with opinions on everything.

"Did you hear about the new airline restrictions?" Pepper started, and when I thought to look up again, it was lunchtime, and Meg and Gracie were walking through the door.

The volunteers went crazy. I guess these two didn't make many in-person appearances. While Gracie sprinted straight at me to report everything that had happened since breakfast, Meg moved slowly through the room, shaking the hand of each of the volunteers, learning their names, thanking them for their help, and in some cases inquiring after family members or mutual acquaintances. She was as warm and comfortable as I'd ever seen her, a campaign video come to life.

She was great at this. It shouldn't have surprised me, but it did.

As soon as we were in the hall, her vibrancy faded like a tablecloth left too long in the sun.

"I'm taking you for a haircut," she said. It took me a confused second to realize that Nancy's task had been reassigned to her.

I hoped she couldn't sense my disappointment. I guess as my stepmother, it did make more sense for her to come along than the Communications Chief of the senator's campaign. Maybe Meg felt bad about last night, for forgetting about me and hiring that babysitter. Maybe she was trying to make up for it.

"I'm getting my hair done too," Gracie said proudly. "Just a trim."

The three of us drove to a salon in DC, trailed by a small security detail. When we pulled into the garden-lined parking lot, I saw a cluster of people waiting by the back entrance. They were holding cameras.

My heart raced as we got out of the car. *Why would the press be here? How did they know we were coming? Did the salon tip them off?*

"Bright smiles!" Meg wrapped her arms around us and gave us both a playful squeeze. She didn't seem fazed at all by the sudden burst of attention.

Of course she's not surprised. The realization washed over me like a cold shower. *They planned this.*

Someone from the campaign must have called the reporters, hoping to orchestrate a photo-op of Meg, her daughter, and notorious orphan/A-student/volunteer Kate Quinn—just three ladies out on the town, enjoying a family day, as if it were all perfectly normal.

This is *normal.* I held Gracie's hand and smiled up at one of the snapping cameras. *It's normal for them.*

I came back to campaign headquarters with pretty much the same long hair, now a few inches shorter and layered so that it swept around my face, making my features softer, my eyes bigger. That's what the stylist had told me, anyway.

I fidgeted with the rubber band on my wrist, itching to throw my hair into its usual ponytail. But this was the Official New Look, and I didn't want to aggravate anybody by messing with it.

A girl came in to do my makeup before the fashion trial. They'd set up a curtained area in my TV lounge where I could change. Nancy met me in the hall to examine outfit number one, low-heeled Mary Janes and a light blue Lilly Pulitzer dress that pinched my waist and grazed my knee-caps. The shoes looked modest, but they were Louboutins. As in, way out of my league. I shouldn't have looked at the label; now I was too nervous about scuffing them to walk straight.

"You don't have to talk much," she told me as we walked down the hall, a note of resignation in her voice. "Just hi, nice to meet you, that sort of thing."

"So I shouldn't give my opinion on US relations with Turkey?" I grinned. "Labor laws?"

Nancy laughed, shooting me a conspiratorial nod. "No. Not today."

In a meeting room at the back of the building, eight random people with clipboards were gathered. And by random, I mean *random*—a college kid wearing a Kudzu Giants T-shirt all the way up to a sour-faced grandma in a pink pantsuit. But they all reacted the same way when Nancy led me into the room. They stared, unblinking, in bald-faced curiosity. I glanced down at my outfit, worried something that shouldn't be was popping out. But it was my face they were watching. They *recognized* me.

I felt a twinge of sympathy for zoo animals.

Elliott stood in the back of the room, observing the proceedings with the impassivity of a god on high.

"Hi," I said. "It's nice to meet you."

The focus group scribbled notes on their clipboards. A few smiled at me first. Others squinted like judges at a sporting event. Olympic standing-in-place—4.8 from the Russian judge.

A half hour later, I repeated the process with a different dress—DKNY, gray, more modest—and a different group of people. This time, I noticed some holding cookies and coffee. One had piled-up masses of hair, like those photos of sister wives you saw in the paper. Where had they *found* these people?

I gulped. "Hi. It's nice to meet you."

Nobody in that group broke a smile.

And then again. Skirt and sweater set—a designer I'd never heard of, which I found weirdly comforting. Brighter colors. Heels higher than I was used to, but hopefully I'd have a chance to practice in them before the press conference.

"It's nice to meet you," I recited to Focus Group Three. Beyond a few faint, pitying smiles, no one reacted. At all. Just like the last two times I'd said it. So, drawing in a breath, I mixed it up a little. "Thanks for coming out today. Hope the cookies are worth it!"

Elliott's poker face drooped into a scowl, but that got a

universal laugh, the tension broken. A middle-aged Asian lady winked kindly at me before starting to scribble.

I didn't hear the results until the senator came back to the office at the end of the day. The volunteers had trickled off one by one, and I'd slipped back into my comfortable jeans and sneakers, pointlessly straightening tomorrow's stacks of bumper stickers, hoping for either a new task or a ride home. I'd even have settled for *Triplecross* at that point.

Hearing the senator's voice in the hall, I decided to fake a trip to the restroom as an excuse to say hi.

But as Nancy's voice rose over the senator's, I slowed my step. "Not great. Not *bad* by any means, but not as positive as we'd hoped. The last group had the best response . . ."

"What was the issue?"

"Low on personality." Nancy sighed. "It may have been the dresses."

Or maybe the fact that I wasn't allowed to say anything?

Stifling a scowl, I peeked around the corner. The senator was leaning heavily against the door frame, one hand cradling his forehead. I wished I could sink back into the wall.

Too late. Nancy's eyes landed on me. She grinned maniacally.

"Good job today, sweetie," she lied. "Tomorrow will be . . ." Her mouth moved soundlessly, hunting for the right sound bite. But for once, the communications guru was at a complete loss for words. I wanted to cry out something too, that I'd do better, help him win, that bringing me along was a good idea, but now I was too worried I'd say the wrong thing to say anything at all. Elliott would be so pleased.

By the time the senator straightened up and turned to me, he had his TV face on—confident, charming.

"Tomorrow will be a big day," he finished for Nancy. "You're right about that, Nance. So what do you say, kiddo? Let's go home and get ready."

∽ 10 ∽

Friday, June 20
The Day America Gawks at Me on Live Television
137 DAYS UNTIL THE GENERAL ELECTION

I woke with a pounding heart.

Press Conference Day.

Dressed and ready, Gracie tiptoed in to shake me awake but found me staring at the ceiling, my mouth already dry.

"Come *onnn*," she groaned. "If you don't come, Gabe won't come, and then I'll have to stay home too!"

As we bumped south along the freeway, the road blurred around us, the noise a rhythmic thud punctuated by occasional car honks and cheers as other drivers recognized the name on the side of the bus: *Cooper for America*. Every so often, the senator opened one of the windows and waved.

I spent the ride feverishly thinking about everything but the event ahead.

Like this bus. The campaign called it the Locomotive, and given the long line of official cars surrounding us, it did feel like we were aboard a train. Ahead were two security SUVs and just behind, two black Secret Service cars. Behind them was a secondary bus filled with staffers—and bringing up the rear, what they called the Caboose, a shabbier bus carrying the press corps who'd been assigned to shadow and report on Senator Cooper's campaign.

Today, they would be reporting on me.

I adjusted my outfit for the twentieth time, feeling the sweater scratching my armpits, the skirt's zipper digging into my waist. Of course, the consultants had picked the highest heels for me to wear. I was having trouble balancing in them. And I was sitting down.

At least the inside of the Locomotive was sleek and comfortable, lined with plush booths currently filled by senior aides, the same lucky-duckies who'd gotten seats at the table on my first day at headquarters.

I tried to settle in. I'd been hoping to sit with Nancy, but she was in the Caboose, giving one-on-one interviews with the more important reporters. And Lou had traveled ahead to meet with the field staff coordinating the press conference. Too bad—I could have used one of his goofy pep talks right about now about how *un*squirmy I was, how there was absolutely no way I would flail in front of the reporters in these heels, fall on my face with my skirt flipped up, then leap to my feet, blowing hair off my lips, smiling and waving—

Think about something else.

In the back was an office—a real one, with a desk, WiFi, a TV that was always on. I craned my head. The senator and Elliott Webb were there, leaning close over the desk in hushed debate. Everyone else on the Locomotive was making laughing, nothing conversation about sports and movies. It was as if they'd all met in secret and agreed not to talk politics.

They probably had. Another campaign strategy—Operation Chitchat.

Next to me, Meg was gazing out the window with an inscrutable expression. I tugged at my skirt again and wondered if she was as anxious as I was. Opposite, Gracie and Gabe were filling out a book of Mad Libs, cracking each other up with each new entry. I got out *The Fountainhead*, half hoping Cal would notice, but he was typing frantically on his laptop.

My eyes landed on the long schedule of events pinned near the front of the bus. I squinted, reading.

"Carsick?" Meg asked, offering me a sip from her water bottle.

"No," I admitted. "Confused."

She set down the bottle, listening.

"Why are we having the press conference in Pennsylvania?" I asked. "Why not DC? Or Massachusetts, at your house there?"

Meg's eyes brightened. "We had a number of events already scheduled in Pennsylvania today, including Senator Tauber's retirement dinner tonight. Elliott thought—"

"So this was Elliott's decision," I said, confirming what I'd already guessed.

"Would you have planned it differently?" Her tone wasn't confrontational. More . . . professorial.

I thought.

"Not necessarily. Keeping to the schedule makes it look like the campaign is on track. Like the press conference is no big deal. And if it doesn't go well, we can redeem ourselves later in the day." Meg smiled faintly, and I sensed that I'd hit on the right answer. "But I wouldn't have picked today."

"Why not?"

"This should be Senator Tauber's big moment. His retirement. We're hijacking it."

Meg looked thrown. Then she let out a sigh. "Bernie's been in Congress for close to twenty-five years, Kate. Trust me—he knows how this game is played."

I knew she was right. Anyone who'd been a career politician that long had probably upstaged more than a few of his own colleagues over the years. Even so, this tactic felt a little too much like Elliott Webb—equal parts savvy and slimy.

So when Nancy climbed onto our bus at a rest stop in Delaware and announced dully, "He's coming. Last-minute schedule change," I enjoyed the dismay on Elliott's face perhaps a little too much.

Gracie stood up. "Who's coming?" She had her Mad Libs pen at the ready, making her look like the world's youngest campaign strategist.

"President Lawrence." Meg sighed, turning to Nancy for confirmation.

Nancy nodded, sinking. "He's going to spout some line about bi-partisanship, about the value of a long record of service, but we know what they're really doing."

Yep. Stealing the spotlight. Just like us.

"I don't see a problem." Senator Cooper emerged from the back office, shrugged, picked up a newspaper. "The more the merrier."

"It's shitty," Nancy blurted. Gabe gasped, Gracie giggled, and even Meg hid a smile. "I apologize, sir."

"Language, *language*." Elliott tsked, not looking up from

his notes, and Nancy, passing him on her way to the back of the bus, shot him the bird. I mentally replayed the exchange all the way to Valley Forge, PA, my smile lingering even as a makeup artist crouched beside me to fix my face.

When we got to Valley Forge, the press army was already gathered in a field lined with old-timey fences and historical plaques, lonely cannons dotting the horizon. As our bus rolled through a police barricade, I saw that a simple stage had been erected in front of the press, security waiting. I spotted James and felt my nerves quiet a little—if the mob descended again, I knew he'd pull me out.

Gracie had to be physically restrained from bounding off of the bus before Elliott could line us up—with Gracie in the rear.

"We have to save the best for last, don't we, Grace?"

She glared at him so viciously he flinched.

In front of me, Gabe's hands trembled. His face was drained of blood, mouth set in a grim line.

"Hey Gabe, hold my hand," I said. He squinted, hesitating, then glanced up at his mom. The makeup girl was dabbing her nose with powder and she didn't look down. I nudged my hand into his balled-up fist and leaned closer. "I'm scared too."

He peered up, blinked, and decided to believe me. Why shouldn't he? It was true. My hand was disgustingly clammy, but I think that was comforting to him, proof that I was as terrified as he was. He squeezed it tight.

"They'll start snapping as soon as the doors open," Nancy murmured, tucking a strand of my hair back into place. "So be ready. You can do this."

I nodded, barely hearing her above the sound of my pulse. "Remember the talking points, if anything—"

"No." Elliott elbowed her aside. "No talking points." His eyes burned into mine. "No talking at all, 'kay? Stand there and . . . look pretty."

He tapped me on the head, and as he walked away, something broke in me—snapped—so forcefully that I could have sworn it made a noise, like two bits of flint knocking together. My pulse stilled to a dead quiet. I blinked, and everything around me became crisp.

Look pretty.

No one had ever talked to me that way before.

As the doors to the campaign bus swished open, I felt my jaw relax, my spine straighten, my hand tighten around Gabe's, but this time, not with fear.

The mob was polite. I didn't wobble in my heels. My smile was set, ready for the camera flashes, and no one called out questions. They knew they'd have their chance in a moment. As we passed by, I heard them murmuring into their microphones and realized they were talking to the audience—all the people watching on TV.

Once we'd arranged ourselves on the stage, the senator read a brief statement I'd heard him reciting in bits and pieces many times over the past week.

"On June the tenth, I learned along with much of the nation . . ." He paused, and if I hadn't overheard the rehearsals, I would have sworn he was choked up. "Something incredible."

He turned here and his eyes were brimming, radiant with joy as he looked at me. I felt my cheeks flush hot. Meg reached around Gabe to give my back a rub, a quick circle like my mom used to do, and for a second, the news crews, onlookers, and supporters dropped away.

But only for a second.

"Seventeen years ago," he went on, his voice now low and serious. I braced myself—this part I hadn't heard. "I developed a relationship with a young campaign volunteer named Emily Quinn. It began very innocently, but evolved into something—inappropriate. We slipped. *I* slipped. I let my wife down. I let my campaign staff down, and the citizens of Massachusetts. I take full responsibility for that. Ms. Quinn and I quickly realized that we'd made a mistake and ended our relationship, at which point she left the campaign, and I . . ."

Here Meg reached out and took his arm. Flash-bulbs went crazy.

"I confessed my indiscretion to my wife and took steps to repair the damage I'd done to my marriage. It took time, but I'm happy to say that we emerged stronger than ever."

He cleared his throat and a campaign aide at the foot of the stage offered him up a glass of water. He waved it off.

"Let me put to rest some of the rumors that have been flying around in the past week. At no point in the past seventeen years have I been in contact with Emily Quinn. I first learned that Kate was my daughter from a *New York Times* reporter who I see in the crowd here today."

The reporters all turned to gawk at a middle-aged woman with dyed black hair. She blinked and raised her recording device. It occurred to me that I could read her article once this was done. And if I could get onto the press bus, maybe I could ask her some questions, starting with, "How on earth did you find out?"

"Meg and I have enjoyed the opportunity to get to know Kate over the past week, as have Gabriel and Grace. Kate's a remarkable young woman, I'm pleased to say."

As the senator beamed over his shoulder at me, my whole body started to tingle.

But then I heard what came next.

Whiteboard Kate.

"Every day after school, Kate volunteered at her mother's food bank, all while maintaining A's in all of her classes. In the past week, she's faced searing scrutiny and incredible upheaval. She's done so bravely and uncomplainingly, even while dealing with her own grief following the *tragic* loss of her mother. She's bright. Caring. And—she plays a mean game of Ping-Pong!"

The crowd laughed and I tried not to let my confusion show. We hadn't played Ping-Pong. As it happened, I'd *never* played Ping-Pong.

"I realize this is a tough sell during an election year, but my family and I would appreciate your discretion and good judgment as we welcome Kate into our family. I'll take a few questions."

The mob started to yell, but he pointed to one among them, like a teacher calling on someone in class.

"Do you plan to drop out of the race?"

"I will not drop out of the race. I don't believe that's the right choice for America, nor do I believe it sets a good example for my children." He nodded to me. "I want my daughter Kate to know that I'm a man who keeps his promises."

"Will she campaign with you?" a female reporter asked.

"Yes," Meg answered this one, leaning into the microphone. "We've asked her to join us and we're thrilled that she's accepted."

"Kate!"

I flinched. A number of reporters were calling out my name. *Most* of them were, in fact. I glanced to my left and saw Elliott frowning up at me.

"Kate—how are you handling the shock . . . ?"

"Kate, did your mother ever . . . ?"

I couldn't make out the questions, but it didn't really matter. I wasn't supposed to talk, was I? Just stand here and smile pretty.

"It's going to be a long day," the senator laughed, motioning the reporters to calm down. "Kate's not used to this, so let's go easy on her."

Then I heard a question rising above the others.

"How did you react to the news? *Were you ashamed?*"

I thought for a second they were yelling to Meg. But no, everyone in the crowd was staring at me, shocked into silence by the question. Even the weasel-faced reporter who'd asked it suddenly looked sheepish. Gabe peered up at me with big eyes, and squeezed my hand twice, silently asking if I was okay.

"All right, that's it for today," the senator said, raising his hand good-bye.

That's it? I thought. *No. This can't be it. That can't be the last thing.* If the question went unanswered, it would stay in the air forever, an assumed "yes," everyone in America believing I felt ashamed of my mother.

The senator stepped away from the microphone and I lurched forward to fill the space. My skin pulsed hot, my hands shaking at the question, but I forced them around the microphone.

"No, I don't feel ashamed."

My voice ricocheted from the speakers, echoed by a shriek of feedback. I guess I'd spoken a little too loudly. The crowd had fallen dead silent. I saw that the senator had come back, his hand hesitating inches from the microphone, but what could he do? I was talking, he couldn't stop me. His hand dropped.

I swallowed.

"There's no shame in being born. I don't have to apologize for that. And as for Senator Cooper—"

My brain flashed to the car ride earlier in the week, the sound bite the senator had liked.

"I feel very *lucky* that he's my father."

Oh-kay, that was really all I could think of to announce and they were all still staring with rapt attention, so I added in a small voice, "Thank you," and campaign-smiled, and they all erupted and started taking photos and talking into their microphones and I got shuffled off the stage with the others. Nancy looked a little green and Elliott like he was planning to strangle me later, but the reporters nodded, impressed, the onlookers cheered and grabbed my hands, and when we got into the bus, my stepmother turned to me with a slow grin and declared, as if it were now official:

"I *like* this girl!"

~11~

The sunlight was stretching dim over rolling hills dotted with cows and lined with long, low fences. Behind me sprawled the glittering tents of Senator Tauber's party, currently a mess of politicos, their voices shrill with forced merriment. But out here, it was still and lovely, and while the senator and his team prepped our official entrance, I had two minutes to breathe.

We'd hopped from one event straight to the next since the press conference, even stopping off at a grocery store for a hand-shaking visit with potential voters. All I'd had to do was wave and smile. Since the press conference they'd been careful to keep microphones away from me. Not that I minded. I was all talked out and a little shaken at having so blatantly disobeyed the one directive they'd given me. My adrenaline rush had rushed back out.

It was harder work than I'd have guessed. I'd flung my arms around like a championship waver for the better part of eight hours. By now, they were hanging like rusted anchors at my sides. At least they'd let me change into ballet flats for our evening event. My feet were grateful.

"Kate!" Nancy motioned me over.

I took one more moment to drink in the sunset, drew a deep breath of hay-scented air, and hurried into the tents to join the Coopers.

There was a receiving line leading to our honored host, the newly retired Senator Tauber. This farm, estate, and grounds all belonged to Tauber's wife, Nancy had dished on the way over. Tauber was the son of a coal miner who'd met and wooed an heiress after the death of his first wife. I took it Wife Two was the woman standing sentinel next to him, her white hair twisted upward like a cone of soft-serve ice cream.

When Senator Cooper stepped forward, the line of Republican well-wishers stumbled over themselves to clear the way for him. The Taubers reacted so cheerily that you'd swear they hadn't known he was coming.

When it was my turn to shake Senator Tauber's hand, he held on, his eyes crinkling with mischief.

"How are you enjoying the spotlight, my dear?" he asked, and I could tell by his expression that he'd seen our little press conference.

"I'm glad to be *out* of the spotlight tonight, sir," I was quick to say. "It's an honor to meet you. Congratulations on your retirement."

He let out a hearty laugh. "She's a natural, Mark!"

I smiled politely, thinking that if I were actually a natural, I wouldn't have had to mentally practice that greeting all afternoon—and my palms wouldn't have gone clammy the second I'd opened my mouth.

The line moved on and I found myself shuffled off to a table in the dining tent with Gracie and Gabe, while Meg and the senator went around shaking hands. Libby, who'd hovered around me since the press conference, had been waylaid by what looked like her male counterpart at another table, hideous brown sweater vest and all.

Gabe tugged on the tablecloth.

"You don't like these parties much, do you?" I asked.

Even Gracie didn't fake enthusiasm.

"We hate them. They're *boring*." The ultimate insult to an eight-year-old.

The wood-paneled bar along the side of the marquee looked less than mobbed for the moment, so I jumped up.

"You guys want some soda?"

It was an innocent offer, but something about the eager look they exchanged made me suspect that soda wasn't usually on the menu. Now that I thought of it, the only beverages in the Coopers' fridge were juices—with an added spritz of seltzer from the soda stream if we were lucky.

Gabe opened his mouth to confess, but Gracie cut him off. "Coke!" Her eyes grew wider as she attempted some sort of twin mind-meld.

"Me too." Gabe's mouth curled upward despite his best efforts to remain poker-faced. "A Coke. Thank you."

Three steps from the bar, I felt the heat of someone sidling up behind me. Before I could look, a wry male voice murmured low into my ear.

"Heya, new girl."

I froze long enough to wipe alarm from my face and replace it with the campaign smile before turning.

Facing me stood a blond boy in an expensive suit, casual

as all get out, hands in his pockets and an easy grin like he'd known me all my life. He did look sort of familiar. My brain spun, trying to figure out where we might have met—headquarters maybe?—but with everything going on today and the blurry memory of all the people who crossed my path this week, I couldn't quite land on an answer. He looked about my age—too young to be a volunteer, let alone a staffer.

"Hi," I tried, thinking that didn't tip my hand one way or the other.

"I liked your moves today."

I blinked, even more confused. He slid one hand from his trouser pocket to mime grabbing something out of thin air. It looked vaguely dirty and I froze.

"Gimme that mic!" he laughed, and I realized with horror that this kid was imitating the press conference. My face started to flush and, not knowing how else to react, I turned away.

He ducked around me to lean against the bar, face contrite and hand raised in apology. He wasn't that tall for a guy, maybe five foot nine, but compared to me, he was a giant—and besides, there was something about him that seemed to take up extra space, like the entire bar area was his stage. I couldn't look past him, let alone *get* past him.

"No no no!" He grinned. "I'm not kidding, that was awesome. If you only knew how many times I've wanted to do that, and seriously—that reporter had it coming. What kind of bullshit question was that?"

I felt a small measure of relief. There was something

dangerous about this kid, something mocking, but at the moment, it didn't seem to be directed at me.

"Thank you for the encouragement," I said, and his cocky expression wavered, as if he hadn't expected a reply.

"You're very . . . polite, aren't you?" He stepped back to get a better look, his gray eyes scanning me like I'd just stepped out of a UFO.

This might have been a good chance to make a break for it, but I didn't want to give him the satisfaction. I crossed my arms so he couldn't get a good look at *all* of me and coolly stared back.

"Why not?" I replied. "There's no reason to be rude to a total stranger."

I was very good at staring contests. An expert, in fact. It was an ability I'd honed through almost a decade of practice with Penny during pockets of weekend boredom. So it was only a few seconds before I had the pleasure of seeing the blond kid look away, masking his failure with a smile.

"Good point," he said. "Touché. For that, I owe you a drink." He knocked on the bar. "What's your poison? Martinis? Tequila shots? You seem like a bourbon girl, am I right . . . ?"

He was obviously kidding—but at the mention of alcohol, I finally realized who he was. How had I not recognized him sooner? The hair, the smirk, the attitude. It was like I was staring into Lily Hornsby's locker.

And so I was only mostly bowled over when in the next blink, a man in a boxy suit entered the room with one hand touching his earpiece and announced:

"Make way for the president!"

The crowd stopped their conversations as President Mitchell Lawrence entered the tent, his hand raised in a jovial greeting, the sweet-faced First Lady on his other arm. I held my breath, trying not to be star-struck and only partially succeeding. They were shorter in person, but wasn't that what everybody said about celebrities? It was like watching wax figures walk into the room. They beelined for Senator Tauber, and I spun around to gape at their son.

"You're . . ."

He extended a hand and I shook numbly. "Andy Lawrence. Nice to finally meet you, *Kate Quinn*." Before I could close my slack jaw, he shot me a wink and leaned in to whisper. "We'd better not talk too long. They're already staring."

He was right. As he strolled off whistling something that sounded suspiciously like "Hail to the Chief," I saw eyes all over the room travel between us. Us—the children of the two men competing for the office of President of the United States, chatting away. At a *bar*.

I feverishly scanned the crowd for Meg and the senator. They were deep in conversation with two couples I didn't know, backs turned to the president.

When I brought the sodas back to our table, Gracie grinned. "That boy likes you."

"I don't think so," I muttered, hesitating by my chair. Over my shoulder, I saw Andy with his parents, shaking Senator Tauber's hand. He was laughing at a joke his father made, but I had the irrational sense that it was at my expense, that he was celebrating somehow—that whatever conversational sport we'd been playing at the bar, he'd scored the winning point by virtue of his last name.

Worse, just as I was about to look away, he caught me staring. *Awesome. Point two to the president's son.* And then, making my defeat that much more spectacular, as I tried to casually take my chair, my ankle twisted and I stumble-sat, sloshing my drink onto the white tablecloth. I'd made it through an entire day of high-heelage without stumbling— and managed to trip in flats. Typical.

Forcing myself not to turn and see Andy's triumphant reaction, I gulped down what remained of my ginger ale, seething with embarrassment.

"Soda, huh?" Meg said dryly behind us. She sat with an indulgent sigh. "I suppose there's no harm—if it's *just this once.*"

She looked right at me when she said it, one eyebrow raised, giving me the sneaking suspicion that she wasn't only referring to my choice of beverage.

We rolled away in the dark of morning the next day, traveling via bus to Ohio. Maybe to test my babysitting prowess, Meg had booked a separate hotel room for me, Gracie, and Gabe the night before. They'd celebrated their freedom by jumping on the beds until two in the morning. When the knock sounded on our door at 4:00 A.M., we all groaned.

Gabe and Gracie piled into the bus in their pajamas to sleep a little longer. I considered dozing in the office chair, but opted for a strong coffee instead.

As I sipped, I studied the day's pinned-up schedule—back-to-back solo events for the senator. The rest of us were off the hook. I decided to spend the morning plowing through *The Fountainhead*, my feet kicked up on the seat next to me.

"*Life-changing*, right?" Cal said, leaning across the aisle.

I wouldn't have gone that far. The death of a parent, the sudden discovery of another one—those were things I'd probably rank more life-changing than a melodrama about architecture. But Cal beamed and I mustered an enthusiastic nod, thinking that this sweet guy, however brilliant a speechwriter, was just this side of clueless.

By the third campaign stop, I'd nearly finished the novel, Gabe and Gracie were up, and Meg was threatening to put an end to their game of Sorry!, observing that both of them were saying "*Sorry*" in a not-very-sportsmanlike manner. It was drizzling outside. The bus felt cozy and calm. A lazy day with the Coopers. I smiled into Cal's paperback. But as the senator mounted the stairs to complete our tableau, Elliott slunk up after him, and my mood took a nosedive.

He pointed at me. "Kate. Get dressed."

I glanced at my jeans and T-shirt in confusion before catching his meaning. Libby scrambled aboard as the doors were closing, clutching a Starbucks cup and a hanging garment draped in plastic. I reached for both, but she handed the coffee to Elliott.

Meg peered up from her newspaper. "I thought we had the day off."

"Not Kate," Elliott grunted. "She's blowing up. But don't get too comfortable. We might need you later too."

"Blowing up?" I asked.

104

Elliott clenched his jaw before answering, like he was fighting to remain civil. "Your little stunt yesterday seems to have paid off. We did some phone polling last night and your likeability quotient skyrocketed. Yours too, Meg," he added with a vicious smile. "Believe it or not."

She ignored him.

"So get dressed. We need you out there, visible. Go."

Another skirt and sweater-set. It was like they'd decided this was the magic outfit, the only one America would like me in. I myself suspected that if I slugged Elliott on live television, my "likeability" would shoot even higher.

Instead, the day called for more waving and smiling alongside the senator—at a local greenmarket, then with the crowd gathering for a town hall meeting. But today, the attention felt different—more focused, not a frantic blur like yesterday. People wanted to talk to me—even more than the senator in some cases.

"Good for you!" a big-haired woman shouted from the steps outside the town hall meeting, getting a round of applause from the crowd, and I thanked her, not really sure what she was congratulating me for.

The more surreal it felt, the easier it became to stand in front of all those people, have my photo taken, hug kids I didn't know, and keep smiling even when my cheeks were shaking. It helped that I *felt* like smiling. Everywhere we went, crowds of people had shown up to tell us how much they *liked* us. An elderly woman in a flower-print dress grabbed my hands and said she was praying for our family. A grinning young couple held up their red-cheeked toddler so he could kiss my cheek. A burly chef at a diner shouted that he'd vote for my father and "tell everyone I know to vote Cooper too!" It was crazy. It was hard not to be affected by it. And even if they were strangers, it was weirdly comforting to hear that they cared what happened to me.

Some of them spoke as quickly as they could while I moved with the senator down the greeting line. One middle-aged woman told me that she'd been unemployed for fifteen months, but knew Senator Cooper would fix the economy. A man in his thirties showed me his prosthetic ankle and teared up when he talked about the country he'd lost that leg defending.

The senator stopped and listened to everyone, wrapped up in their stories, their questions and concerns. I watched along with everyone else, buoyed by the waves of hope radiating out from him through the crowd. This wasn't a political act. It was what drove him. At every stop that afternoon, the senator lingered so long chatting that Elliott and Nancy had to practically drag him back onto the bus. He cared about these people—you could see it.

Sunday was much the same, as we rolled deeper into the Midwest, from a visit to a mega-church in Michigan to a private dinner with high-level Chicago donors that I hadn't been invited to—until the hostess called and said I "must, simply *must* come along."

At the crystal-laden dinner table that night, I felt a surge of gratitude to my mom for having drilled etiquette into me. I knew which fork did what and when to put my napkin in my lap, to speak when spoken to and at the correct volume. But this turned out to be an easy crowd. They asked about school, how I was enjoying the campaign trail, nothing tricky. They all agreed that the "impertinent reporter" was completely unprofessional and should be fired. When I spoke up in his defense, the ballerina-thin hostess pressed her hand to her heart.

"She is *dear*, Mark. What a blessing."

After dessert, the senator got up to talk business in the study with some of the gathered men, and I suddenly felt like we were in some period piece movie where the ladies were now supposed to go play the pianoforte or embroider. Meg stifled a yawn, but as the senator passed my chair, he patted my shoulder and smiled, his blue eyes crinkling at the corners. It was enough to get me through the next half hour of polite chitchat, back to our latest hotel, and into another unfamiliar bed.

Before I sunk into sleep, I mulled over the utter implausibility of being in this hotel room—the Ritz Carlton or Four Seasons or wherever on earth I was—being out on the campaign trail, my name and face all over the Internet, on the cover of newspapers across the world, my likeability being polled, tested, reported on. Was there anybody in the world who could understand how strange this was?

Of course there was, I realized. *Andy Lawrence.*

In only two minutes of conversation at Senator Tauber's party, Andy had struck me as overconfident. Sly. Defensive too, like he was watching at every moment for a weakness he could make a joke out of.

And yet—he really did seem impressed by my maneuver

at the press conference. It was like he thought I'd done it as a dare, managing to one-up both Sexy Ronald Reagan and the cow prank at his prep school in one fell swoop. When I replayed the conversation in my head, he seemed . . . envious.

I tried my best not to waste valuable sleep time thinking about the president's son. But his face lingered in my mind even as I started drifting off, and all through the next day, I wondered whether he was on the road too, whether we were waving and smiling at the exact same time.

~12~

"Can you explain these numbers?"

The cable news pundit squirmed. *"Only in part. I mean . . ."* He let out a desperate laugh. *"This is a massive bump."*

A cheer rippled through the clutch of staffers surrounding the Locomotive's office TV. I craned my head to see past them.

Mustached Chuck snorted. *"I can't explain these numbers—and I'm the pollster."*

Nancy shot me a wink over her shoulder. "I've got a theory."

Before I could ask her to elaborate, Lou barreled aboard the bus, hoisting a box of doughnuts as a trophy, his bald head shining under the bus lights like a beacon.

"Eight points!" he shouted, and the bus went wild. I tapped my lips with my fingers, glowing with exhilaration. I wasn't sure what the senator's numbers were before, but I guessed that eight percentage points were enough to put him back in the game—maybe even ahead of President Lawrence.

As the crowd broke, clamoring for doughnuts, I crept closer to the TV.

"*This press conference was a big win,*" another pundit was saying, holding up a hand as if to stave off argument. "*He moved quickly, he owned up to it. Personally, I think Cooper's decision to mend his family was* heroic, *given the circumstances.*"

I glanced at Nancy, wondering if she'd caught that word. Then my eyes shot back to the TV, suspicious. Was this guy on the Cooper payroll?

"*You talk about family values. I think the numbers we're seeing reflect the reality of family values in today's America. Listen—nobody's perfect, but this man is dealing with his issues in a way that Americans see as very honest and brave.*"

Campaign plant or no, the others on the news program seemed to agree.

"*And don't forget Meg Cooper,*" interjected a female pundit. "*The power of a woman scorned.*"

Reel footage appeared on screen, Meg waving in front of a red, white, and blue banner, an almost sardonic smile on her face.

"*She's often come across as aloof, prickly—something the campaign's worked hard to combat, but this has really humanized her. I mean, this is not as simple as a Stand By Your Man scenario. The fact that she's embraced Kate Quinn is remarkable. This girl is the very symbol of her husband's betrayal. Talk about generosity.*"

I drew in a sharp breath, wishing I could rewind the last ten seconds and unhear what I'd just heard.

"At the risk of sounding *aloof* and *prickly* . . ." I turned to find Meg squinting at the TV with an expression of weary amusement. "Don't we have better things to do than watch this trash?"

As I winced in agreement, she walked away, eyes closed, cradling her hot coffee in her palms while reciting, "One hundred thirty-two days to go."

Taking Meg's advice, I managed to avoid listening to the TV for the next few hours. But at the next campaign stop, still stinging, I couldn't resist asking Nancy to spell out her theory on the senator's sudden success.

She raised her eyebrows. "*You*, silly. Isn't it obvious?"

I flushed, shaking my head. "Some lady on the news just called me a 'symbol of betrayal.'"

"Don't listen to the news." Nancy turned to face me. "Listen to me. We're polling better now than before that *New York Times* article broke. How do *you* explain that?"

Was it really possible that I'd gone from "symbol of betrayal" to valuable member of the team in a matter of days? And if it was that easy for numbers to jump sky high, what was preventing them from dropping off a cliff again—and me with them?

Before I could answer, Nancy nudged me with her elbow.

"Voters like that you grabbed that mic." Her step was bouncy with triumph as she walked away past Elliott. "Ask Chuck—he's got the polling to prove it."

Voters wanted me to grab a lot more mics. I soon learned that the campaign was fielding a barrage of solo interview requests, from late-night talk shows, *People* magazine, MTV. The thought sent me into cold sweats at night, worrying there'd be a knock on my hotel door at 6:00 A.M., Elliott's voice shouting *"You're going on* The Today Show, *put on a dress!"*

But that didn't happen, thanks to Nancy, who made sure that all requests were met with a polite but firm no. I thought she was shielding me. But on the bus Wednesday, Cal leaned low over his laptop to whisper, "ATV's got an exclusive. Shawna Wells. Family interview. It'll air as a one-hour special. Pretty cool, huh?"

I couldn't answer. Shawna Wells used to be the co-host of a morning show that my mom watched every day before work. Now she anchored the evening news on ATV. I remembered watching her one night as she sat with the president of a country in Eastern Europe and charmingly eviscerated him for human rights violations.

When I saw that, I was in awe of her.

And now I was terrified.

"We'll do it in Massachusetts," Elliott decided. "I'll send some folks up to air the place out."

He convinced Nancy to push the interview a month so that the team could "prep" me better. I had to admit, a month away sounded a whole lot better than first thing tomorrow.

Maybe by late July, this would all feel like no big deal.

My life consisted of rolling panic attacks at the very mention of the word *interview,* along with recurring nightmares about being filmed in something embarrassing—zit cream, a too-small towel, my old nightgown with bunnies spelling out "I Love You" in balloons. So you'd think the last people

I'd want to hang out with would be members of the press.

But all along the campaign route, I found myself perversely drawn to the Caboose—that last, shabby bus in line, full to bursting with chattering reporters.

As we caravanned our way across the country, we often stopped at the same lunch spots, staffers and press interchangeable as they stood in clusters, waiting for their sandwich orders to come up. They seemed to all know each other.

Cal made a running joke of it, teasing the Caboosers with the prospect of a scoop. In Indiana, he whispered to a young blogger with a hipster haircut, "Off the record? I like your T-shirt," and later in the week groaned, "Off the record? I'm hung over," to a clutch of cable news reporters he'd obviously shared drinks with at the last hotel stopover in St. Louis. I laughed, and then hid it, feeling like they were all at a secret party that I hadn't been invited to. Later, I watched them loudly board their bus with a twinge of envy—especially when I saw that black-haired *New York Times* reporter getting on, tucking her laptop into her saddlebag and all her top-secret information along with it.

Her name was Dina Thomas, I'd learned. She'd been on the political beat for fifteen years. She won the Pulitzer three years ago for reporting that a big-city mayor was embezzling city funds to build a vacation home.

When we stopped for burgers at a roadside stand in Kentucky, she went to eat at a picnic table away from the rabble. The senator stayed on the bus with Louis, going over the campaign budget, while Meg tried to get Gracie to stop stealing a road-sick Gabe's French fries. Unnoticed, I slipped away.

Dina looked up from her laptop with a curious expression when I approached, pushing her sunglasses on top of her glossy black hair.

Maybe it was learning that I'd be interviewed by Shawna Wells on national television. Or maybe the fact that I'd recently—finally—allowed myself to read that fateful *New York Times* article, which even after all the buildup was staggering in its details about my life. Whatever was spurring me on, it had managed to shove me out of my comfort zone. This was my chance.

I sat.

"You sure you want to be seen chatting with me?" she asked, clearing her throat. "They seem to have you on a pretty tight leash."

I flushed at that, but didn't flinch. "I have some questions," I said, then quickly added, "Off the record."

Dina's eyes twinkled. "I thought you might." She shut her laptop and rested her hands on it. Her fingernails were trimmed short, bitten maybe. "If you want to know how I found out about you, I'm sorry, but I can't help. I protect my sources. I've been subpoenaed, court-martialed, physically threatened—but I've never revealed a source who didn't want to be revealed."

"I, um . . . okay." Thrown, I glanced over my shoulder, but nobody seemed to have taken notice of me over here. "It's just—*I* didn't know who my father was. My mom never told me. So I don't understand how anyone could have—"

She cut me off, but kindly. "Kate. I can't imagine how difficult this is for you. I wish I could help you understand, but I can't. All I can say is, in my experience, the truth always comes out in time."

There was so much I wanted to ask. Like how she'd found out about my mother. Not just the bare facts: college degree, profession, date of accident, but the impression Mom had made on everyone around her. The words she'd used to describe my mom were sparing, but unnervingly spot on.

"... *A community leader known as much for her relaxed warmth and constant humor as for her passionate advocacy on behalf of the East LA residents her organization served, Emily Quinn raised Kate privately, shielding her from the spotlight of her own often public role* ..."

Dina was crumpling her ketchup-stained napkin. She gave me a smile that indicated good-bye and I knew better than to argue.

Cal watched me get up from the table and return to my waiting burger, his eyebrows raised.

"I asked her where she got her sunglasses," I said.

He grinned. "Ask Nancy—she'll get you a pair."

After that, I kept my distance from the press corps, contenting myself with watching and eavesdropping. Dina was a brick wall, a nice one, but obviously unmovable. I focused instead on mentally preparing myself for the interview to come, hoping that Dina was right, that one day soon it would all become clear.

When we got back to Maryland on Thursday, a fresh hell awaited me.

Almost all of the campaign's television ads and print

materials featured the senator's family. Now that I was an honorary Cooper, it was time for new ones.

But that wasn't even the problem.

The day of the commercial shoot, I woke from a nervous night of half-sleep and checked my flip phone for the time.

I checked it again.

Then I sat bolt upright in bed and clutched it with both hands.

I had 213 missed calls. Over a thousand texts. From what I could scan, all of them were from strangers, some so profane that I threw the phone onto the bedroom floor and stared at it unblinking as it buzzed.

And buzzed again.

Downstairs, Libby was waiting for me, bearing a brand-new smart-phone and a wince of apology.

"We have no idea how it happened." She shook her head as if traumatized. "A campaign contact list leaked. Some *awful* blog posted it online last night. I hope nobody prank-called you yet!"

I handed her my phone, and her face went pale. As she helpfully imported my contacts into the new phone, she chattered away about how the Internet had already exploded into a heated debate over protecting the privacy of minors.

"So in a way, it's a good—"

Another text came in and her nose wrinkled.

I didn't ask.

By the time we left the house, I was still creeped out, but took comfort in the now familiar sight of James waiting by the car in his crisp suit, somehow looking both friendly and dead-freaking-serious.

They're just words on a phone, I reminded myself. *And photos,* my brain added before I shoved that lovely thought away. Either way, nobody was ever going to get past James. My attention was drawn anew to the guards manning the gate as we drove past the press siege. They were here to protect us, buffer us from all the people out there who didn't support us, who wanted to find dirt on us, or make malicious contact for the thrill of it, or worse.

There are people out there—total strangers—who hate *me,* I realized, and rubbed my arms against an imaginary chill. The glass of the car window felt flimsy all of a sudden. But that was silly. I knew it was bulletproof.

The commercial shoot only added to the bizarreness of the day. We filmed it an hour away at a supporter's house that none of us had ever been to. However random, the place was lovely—green lawns flanking an artificial pond full of non-artificial ducks. The crew had set up a picnic and Gabe got confused when the cameraman told him not to eat the food.

"Think Christmas cards, Gabe," the senator laughed. "Real life—but prettier."

It took us a while to get to pretty. They tried some shots of us all piled onto a red-and-white checkered picnic blanket, awkwardly leaning over each other to grab prop food, and when they yelled "More chatting, please!" the senator blurted, "How was your day, dear?" to which Meg replied, "It was very odd. I put together this lovely meal and then strangers showed up with cameras and started ordering us around!" Pretty soon we were all actually laughing, even Gabe, who had to be constantly admonished for looking straight into the lens in abject terror.

Next came shots of us strolling the grounds in different combinations: the senator and his wife, me and the twins, me and Meg, and finally me and the senator. As the cameras rolled, our fake conversation morphed into a real one.

"You're doing great," the senator said. I laughed, thinking he meant the commercial, but he patted my back. "Everybody tells me what a trouper you've been, kiddo. Keep it up."

I flashed a very real smile and the crew yelled, "Cut!"

On our way back to campaign headquarters, my brain replayed the senator's comment in a broken-record loop. Was there a promise implied in that "Keep it up"? Keep it up . . . and then what? If I kept trying hard, kept inexplicably boosting his polling numbers, maybe this could stretch longer than just the summer, all the way to November fourth. And by then, they'd be so used to me, it would make all the sense in the world to invite me along to the White House.

At the thought of that big, columned building, my brain shut down. 1600 Pennsylvania Avenue. I'd still never seen it except on the news and in movies. It seemed like a jump too far, ridiculous, like we were all campaigning for the chance to teleport to Jupiter. But the White House wasn't a fantasy to the senator. It was the reason he got out of bed every morning. And if I could help put him there, I would.

It was a future. A possible future. It had been a long time since I'd dared think that far ahead.

As soon as we walked into HQ, Tim the Surly Campaign Aide blocked my way.

"There's someone on the phone for you." His Adam's apple rose with indignation. "The *campaign* phone. A friend from South Carolina?"

Rolling my eyes, I pried the phone from his clenched hand. It had to be Lily Hornsby—my *only* friend from South Carolina. We weren't exactly on phone-catch-up terms, but maybe she wanted to say hi. She must have called my dead cell number and thought to try me via the campaign. But when I picked up the receiver, the voice on the other end was male.

"Greetings from the Palmetto State." His voice was teasingly familiar, dry and ironic, with no Southern drawl whatsoever. "Your cell number's not working. FYI."

My brain sputtered like a beached fish. Was this a stranger? Someone from school I'd never paid attention to? Or . . . oh my God. Oh. My—

"This is Andy Lawrence, by the way."

"*Why are you calling me?*" I glanced over my shoulder at the staffers passing in the hall and ducked behind a cubicle wall.

"I'm bored," Andy replied. "I actually am in South Carolina, you know, so it wasn't technically a lie. My dad's got us going to three backyard barbecues today. *Three.* Have you dealt with this yet? You have to eat at all of them or it's rude, and people keep pushing food at you like you're their Save the Children sponsor child. I don't know how I'm gonna get down another rack of ribs. It might not be physically possible. Seriously, I'm thinking of becoming a vegan for the next five hours. What are you doing?"

I froze. "*Why?*"

"Just curious." I could almost hear him smiling on the other end of the line. "Not much of a phone talker, are you, Quinn?"

"No, I . . ." I let out a flustered breath. What was the matter with me? *Just find out what he wants and get him off the phone.* "I'm a little rusty, is all. We've been shooting campaign ads today, so I haven't had to do much besides smile and mime eating."

"*Mime eating?*" He laughed. "Yikes. Want some ribs? I've got an endless supply. I'll deliver them to you myself."

Just then, an aide walked by with a stack of pizzas and I almost floated after the smell like a cartoon animal.

"Dammit, I'm on." Andy let out a mournful sigh. "Nice talkin' to you, Kate Quinn. 'Til next time."

And click.

Tim craned his head around the corner, his eyebrows knotted in accusation. I held my breath, wondering if he'd known all along who I was talking to.

"Personal calls are *not allowed* on the campaign line," he hissed, snatching the phone back.

As Tim stomped away, I collapsed against the cubicle, buzzing, replaying the nonsensical conversation in my head, hoping I hadn't just done something stupid by mentioning campaign ads to the president's son.

He is the enemy, I reminded myself. *Beware.*

I was sitting on the floor in Gracie's room on Friday afternoon, teaching her to play Spit, when Senator Cooper popped his head in.

"I'm heading to Oklahoma for a fundraiser—wanna tag along?"

Gracie's face lit up, game forgotten. I glanced up at the senator, and was surprised to find him looking past Grace at me. He cleared his throat, uncomfortable.

"Well?"

"Yeah!" I blurted. "Sounds great."

Gracie stood, scattering our cards across the carpet. "What about me?"

"Mom says no this time." He put on a fake stern expression. "And she's the boss."

As soon as he was out of sight, Gracie fled downstairs. A few seconds later, I heard a door slam.

"Yikes," I muttered. Did she do this every time she wasn't allowed on the road?

I straightened up the game and went back to my room to pack—but no need. A full bag was already waiting for me at the end of the bed.

This fundraiser was a special one—a benefit concert, Winchaw Junction headlining. I knew they were a country band, but wasn't sure I'd recognize their music.

"Should be a good time," the senator said. It already was. We were traveling to the event via a donor's private jet, most definitely the first time I'd ever skipped security lines and hopped straight onto a plane from the tarmac like an old-time movie star. It was thrilling—until we climbed the stairs and saw Elliott Webb inside, laughing raucously with the portly older man who owned the plane.

As the senator joined them, I retreated to a seat in the back and belted myself in, glad I'd brought a book along. But when we started to roll down the runway, Senator Cooper came to sit beside me.

After takeoff, the silence stretched from comfortable to awkward. I forced myself to turn from the window and smile at the senator.

"So, are you a big country music fan?"

"Sure." Something in his expression made me suspect otherwise. I raised my eyebrows and he chuckled. "Full disclosure? It's not my favorite. I'm more of a blues guy, myself. Don't tell anybody."

"Blues." I stared at him, still skeptical. But then he slid lower in his chair and kicked his feet out, a sly smile spreading across his face, and a different man started emerging—someone I'd actually believe was a blues fan. The salt and pepper in his brown hair suddenly looked less perfectly distributed. I could picture him on a porch swing, coaching a soccer game, shopping for power tools. He seemed like a dad. Was this how voters saw him too?

"I do like *some* country," he admitted. "The classics. Johnny Cash. And stuff that veers more toward folk. I've got a million old Bob Dylan tracks."

I had to cut him off there. *"Bob Dylan?* But . . . you're a *Republican."*

He laughed. "I won't say I align with all his *views*, but I appreciate the spirit behind his lyrics. And I love the music itself."

"That's—awesome."

I didn't blurt out what popped into my head next, that my mom loved Bob Dylan. She had a million old records too.

Maybe he already knew. Maybe they'd bonded over that when she worked for his campaign. Maybe Bob Dylan was the first crack that led to the dam bursting, to infidelity, to me.

The concert was held at a huge fairground in what had looked from the air like Middle of Nowhere, Oklahoma. The whole place was festooned with campaign banners, posters homemade and official, streamers and balloons, a massive *Cooper for America* backdrop hanging behind the stage.

As a local politician took the stage to introduce us, the senator turned to me in mock concern, fidgeting with his tie.

"What do you think, kiddo? Presentable?"

"You look fine to me, but . . ." I put my hand to my jaw, the way I'd seen Elliott do when he was thinking. "We'd better bring in some consultants and run a quick poll. Too risky otherwise."

The senator let out a laugh so loud and sudden that the

staffers watching the stage for us turned in alarm. He shot them his trademark thumbs-up, me a wink, and then as his name rang out, strode away onto the darkened field, and I stayed behind, glowing. It was just a stupid little joke, but he'd liked it. My father thought I was funny.

As the spotlight flashed across the entranceway, there came a roar that seemed to rise from the ground itself. The place was going crazy, guitars twanging, the lead singer taking the stage to introduce "The man who will restore the country that *we* know and love . . . !"

Easy crowd, I told myself to calm my nerves. *All of these people are supporters of Senator Cooper. And they won't be looking at me. There are lots of people on stage, I'll slip right in once security cues me that it's safe to go.*

But if it's no big deal—why am I entering by myself?

As if in answer, my name blared from speakers all over the field. The crowd started screaming again.

A local coordinator turned to me, her face glowing with fervor. "It's *you*, Kate! You're on!"

I walked out of the safe zone into the roaming spotlight and felt it catch me and stick, hot and blinding, vaguely registered the Jumbotron broadcasting my giant face, remembered late to smile and wave, and thought, of all things, of Andy Lawrence, what he'd said on the phone last week.

"I'm on."

I thought I'd known then what he meant. Now I *really* did.

The senator sat with Elliott on the way home, talking strategy, tomorrow's visit to a factory in Ohio, the dietary habits of koalas, for all I knew. I was asleep before the plane took off, my ears still ringing and my cheeks sore from smiling.

I half woke when I thought I heard my name. Somebody had tucked a blanket over me.

"She did well," the senator was saying, his back to me a few seats away.

"You got lucky with her," Elliott said, and I perked up a little, surprised at his sentimental tone. "We all did. It's amazing—she's the most *docile* teenager I've ever seen."

What?

Docile. Like a barnyard animal.

A branded cow.

"She's a good kid," the senator said.

No matter how many times I replayed it in my head that night—as the plane descended and touched down, as we drove away, as my body welcomed my bed but my brain refused to yield—it still sounded like he was talking about somebody else. An intern, maybe, or a friend's child. Not his own.

"She's a good kid" was the beginning and the end of that thought. It was the sentiment of somebody who wasn't curious to learn any more.

"Steelworkers built this country," cried the senator the next day, his stage surrounded by industrial equipment. "And together, we can move it forward!"

A healthy smattering of applause rose up from the crowd of factory workers who'd stopped work for the senator's visit. We were all dressed down today, the senator forgoing a jacket and tie, sleeves rolled messily up, as if to demonstrate that he too had experience working in factories.

When the senator came down from the stage and made for the crowd, Lou smiled at the rest of us.

"Not bad, huh?"

Cal shrugged, texting someone on his BlackBerry. "He skipped a line."

"No," Nancy blurted, staring at her own phone. "No! This cannot be happening *again!*"

A few startled factory workers turned to stare, but Nancy was already stalking out of the cavernous industrial space before we could ask what happened.

Before she got to the door, we found out for ourselves. Five black-suited men with fingers pressed to their ears flanked the entrance, staring in confusion at the gathered crowd.

"Oh fu—jeez," said Lou, eyes cutting to me and then back to them. He ran a hand over his bald head. "Can you spell snafu?"

"S. N . . ." Cal looked up. "Ohhhh shit."

"What is it?" I asked, already guessing the answer. No wonder Nancy was upset.

"Prepare to hail the chief," Cal groaned, pocketing his phone and hurrying to flank Nancy, who was jabbering irately at the Secret Service agents, as if they were responsible for what had to be an epic scheduling mishap—the senator and the president making the same campaign stop on the same day.

Even Meg's eyes were wild as she made her way out of the throng. "How did this happen?"

"I'm gonna find out," Elliott growled, appearing from nowhere. "For now, let's speed this up. Everyone get in, get out. On the bus in five, before anybody gets any photos."

In the fake-cheerful chaos that followed, I decided to beat the crowd to the Locomotive. Gabe and Gracie met me at the bus's door.

"Can you get us a bag of Doritos?" Gabe whispered.

"Just one." Gracie smiled. "We can all share it. It's hardly anything!"

"Please? We're *starving*." The way Gabe moaned it, you'd think he was a dying street urchin.

Doritos were clearly not part of the Approved Cooper Family Diet. But . . . I didn't know that, did I? I could do this for them. I had five minutes.

Okay, three.

Entering through the side of the factory, I jogged down a dim hallway, toward the vacant break room I'd spotted as we paraded into the event.

It wasn't so vacant anymore. A smash sounded from inside the room.

"Come on, you asshole!"

I hesitated a second before rounding the corner—just long enough to smother a laugh.

Andy Lawrence and the snack machine were locked in battle, his hands grasping its broad sides and leg ratcheted back, ready to kick.

This was too good.

I cleared my throat. Andy turned, his face flooding gloriously red at the sight of me.

"Quinn . . ." His eyes blinked hard. "Fancy, uh, meeting you here."

I stepped between him and the machine, spotting a Cheetos bag dangling teasingly off the end of its coil. I gave the glass a gentle flick and through sheer dumb luck, it dropped with a soft thunk into the dispenser.

Luxuriating in his thrown expression, I handed Andy the Cheetos.

"How did you do that?" He squinted suspiciously at the machine.

I shrugged. "Maybe it just wanted someone to be nice to it."

A smile stretched across his face, one crooked corner at a time. "You're a very wise girl, Kate Quinn."

I felt my ears go red and knew my face would follow. "Gotta go!" I said, and hurried out with a backward wave before he could seize the upper hand once again.

I made it to the bus seconds after Elliott, but he was already glaring at his watch as if I were hours late. Ignoring him, I plopped myself down next to Gracie and stared out the window at the president's limousine, hoping no one would notice that I was trying to wrestle away a smile.

"Kate?" Gracie whispered.

I held my breath as I turned to her, but still couldn't squelch my giddiness.

She raised her little eyebrows. *"Doritos?"*

"Oh." My grin evaporated. "Shoot."

The senator was touring the West Coast for the next few days, the rest of us given time to "unwind." Easier said than done. On the second morning, while Meg was outside watching Gabe demonstrate his new and improved cannonball, Gracie and I snuck a curious look at the news.

On CNN, some guy in a bow tie was jabbering on about what voters want.

"*They don't care about his life—they care about their own, first and foremost. This extramarital affair, the Kate Quinn scandal—it's becoming, increasingly, a non-issue . . .*"

The anchor interrupted to argue. "*We're talking about a secret child here—let's not oversimplify . . .*"

The ticker scrolled by: "*Kate Quinn Scandal a 'Non-Issue.'*"

I heaved a sigh. "At least they've stopped calling me a love child."

"Yeah." Gracie snickered. Then her face dropped. "What's 'love child'?"

A throat cleared behind us, and I spun. Meg's mouth twitched—with suppressed amusement? Hopefully?

"Outside," she ordered. "You will spend the rest of the day acting like normal children. Go."

As we skulked out of the living room, Meg went for the remote. But before she could flip off the TV, I heard the anchor plug the next segment:

"*Next up, Cooper's hard line on immigration, and what it means for the Hispanic vote . . .*"

The words *hard line* echoed chillingly in my head long after the TV fell silent. When Penny called after lunch, I almost blurted them out in place of a greeting. She'd know what they meant. But I hesitated to bring it up. She was so upbeat, so eager to hear how everything was going that I didn't want to spoil her mood. Or mine.

And besides, we had more pertinent things to discuss. Like:

"*What* is with all the *dresses*? Every time I see you on TV, you look like you're wearing an American Girl costume."

"Yes, I'm dressed as Katie Cooper," I deadpanned. "I'm from 1950. I'm twelve years old, and I love ponies and playing the trombone."

Penny laughed. "Please tell me you have a doll that looks just like you."

"I don't, but if you can find me one, I promise I will carry it around to all of the campaign stops. It'll be terrifying."

That was as close as we got to talking politics. We talked about almost everything else—my LA friends, my old school, how she was going to have to share a room with her little sister Eva when her brother Enrico was home on leave from the marines in a few weeks, how tragic it was that our favorite K-town restaurant had closed down. We didn't talk about my mom. Penny had always been careful to let me bring her up first, and I didn't this time.

I didn't tell her about Andy either.

I wasn't sure why.

It felt like a secret—not so much that I'd seen him, twice now, or that he'd called me . . . but that I still thought about him calling, wondered if he would again. Maybe I didn't want to admit that the opponent's son took up so much space in my brain. Not even to Penny. Not even to myself.

⌥ 14 ⌥

Tuesday, July 1
Gearing Up for a Week of Barbecue,
Flag Waving, and Cowgirl Training (Probably)
126 DAYS UNTIL THE GENERAL ELECTION

We had a trip planned for July Fourth that, judging by the ambient stress level, seemed to carry a lot more weight than a simple jaunt to Texas.

Even Meg was wound up tight and letting it show. Her daily recitation of how many days were left in the campaign had gotten louder and a lot less soothing in the past week. And in direct violation of her self-imposed "Campaign-free Zone" policy, she'd started inviting her own staff to the house every day that she wasn't out campaigning. In a weird way, it reminded me of home, how my mom used to have her directors and board members over on weekends and evenings, everyone pitching in on behalf of the Cocina. It was a familiar environment, one that I felt comfortable slipping into.

Since the press conference, something had shifted for Meg. She was alert now, actively involved, maybe even enjoying herself. Seeing how curious I was about the campaign, she'd started giving me things to do, local events to attend along-side her—small ones so far, meetings with supporters who'd asked about me. I jumped at the chance to help, hoping that the more I understood how the campaign machine worked, the more comfortable I would feel as a part of it—not just out on the road or at events, but in day-to-day life too. I kept waiting for the morning I would wake up at the Coopers' house and not blink hard with shock at the still unfamiliar guest room surrounding me.

Any day now.

The Tuesday before July Fourth, Meg invited me to a women's Political Action Committee luncheon where she'd be the keynote speaker. Since she knew most of the ladies in the room already, I assumed it would be another easy crowd. But that morning, Meg began to pace. Over breakfast, she asked me to critique her speech, wanted my opinion on whether the phrase "seminal moment" made her sound too elitist.

And that afternoon, when she took the podium, she introduced me as "My stepdaughter, Kate," saying the word so casually that it felt as though I'd lived with her for years, not weeks.

"Poor Susan," Meg gossiped on the ride home, referring to the event's hostess. "She's running for state senate again."

"You don't think she'll win?"

Meg's mouth quirked. "Considering she's lost the last seven times she's tried, I'd say the odds aren't great."

I choked back a giggle. "This is her *eighth* try? That's crazy!"

Meg raised her eyebrows. "You think that's crazy? Lydia Danforth, the one I introduced you to—"

"The one who kept talking about her kids back in the Hamptons?"

"They weren't her kids. They were her llamas."

I blinked, not understanding.

"She keeps llamas in her beach house. Not at. *In*. Ten of them." She clamped her lips together. "I shouldn't laugh. She's one of our biggest supporters."

I stared at Meg, my jaw hanging open. She burst out laughing anyway.

We were both still giggling when we entered the house and rounded the corner into the family room, where Gabe was leaning over the coffee table, hard at work on something. When he saw me, his face went blank. He scrambled away, clutching his project behind his back.

"That was odd," Meg said.

I shrugged, thinking it wasn't, really. It was just Gabe.

But that wasn't quite true, was it? It had been a long time since he'd acted so uncomfortable around me. I'd worked at it, steadily. Every time he was playing a video game or watching TV, I'd quietly, casually sit next to him, reading my book. Eventually he'd stopped reacting so weirdly to me. Until today, anyway.

That night, I went up to my room to find a sketch of a seagull lying on the bed. I traced the edge of it, realizing why he'd had his hands behind his back when he fled the room. At the bottom, he'd written, "For Kate. Your brother, Gabe."

I smiled at the sketch again. Propped it on my dresser and sat down on my bed to smile at it from across the room. I had a brother now. A sister and a stepmom.

It was nearly perfect. Except . . .

I sank backward to stare at the ceiling.

Despite fleeting moments here and there, the senator still

felt like "The Senator," the friendly politician whose campaign I was working on. Once again, I reminded myself of Louis's words.

Stick it out. He's worth it.

On July second, the senator flew home from Oregon just in time to reboard the campaign's plane, this time with us in tow. The press was assembled on the tarmac to document our departure from the DC airfield, buzzing with some fresh excitement that I didn't really understand. By now, the photographers didn't surprise me, not even at 6:00 A.M.

When we landed in Texas, two luxury SUVs were waiting for us. In the back of the "kids' car," as Gracie dubbed it, the twins stared upward for most of the ride, mesmerized by the cartoons playing on the backseat's TV. But my eyes were fixed elsewhere—on the flat landscape that stretched around us, the long straight roads and endless fields where long-horned cattle grazed. There were signs in Spanish that reminded me of home, rusted water towers and dingy billboards shouting "God Saves" or "This is Panther Country," and quite a few "Cooper for America" yard signs too. The longer we drove, the more barren the landscape became. I found myself calculating how many miles we were from each tiny town we passed, in case we needed rescue.

We were headed to the family ranch of the governor of Texas. I knew that much. Eric McReady had been a rival candidate during the primaries, the senator's fiercest competitor. It struck me as odd that only a few months after a round of primaries that Meg had called "brutal," we were vacationing with the former opponent's family. Something else had to be going on.

When we passed through the iron gates of the ranch, we entered a completely new world. The plants around the long drive were lush and manicured, not scrubby and sparse like the ones dotting the highway. We rolled past a tennis court, a rose garden, stables, and horse paddocks before finally arriving at the sprawling compound where the McReadys lived when they weren't in the state capital. It was like the Emerald City emerging out of a poppy field.

When the family came to greet us, I slipped out of the car wearing my practiced smile, guessing that more camera crews would be here to document the oh-so-friendly moment. But to my surprise, we were alone—apart from the twenty-plus staffers who bustled around coordinating each handshake.

The senator and governor greeted each other warmly, as did Meg and Mrs. McReady. They all commented on how big the twins had gotten, which made Gabe slump and Gracie stand up even straighter. Then they introduced me to the governor's blond daughter, Carolee, who looked about my age.

Sure enough, as Carolee and I exchanged hellos, her perfectly coiffed mother chimed in. "Carolee is *also* sixteen!"

Everyone reacted as if this were the most incredible coincidence they'd ever heard, like they'd just learned we were both badminton champions or shared the same bone marrow type and one of us was due for a transplant. Carolee twirled her ponytail and shot me a shy smile.

"It'll be nice to have somebody new to hang out with," she said, and I instantly relaxed. "I thought maybe we could go riding tomorrow, if that's cool with you?"

We had a big barbecue for dinner that night, and I slept in the guest room that shared a wall with Carolee's ridiculously luxurious bedroom suite. She'd said she was tired and ducked off to bed earlier than everybody else, but I heard her cell phone beeping with texts until well after midnight. I finally managed to doze off, listening to the sounds of an unfamiliar terrain, and dreamed of coyotes and horses and scrubby land a thousand miles away, flanked by ocean and mountains, me and Mom in the middle of it.

Mrs. McReady outfitted me with a pair of Carolee's old boots and a cowboy hat while the horses were being brought around to the front of the house the next afternoon. The senator and Governor McReady had taken a break from their discussions to see us off. I'd ridden horses before in the canyons surrounding LA, so I wasn't too worried about making a fool of myself in front of them—until I saw Carolee.

She was wearing a tank top and jeans, like me, but hers looked painted on, her hat perfectly perched over a ponytail that spilled like spun gold down her back. Carolee rode without effort, one hand lightly clutching the reins of the second horse that trotted obediently beside her. Once I'd clambered into the saddle, I peeled my hair from my forehead and shoved it under the wide-brimmed hat, hoping I didn't look as sweaty as I felt. Carolee waved cheerily at our families, but as soon as we cut off the driveway onto a horse trail and out of sight of the house, her face dropped into a mask of tragedy.

She squinted over her shoulder. "Have you ridden before?"

"Yeah, I—" Before I could regale her with tales of sunset rides to Mexican restaurants in the Valley, she cut me off.

"Cool."

Carolee beeped. She dug a cell phone out of the back pocket of her jeans and slowed the horse so she could text a reply. I watched her with a mix of horror and admiration. It was as if she were transforming into a mermaid in front of me, or some other magical creature, the mythical Texan Teenager— who brings a *cell phone* out on a trail ride. I was surprised you could even get reception out here.

Once she'd sent her text, she collapsed over the horse with a groan, arms dangling like she was settling in for a nap.

After we'd gone past a cow field, skirting the edge of a barbed wire fence, and listed left for no good reason, I glanced at her with concern. "Are you okay?"

She sat up, grudgingly. "I hate riding. It's just like . . . ughh."

I waited for more of an explanation, but apparently that was all she had. Her horse swished its tail and she swatted peevishly at a fly with her hat.

"It's so fucking hot."

I had to agree. "But you must be used to it, right? Being from Texas and all."

"Yeah but . . ." She squinted up at me like it had just occurred to her that I was an idiot. "We have a *pool.*"

"Oh."

"I wanted to hang out there today, not ride out on a fucking

137

vision quest, but whatever. They wanted the house because Senator Cooper's gonna ask my dad to be his runnin' mate."

She turned to me, eyebrows raised, waiting for a reaction.

"That's what I figured."

Her eyes narrowed. I must not have acted sufficiently impressed. And then her smirk plummeted, as she remembered who *my* father was—the one who'd kicked her dad's butt in the primaries. The top name on the ticket.

Be nice, I reminded myself. *If she's right, then you're going to be seeing more of her.*

Beep. She whipped out her cell phone and texted.

We passed a gnarled old split tree with an actual buzzard sitting in it. Our horses seemed to be ambling along directionless.

"Where are we going?"

Carolee blinked blearily up at me from her phone. "The other stable."

I found myself scanning the grassy horizon, praying for the faintest glimpse of it.

Another text came in and Carolee's spine straightened. She held up her cell phone. "So there's a party. I kinda want to go. Do you mind?"

"Right now?" I asked, but she was texting again. "Yeah, that's fine."

"Cool, so let's just drop the horses at the other stable."

"Sounds good." Suddenly my tank top felt twice as crusty, the backs of my knees soggy with sweat. I hoped we'd have a chance to shower first.

When we reached the stables, a shabbier version of the

ones near her house, a shiny red pickup truck was parked on the dirt road that stretched beside the old wooden building. Its engine was running.

Carolee helped me out of the saddle and put the horses away with sudden friendliness, shutting and locking the stable doors behind us. Then she turned to me with a sympathetic wince.

"So . . . my boyfriend's here and I think we're just gonna head straight there. Can you call one of your dad's people to pick you up?"

I blinked, confused.

Then it hit me, in mortifying stages. Oh. I wasn't invited to the party. I'd misunderstood. And oh. She *wasn't even giving me a ride back*. This was actually happening.

"Um, sure," I said, my head swimming from the heat and the complete ridiculousness of the situation.

"Cool," she said, and before I could even really process what was going on, she and the red truck were a dusty line receding into the distance.

It was right about then that I saw the logic in bringing a cell phone on a trail ride.

When I finally found my way past stray bulls, cow patties, razor-sharp shrubs, and heat-induced hallucinations to the paved driveway leading to the ranch house, my feet were blistered inside Carolee's boots and my shirt so stuck to my back that I suspected it would have to be surgically removed.

Bracing myself for a big fuss from the assembled Coopers, McReadys, and staff, I opened the front door instead to an empty house, the sound of a distant TV echoing through the vacant hallways. An elderly Hispanic woman in a ridiculous uniform poked her head in.

"They're out," she said, and started the vacuum.

I staggered to the open-space living room and stared through dancing sunspots at the massive television that hung beneath a mounted stag's head. Fox News was on—broadcasting a press conference in the town square we'd passed through yesterday. The senator was speaking, turning it over to Governor McReady—his new running mate. So that's where they all were.

A cool shower, a greedy gulp of water from the tap, then I stumbled into bed for an unavoidable nap—and woke up after God knows how many minutes to the sound of my cell phone ringing.

I picked up, expecting Meg's voice or a staffer's. Instead, it took me several blinks to realize I wasn't still asleep.

"Heya, new girl. How's Texas?"

Andy pronounced it the Spanish way, with an *H* in place of an *X*.

I sat up so quickly my head spun. *"How did you get this number?"*

"Charming as always, Quinn. Aren't you supposed to be the polite one?"

"Sorry. Rough day. Just out of curiosity—are you using the FBI to stalk me?"

"Let me guess," he said, ignoring the question. "They made you hang out with *Carolee*." The name was a groan.

I glanced out the window at the empty front drive. "How did you—"

"Nightmare, am I right?"

"No." I flushed. "She's really nice."

"Oh man!" Andy laughed ruefully. "That's a diplomatic answer. Some might call it a *politic* answer. Or a *lie*. I've met her, you know."

Call me crazy, but it didn't feel right to complain about the daughter of my dad's running mate to the son of his competition.

"She's totally fine," I started, but he cut me off.

"What happened?" There was a long pause. "Seriously, tell me."

I drew in a breath. "She ditched me like five miles away at the other end of the ranch to go to some party and I had to walk back in cowboy boots and it's a hundred degrees and I'm lucky I even got into the house because nobody's here and I don't know why people go on about dry heat being better because it absolutely full-on sucks."

"Oh my God." Andy at least had the good grace to stifle his laughter. "Why did you say she was nice?!"

"She is!" I let out a bewildered laugh. "When other people are around."

"She's a stone-cold bitch, but I'm proud of you for trying here, Quinn." I smiled. I couldn't help it. It felt good to get all that out, like the first gasp of air after holding your breath underwater.

A car pulled up outside. No, several. They were back, loud voices filling the house. I glanced at the doorway. *I should get off the phone.* Instead, I jumped up, flipped the lock on the bedroom door, and leaned against it, heart pounding.

Nobody came down the hall. Why would they? I was supposed to be with Carolee, having wholesome fun out on the trail, or whatever else they imagined good Republican teenagers doing.

Andy cleared his throat. "You still there?"

I sat on the edge of the bed. "Yeah."

And then the unthinkable happened—

We talked.

More precisely, he asked questions, and I kept answering them, my finger hovering near the END CALL button but never able to press it, never quite able to get to "I've gotta go," until before I knew it, an hour had passed, and I was in a full-fledged conversation.

"Have you done the 'Just popping into a local diner to grab some ice cream' yet?"

"Yeah, on like day two!" I laughed. "Everyone in the place looked so confused. It wasn't ice cream, though. We got these disgusting loaded hot dogs."

"Which you were then forced to enjoy on camera."

"Yes! Because they're the official food of Skokie, Indiana. I have no idea why. I've had nightmares about them."

"I can beat you. I had to eat haggis last week at a donor party hosted by some rich dude in Florida whose ancestors were Scottish."

I covered my mouth. "That's sheep guts?"

"Sheep organs, actually. *Wrapped* in guts. That wasn't even the worst part. The bagpipe player stood behind my chair for the entire meal. We were pretending our family was part

Scottish too, so I had to act like I was really into it. I'm just glad they didn't make me wear a kilt."

"There's always next time. Gotta be more Scottish donors out there."

"It wouldn't even matter at this point. I think the campaign has reached peak embarrassment for me."

I hesitated, surprised he felt it so keenly. I'd sort of assumed it was my inexperience that made me feel that way.

Andy groaned. "I just doomed myself by saying that. We're taping a warm and fuzzy family interview with some Spanish language news channel this weekend and I know they're going to expect me to rattle off perfect español for the audience, since I'm in Spanish 4 and my dad can only say, '*Somos una* America!' He really lays it on thick too, like Speedy Gonzalez. He doesn't even know how insulting he sounds."

Andy's next question cut my laugh off.

"Have you done that yet? The big family interview?"

I blinked at the ceiling fan, my pulse quickening at the thought of the top secret Shawna Wells exclusive, now only a few weeks away. "Nope. Not yet."

"You're lucky. They're excruciating. You can't scratch an itch without the cameras zooming in and using that shot as an opener."

I decided to change the subject. "Do you have a list of approved sound bites?"

"What, like, in a binder? Yep. But my list pretty much just says, 'Don't talk to anyone.'"

I rolled onto my stomach. "They keep pulling me aside

and giving me notes on how I veered off script when I was, like, asking somebody at a rally where the restroom was. Am I supposed to randomly drop taglines into everyday conversation?"

"You could try it," Andy suggested. "'Nice weather, isn't it?' 'Yes! But it'll be even better with a healthy investment in clean energy!'"

"Except our campaign would be: 'Sure is beautiful out! Kinda makes you question the scientific validity of climate change, doesn't it?'"

"Wow, you're good at this."

"Why thank you."

Andy's laughter died in a sigh. "You got me in trouble, you know."

"I—what?"

"Your famous line! 'I'm *proud* that Senator Cooper is my father.' Don't get me wrong, I liked it at the time, but now it's like the catch-all question for me. Every freaking reporter. 'Andy—are *you* proud of your father?' I'm not supposed to talk to the press, but I finally got fed up and answered the goddamn question just so they'd stop asking."

I grinned slowly. "What did you say?"

"What do you think I said? I was like 'Yeah, of course I'm proud of him. My father's the *president*.' I mean, what else was I gonna say? 'No, I'm not proud, I think he really blew that meeting with the German chancellor?' Of *course* I'm proud. Whatever, they took it the wrong way. I guess I kind of sounded like an asshole, like I was bragging, and they keep playing it on TV."

I cringed in sympathy.

"Plus side is the campaign won't even let me *near* reporters now. But I'm stuck in DC and I'm completely bored, which leads me to my next question. Um. Do you want to go out sometime?"

"What?"

The other end of the line got really quiet.

"I'm sorry," I said. "Are you asking me . . . ?"

This couldn't be happening. This defied explanation.

"Okay, let me rephrase: Do you want to *hang* out some time? Do something? For fun?"

I tried to speak but couldn't.

"I'll take that for a yes and hang up before you can change your mind. See you soon, Quinn."

Out in the living room, the strategists were watching Fox News, and sure enough, there was the video of Andy, saying, "Um . . . yeah. My dad's the *president*." And sure enough, he did sound like an asshole. I burst out laughing and Nancy turned from the news to nod at me.

"Thank God we've got you and not him," she said, to re-sounding agreement from all the gathered staff.

The next day, at a huge Fourth of July picnic and rally, I smiled for the cameras wondering whether Andy was watching, wanting to send him some sort of a code, but unwilling to risk it.

I barely noticed the fireworks.

Wednesday, July 9

Swimming Laps

118 DAYS UNTIL THE GENERAL ELECTION

Back in Maryland, the walls were pressing in.

At first, I was thrilled that Meg had negotiated a week off for me. The senator was campaigning in the Southeast, Meg busy scheduling her own events, and Gracie and Gabe working through a backlog of play dates. I told myself I was content enough to dig through the Coopers' oak-paneled library for books to read poolside—especially after Meg complimented me by noting that she was an avid reader at my age too. But then I found myself pacing the grounds like one of the guards, rereading the same page for the better part of an afternoon, and finally practicing the freestyle stroke I hadn't used since I was nine and forced to take classes at the Y. My form had not improved. And my mind wasn't in it. It was on a bus.

Yep—I missed the campaign.

Not the cameras or the waving—oh *God*, the waving—but the momentum of it, the sense that at any given moment I was exactly where I was supposed to be.

And I missed the senator too.

One night I heard Meg on the phone with him, a now typical conversation, strained in its courtesy. She handed the phone to Gabe, and then to Gracie, who chatted for a few minutes and then hung up.

Gabe noticed. "You didn't let Dad talk to Kate!"

But then, he hadn't asked, had he?

Uncle Barry called a few minutes later, right on cue for his weekly check-in, and it was my turn to get on the phone.

"Everything good?" he asked. "Having a good time? Getting along with the Coopers? Need anything from here?"

It was almost as if Barry were reading from a list and ticking off each item when I answered. I knew he wasn't the chattiest person over the phone—or in person—so I didn't take it personally. But when he started to say the usual, "Whelp, have a good one," I found myself scrambling for ways to extend the conversation, just to kill time.

Before I could ask how hot it had gotten down there, he'd already hung up.

On Thursday, out in the garden, Meg watched me methodically rip apart a dandelion head. Her forehead knotted.

"We need to introduce you to some kids your age. It's too bad Carolee doesn't live close."

"Yeah!" I sighed. "Oh well."

I guess I wasn't too convincing, because Meg cracked a smile.

"I thought that might have been a stretch. But there are some nice families around here, with kids who actually have half a brain cell. I'll see who's around."

"I'm fine, really. I like hanging out here. It's . . . downtime. I love downtime." To prove it, I cracked their leather-bound copy of *War and Peace*.

But an hour later, by some perverse magic, Meg got an out-of-the-blue e-mail inviting me to a birthday party. It wasn't a politician's kid, at least. Saturday night was the sixteenth birthday of Jacob Spinnaker, the son of an editor at the *Washington Post*. Jacob went to Farnwell Prep, the same school as Gabe and Gracie. I guessed that that was how the Spinnakers got Meg's e-mail address. They probably figured I was bored, not knowing anybody but the Coopers.

It was a nice gesture. I tried to get out of it.

"I'm not much of a party person."

"That's not true," Meg admonished. "You're great in groups."

"I should probably rest up, though. That Shawna Wells interview is only twelve days away."

"And this will be a good opportunity for you to get your mind off of it."

"The restaurant's in DC? I don't know how I'd get there . . ."

"They're sending a car." She raised her eyebrows. "Isn't that *nice?*"

I was going.

Sifting through a closet jammed with dresses and skirts, I surfaced a pair of jeans, thinking this was, at last, a chance to dress like myself in public. But then . . . how public was this actually going to be? Would there be cameras? I finally settled for a green campaign-approved sundress, less dowdy than the others.

As I was getting ready, I heard a familiar voice booming through the downstairs foyer. The senator was back.

As Gracie and Gabe ran screaming from their playroom,

I followed, taking the steps two at a time. He smiled over Gracie's stubby ponytail at me.

"Heard you're Miss Popularity!" Then he frowned, considering. "Do you want James with you? Might be a good idea . . ."

Oh God, just what I needed—to walk into a party full of strangers, flanked by a guy with a gun.

"I'll be fine," I said as my Town Car pulled up outside. He didn't look convinced.

But then, giggling, Gracie and Gabe climbed onto the senator's legs, and his wary expression changed to a playful one. As the three of them stumbled away down the hall making Godzilla noises, I hesitated on the porch, wondering if I should just go.

"I'll be back by eleven," I called out, guessing that was a pretty good curfew. Nobody seemed to hear me.

On the ride into DC, jitters set in. This was weird. A random invitation to a party full of strangers? It might have made sense as an excuse for the parents to mingle with the Coopers—but when Meg called the Spinnakers, they'd told her the party was "kids only."

The car pulled up outside a restaurant with towering glass windows that revealed an interior so swanky, I instantly regretted my choice of clothes. Cotton? Did I look wrinkled? Would they notice? I tried to pay the driver, in case the Spinnakers hadn't, but he laughed and told me it wasn't necessary. Come to think of it, there was an eagle symbol where the toll meter should go.

As I was mustering the courage to open the car door,

someone else beat me to it. His hair was carefully mussed like the first time I'd met him, his sleeves rolled up over lean arms, and his gray eyes flashing mischief. A Secret Service agent hovered five feet behind him.

Now I wished I'd brought James.

"You made it!" Andy offered his hand. I clambered out without taking it, a new picture forming in my mind.

"There was no party?" The sidewalk seemed wobbly all of a sudden. "*You* did all this—sent this car?"

"No, there's a party. It's Jake's birthday—I just got you on the list."

I blinked again, dazed, and Andy added, "I go to Farnwell Prep with these guys." He shrugged. "I told them they'd be idiots not to invite you."

The car drove away, leaving me with no other option than to trail after Andy. I had to admit, it did feel better walking into the restaurant with someone I knew, however strange the connection between us.

In a private room in the back, five boys and four girls were seated around a long table laden with appetizers and what looked like cocktails but probably weren't, given the eagle-eyed waiter hovering in the corner.

"Guys, this is Kate," Andy said, pulling out a chair for me.

"Finally!" A red-haired kid with giant ears and a nice smile stood to greet me. "Andy won't shut up about you."

I glanced at Andy, surprised, but he was doing some kind of complicated hand thing with one of the guys down the table.

The dreadlocked girl next to me had a comically full mouth. "Nifftometchoo," she got out. "Mini pizza?"

We ate, drank Italian sodas in martini glasses, and talked, mostly about stupid stuff, the superhero movie that came out last weekend, the worst book on their summer reading list. They were possibly the most normal group of people I'd met since leaving South Carolina. They didn't seem at all snooty like I'd worried they would be, given their prestigious school and the pedigrees of their families. And if they knew anything about me from the news, they made a really good show of pretending otherwise. Tonight, I wasn't the top story. I was just the new girl that their friend Andy wouldn't shut up about.

I stole glances at him over dinner, noticing the way his fingers grazed mine as he passed me plates of food, how he made a point of including me in the conversation—and yeah, okay, I might have also noticed that he was weirdly handsome, sort of rakish when he grinned and probably still as athletic as that *US Weekly* photo underneath his preppy blazer. He caught me looking once and I thought for a horrifying second he'd tease me, but he just kind of flushed and Lucy, the girl sitting opposite, smiled at us like we were a basket of kittens.

Did she think we were on a date? Did *he*?

Once the meal was cleared and the party seemed to be dwindling, I wished red-haired Jake a happy birthday and thanked him sincerely for including me.

He glanced at Andy. "Isn't she coming?"

"Hopefully," Andy said.

Jake grinned appreciatively. "Badass."

"Coming to what?" I asked.

"I was getting to that." Andy stuck his hands in his pockets. "So there's this concert. Kudzu Giants. Do you know them?"

I laughed. "Uh, yeah!"

Everyone knew them. They were huge, in constant rotation on the radio but still completely indie in sensibility. Penny and I were both obsessed with them, but our parents had never let us see them play live.

Andy grinned. "Wanna come?"

We hopped in an armored SUV with four others, including Secret Service. A guy with a camera ran out of the restaurant after us and Andy *just* managed to slam the car door before he could snap a shot.

And, like that, I realized what a stupid idea this was.

That photographer had missed his chance of landing the front page of tomorrow's tabloids by less than a second. I could picture the headline now:

"Bipartisan Partying: Andy and Kate Hit the Town."

If this got out, it would be humiliating—not just for me, but for the senator and his staffers, whose jobs revolved around demonstrating how different I was from the president's son.

Sensing my mood shift, Andy squeezed my arm. "I won't let them take a picture of us. I'd be in bigger shit than you, trust me."

That should have been comforting. But somehow I sensed that Andy didn't really care how much trouble he got into. He was courting it just by calling me, inviting me out. Was that the real reason I was here? So Andy could feel the thrill of rebellion?

The thought hit me dully. It felt uncomfortably like truth.

The car was moving, and I wasn't dramatic enough to open the door at a stoplight and bolt, especially given the security detail surrounding us. But as we drove, I forged a plan. Once we got to the concert, I would call a cab and head straight back to the Coopers' house, no matter how much I was dying to hear Kudzu Giants—see them, live, in person . . .

No. Whatever game Andy was playing, I didn't want any part of it.

As the car pulled into the back alley of the concert venue, I slid my hand into my bag. My fingers scrambled around my wallet, my set of house keys, a tube of Cherry ChapStick. Where was my cell phone?

Andy held the car door open for me and I reluctantly climbed out, scanning the building for its name, location, any tidbit I could tell the taxi company so they'd know where to get me. Finally my eyes landed on a sign—a red, white, and blue one.

"Reelect Lawrence ~ Benefit Concert."

My bag dropped to the ground.

Everyone had piled happily out of the two cars behind me, but I let them pass, staring up at the campaign poster on the VIP door. Andy doubled back, his hand extended.

I picked up my bag and clutched it to me. Backed away. "Why did you bring me here?"

He grinned, all innocence. "I told you. For the band." His friends waited impatiently at the back entrance, waving for us to join them. "Come on, Quinn, I snuck out of the White House for this."

I relaxed. A little. "You're not supposed to be here either?"

"No, I told you. House arrest until they can figure out how to spin me for the campaign. We're gonna watch from the wings—I've got a buddy that fundraises for my dad, he's hooking us up. Secret Service won't tell my folks unless they ask, which they won't. They won't even come in this way. They'll never know."

I made one more attempt to find my phone, and then I pictured it—sitting on my bedside table back at the Coopers, still attached to its charger. And like that, the charge got sapped right out of *me*. In my nervousness about coming out tonight, I'd forgotten my cell phone. How could I be so stupid?

Behind me, the alley was empty, the cars that brought us already gone. As Andy glanced over his shoulder, I pressed my hand to my forehead. I could borrow a phone—call a taxi and bribe the driver not to say where he picked me up, but I didn't like the odds that he'd keep quiet, given how much Nancy had told me tabloids paid for scoops. And this was a scoop.

I could walk away. Find a payphone on the street. Did street payphones even exist in neighborhoods like this?

A low rumble rose up from the building—a thrumming bass line, and then drums. They were starting.

"Nobody will know we're here." I declared it more than asked it. Willed it to be true. "You *promise*."

Andy pressed his hands against my shoulders like he was holding me together.

"I promise."

There was something solid about the way he said it, like his feet were rooted into the ground. I decided to trust him. For now. Just this once.

❧ 16 ❧

The show was amazing, euphoric, glorious—by Cal's definition, I might even have classified it life-changing. I tried to memorize every detail to report back to Penny, but there was such a blur of activity back in the wings that I had no choice but to blur with it.

When we first walked in, the backstage area was jammed with people—some working, whispering into headsets, most of the others getting themselves into prime position to enjoy the show.

They won't notice you, I told myself. *You're only five-two. You probably can't even be seen in this crowd.* A guy wearing a baseball cap and a Reelect Lawrence lanyard nudged past me to greet Andy and I flinched. At my movement, he turned with a quizzical smile. His eyes grew wide.

"Jesus Christ Almighty." The man put his hands around Andy's shoulders and shook him, his mouth forming silent curse words. *"What are you—"*

"It's fine, Steve, she's a friend of mine."

Poor Steve, the "cool" fundraiser, let out a helpless laugh.

I extended my hand. "I'm—"

He cut me off, turning and motioning for us to follow. "I

don't want to know, I haven't seen you, you were never here, and I don't *ever* want this coming back to bite me in the ass." That last part was directed at Andy.

He'd led us behind the backdrop, where we couldn't see anything except a ladder leading up into the lighting rig.

"Awesome, man," Andy said, shaking his head. "I owe you."

"You have no idea." Steve sighed and pulled the baseball cap from his head, shoving it onto mine before disappearing back toward the wings, grumbling something about early retirement.

Andy faced me with a serious expression and lifted his hands to my face. I held my breath. He straightened the hat. Then he smiled, stepped onto the ladder, and offered me a hand up.

A short climb later, we were overlooking the stage from a sturdy lighting platform, hidden from the audience, only a few vertical yards away from my favorite band in the world. By the time I was sitting cross-legged next to Andy, sure I wouldn't fall, listening to the music flooding the rafters, I'd completely forgotten that I wasn't supposed to be here in the first place.

"This is amazing," I yell-whispered into Andy's ear.

He shrugged like this was something he did every night, but then his face relaxed again, his gray eyes widening, and I could tell he was just as transported as I was. It was easy to be swept up by this band, a musical collective with more than a dozen members who swapped instruments, danced and sang under dizzying lights. I got so caught up in the moment that when, after an hour-long set, the music died down and the lead singer strode to the front of the stage to bring up the man himself, President Lawrence, I started screaming along with everyone else.

Andy turned just in time to see my face go pale. He linked his arm through mine. "Annnnnd it's time to get some air."

It wasn't until we got outside that I realized only the two of us had left—the others must have stayed behind in the wings to hear the president's speech and the band's second set.

"So?" Andy raised his eyebrows. "Was it worth the risk?"

A smile flooded my face. "Yes. That was . . . incredible."

"As good as Winchaw Junction?" Seeing me blush, he gave me a nudge. "That's what made me think of this. I watched you on TV pretending to like country music—and I thought this might make up for it."

"Thank you." I laughed, shaking my head. "I don't know what it is, but Republicans and quality music just don't seem to click."

"It's all those Republican 'values.'" He winked. "Liberals will look the other way when rock stars act like rock stars."

"Aha."

Andy stared suddenly at the ground. The light hit his cheek, and I noticed for the first time a tiny white scar under his left eye in the shape of a boomerang. I was stifling the urge to reach out and touch it when he looked up with a shrug.

"So I don't feel like going home yet," he said. "There's a park near here. You wanna take a stroll or something?"

The music from the arena had started again. I could still

feel the bass thrumming in my veins. The night air was cool and sweet.

I smiled. "A stroll sounds good."

The streets surrounding us were lamp-lit, circles of orange light spilling onto the silent asphalt. All of the storefronts were closed for the day. There was nobody in sight.

"Is it safe here?" I asked.

"I've got Tom." Andy pointed behind himself to the Secret Service guy I hadn't even noticed lingering a few yards away. Right—you couldn't get much safer. And yet my stomach was in knots, my skin tingling, hands restless at my sides.

It's Andy, I realized. *He makes me nervous.*

"Just a couple blocks." Andy started to whistle.

I followed, hoping he knew where he was going. And then, as we rounded the corner of a huge building lined with columns, I saw it.

"That's where I live," Andy said, then motioned me in the other direction. My body followed, but my head wouldn't turn. I had to keep staring.

Because there it was, brightly illuminated against the night, its fountain splashing, flag flying, profile unmistakable. My brain fell numb.

It looked like a very nice house. It was on *money.* How could anybody live in it?

And yet, we *would* live here, wouldn't we? Starting in January, if the senator's numbers kept up, the Coopers would move into this big iconic building, and maybe, just maybe, I'd come with them.

I thought that seeing the White House in person would

make it all seem more plausible. There it was—a real thing. You could touch it. Enter through a doorway and sit on its furniture. *Sleep* on its furniture.

It just took years, half a billion dollars, and millions of votes. Then it was all yours.

"And here's the park."

I shook my head. "You're taking me to the *National Mall?*"

"This is Lafayette Square," Andy corrected. He pointed over my head, grinning. "The Mall's over there. Don't worry, I'll take you there next time."

As we passed a statue of somebody who looked like George Washington but, given the name of the park, was probably the Marquis de Lafayette, Andy grabbed my hand and pulled me off the path.

"I like the lawns better," he said, and I nodded as if that were a perfectly normal sentiment, as if it were completely normal to take a nighttime stroll outside the White House with somebody who lived there. He kept a firm, easy hold on my hand, and for some reason I couldn't explain away, I didn't pull back. I glanced at him, wondering whether he'd brought me here to show off or to intimidate me, but there was no hint of that in his expression. In fact, he squinted, pointed to the side of the building, and said lightly, "Maybe next year, you'll be living there. They'll probably give you my room. There's a loose floorboard under the bed. I'll hide notes for you."

I smiled. "Sounds great."

It sounded insane.

Andy sighed. "Did you see my mom in the audience tonight?" I hadn't. "She was doing her Barbie face. I keep telling her not to."

"Barbie face?"

He demonstrated and I burst out laughing. It wasn't exactly Barbie, more like a sock puppet, a delirious, open-mouthed grin. His imitation dropped into an eye roll.

"The woman is a serious intellectual. She's got a master's in French literature, but you'd never know it. As soon as a camera's on, it's . . ." He made the face again, even doofier.

I smiled again, but this time when he looked at me, he flinched. He squeezed my hand once more and let it go.

"I shouldn't make fun of my mom. She's a great lady."

He'd lapsed into such sudden seriousness that I wondered if something had happened at home that he hadn't told me about. Then he stopped and turned to me, his face grave.

"What was your mom like?"

My breath caught. It was like he'd slapped me.

"I'm sorry, I shouldn't have asked that." His head rocked forward, eyes dimming, and just like with Gabe, I felt an instinct to reassure him.

But I hung back instead. I hadn't talked much about my mom in the last year. Not since her funeral, anyway, when I said what I could in a letter that Penny read for me in front of everybody because I couldn't get my voice to work. And if I was going to be perfectly honest with myself, I hadn't thought much about my mom since then either. Not really. Not bravely. She was always present in my mind, like something you keep seeing out of the corner of your eye, but I wouldn't look at her directly, couldn't. I'd allowed myself only brief glimpses, quick, easy memories, nothing lingering. Nothing that hurt too much.

"She was wonderful," I said, and even that was difficult. "She was a great mother."

She was a mystery, my mind added. *She wasn't who I thought she was.*

Andy shook his head. "This has been a seriously fucked-up year for you, huh?"

I let out a startled laugh. It was such a perfectly accurate description.

"Yeah," I answered. "But the campaign keeps me distracted."

He snorted. "Sorry. I—yeah, sorry."

He didn't look sorry.

"You don't care much about the campaign, do you?" My voice sounded exactly as critical as I meant it to. I was remembering stories about Andy now, those items Elliott had gleefully listed on the whiteboard.

"It's a hard thing to care about," Andy said. "I mean, I want my dad to be reelected and all, but the campaign is pretty much a joke. It's a game that powerful people play. And I'm not interested in being a pawn. Or even a—what do you call it—rook? What is a rook anyway?"

He started yammering about birds. I wasn't that easily put off.

"Is that why you got drunk at the Correspondents' Dinner? To show them you weren't a pawn?"

He stopped short, surprised, and I felt a thrill from having thrown him.

"I wasn't drunk." He walked into my path to face me. I raised my eyebrows. "Seriously! You think that bar would have served me, with an entire press corps and half the government there? I was *pretending*. I wanted to see if anybody would report on it. And guess what? Nobody did."

"People talked, though. They talk about it in the campaign office."

"Well, that's encouraging. I guess. It's all just such a load of bullshit."

I felt exposed all of a sudden, like Angry Campaign Aide Tim was going to jump from the bushes, screaming, "Traitor!"

My jaw tightened. "I don't see it that way."

"Okay. Good for you. No, I mean it. Just . . . be careful." He gazed up at the elms silhouetted along the edge of the square. "They'll keep trying to shut you up, or make you say exactly what they've written. Which is all good, unless you disagree with the party line." His eyes shot to mine. "And I'm guessing you do."

The words *hard line* flashed across my brain.

"No, I don't," I countered. Maybe too quickly. Andy didn't look convinced. "I haven't really had time to think about it. I mean, I'm sixteen. They're not asking me to comment on specific issues."

"Not yet."

I turned to Andy, whose gray eyes were sympathetic, Andy, who didn't play the campaign game, who fought it at every turn, and that uneasy feeling in my stomach formed words.

"What is this? Calling me. Bringing me here. What am I, some act of revenge against your dad's campaign? A joke, a prank? What?"

He didn't answer.

"Just admit it."

He opened his mouth but nothing came out. It was as good as confirmation. God, I was so, so stupid.

I turned around to hide my face, then started to walk away, which I now sensed I should have done several hours ago.

"Wait, Quinn!"

I could hear him running behind me until his hand found my wrist and stopped me with a tug.

I mustered every remaining scrap of dignity. "Thank you for the concert, Andy. But—I'm not interested in being a pawn either."

"It's not like that." He stared me down. Tried to, anyway. Again—I was freakishly good at staring contests.

Finally he sighed, his body releasing the usual cocky stance. "Okay, so at first, yeah, I thought it would be funny to mess with the people at Tauber's party, to be seen talking to you. But then . . . I don't know, I just . . . I found you interesting. And every time I talk to you, you get more interesting. Which is why I keep harassing you."

I could tell from his goofy wink that he didn't really consider it harassment. And okay, fine. I didn't either.

He was the only real friend I'd made all summer. Maybe longer than that—since California, since Penny became a voice on the phone, and the one person who knew me better than I knew myself became no more than a memory—a dubious one, at that.

Whatever Andy's faults, he was here. Living, breathing. He cared whether I walked away or not.

"I'm an honest person," he said, swiping his hand nervously through his hair. "Which, okay, is exactly what a liar would say. But I'm serious. I'll never lie to you. I'll tell you anything. Just ask me."

I raised my eyebrows at that dare. So many things I could ask. I chose the easiest one.

"How did you get that scar?"

His hand flew to his cheek. "Lacrosse. Another inch and I'd have lost the eye. Secret Service massively overreacted."

"Okay," I said, a mutinous smile rising to my lips. "I believe you."

"Yeah?" he asked, his hand extended. "We're good? You trust me now?"

I shook his hand. Didn't answer. We were good—but I still knew better than to trust him.

As we walked past Andrew Jackson, Andy's shoulder bumped mine and his fingers grazed the inside of my wrist. I could feel the warmth of the two inches between us as we strolled back to the street, where the same car that had picked me up was waiting. When we reached it, Andy stood beside the back door, ready to open it for me.

"Thanks," he said.

"For what?"

"I don't know." He shrugged. "Existing?"

I rolled my eyes, secretly glowing. As Andy widened the

door so that I could pass through, he leaned in. I thought he was trying to whisper something to me, so I turned my head—just in time for the kiss he'd intended for my cheek to land somewhere a lot closer to my mouth. Like . . . *on* it.

I barely had time to register what was happening before we broke apart, his startled expression probably matching mine. Then he grinned.

"Okay then! Night, Quinn."

I was too mortified to reply with anything but a wave as the car pulled away. Did Andy think I'd gone for the kiss? Did it count as a kiss if it was accidental?

Did he like it? Oh God, strike that thought.

Either way, I felt like a shaken snow globe, little sparkles swirling in me, never settling. They stayed there, shimmering, the whole drive home, so that I didn't even notice the time, or that all the lights were off except for the front foyer, and one tiny bulb lit in the small window off to the side of the front porch—the senator's study.

When I opened the front door, he was sitting on the stairs. He jumped up, and I moved to greet him—but his face froze me to the spot. I'd seen the senator tense and relaxed, seen him joking around with his staff, seen him nervous and contrite. But never had I seen him like this.

He was furious.

"Where the hell have you *been*? I've had people all over town looking for you!"

"I—I'm sorry." I scrambled for an explanation, my brain landing on the cover story we'd all agreed on before the concert, praying one of those people looking for me hadn't found me at exactly the wrong moment. "After dinner we went to Lucy Davison's house and I guess time just got away from me."

"You *call* next time!" He shouted so loud that startled tears sprang to my eyes.

"I left my phone here, I . . ." I dropped my head and let my voice die, shrinking into the marble floor. "I'm sorry."

Seeing my face, he collapsed against the railing. "You scared me to death, Kate. We thought you'd been kidnapped. Do you understand that that's not a metaphor? We *literally* thought you'd been kidnapped."

I mustered a small "Oh."

"Bed. Now. We'll talk about this in the morning."

Before I got to the top of the stairs, he called after me again.

"Kate?" I looked down to see him running a hand over his graying hair, his wide shoulders slumped with fatigue and worry. "I'm sorry I lost my temper. And I'm glad you've made some friends. We just need to establish some ground rules."

In the darkened upstairs hallway, Gabe was peeking past his door. "Are you okay?"

"Go back to bed," I answered, beaming. "Everything is wonderful."

I hit the mattress and it seemed to float. My first fight with my father. The first time I'd ever really thought of him as my father—the first time he'd acted like one.

It was like something out of a movie.

Before I fell into giddy dreams, I replayed the events of the evening in my head, realizing with an almost electric charge that I'd just gone on a pseudo-date and shared a pseudo-kiss with the president's son, strolled past the White House, watched a world-famous band from up in the lighting rig, dodged the paparazzi—and somehow it had turned out to be the most normal, stereotypically teenaged night of my life.

The next day, there was no talk of ground rules. But the senator did stay home the whole morning, sipping coffee and flipping through the sports section. When I sat nervously next to him on the sofa, he gave my hair a ruffle.

After Meg made breakfast, he helped her carry the plates to the patio table. On my pancake, someone had drawn a happy face in syrup.

~17~

Friday, July 18
Welcome Home, Coopers!
109 DAYS UNTIL THE GENERAL ELECTION

Rain splattered the windows of the campaign plane as we descended over Massachusetts. I felt an irrational stab of disappointment, as though the Coopers' home state was rejecting me already.

But then, peering down at the wet airfield, I saw the waiting crowd.

They held homemade signs and cheered at a deafening pitch, their voices rising even louder when the local coordinator shouted on his loudspeaker to rev them up. The senator was grinning even before he stepped off the plane, his hand held high in greeting. Over the past month and a half, I'd seen how good he was at the unforced smile, the confident gait, but there was something different about him here. Something real. He was home.

After passing through the handshake line, we ducked inside the waiting limo to find Elliott Webb reclining in the seat opposite us. He put down his newspaper, shook hands with the senator and Meg, ruffled Gabe's rain-doused hair, and playfully poked Gracie in the side.

"The house is ready," he announced. "Some new flowerbeds

for you to plant when the cameras are rolling, Meg, assuming the rain lets up."

"Just what I wanted to do this weekend," she chuckled.

I stared unblinking at Elliott, waiting for him to acknowledge me. Then I remembered the word he'd used on that plane ride. *Docile.* No wonder he wouldn't deign to say hello. Would you say hello to a cow grazing in a pasture?

Actually, I thought wryly. *I probably would.*

I sighed and stared through the window, trying to block out both Elliott and anxious thoughts about the upcoming interview. The view was a good distraction. This was my first time in New England and I was curious to see how closely it matched my impressions of it from the John Adams miniseries, my much-loved copy of *Little Women*, and the Stephen King novels I'd snuck from my mom's library when I was way too young to read them. I hoped it was more like the first two than the last one.

We exited the highway and reached a more scenic, forested area, then drove through a charmingly old-fashioned town.

"That's where I used to take ballet," Gracie called out. "And that's where we go get ice cream."

"Can we get ice cream?" Gabe asked, but the Coopers were deep in conversation with Elliott.

"How much time is allocated?" the senator was asking.

"I gave them all day Sunday."

"That's where we pick blackberries!" Gabe cried out, and I saw a long, paint-chipped fence with briars stretching over it, and behind, an old converted farmhouse, with stone walls and wooden ones painted dark green, a pond glittering gold to one side. The weather chose this moment to break, the sun falling gently on the house and grounds. I pressed my fingertips to the window. It was like going back in time. We might as easily have been driving in a buggy to visit Jo March and her sisters at that very house.

To my delight, we pulled in.

This was where the twins were born, where they'd lived on and off for all of their eight years. Home.

Their home.

I had just enough time to deposit my bags in the hall and steal a quick look at the low doorways and knotted planks of wood in the floor, listening to the happy racket of birds and bugs outside, taking in the heavy scent of wooded summer before I was shepherded into the dusty SUV parked in the garage.

"She insists," Meg was saying. "Best to just get it over with."

"Fifteen minutes," the senator said from the driver's seat. "No more, I'm serious."

"Where are we going?" I asked.

Gracie glanced over. "To see Grandma."

"Oh."

The car suddenly felt very small and very rapid. I wondered how Meg's mother would respond to me, given that there was no direct connection between us. Judging by the lack of enthusiasm shown by every member of the family, I was guessing she wasn't a bundle of sunshine either.

I was right about their reaction. Wrong about the person.

"Hello Mom," the senator said as we clambered out of the car. My breath caught.

His mother? That would make her *my*—

She waited for us, hands on hips, a ray of dusty light falling from between the boughs of thick trees above, obscuring her face. Behind her stood a whitewashed house with a long front porch, chickens scrabbling between us in the damp dirt. The light shifted, and I saw that her face was prettily lined, graying hair swept up in a genteel bun. Her eyes, however, were sharp as daggers—and aimed at me. I sensed somehow that she was testing me, and so I didn't flinch.

My grandmother smiled.

The senator cleared his throat, uncomfortable. This was probably new to him—the sensation of being ignored. I could've taught him a thing or two about it.

"Evelyn, this is Kate." Meg's voice was flat, almost hostile. "Your granddaughter."

"I know who she is," Evelyn said. "Just look at her. Well, are you gonna come inside or stand there letting flies land on you?"

She turned on her boot heel and stomped into the house, the screen door slapping shut behind her.

With great effort, the senator smiled. "Shall we?"

Evelyn spent a few minutes fussing grouchily over the twins, continuing to pretend her son wasn't in the room. Then it was my turn.

"Need to check on the potatoes," she said. "Kate, you come along. I've got things to say."

As Evelyn marched outside, I stared at Meg in helpless appeal, but she just raised her eyebrows and waved me on

172

while the senator slumped into a kitchen chair with a groan of relief.

I found Evelyn in the wire-fenced garden stepping lightly through low rows of plants, and noticed with new interest how rural it was here. The Coopers' farmhouse was a farm in name only, its natural surroundings purely decorative. This one was a working farm, small but real. It surprised me—whether it was Meg's mother or the senator's, I guess I would've expected her to live in a fancy condo or a house even grander than the Coopers' place in DC. But Evelyn moved through the hedges with purpose, and more than that, pride. This little farm was her kingdom. No wonder she acted like a despot.

When we got far enough from the house, she turned on me with a scowl.

"Don't you let them push you around. They've got no right."

I had no response to that.

"Oh," I tried. "They aren't—"

"You're a strong-willed girl," she interrupted. "You know how I can tell?"

I shook my head, but felt my spine straighten at the compliment.

"Because you come from a long line of Goodwin women, that's why." She grinned, her cheeks crinkling, and all the age spots on her face transformed into girlish freckles.

Goodwin. That must have been her maiden name. So now I was a Quinn, and a Cooper, and a Goodwin too.

"Gracie's a tough one and so are you." She winked and

poked me hard in the chest. Then she nodded as if that touch had confirmed it. "I can see it."

I had a sense all of a sudden of why Gracie had called her "*my* grandma," so emphatically taking ownership over Evelyn back in DC when I'd first asked about grandparents. They had a bond. But maybe we could too.

As we walked back to the house, she slung an arm around me.

"You're one of us. And we look out for our own. Always have done. Don't forget that."

On the drive back, I wondered exactly what Evelyn had seen in me, what Goodwin trait had jumped out at her. Was it my freckles, my stubborn nose, or had she really read character in my face? I'd never thought of myself as strong, especially not now, after everything I'd been pelted with in the past year.

I pictured myself as an old woman living by myself on an organic farm. It was surprisingly easy to imagine.

It didn't matter, though. She was wrong about the Coopers. Nobody was pushing me around. This was just the way campaigns worked. It was fine.

Saturday night turned out to be equal parts Stephen King and *Little Women*.

In the early evening, we did last-minute interview prep. Nancy sat with me and asked questions, and I answered the way we'd rehearsed in front of cameras back at headquarters. Gracie lingered with us for a while, making a game of trying to answer the questions before me until Nancy shooed her away. By the end of the evening, I felt ready. Nervous—but prepped.

Meg had insisted we all have an early night, but the twins' anxiety over tomorrow had turned into giggle fits and races through the house's uneven corridors. Keeping well out of that fight, I retreated to the sweet little room they'd given me, with its slanted roof and a window that looked out over the pond through wobbly panes of glass. I went to air out the dress I'd be wearing tomorrow morning. Nancy had carefully selected it, and when she presented it to me before we left for Massachusetts, I'd been pleasantly surprised. It was simple, comfortable but cute, something I might have actually picked out for myself. It was Marc Jacobs too—a label even Penny would be impressed by.

But when I went to look for it, my bag was already open, and inside, all I found were tatters. Someone had sliced my dress into pieces.

I stared around the room, chilled, clutching the shreds of fabric to my chest. The bedroom window was locked. No one was hiding behind the hope chest at the end of the quilted bed. But a pair of blue craft scissors was lying open on the antique dresser.

Downstairs, Meg had gotten Gabe into his twin bed, but Gracie was still jumping up and down on hers. The second she saw me—and the blue silk in my hands—her face went ghost white. In the next blink, she was a blur, streaking past me out the bedroom door.

I streaked after her, shouting. Gracie careened around the corner, passing the stunned senator so narrowly that she

175

made him drop his notes. I ran faster, letting go of what was left of the dress. She was fumbling for the handle of the door to the backyard, but it was locked. As I cornered her, she turned to face me, her chin jutted out in defiance.

"Why would you do this?" I crouched to grab her arm, so mad I trembled, which made her shake too. "Why? What is your *problem*?"

She just stared at me, her jaw grinding. Confused tears prickled my eyes. I thought frantically of the last few days, of what I might have done to make her lash out.

At last, Gracie opened her mouth, but before she could answer, Meg's voice rose up behind us.

"Grace Eleanor Cooper." Her tone was icier than anything I could have mustered. I looked over my shoulder to see her fingers streaming with blue fabric. "You have some serious explaining to do."

Whatever explanation there was, Gracie gave it to Meg behind a thick, mottled old kitchen door. When she came out again, it was only long enough to say a sullen "I'm *sorry*" before Meg ordered us both to bed.

Andy called at almost midnight, waking me up. I wasn't sure how thin these walls were, so I pulled the quilt over me like a tent to muffle my voice.

"Why are we whispering?" Andy whispered.

"Everyone's asleep."

"Ah." His voice went back to normal. "So. Are you around this weekend?"

I flushed, wondering if he was about to ask me out again. Neither of us had mentioned the accidental kiss from the night of the concert; the fact that he was still calling gave me hope that it wasn't quite as awkward as I remembered it.

"Actually, no." I sighed. "We're in Massachusetts, getting ready for this—"

My mouth clamped shut, putting the brakes on what I was about to tell him. The campaign was keeping this interview secret. I didn't *really* see the harm in telling him, and he might even be able to give me pointers on surviving the dreaded family interview, but still . . .

"Top secret something or other?" he offered. "That's too bad. I was gonna sneak out for a movie or something. Thought we could rendezvous."

"Next time," I promised, knowing as I said it that it was a terrible, terrible, wonderful idea.

Sunday morning, just before dawn, Meg shook me gently awake. The makeup crew had arrived, along with a full battalion of staffers.

They'd flown my usual makeup girl up for the interview. She was more nervous than I was. "Do you think I'll get to meet Shawna?" she asked, dabbing my cheeks with liquid blush.

When I emerged from makeup and hair, Nancy was pacing the perimeter of the house with her earpiece in, conversing with the air and delegating tasks to aides in hushed asides.

She interrupted her march when she saw what I was wearing—a blue short-sleeved shirt and black skirt, the closest match to the ruined dress that I could muster from my luggage.

"What happened to what we talked about?" Her voice was quiet but sharp-edged.

Gracie chose that moment to walk into the hall. Hearing the conversation, she halted mid-stomp, her eyes frozen wide.

"I spilled something on it."

"*Kate,*" Nancy sighed. "Well, that'll have to do."

Gracie looked wary as I approached, eyes turned up and head hung like a dog expecting a beating. I was still angry, but I confined my revenge to bumping her with my hip as I sauntered past.

"Thank you," she said, so quietly I could barely hear it. She trailed me into the kitchen, where Meg was trying to cajole Gabe into eating some cereal. I poured my second coffee of the morning and continued into the living room. The TV was on, of course. There didn't seem to be anything new in the news ticker.

The back door opened with a creak. Elliott strode in and held it for the senator, looking, as usual, like he owned the place.

When he saw me, his face contorted. "No!"

I flinched.

"I told you, hair up! Ponytail!"

My mouth fell open in disbelief, sure that he was yelling at me—until I saw my makeup artist cringing in the doorway behind me. My fists balled up.

"It's hair, Elliott," I found myself snapping. "It's just *hair.*"

Before he could start screaming about the importance of minute stylistic details, I smiled. That shut him up.

"We'll fix it!" I spun, grabbed the stunned makeup girl, and left the room.

Everyone's wound up, I reminded myself. *Let's just get through this.*

Once my horrifying hairdo error was fixed, the staff fled the house like it was on fire—first stylists, aides, and then, finally, thankfully, Elliott himself—until only Nancy remained.

As she trotted past me in the hall, she tugged on my ponytail. "You look *so cute!* Good call on the outfit."

I was still glowing from the compliment when the senator opened the front door and Shawna Freaking Wells walked in with her camera crew.

She looked exactly the same as she did on TV, a tall, beautiful black woman with a chin-length bob and skin that seemed never to age. Seeing her here, in the flesh, right in front of me, felt somehow more surreal than any of the other celebrity encounters of the past several weeks. When I shook her hand—her warm, soft, actual hand!—my words of greeting sputtered and died in my mouth.

Shawna had been a morning fixture in our house in LA for as long as I could remember, practically an alarm clock. Every day, without fail, *"I'm Shawna Wells and here's this morning's news . . ."*

If seeing the president and his wife was like watching wax figures come to life, today was that much stranger—I was meeting someone I'd known my whole life. And what was even more amazing, Shawna greeted us the same way—as old friends, a family that she was thrilled to catch up with at long last.

"Senator." She clasped both of his hands in hers. "Thank you for welcoming me into your home."

They started by getting what they called "B-roll" shots of all of us hanging out around the house. I noticed again what a nice job the campaign staff had done here, making it look lived-in, cozy, even a little messy. Shawna chatted with us the whole time, small-talk questions, off-the-record, like "What's the best place you've visited so far, Kate?" I knew it was to warm us up, to get us relaxed so she could ask more pointed questions. They'd prepped me on that. Even so, I liked her for it.

When it came time for the first set of on-the-record questions, we all sat on the sofa, Gabe and Gracie to my right, and the senator and Meg to my left. Nancy orchestrated it carefully as the crew was setting up, making me wonder how long the aides had deliberated on the right seating arrangement for this shot.

The camera turned on and I gave Gabe's hand a squeeze. Shawna noticed it, motioned to her cameraman. When she asked the twins how they liked having a new big sister, they stayed with what we'd practiced. Then Gracie added something of her own.

"I like that she's pretty and that she's smart." She glanced at me, an apology in her eyes. "She's a really good sister."

In answer, I broke from the polite posture we'd practiced in "media training" to gather Gracie up in a hug. Gabe crumpled out of the way and we all started laughing.

"That was great, Kate," Nancy whispered when we broke for a new setup. "They'll use that. Nice work."

During planning, they'd asked me whether I'd prefer to be

interviewed with just the senator or both Coopers. "Both," I'd said quickly. Nancy seemed pleased, Elliott less so. I guess he hadn't noticed how stilted my conversations with the senator still were, how much closer I was with Meg.

We shot this portion in another corner of the living room where the crew had rigged up a draped backdrop and a set of blinding lights. Shawna was studying note cards when we sat down.

Here we go.

We were prepared for most of the questions. Nancy and Elliott had been smart to focus so much on prepping us—and accurate in their predictions of what "America" would want to know.

"What was your first reaction?" Shawna asked me. "When you learned about your father."

"Mostly shock," I said, the honest answer we'd arrived at by committee. "But once I met my dad—and then Gabe and Gracie and Meg—it all kind of clicked that this was my family and this was where I was meant to be."

Judging by Shawna's glowing reaction, my answer was a winner. I relaxed even more as she asked Meg and the senator how they'd told the twins about me. It was as though she was following the campaign's script for how this interview would go.

Off on the sidelines, Nancy had a tight almost-smile, like a coach watching her team taking the lead.

The first surprise came after the cameras stopped rolling. Shawna stood and touched me lightly on the shoulder.

"I'd like to do a one-on-one with you, Kate, if you don't object."

We hadn't planned this, but it seemed like a reasonable request, so I said "Sure," just as Nancy stepped in to decline. Shawna looked to each of us for a response and I shot Nancy a reassuring smile. "It's fine."

She nodded, trust in her eyes. I was prepped. And besides, I came from a long line of Goodwin women, all of them strong. I could handle this.

But none of these questions were on our list.

"Tell me about your mother," she started, and I pressed my lips together to keep from showing alarm.

We strolled along the edge of the woods outside the house, the cameraman walking backward just ahead.

"She was wonderful," I answered, remembering the words I'd used when Andy asked. I smiled at the memory. "She was a great mom."

"Did it surprise you to find out that she and the senator had an affair?"

The only reply that sprung to mind was the truth. I hesitated. But the cameras were rolling. It was easier just to answer.

"It *still* surprises me, actually," I said, and felt my whole body relax the second those off-script words spilled out. "It doesn't really fit with everything I know about my mom. She was an incredibly moral person, talked all the time about how even little actions can affect other people, how respon- sible you have to be."

As Shawna nodded thoughtfully, my mind began to whir.

"Maybe it took this happening for her to learn that lesson. I don't think she set out to hurt anyone, but she did—and maybe I was a reminder of it."

It wasn't a happy thought. My eyes hit the ground and it took effort to force them up again. Look out at the horizon, they'd told me in media training. It conveys optimism. Trustworthiness.

"You mentioned responsibility," Shawna said. "Is that something you learned helping your mother at her nonprofit?"

"Definitely." We'd touched on this a little in prep. "It gave me a sense of perspective—and it taught me how important it is to help people in need."

That seemed like a safe statement, in line with my other sound bites, but Shawna's gaze intensified. "Do you think your father shares those values?"

"I . . . um." I swallowed, suddenly flushing hot. "Sure. Yeah, probably." My forehead was prickling. "I mean—absolutely!"

I blinked hard, wishing I could take back all those ums and go straight to "absolutely." What was the matter with me?

Shawna winced.

"Let's switch gears," she said, waving a finger for the cameraman to keep rolling. I nodded, grateful for the reprieve.

Then she said, "Is there a special someone in your life?" and my mouth went dry all over again.

"Um—n-no!" I stammered, newly suspicious of the twinkle in Shawna's eye. She'd started her career as an investigative journalist. Did she know about Andy? The street had been deserted that night in DC. But what if someone had seen? What if there was a rumor going around and I had no idea about it?

I drew in a steadying breath. "I'm pretty focused on family right now."

"And they certainly seem to be focused on you." *Phew.* She cocked her head for the follow-up question. "How do you get along with Mrs. Cooper?"

"Meg?" I grinned. This was an easy one. "She's great. She—"

She should hate me, but she doesn't, I thought. *She's a miracle.*

Oh God, here it came. I was absolutely not supposed to cry.

I started to cry. Shawna touched my shoulder in sympathy.

"She's been so accepting," I managed, swiping the corner of my eye with my pinkie, praying my makeup hadn't smeared on top of everything else. "She's a wonderful mother too."

"And your father?"

My tears evaporated. That question I had an answer for. One I'd rehearsed in front of Elliott Webb.

"He's everything I always dreamed my dad would be."

"So . . ." Shawna beamed down at me, that comfortingly familiar face, everybody's best friend. "What happens after the campaign, Kate?"

My mouth opened—and nothing came out.

Because nothing could come out. I didn't have an answer.

"I think that's all we have time for!" Nancy ran into the shot and latched on to my arm. I held on to her as she whirled around and walked us away from Shawna and the crew.

Behind us, I heard them setting up for the last part of the day, a sit-down with Meg and the senator.

Why didn't we prep that question? I wondered.

And—more importantly—why did I still not know the answer?

Wednesday, July 23
Paying Respects
104 DAYS UNTIL THE GENERAL ELECTION

The Maine sky was a bright, cheerful blue. The mourners lining up to enter the little stone chapel cast their faces down as if to block it out.

The senator hadn't spoken a word since we'd landed for this unwelcome visit. He'd stared at his speech with heavy-lidded eyes, his thumb rubbing the page as if to erase the words he'd written.

This was the kind of funeral that politicians had to attend. Supreme Court Justice Thomas Bellamy was well-liked by many in DC. And because he'd died so suddenly—during an election cycle—the press would be on hand to document exactly who showed up to pay respects.

But for the senator, this funeral was different. In law school, it was young Professor Bellamy who'd taken Mark Cooper under his wing and encouraged him to turn his attention toward a life in the public eye. I remembered Nancy saying that he'd given a thoughtful quote to the press right after my existence had come to light, and I'd heard the senator laughing on the phone with him from time to time. Apparently, Justice Bellamy had suggested we get our families together after the election was done.

But now, at the age of only fifty-nine, he was gone.

The press waited a respectful distance from the small church where Justice Bellamy was being laid to rest, cameras rolling. The senator didn't open the car window when we arrived. Didn't raise his eyes from the page. Meg watched him, one hand placed gently against his knee. The twins, oblivious, fussed in their black outfits, nudging each other with their elbows.

A large security detail flanked the church, their sleek suits clashing with the centuries-old stone walls surrounding the chapel. As we passed into the church, one of them pressed a finger to his earpiece, muttering softly.

Sure enough, the president was here. He and his family stood near the organ, the First Lady grasping Bellamy's widow's hand with both of her own. I could see the back of Andy's head. He didn't turn.

Mrs. Bellamy glanced around the president's shoulder, spotting Meg and the senator. At the sight of friends, her face relaxed, grief showing even more plainly through.

To her right, three children stood in a staggered row, watching the crowd with hollow eyes. The youngest, about five, had her mouth pursed tight to keep tears in check. The oldest was a boy a little younger than me. He looked like he had just woken up to a nightmare.

As I watched him, the church seemed to tilt and then to sink. The room felt small, more people walking in behind us, and I reached my hand out as if to grasp Penny's, but she wasn't here, and my breath caught, my eyes pooling.

Meg glanced at me in alarm. I tried to croak an excuse,

but instead just squeezed past all the mourners and out the side door of the chapel, spots gathering.

I drew in a greedy, cool breath, smelling salt in the air. It took me a few seconds to realize I'd emerged into a graveyard. Past the crumbling headstones, I could see a lighthouse and the ocean.

"You all right?"

I spun to find Andy Lawrence a few feet away, his hand half extended, like he was waiting to grab me if I passed out.

"Yeah," I lied. The word hardly came out.

Andy squinted, his head cocked. "It's a little soon, isn't it?"

"I think it might always be." I steadied my breath as I stared at the glittering ocean.

Andy circled a stone angel, looping closer.

This isn't safe, I thought. *Anyone could see us.* All the same, I felt my shoulders loosen, my hands unclench as he walked over.

"This doesn't bother you?" Andy motioned to the graves.

"Not really." I tried to smile. "She was cremated. After the funeral, we sprinkled her ashes up the coast at her favorite beach."

"In the ocean?" Andy stood next to me and turned toward the view.

I nodded, watching a boat draw its wake across the water. Andy's pinkie grazed mine.

"That's smart. You don't have to go to a specific grave to visit her. The earth is seventy percent water, and it's all connected. So in a way, you're visiting her right now."

I blinked away tears, the light from the ocean glittering

bright, blinding me. Andy's fingers found mine and danced against them until they were entwined. I dared a glance. He was watching me—with concern, but something else too. Something I was suddenly desperate to define.

"Andrew." A sharp voice sounded behind us and we jolted away from each other. I turned to see the First Lady's expression travel from annoyance to shock and then back to placid politeness. Barbie face.

"The funeral is starting," she said softly. Her eyes traveled to mine, a worry-line creasing her forehead, then darted away again. "I need you inside."

Does she know? I wondered, the usual question following on its heels. *Know what?*

As Andy walked away, I imagined a cord connecting our hands, pulling me after him. Even once I'd sat down in the chapel between Gabe and Gracie, other people's grief settling on me like a sodden blanket, I could almost feel Andy's fingers sliding over mine, telling me through touch that he understood.

I woke from my daze to see the senator rise to the podium and begin his speech.

"In a time like this, a time of grief, of shock—a time when the world seems unfair, the universe uncaring, it is important to hear words of comfort. Of reassurance. But I'm here today as someone who was lucky to know Thomas Bellamy—and to love him, like a brother. So those reassuring words are hard to find." He swallowed. "I'm angry. Tom was taken too young. And I'm angry about it."

Everyone leaned forward. This was not the usual eulogy.

"But Tom believed in objectivity." The senator paused, grinning as if someone had just whispered a joke into his ear. "His favorite quote at Yale was, 'Let's look at this from another angle.' I'm sure his colleagues in the Supreme Court heard those words on more than one occasion—probably pretty maddening if you were about to break for lunch."

Several people in the congregation chuckled in recognition.

"So, to honor Tom, why don't we look at this from another angle. Thomas Bellamy's time on this earth has ended. Let's take a look at his life."

As the senator's words rolled over the chapel, it seemed to settle back into its foundation. The world felt orderly again. Safer. Looking around at the other mourners, I could see their own expressions changing as the senator's speech unfurled. His words—they were helping.

I stared at the senator with new wonder as he concluded his speech. He seemed to fill the room, the churchyard, the coastline. It wasn't just that he was charismatic.

He was presidential.

As we left the church, I searched for Andy, hoping to convey with a look my gratitude. But it was his father's expression that caught my attention and held it.

The president looked worried.

～19～

Friday, July 25

Winging Our Way to the City of Angels

102 DAYS UNTIL THE GENERAL ELECTION

My birthday was the same week as the Republican National Convention.

When Meg found out, her first reaction was, "Oh no!" followed by an anxious, "And what's on your birthday list this year?"

I was already getting what I wanted. This year's GOP convention was in Los Angeles. For weeks, I'd been alternating between cold panic and breathless excitement at the thought of this visit. On the one hand, we were all preparing to step onto the biggest stage of our lives in front of an audience of millions of viewers, the fate of the country hanging in the balance. On the other hand, I'd have nine whole days back home. The scales were balanced as far as I was concerned.

Penny had been counting down to my arrival for weeks. "You'd better come straight over, or I'm going to kidnap you. I don't even care if Secret Service is listening right now. Consider this your warning."

I promised her I'd see her first, even though I knew I'd still be scheduled to within an inch of my waking life. Probably my sleeping life too. There had to be pockets of time I could steal, though, and maybe even times that Penny could tag along, see what the campaign was like. I couldn't wait.

When we boarded the plane, Meg presented me with a stack of books that she was careful to say were *not* birthday gifts, just something for our long plane and bus rides. The titles were familiar, some because they were classics, and the others because I'd heard them mentioned recently—by Andy and Jake and Lucy.

Meg had bought me the Farnwell Prep summer reading list.

I wondered what it meant, but didn't quite know how to ask. I just thanked her and started to read. The books were almost, but not quite, interesting enough to keep my mind off the trip ahead—and the Shawna Wells interview.

It had aired yesterday while we were "getting an early night," as per Meg's orders. I knew Meg well enough to have already suspected we wouldn't be gathering with a bowl of popcorn to gawk at ourselves on the Coopers' flat screen. And for once, Nancy had agreed with Meg.

"You did great, now let it go," she said, echoing Lou's advice from back in June. "Trust me—the more you watch yourself on TV, the more it changes you. And we want you to stay exactly the way you are!"

Judging by the cheery attitude of the campaign staff who'd boarded the Cooper for America plane with us, it had gone well. I told myself that that was all I needed to know and almost, sort of, kind of believed it. At least this week would be full of distractions.

As our flight descended, I leaned over Gabe to get a view of the wide crescent of the Pacific coast, the endless buildings like tiles in a mosaic, the mountains in the distance, the beautiful smog. Yep. I'd even missed the smog.

My home for the next nine days would be very different from the little house I'd shared with my mom. The campaign was housed downtown in a high-rise hotel across the street from the convention. The staffers had rooms all over the hotel, but the sprawling penthouse suite was ours. It had three bathrooms with Jacuzzis, oil paintings on the gilded walls, a chandeliered dining room that the campaign staff immediately claimed as an office. Gazing over the city from my own private balcony, I promised myself I'd invite Penny to join me here this week. Maybe she could even stay the night for my birthday.

Once we'd checked in, we had two hours to kill before the first afternoon event. After I'd explained my solemn vow, the senator laughed and agreed to let me visit Penny. It wasn't until I said I'd take the Metro that he started to worry.

"Where does she live?" he asked. "I didn't even know there was a subway in LA."

"Of course there is!" I chirped. "I can hop on the Gold Line. Atlantic's only like eight stops from here."

From his bemused squint, I realized he was thinking only of Beverly Hills, Brentwood, places he'd visited on donor calls.

"And this is a safe neighborhood?"

I just kept smiling. "It's where I used to live?"

He sighed, defeated. "Back by five. No subway. James will escort you."

I giggled on the ride over, picturing Penny's face when I rolled up in a Town Car with my very own Secret Service agent. But as we rounded the corner onto her street, gliding past a familiar row of faded bungalows with dry, carefully tended lawns, I was the one whose mouth fell open.

Between two spindly palms in her front yard, a giant banner read "Welcome Home, Kate!" and under it, at least two dozen people were gathered. At the sight of the car, they jumped in celebration.

I smiled so wide my cheeks burned, spotting friends from school I hadn't spoken to since I left—Kevin, my old lab partner and sophomore semi-formal date; Irina, my gorgeous Latvian friend who still wore her crazy hair in pigtails; Chester, who was much taller than I remembered; Topes and his little sister, Angie; the still teensy Eva; and was that Enrico? I hadn't seen Penny's big brother since he'd joined the marines two years ago.

And there in the middle of it all was Miss Penelope Diaz, black hair braided prettily and eyes welling up, her parents standing behind her.

The moment I got one foot out of the car, they swarmed me. I glanced nervously back at James, but he was busy trying to stifle an unprofessional smile.

"Look at you!" Penny released me from a bear hug and clapped her hands under her chin. "You're still in costume! That. Is. Awesome."

I glanced down, realizing I was still wearing the photo-op floral dress from the airplane. In my rush to get down here, I'd forgotten to change into something less ridiculous. Enrico's eyes were wide.

"You've grown up, Skinny Kate," he said, making me blush.

By the time Penny's mom made her way over to gather me up in a plush hug, my friends were all around me, asking a million questions a minute, mostly "What's your dad like?" and "How are you *doing* with all this?" I answered as well as I could, overwhelmed and delighted. And then Penny's little sister, Eva, tugged on my wrist with her own question.

"Do you have a boyfriend?"

Everybody laughed—and, at my dumbstruck reaction, laughed harder. "I—Um . . . not really."

Penny narrowed her eyes. "Not *really*?"

"There's a boy," I admitted, to general whooping. "But it's not really anything."

Penny's mouth fell open, her hands landing on her hips. This was an act, I knew—over-the-top indignant—designed to mask her hurt that I'd withheld such crucial information. I'd be hearing about this later.

Enrico put his hands out like a bodyguard, quieting the group. "No more questions. Kate's probably dating, like, the president's kid. It's top secret—classified. If she tells you, she'll have to kill you."

My friends cracked up, not noticing that all the blood had just left my face. Except Penny. Her suspicious squint had only deepened. Enrico nudged me.

"Just messin' with you, K."

Faking a laugh, I punched him in the arm. His beer spilled

and something flashed. At first I thought it was lightning, but we never got thunderstorms here. The voices of the group fell lower, confused, and Penny stood up on tiptoes, peering past the crowd.

It was a photographer, his head poking out of the driver's-side window of a car idling on the other side of the street. And from the other direction, a news van had just shown up, the crew rushing out to get a shot.

I groaned. "Let's just pose for them, then they'll go away."

"Why are they here?" Mr. Diaz shook his head, bewildered. "Did they follow you?"

"Maybe." I grinned, pointing. "Or maybe it's the ginormous sign. You tipped them off, Mr. Diaz."

"This is, like, normal for you now?" Irina asked. "People following you around to take your picture?"

She pinched the flouncy skirt of my dress and I wondered with a start whether she was jealous of the attention. She was Miss Drama Club in school, hoping to start auditioning professionally as soon as her conservative mother would allow it. But for now, she was just another high school junior, languishing in obscurity. Didn't she know I'd swap places with her in a heartbeat?

Except for the Coopers. Them I'd keep.

We gathered the group into a goofy pose and sure enough, the photographer thanked us and drove on. The film crew rushed in, ready for an interview, but I wasn't going to sign on for that, not without Nancy here to okay it.

"I'd better go," I sighed, hugging Penny. "But I'll be back."

"Every day, right?" She had her arms crossed to show me she meant it.

I grabbed her pinkie with my own. "As much as I can."

As we drove away, I watched the light become more golden, dustier, noticed the lawns growing first greener, then gated and sprawling, talked James out of taking the freeway, got stuck in traffic anyway, and made it back for the first event just in time, feeling like Cinderella—except for the whole covered in dirt thing.

Or so I thought.

That photo was everywhere. In less than five hours, it hit the web, the evening papers, the top right corner of every cable news station. And not just the posed photo—video too. That crew had managed to get an impressive amount of party footage, mostly of me trying to ignore them.

Elliott was inexplicably livid. He stormed into the living room of our suite with his finger pointed at the TV like he was going to stab it, yelling, "Why wasn't I told about this?"

"Whoa—what?" I muttered, my own temper flaring.

"You need to keep a better handle on her!" he yelled, never so much as glancing at me.

"Lay off, Elliott," Nancy snapped. Seeing her blanch, I remembered that day back in South Carolina when he told her that I was her responsibility.

The senator stepped between them, while Meg positioned herself in front of me. I appreciated the protective gesture, but it wasn't necessary. I wasn't the one Elliott was furious at. It was the one up on the screen, the one who went off-plan to visit friends in a "bad" part of town.

"Just lower your voices and look," the senator said, calmly motioning to the TV. "This is not a crisis."

"*Kate Quinn celebrated her return to her hometown of Los Angeles by paying a visit to old friends,*" the busty cable anchor was saying. So far so bland. What was Elliott so pissed off about? "*But some are wondering whether this is a move by the Cooper campaign to pander to Hispanic voters. We have with us Carlos Muños, Professor of . . .*"

My mouth fell open. "'*Pander*'? What the—"

Elliott whirled on me. Oops. *Really* should have kept my mouth shut.

"Everything. We do. Has. Impact. *Everything!*" He paced away. "Why am I explaining this to her, it's a waste of—" He pointed to Nancy. "Do your job!"

And he stormed out of the suite.

The senator sighed, putting his hands up in response to Nancy's death-glare. "I'll talk him down."

Why? I wondered, and not for the first time. Elliott was disrespectful, bad-tempered, arrogant. No one liked him, as far as I could tell. And he'd never even pretended to be nice to me—not for a second. So why not fire him?

He must be really good. Which means—he must be right.

I gulped and looked at the carpet. "Well, that was awkward."

"Out of line is what that was. Elliott . . ." Meg sighed, not finishing the thought. She wrapped an arm around me. "But listen—you're learning. We all are. Deep breaths."

When she called that night, I thought Penny might be reeling from her first dose of media exposure. But she had other things on her mind.

"You gonna tell me about the president's kid?"

I crept off my hotel bed and quietly shut the door. Then, with an extra burst of paranoia, I slid two pillows along the bottom of the doorframe.

"You can't tell anybody," I whispered.

"What could I tell? You haven't told me *anything*!"

"There's nothing really *to* tell." I didn't know until I said it how much of a lie that was. My heart started thudding. "He's a friend, but it's obviously not a great idea, so it's a secret."

"He's a friend. That's it, huh?" The other end of the line was suspiciously quiet.

"Yeah."

Penny let out a very long sigh. "Okay, Kate. That's how you want to play it, that's how we'll play it. Now tell me about your hotel. Rate the pool. One through ten."

She was only letting me get away with this because her pride was hurt. Still, I was relieved. It wasn't just that I knew Andy was a bad idea, that if word got out about him, it would be a disaster, that the delicate balance of my life right now depended on keeping him a secret. It was that he was *my* secret. It felt wrong to tell Penny—like whatever strange connection I had with Andy, it would disintegrate if anybody else in my life knew about it.

I felt uneasy enough after hanging up that when Andy

called a little after eleven, I silenced the phone and let it ring out without answering.

And then I listened to Andy's forlorn voicemail ten times before falling asleep, knowing that the next time he called, I'd pick up.

∽ 20 ∽

Saturday, July 26
Two Days Until the RNC
101 DAYS UNTIL THE GENERAL ELECTION

The next morning, Libby brought fancy coffees to the suite for Nancy and me, and I thanked her with a guilty smile—when Nancy had asked me where the best coffee in LA was, I'd blurted, "The Bean and Steam on Franklin," before realizing they were sending Liberty clear across town to fetch beverages just as easily purchased from the Starbucks in the hotel lobby.

At least it had given her a chance to see the city. Spying loose wisps of hair around her usual tight bun, I wondered if she'd driven over with the windows down, and felt a surge of envy that lingered until she too ducked away, leaving Nancy and me with two lukewarm cups of the best coffee in LA. The senator and Meg were out to a private breakfast, Gabe and Gracie lolling on the sofa watching Saturday morning cartoons, so we had the terraced deck to ourselves.

"Your dad and Meg are meeting with delegates tomorrow," Nancy told me, pushing her half-full latte away with a grimace. "So we thought you and Gracie and Gabe might want to go out and do something fun, just the three of you."

If I could raise one eyebrow, I would have. "Just the three of us—plus security, you mean?"

She smiled, caught. "And a camera crew. *Ours* this time. Any ideas? The beach maybe, or a studio tour? That could be fun, right?"

"How about Magic Mountain?"

I'd been hoping to go back ever since the end of the school year, when Penny told me I'd missed out on their junior trip. The twins were tall enough to go on a lot of the rides. And I couldn't wait to introduce them to Penny.

"*Great* idea." Nancy nodded and started making notes on that ubiquitous legal pad of hers.

"Maybe I could invite some friends along too?"

Her smile evaporated. "*Just the three of you.* Did I not make that clear?" She laughed lightly, but there was no warmth in it. It was like she was mocking me.

I froze, thrown by her mood change. The stress of the campaign must have been getting to her more than I'd realized.

Penny and I had talked for months about going together. It wouldn't be the same without her. But with tensions this high, did I really want to risk a blowout over a trip to an amusement park?

"Yeah, okay," I said. "The three of us sounds great."

I didn't find out until the next morning that this would be a first for the twins. They'd never been to an amusement park in their lives—never even gone on a roller coaster.

"I mean, we've done *spinny* rides," Gracie said, trying to save face.

Gabe nodded sagely. "We went on lots of rides at the Iowa State Fair and I almost threw up but then I didn't."

"Good man," I said. When he blinked up at me, I caught a proud gleam in his eye that hadn't been there before.

The camera crew was young—local volunteers who worked in the film industry. They made for a rowdy van ride up the 5 into Valencia. When the roller coasters rose into view, I watched my siblings fire up like rockets, ready to launch.

The park offered to let us skip the lines, but Nancy thought it would make us look elitist. I saw her point—although I'd secretly always dreamed of being a line jumper like the VIPs Penny and I used to grumble about in our hour-plus waits.

When we finally reached the end of the line for our warm-up ride, a steel coaster with a couple of serious drops but no loops, I took extra care to help Gabe get seated and belted in. But when our train started away, it was Gracie's hands I noticed shaking.

"I can do this," she muttered through a tight-locked jaw. Then she said it again. And again, a frantic mantra that increased in volume as the train car *click click clicked* its way upward. I had to nudge her twice to get her to wave for our camera guy in the seat behind us.

As we reached the apex, Gracie let out a keening whine, the prelude to a sobbing fit. My heart started to ratchet up, and not in a good way.

As we tilted over the rim, I lifted my hands and grinned at the twins. Their eyes were glassy, mouths agape, and then we dropped and they let out noncommittal screams as if they hadn't yet decided if this was fun. I shot the cameraman a thumbs-up, hoping the movement covered Gracie's horrified face.

As the train careened back into the station, I was brain-storming ways to salvage the day. *Spinny rides. Or we could go watch a stunt show?* But when the twins staggered onto the platform, they erupted into delirious laughter.

Gabe jumped up and down, electrified by sudden mania. "Let's do a loopy one!"

Gracie blanched. "Loops. Sounds . . . great."

Despite Gabe's pleas, I didn't push it. There were more than enough easy rides to fill the day, especially given the long waits and near-constant photo op breaks. Gracie buried her fear under a brave mask and eventually even that dropped away. By roller coaster three, she was doing the happy terror dance at the end of the line with everybody else.

And for those next seven hours, Gabe was a different kid, a puppy whose leash had been dropped. For one whole day, he took a break from caution, from waiting for others to react first. He didn't even hide from the cameras, hardly noticing them in his mad rush from ride to ride. For the first time in months, I saw the kid that he could be, glowing and relaxed. Free.

As the sun was dipping low and the Ferris wheel's lights were blinking on, the crew got one last shot, all three of us relishing the official last treat of the day—funnel cake. We took polite, teensy bites until the cameras stopped rolling. Then we dug in like wild pigs.

"My mom used to tell me you have to eat funnel cake after riding roller coasters, or you'll feel dizzy the next day." I laughed, spilling powdered sugar down my shirt.

Gracie squinted at the plate. "Is that true?"

"Nah. She just liked funnel cake."

I peered up at the lights, remembering all the trips here we'd taken, just the two of us. I was younger than Gabe and Gracie the first time we came. After my first ride on a roller coaster, I'd burst into phlegmy tears. Mom was determined to raise a daughter who could ride the loops with her, though, so I tried again. It took me two visits before I actually enjoyed myself. I was about to admit to the twins how much braver they were than me, when Gabe cut in quietly.

"You never talk about your mom."

The twins watched me try to form a response. "It's because I miss her. So every time I talk about her, I get sad."

As Gabe took my hand, Gracie stood, sending the last bits of funnel cake scattering onto the ground.

"*We're* your family now."

I smiled, but there was an odd steeliness to Gracie's voice, making the sweet statement come across as more of an accusation. Her chin was thrust upward, her eyes stubborn and pained, a mirror of that night in Massachusetts when she'd cut up my dress and wouldn't tell me why.

I watched her as we made our way to the parking lot. I still didn't understand this side of Gracie, but a picture was starting to emerge. She'd felt threatened by me that day, for whatever reason. And today, she felt threatened by my mother, the huge part of my life that Gracie didn't, couldn't, wouldn't understand.

As we rode back along the freeway, passing hills lit neon by the sunset, more memories rose up, creeping through the crack in the door that Magic Mountain had opened. I let them in, recalling the day I went to the LA County Fair with Mom and her best friend Marta when I wasn't much older than a toddler. One of my earliest memories was sitting between them on the scrambler. As we smushed each other, Marta's soda spilled on Mom's shoes, but they just cracked up.

They were so young, I realized now. *Mom was so young to have me. And so young to already be gone.*

I caught Gracie watching me, but kept my thoughts to myself. Gabe might have wanted to know more, but Gracie couldn't process it. In that way too, Gabe was braver than his sister.

When we got back to the hotel, an e-mail was waiting for me as if conjured by magical thinking. Marta had sent it this morning.

"It's been so long," she wrote. "I'd like to catch up."

I was a little surprised to hear from her. She'd been a constant part of my life in LA, since she was Mom's best friend and close colleague at the food bank. Still, we were never what I would call close. It wasn't as though I shared secrets with her or came to her for advice. I'd had Mom for that. Over the past year, Marta had checked in with me in South Carolina from time to time, probably feeling like she owed it to my mom in some way. But calls from her had gotten more and more uncomfortable, and then more and more infrequent. This was the first time I'd heard from her since a few months before the Great Revelation, so it was no wonder she wanted to see me. There was plenty to catch up on.

But there was something oddly formal about the wording

of her e-mail, like she was setting an agenda for a meeting at the food bank.

"I realize you must be busy, but I'd really welcome the opportunity to sit and talk."

As awkward as her e-mail was, my response was probably worse.

"I can do Wednesday between 11:40 A.M. and 12:25 P.M.—would that work for you?" I tried to soften it with a smiley face. "Sorry to be so specific, but it's been crazy. Maybe we could grab lunch?"

I wanted more wiggle room in the time, so I didn't sound like such a self-important jerk, but Nancy had insisted I write the exact allotted window. She watched over my shoulder as I typed my reply.

"We need you at the Costco meet and greet and then you've really got to be on time for the AIPAC luncheon," she reminded me, running her hand anxiously through her hair. "But that should give you enough time to catch up with your friend, yeah?"

It was better than nothing. Marta's reply came in almost instantly.

"Great! How about a neutral spot—remember our diner on La Cienega?"

I smiled, recalling our old tradition of bimonthly brunches there—just me, Mom, Marta, her little Yorkie Freddie, and occasionally one of Marta's boyfriends, the poor guys she seemed to swap out every four months like clockwork. I wondered if she'd bring Freddie along on Wednesday.

Then I noticed, again, Marta's odd word choice. *Neutral spot.*

Were we fighting and I didn't know it?

I'd have a few days before I found out. And they would be full.

Monday morning, the first day of the convention, I woke up at 6:00 A.M. to voices in our suite's living room. One of them grew unnaturally loud, and it took me a few groggy blinks to realize that the TV was being turned up.

Throwing on presentable clothes, I lumbered from my room to see Meg glaring at the screen. She hadn't brushed her hair yet, which wasn't like her, and she was clutching her coffee mug to her chest as if it were a teddy bear. Nancy and Louis stood behind her with their arms crossed James-style, and in the corridor that led out of the suite, Elliott paced, hissing into his cell phone. I pitied whoever was at the other end of the line.

Meg's glare broke when she spotted me. "Morning, Kate. Coffee?"

I followed her as she shuffled to the kitchen and poured us both a wakeup dosage. It was only then that I saw the senator across the room, slumped against the glass doors to the terrace, squinting at the sunrise. That was not his get-up-and-go posture.

"What's going on this time?" I asked Meg.

She pointed to the TV.

"Oh *no*." It was me again. Of *course*. Me and Gabe and Gracie, the photograph from yesterday, the three of us on the roller coaster. All of us . . . smiling? "Wait."

I put down my coffee mug with a clunk.

"What's wrong with *that*?"

"Absolutely *nothing*," Meg growled a sigh.

A box popped up, framing a woman I didn't recognize standing outside a church I did recognize, surrounded by congregants.

Nancy turned the TV up even louder.

"Don't get me wrooooong," the woman drawled, dragging the word out like a schoolyard taunt. "I've got nothing against kids going out, having a good time, riding the rides. But to do it on the *Lord's* day?" She let out a helpless laugh, glancing over her shoulder at the white steeple I'd driven past countless times on Santa Monica Boulevard. "*My* family found a church here in Los Angel-ease. It wasn't hard. It makes me wonder how conservative the Coopers really are. It raises questions about values. I think a lot of people are wondering about that."

The senator spun around, brought back to life by the sound of this vapid woman's voice. "Why would she do this? What can they hope to gain by undermining us?"

The way he said it made me suspect this wasn't some random, woman-on-the-street interview. Her last name was the same as one of the candidates from the primaries. His wife?

"Fred's an asshole," Louis said, his affable shrug making the insult seem charming. "This is his Hail Mary pass." He chuckled. "Excuse the pun."

"It's the same old rhino accusation." Nancy sighed.

"Rhino?" I whispered to Meg.

"Republican In Name Only," she explained, and I respelled it in my head.

"Wait." I stepped forward, confused. "She's a Republican too?"

Lou chuckled. "*Oh* yeah. Just ask her. She'll tell you. She'll never stop tellin' you."

"So isn't she on our side?"

Senator Cooper raised his hands in the air. "Thank you, Kate. That's just what—"

Elliott slammed his phone on the dining room table and glowered through the doorway at us.

"Nobody's on our side, Mark. Not until the instant the nomination is ratified on Wednesday. *Nobody* gets to relax until then."

That last part was directed at me. If Elliott wanted me to feel the pressure, he could have spared himself the trouble. I'd hardly slept last night, thinking about the day ahead, all the events that would lead up to my first appearance in front of a packed Staples Center audience, and oh. Right. *America* watching live.

Tonight would be a smile-and-wave on the biggest scale imaginable. The theme of our appearance was "Proud Conservative Women"—we'd parade in after a speech by the female mayor of San Diego. But Nancy deemed the whole day so important that she insisted I be camera-ready from 8:00 A.M. on. One look at the four-page schedule told me why. This day was going to be crazy.

Somehow, the pages flew by, one lightning-quick event blurring into the next. Libby and other aides had refreshments handy as we walked between meetings, calling on other hotel suites, popping in on a few joint press appearances and rallies, until at around 5:00 P.M., we finally reached the wide courtyard of the Staples Center itself.

"Wow," I said, seeing the first hordes waiting to be admitted, bearing bedazzled outfits, huge signs, crazy hats. A bus pulled up and as twenty more people piled out, a group in the crowd shouted "Minnesota!" and the bus people whooped.

"Exciting, huh?" Libby skipped in place as she passed me my fifth water bottle of the day. I nodded, gulping it back, trying to drown out my mounting terror.

Inside, I stole a quick glance at the cavernous arena, expecting to be even more terrified by the size of it. But the first association that popped up, unbidden, was Kudzu Giants. No—Andy. Even more mutinous, a sudden sharp pang, wishing I could sneak him in here like he'd done for me. The thought barely had time to form before an aide motioned me backstage.

That quick glance was the longest moment I got to myself all day. By 6:00 P.M., after all those water bottles, I was beyond ready for a bathroom break. I figured they'd probably scheduled us one, but when Gracie complained that she needed to go and Gabe ran after her, three staffers stopped me at the door.

"Makeup," Libby explained, checking her watch with such frenzied eyes that I took pity and went along. Makeup and hair took an hour. I sat patiently, my legs crossed tight and my bladder beginning to bulge.

Nancy poked her head in for a final check. "You look great!"

I lifted myself carefully out of the chair. "Which way are the restrooms?"

"Out right." She stopped me with her hand. "Uh-uh. There's press out there now, getting behind-the-scenes shots. We don't want them to catch you running for the bathroom."

She laughed.

I managed a tepid smile. "I won't run."

Nancy's phone beeped. "They're ready for us."

As she started away, I realized I had two options. Follow her or rebel—dash past the assembled journalists and duck into the bathroom before anybody got a shot off. My bladder was so full I could barely move, so sprinting wasn't a viable option. With a wince of pain, I waddled off beside Nancy, praying we'd have one more break before the big moment.

My prayers went unanswered. Whether it was because I'd gone to a theme park on a Sunday, I couldn't have told you, but this giant venue suddenly seemed to have only one bathroom, and that was the one I was plodding away from, my hopes of relief dying with every plod. Finally, Nancy led me into the wings of the arena where a gaggle of brightly suited ladies were waiting in uncompanionable silence, tapping their stilettos in anticipation.

I recognized Mrs. McReady before I spotted her daughter. Carolee glanced lazily over her shoulder at me, scanning my outfit. I winced a smile and she quickly looked away.

There were a lot of women I didn't recognize, and others I'd met so briefly that I couldn't possibly recite their names. The churchy lady wasn't there. I wondered whether she'd been booted from the appearance for her comments yesterday.

Gracie ran from Meg's side to hug me around the waist.

I gasped. "Not too tight!"

"Okay, ladies, let's go!" said the earphoned coordinator, and we walked into the arena to a deafening cheer that seemed to ricochet back on itself like the roar of a waterfall. The first thing I took in was color everywhere, red, white, and blue—strange to see when it wasn't July Fourth. Then faces poked out from the mess of signs, and waving hands, and oh my God, there were so many of them. The lights scanned the stadium like they were searching for escapees, and as they found us, the crowd got even louder, music blasting from the stage's speakers. Everyone surrounding our path stood, applauding.

"What's wrong with you?" Gracie yelled up at me.

"What do you mean?" I asked through gritted teeth.

"You look really weird!"

I leaned down as far as my bladder would allow. "I haven't peed since we left this morning," I hissed, and Gracie let out a laugh so loud that the cameras beside the stage swerved to focus on us.

Great. I grimaced a grin and kept taking mini steps forward, one at a time.

On the stage, we lined up as rehearsed, and after endless silent seconds and even more endless announcements of our names—like anybody here didn't know who we were!—followed by absolutely interminable, but very kind, really, applause from the audience, we were free and I smiled and waved my way back off the stage and through the crowd, hit the edge of the wings, and speed-waddled down the empty corridor to the bathrooms, marveling at the miracle that had just occurred. I had somehow managed not to humiliate myself on national television.

Or so I thought.

The first call back at the hotel was Penny. "You looked so pretty up there! But. Um . . . what was going on with your walking?"

Oh God.

She was my best friend, I reminded myself. Only someone who'd known me since first grade could possibly notice something as subtle as that.

Andy called while I was still on with Penny. I clicked over, heart pounding.

"Quinn. I don't know how to ask this without sounding like an asshole . . ." He didn't wait for permission. "Did you have to pay a visit to the *bathroom*, by chance?"

I blushed so violently that my knees nearly crumpled from lack of blood.

"I only know because I've been there." He laughed. "You've gotta make them wait for you—even if you have to make a run for it, fight for your right to urinate!"

"Next time," I got out, covering my hot cheeks with my hands.

"You looked great, though," he added. "It was nice to see your face."

I started to smile.

"Your pained . . . sweating face . . ."

"I hate you."

I could hear him grin. *"Liar."*

The news commentary was instant. Nancy shushed every-body when the cable stations mentioned my name in their recap of the evening.

"Kate Quinn made a charmingly nervous first appearance on the convention stage . . ."

Up on the screen, there I was, tiny, waddling up the steps and crossing the stage with my knees pressed together, my eyes fluttering with panic.

How could they not tell?!

Nancy gave me a hug. "Charmingly nervous. I'd say that's pretty close to perfect."

"Nice job, kiddo," the senator said. He shot me a wink and I turned to hide what had to be the goofiest grin in the world.

"I've got a wardrobe note," Elliott said.

"Of course you do," I muttered under my breath.

Elliott didn't deign to look at me. "Can we get her some freaking high heels? Next to Carolee, she looks like a munch-kin."

"Hey now!" Lou put his hands in the air. "Let's not insult the vertically challenged—myself included. Shorties vote too, you know."

He nodded to me with mock-seriousness and I let out a laugh. It had been nice to see more of Lou during the lead-up to the convention. He'd traveled here with his wife and their four-month-old baby, and I'd enjoyed watching him in dad mode, cradling his daughter while directing traffic over his cell phone.

Nancy waved everybody silent again and turned up the TV.

"Kate's one to watch in the coming days," said the news pundit. *"She's her father's daughter and I expect we'll see that Cooper confidence come out more and more as the campaign progresses . . ."*

That Cooper confidence. I glanced at the senator in the hallway, wondering whether what Lou said that first week at headquarters was actually true. Maybe we were alike after all. Judging by the giddiness I felt right now, the idea was clearly starting to grow on me.

Along one edge of the living room, I spotted Gracie in her pajamas, poking her head around the corner to stare at the television with a furrowed brow. As her blue eyes veered to mine, I cocked my head to ask what was wrong, but she gave me no more than a blank blink before disappearing back into her room.

21

It was Meg's turn to be a nervous wreck. And the senator was teasing her mercilessly for it.

"Come on, Meggie," he said, using a name I'd never heard uttered before, and judging by her death-glare, might never hear again. "'It's just like an undergrad lecture, except all of these people actually want to be there.' Isn't that what you always tell me, Miss Cool as a Cucumber?"

He grinned and tried to poke her in the side, but she whapped him away, laughing.

"Let me concentrate!"

She went back to scribbling last-minute changes to tonight's speech. I stayed close, wondering whether she'd ask me to weigh in, like usual. I suspected the professor in her was using the campaign as a teaching opportunity, especially when she'd point to key phrases and say, "What does this convey, Kate? What will voters pick up on?" She knew the answers already, that much was obvious, but she wanted me to come up with my own response. Or maybe she wanted my perspective as a younger person.

In any case, she didn't ask and I didn't mind. Today was as close to a day off as I would get during the convention, my responsibilities limited to tagging along for a few family appearances, then looking after the twins in the suite until tonight's televised events. Around six o'clock, Gabe, Gracie, and I would sit in a special box seat and watch Meg deliver her address while the senator watched backstage, hidden until his big moment at the end of the convention.

The crowd was as galvanized Tuesday as they'd been on night one, and this time, I was actually able to enjoy it. There were several speeches before Meg's, a bunch of junior congressmen, then the petite, energetic governor of Wisconsin, who'd walked with us in the Conservative Women Parade yesterday. Nancy had told me that all of these people were up-and-comers in the Republican party, many of them on a national stage for the first time in their careers. I could only imagine how anxious they must be, experiencing a single moment that could affect the entire trajectory of their lives. I cheered as loud as I could.

But when I started listening to what they were actually saying, my voice faltered. Underneath the feel-good sound bites and battle cries that sent the crowd into an ecstatic frenzy, there was an undercurrent that set my teeth on edge.

"I believe this is the Greatest. Nation. In the World," one junior senator said, to resounding applause. "President Lawrence says he considers us citizens of the world. Well, my friends, I don't know about you. But I am first and foremost— an American!"

Can't you be both? I wondered.

The petite Wisconsin governor spoke to more specific issues. "Our opponents want to bury their heads in the sand.

About terrorism abroad. An educational system that isn't serving our students. Unchecked illegal immigration—all the insidious undercurrents that threaten the very fabric of our way of life. Mark Cooper is a man who has proven that he can face difficult issues head-on. He's what this country needs!"

I pictured myself wearing a T-shirt that read "Difficult Issue." *Maybe after the election.* But then my mind looped back over her list of "insidious undercurrents," and I felt myself shrink, praying that against all probability, Penny wasn't watching with her family.

"Our vision for the country is the same as my parents' and grandparents'," one extremely pale congressman said. "One with strong, wholesome values. One that respects and upholds the Constitution. One that defends the freedom of *true* Americans, like you and me."

As their speeches rolled out, I started to develop a much crisper picture of what "The America We Know" looked like. It sure didn't look like the neighborhood where I grew up. And it *really* didn't look like the Diazes'. I felt bile rising in my throat.

All summer, I'd managed to keep that policy binder buried, ignoring any mention of immigration on the news or in the senator's stump speeches. But here, surrounded by thousands of screaming supporters, there was no escaping the party line. It was a hard line, all right.

More than hard. Unbearable.

So it was both a thrill and a relief when at long last, Meg took the stage, wearing a dark green suit, her blond hair elegantly bobbed, her smile flashing white even from back here. As I stood, pulling Gracie and Gabe up with me, a cameraman scuttled in front of us and crouched to film our reactions.

"I can't see!" Gracie pouted directly into the camera. I hurriedly lifted her so that she was standing on her chair, her head well above the cameraman's. In the row behind us, Governor Rizzo's family laughed and tapped Gracie's shoulder to give her a high five.

Gabe grabbed my elbow, his face grave. I held my breath, hoping he wasn't having a panic attack from the attention. But then he gripped more tightly, boosting himself onto his own seat—and grinned like he was looking down at Magic Mountain from the top of a roller coaster.

Up on stage, Meg made her way out of a small crowd of cheering bigwigs and approached the podium. Gabe waved wildly. Spotting us in our box, Meg's mouth dropped open in surprise. She shot him a delighted thumbs-up, then stepped behind the microphone—and proceeded to blow all the other speakers out of the water.

Meg was articulate but relatable, warm but forceful. She talked about the regular Americans she'd met through-out the campaign, who were going through tough econom-ic times. She made a gentle allusion to the "challenges and unexpected blessings" that had recently come into her life, and at the mention, I could feel the heat of the camera lens focusing on my face.

As she concluded, she turned to our section with a warm smile.

"Like me, my stepdaughter, Kate, is a history buff. One night recently, she told me something that really resonated. 'History is about people,' she said. 'It's amazing how much one person can change the world, even if they don't know they're doing it.'"

The audience fell into a hush as she paused. I covered my grin with the tips of my fingers.

"I want to say this to everyone who's watching. *You* are that one person. You have a vote, a voice, a say. And no one can take that away from you. So on November the fourth— let's go out there and change the world. God bless you all, and God bless America!"

"Nice quote, Kate," Penny said later as I curled up in my hotel room, relishing the feel of my ratty old pajamas. "She seems like a really nice lady. And smart—why isn't *she* running for president?"

I laughed, thinking of Meg's daily countdown. "Only one hundred and thirteen more days." "Only one hundred and six more days." She still said it every morning. As skilled as Meg had proven to be at politics, I knew that she saw the campaign as an intellectual exercise at its best and a grueling test of will the rest of the time.

"Or maybe you should run," Penny suggested.

I snorted. "Fat chance."

"I could see it." Her voice was flat. "Kate Quinn Cooper. *Republican* from California."

She was trying to bait me. I didn't respond.

"I mean, you're Miss Junior Republican now, right? Somebody at the convention called you 'The next generation of the GOP.' What does GOP even *mean*?"

"Grand Old Party," I answered. I could hear her choking on the other end of the line.

"*What? I* always thought it stood for something serious."

"It's a nickname. Like the elephant's our mascot."

"'*Our*'?"

My defenses started to flare. "Yes. *Our.* I'm a part of this campaign, so I'm a part of the party too."

She didn't say anything. So I kept going.

"Question, Penny—when I was asking for advice back in June, weren't *you* the one who told me I *had* to do this?"

"Go along on the campaign, not go along with every-thing—"

She cut herself off with a sigh. I knew what she meant. I ignored it.

"It's not so horrible, you know. They're good people with worthwhile goals. Freedom is a good thing. Personal respon-sibility is a good thing."

"Wow, you're *really* into this." Her voice was quiet. "That must be why I've hardly seen you this week."

I started to apologize. "There's just so much going on—"

"I know," she said. "I'm watching it on TV."

I couldn't sleep that night, and not just from my conversation with Penny. There were no huge events planned Wednesday, just the usual succession of breakfasts, donor handshakes, and volunteer meet and greets. Nothing I hadn't done a million times this summer. But my stomach was in knots, my limbs jumpy under the covers.

It was Marta, I realized. I was nervous to see her and I couldn't put my finger on why.

When my car arrived at the Starlight Diner the next morning, I felt my nerves sink into dread. More than that, something familiar and unwelcome. Grief.

I asked the driver to pick me up in exactly forty-five minutes. He was hesitant to leave me, but there were no cameras in sight, the street was quiet, and the diner empty, except for Marta's slumped silhouette in the usual corner booth.

Opposite her was an empty seat. The one my mom used to take.

I drew in a breath and held it as I clomped in my low heels across the shiny diner floor, too nervous to exhale until Marta jumped up to hug the air out of me, her eyes glittering.

"Look at you," she said. "You look . . . different."

"Thank you," I said, but I sensed that it wasn't quite a compliment.

After we'd ordered, Marta asked tentative questions about how my life had changed since the last time we'd talked.

"Do you like the Coopers?"

"Yes, very much," I answered. "They've been wonderful. I haven't gotten to know the senator as much because of the campaign . . ."

Marta blanched. Before I could ask her why, she smiled. "And you're a big sister!"

"Yeah! They're great. We get plenty of bonding time out on the road. The campaign bus is big, but—"

"Have you seen Penny since you've been back?"

After chatting for a few more minutes, it occurred to me that Marta was changing the subject every time the campaign came up. If I didn't know her so well, I would've suspected she hated talking politics. Something was off.

"No Freddie today?" I asked, thinking that question would be safe enough.

She took a gulp of water. "Freddie actually passed back in May."

"Oh no." *Freddie too.* "I'm so sorry."

Marta's fingers kept tapping the edge of the booth, as if she were waiting for a buzzer to go off. It wasn't like her to be this antsy.

She's feeling what I am, I told myself. *The emptiness of the booth. Last time there were three of us, four with Freddie, and now it's just us. And we don't know how to talk to each other anymore.*

I tried again to break the ice. "How's the Cocina?"

She froze even more at that, eyes wide like I'd caught her with her hand in a cash register. "I actually moved on a few months ago."

So that was why she was anxious. She felt guilty about leaving my mom's organization. Maybe she saw it as breaking a promise to her best friend, but who was I to hold that against her? I reached out to put my hand on top of her restless one. It balled up under my palm.

I tried to smile. "So where are you working now?"

She swallowed, pulled her arm back.

"I'm fundraising for the Lawrence campaign, actually.

I've always been an active Democrat and it was too big an opportunity to pass up."

She said it quickly, defensively. It did come as a bit of a shock to hear that she was working on the opponent's campaign, but I made sure not to show it.

"That's amazing, Marta—"

"You're happy, right?"

She was holding on to the booth, staring at me so intently that it was impossible not to read the bare emotion in her eyes. The fear, the doubt. No.

The guilt.

And then I realized. Had I been standing, I would have staggered back.

The waitress brought our lunch plates. Neither of us looked at them.

"It was you," I said. Her head fell in acknowledgment, but I had to say it anyway. All of it. "Mom told you who my father was. And you told *them.*"

Her eyes flashed. "I thought—he *had* to know! Cooper, I mean." She shook her head, correcting herself. "Your *father.* He had to have known about you by then. All those experts around him, researching every single angle—it seemed impossible that he wouldn't have found out. And if he knew, then he was the biggest hypocrite I'd ever seen. I owed it to *you,* Kate, to make it known. Make him acknowledge you."

My voice barely came out and when it did, I didn't recognize it. "Who did you tell first? The Lawrence campaign? Dina Thomas?"

Her eyes widened at the name, as if she were surprised

that I knew the reporter. How naïve did she think I was? But she recovered.

"The campaign first. They encouraged me to contact the *Times*, so—"

"Why not . . ." I shrugged, cutting her off. "I don't know, *me?* If this was really about me, Marta, not your career, it seems like I should have been the first to know."

She winced. "It was a mistake. I acknowledge that. And I also acknowledge that I was wrong about Cooper. He didn't know, Kate. About you."

I stood, roiling with anger. "I know he didn't! I *live* with him, he's my father. I'm not an idiot, or—or a victim. I know *everything.*"

"Okay," she said, even though I'm sure she suspected I was lying. I didn't know everything. Not even close. The affair was a big black hole, a blank spot in history, and my impression of the man himself was still fuzzy after weeks of traveling and living with him.

The only reason I knew that he hadn't found out about me, hadn't abandoned me, was that I'd seen his face the first time I met him, the shock on it, the raw truth behind the politician's mask he so rarely took off.

"Can you forgive me?" Marta was asking, and I didn't have an answer, so I just slapped some money on the table and said:

"Maybe I'll see you at the debates."

And strode out the door, clutching my cell.

"I'm done early," I said when the driver answered his phone. "You can get me now."

～22～

Back at the hotel, our suite was empty, the TV still on, Fox News interviewing manic convention-goers. There were two publications sitting on the coffee table, *Time* magazine and the *Washington Post*. I was too riled up even to sit, but the cover of the magazine stopped me like a whip crack.

I was on it.

It was the last photo they'd taken on Sunday—me, Gracie, and Gabe, sharing funnel cake at Magic Mountain. The caption stretched wide across the bottom of the page.

"The New American Family."

I sat and touched the magazine lightly, my anger giving way to dizzy wonderment, not just because I was on the freaking cover of *Time* magazine—but because of the warmth I felt reading the headline.

For once, the public's spin was right. We *were* a family. The photo was proof. On the cover, Gabe was smiling up at me, Gracie going for a corner of the funnel cake as I watched her, laughing. We looked glittering, strong. Blessed.

This cover was evidence of something amazing. I had become a sister, really and truly, and a stepdaughter to Meg, who cared what I thought, who wanted to know my hopes and help me achieve them. The Coopers cared about me. They belonged to me.

The door to the suite flew open. Elliott's eyes landed on me and narrowed.

"You satisfied?"

With the *Time* cover? What was wrong? This seemed totally innocent. More than that—positive.

He leaned over the coffee table, picked up the *Post,* and threw it at me—actually *threw* it at me—sending pages fluttering wild as he stalked to the window. Meg walked in as I was trying to gather the paper, Nancy close behind, chattering into the senator's ear.

"We blame it on the mother, on the school district. We make Kate the victim here—"

She cut off when she saw me. I riffled shakily through the pages, seeing nothing about me except an image from the convention that showed half my face on the edge of the frame. Nancy looked to the senator, whose eyes were locked on the carpet, his mouth frozen in a frown. Even Meg wouldn't look at me.

I turned another page and finally found something, just as Nancy murmured, "We'll have to change your speech, Mark."

It was the photo of me with my friends, the one that had appeared on the news, making CNN accuse us of pandering to the Hispanic vote. This article took a different slant.

Cooper Daughter's Checkered Friendships, it began.

Kate Quinn attracted national attention earlier this week when she was photographed at a gathering of friends in East LA. Now reports have surfaced that shed new light on the life of the sixteen-year-old prior to her joining the Cooper campaign.

The neighborhood of East Los Angeles in which a group of thirty friends hosted a welcome home party for Quinn is widely known as a haven for undocumented immigrants. In fact, our investigations found that several of those photographed that day—who have declined to be interviewed—are the children of parents who have been incarcerated and deported, and another, Chester Washington, is himself a convicted criminal . . .

"*Convicted criminal?*" I bolted from the sofa and threw down the paper. "Chester? He shoplifted when he was eleven! He was in juvie for like six months and won't so much as jaywalk now because of it—"

"Quiet."

Everyone froze, staring at the senator. He hadn't yelled the word, but he'd said it sharply enough to make even Elliott and Nancy retreat to the edges of the room. Meg sat and took my wrist, trying to pull me down next to her, but, my heart racing, I stayed where I was, daring the senator to look up at me.

He did, slowly.

"What. Were. You. Thinking."

He squinted, waiting for an answer, and the anger that had been thrumming through my veins since seeing Marta flared like alcohol thrown on a bonfire.

"I was thinking I'd be able to see my friends and be *myself* for one day. Apparently I was wrong."

He flinched, surprised by my tone. I was surprised too. I hadn't heard that voice come out of myself in a long time, maybe ever.

The senator breathed in, controlling himself, rinsing the anger from his face but only partly succeeding.

"Did you know that your friends were the children of illegal immigrants?" His eyes were wide now, imploring, though his face remained grave.

I sucked in a breath. "I—I don't think of them that way. I went to school with them. A *magnet* school, by the way."

"That's not the question." Nancy's voice rose up from across the room. I saw Meg's eyes darting to her but couldn't read them.

The senator was still watching, still hopeful.

"No," I answered. "I'm just as surprised as you are."

As the room fractionally relaxed, I steadied my footing, reeling from my own lie. I did know, of course. Not about the two boys who were mentioned in the article along with Chester. But about others much closer to me, who, thank God, had not been exposed. Yet.

My breath came ragged, my skin prickling with panic. They were right to be mad at me, I realized now—but for the wrong reason.

What was *I thinking, putting the Diazes in the spotlight? How could I be so stupid?*

"That's what I thought." The senator sat down and patted the seat opposite him. I obeyed, still shaking a little.

Elliott strode quickly over. "She'll need to make a statement."

"I'm sitting right here," I snapped. Meg reached out to hold my arm. "You can drop the third person."

As Elliott smiled, his eyes narrowed, a cat watching a

mouse. "*You. Need. To make a statement.* We'll write it. You read it."

"Saying what?"

The senator cleared his throat. "Exactly what you just told us. You weren't aware that these people were in the country illegally, and you apologize for your association with them."

I could hear an echo of Andy's voice from that night outside the White House, so sudden and vivid it was as if he were whispering in my ear right now.

They'll keep trying to shut you up, or make you say exactly what they've written . . .

I stayed silent for a long time, maybe too long, because when I looked up, Nancy was crouched in front of me, her hands pressed together as if in prayer.

"Our position is to firmly oppose illegal immigration," she explained, and my throat went dry. "It's one of our major policy issues."

Our. I turned to the senator, but he was peering at Nancy like a student watches a teacher.

"It's important that you fall in line with that."

It seemed so reasonable coming from her that I took the legal pad she was handing me, on which she'd hurriedly scribbled a paragraph.

The words swam on the paper. I pressed my hand over the page to cover them.

"I won't read this."

Elliott laughed sharply and stalked away, shouting over his shoulder, "I told you. It was *only* a matter of time before the liberal mother reared her head from beyond the grave."

231

"How *dare* you!"

I'm not sure whether Meg said it or I did, but I was the one who stood so quickly that Nancy nearly stumbled onto her backside getting out of my way.

For one endless moment, I contemplated crossing the room and slapping Elliott across the face. It would be so easy. Instead, I barely managed to get my legs to move me out of the living room and into my own.

I sat with my back to the door, muffling my tears, wishing my dead liberal mother were here, to tell them all to leave me alone, pack my bags for me, and take me home to our little stucco house a few short blocks from Penny, my best friend, who didn't deserve to be a "major policy issue," who I swore, I swore, I would never, ever apologize for.

We were in sixth grade when Penny got up the nerve to tell me. It was a sleepover night and she'd muted the TV in my bedroom to whisper the secret she'd been keeping since the day we met. I remember sitting cross-legged on the floor, our knees touching, her eyes on the ground.

"Do you still want to be my friend?" she'd asked, and I'd hugged her and promised that we'd be friends forever. I'd kept that promise for five years. I wasn't about to abandon it now.

My stomach ached with shame. How could I not have seen this coming? No. How could I have *ignored* it? Because that was the truth, wasn't it? I hadn't wanted to see it. That first day at headquarters, the senator's stance on immigration felt like a roadblock between us. Now it felt like the Grand Canyon.

Out in the living room, Meg's voice rose up in anger, then the door slammed shut into silence.

After a few minutes, Meg knocked softly. "Kate? You want to come out and talk about this?"

I opened my mouth, but didn't trust myself to answer. A few shaky breaths later, I heard her footsteps moving away, and a little while after that, the door to the suite quietly thudding shut.

The suite was silent after that. I realized slowly, dully, that they'd left me here. I crawled into my bed, pulled up the covers, and watched the commentary on my room's TV, the scrolling news tickers finding gleefully creative ways to publicize the burgeoning scandal. After two hours of coverage, three different stations were calling it "Kategate." I had to admit, it was pretty catchy.

And then, at about 3:00 P.M., I watched the spin kick in. As the senator left that afternoon's luncheon, swarmed by reporters, he made light of the situation.

"Look, this is a non-issue," he laughed. "These are friends Kate knew from her *magnet* school, where she and a number of other kids in this photo were straight-A students."

There was a flurry of voices, and then he raised his hand.

"My views on immigration remain the same, but that's not what this is about—this is an attack on my daughter and my family, and I won't respond to such low tactics. Thank you."

He was so convincing.

The news footage showed Meg and Gracie behind him as he walked away. No Gabe.

I muted the TV, confused, and heard a tiny sound, glass

233

clinking against glass. Creeping out of my room, I saw Gabe on the sofa, playing a game on the suite's Xbox with the volume turned down, a half-full glass of orange juice sitting on the coffee table in front of him.

"How long have you been here?"

He shrugged. I curled up beside him, watching as he shot down zombies from a helicopter.

He paused the game to turn to me. "Are you in trouble?"

"Yeah." I sighed and settled back against the sofa. "Why aren't you at—"

"I didn't feel like it," he said, but there was something in his watchful stare that made me smile.

"You didn't want me to be alone?"

He blinked slowly. "I didn't want you to *leave*."

His words hit me like a cold wave. I felt first the impact, then the shock.

He cared about me. My little brother was worried. But it was more startling than that too—a reminder. This was my choice. Sometime in the last two months, I'd forgotten that leaving was even an option, that my real home was in South Carolina with my aunt and uncle. So what if they only called me once a week, the bare minimum of check-in: "Are you having a good time? Do you need anything? Talk to you next week!" They were still my legal guardians. I could pack up and go any time I wanted. I had a choice.

I forced a smile and ruffled Gabe's hair as he restarted the game. "I'm not going anywhere."

～23～

The sun was inching toward the hills when Meg and Gracie came back, bearing fat paper bags from In-N-Out Burger.

"This is the good one, right?" Meg asked, a weary peace offering. "The one you told us about."

Something in the way she watched me as we ate set my nerves on edge. And sure enough, once the empty wrappers were crumpled into the trash, she invited me onto the patio to talk.

I wondered where the senator was, whether Meg was his proxy in this conversation. But then, had I ever had a meaningful conversation with the senator? Had Gracie or Gabe, while I'd been here? Meg was the official representative of both parents and probably always would be.

"None of this is your fault," she started, surprising me. "But you're a smart girl. *You know* how to be helpful to this campaign."

"I wasn't trying to screw anything up." My anger was starting to crumble. I clenched my fists, fighting to keep it. "I was just living my life. My old one, I guess."

She rubbed my back in a circle and I found I couldn't look at her. I turned instead to stare over the patio rail at the hazy LA skyline, the hills beyond, and the mountains you could only see if you squinted. Meg's arm rested warm against mine as she gazed out with me.

"In two hours, the delegate votes will be in and your father will officially become the Republican nominee." There was a note of sadness in her voice. "And then it'll be fourteen more weeks until the election. Weeks like this. Some easier, some worse." She gave my wrist a gentle squeeze. "And they've done it—the press has crossed the Rubicon where you're concerned. From now on, it'll be fair game to criticize you. It's not fair, but it's the way it is."

Our team will go after Andy now, I realized. *He might enjoy it in some perverse way.*

"Are you up for this?" Meg had turned to face me. The red sun shone on half of her, so that on one side she glowed like an avenging angel, and the rest of her just seemed kind of exhausted.

"What if I'm not?" I swallowed dry. "Up for this."

She wouldn't answer. Not directly.

"It's still *your* choice, Kate."

She went inside after that, leaving me to replay the conversation, wondering what the dark note in her voice had meant. Was she concerned for me? Or for them?

Did she *want* me to leave the campaign?

She popped on Fox News for the twins and me before she left to join the senator and a number of supporters in the wings of the arena, where they would watch Governor McReady accept his vice presidential nomination.

When the camera showed Carolee in the front row, her whitened teeth glittering under the lights, fake eyelashes fluttering, Gabe, Gracie, and I grimaced in unison. I clicked off Fox News, and turned the Xbox on so Gabe could continue his fight against the zombie horde.

The next morning, I woke still uneasy. I'd always believed that Meg had my best interests at heart. Was that changing, now that my hopes and the campaign's weren't perfectly aligned?

I didn't doubt that she cared about me. But caring about my life and wanting to be a part of it were two different things.

When the wake-up knock sounded on my door, it was Nancy, not Meg in the doorway. Her red hair was swept up in a sculptural simulation of a messy bun, and she was dressed down in jeans that I was sure had never seen the inside of a shopping mall, unless you counted Neiman Marcus.

And speaking of Neiman Marcus, she was holding a garment bag.

"For tonight." She swept past me and unzipped the bag, revealing an unbelievably gorgeous pale pink dress with silk layers that sunk against each other like rose petals. A discreet label with cursive stitching inside the low backline read MONIQUE LHUILLIER.

As in celebrity weddings Monique Lhuillier. *Vogue* five-page spreads Lhuillier.

"Whoa," I breathed. "Nancy, I'm not sure I can pull this off."

She raised an eyebrow. "I respectfully disagree."

"Did you pick this out yourself?" I touched the soft hem, fearful of leaving so much as a fingerprint.

"You think I'd delegate something this important to one of my staff?" She snorted, and even that sounded elegant somehow. "Tonight's your big night, Kate. It's time to bring out the couture."

I knew what she was doing, and I didn't complain. With one zip, she'd managed to make me start the day glowing, believing that tonight represented a big moment for me, Kate Quinn, that I was a key component of my father's success. It was enough to take away the sting of yesterday, the queasy mix of guilt, defiance, and worry that I'd woken up with.

The pampering helped too. I felt quite couture all day, even in my lounge-around clothes, while catered trays of fruit and hors d'oeuvres were brought up by the hotel staff. Admiring my hung-up dress—no, I'm sorry . . . *gown*—I couldn't help smiling, thinking of Andy, who had called me late last night to complain that I hadn't made a TV appearance to defend myself against Kategate.

"I'll be on tomorrow," I'd said. "Just to listen to speeches. Not to make any."

"What are you wearing?"

"Not sure yet."

"No, right now."

"Shut up."

"Fuzzy slippers. Nothing else. Got it."

When I examined my made-up reflection in the tall bathroom mirror, I saw someone else. Not a stranger exactly. I knew this girl. She was Whiteboard Kate 2.0, the one polling groups and consultants liked, the one who had law-abiding friends or, even better, no friends at all, who did as she was told without question.

"Smile," the makeup artist said, applying more blush to the apple cheeks of that nice girl in the mirror.

Andy wouldn't see me on TV tonight either. He'd see Kate Cooper.

Even so, Kate Quinn couldn't resist feeling a frisson of delight when Libby carefully zipped the dress and it fit like it was made to measure.

And when I took my place in the arena next to Meg, Grace, and Gabe and watched Senator Cooper stride across the stage, wearing a dark suit and red tie like the first time I'd met him, my own voice drowned in the roar of approval from the thousands of supporters around us, and I thrilled along with them.

I *had* helped him get here. All of us had. His family, the people who voted for him—even the people who ran against him—we were all an intrinsic part of history.

"My friends!" He waved, and the crowd settled. Then he laughed. "It's been a *long road to get here!*"

The sound the arena made was a dam bursting, an echoing tumult that crashed, crested, and fell again into a hum when the senator raised his hand to speak once more. I felt like I was being carried by the noise.

"And tonight I am pleased and *proud* to accept your nomination for President of the United States of America."

With that announcement, we were pulled to our feet, all

twenty thousand of us lifted by some invisible force, and I was beaming, joyful, yesterday's conflicts forgotten, especially when the senator said, "I want to thank a lot of people for their hard work and dedication to this country, but first I want to give a special thanks to my daughter Kate."

It wasn't one of Cal's "applause lines," designed with a pause so that the audience would clap. The senator phrased it simply, as if it were something he said every day. And when he peered down from the stage, he looked right at me, his eyes warm in acknowledgment.

"Kate is a daily inspiration to me. She's living proof that miracles can happen. Seventeen years ago, I went through a dark time. A challenging time. For a little while, I wasn't sure if my marriage would come out of it intact. But it did, thanks to the love and strength of my incredible wife, Meg."

I clapped along with the audience, not sure where the senator was going.

"And in June, I learned along with the rest of the country what else had come out of that challenging time seventeen years ago. I'll tell you what that was—a blessing. A miracle. My daughter Kate."

The audience applauded but it seemed muffled to me. Inconsequential. All I could focus on was up on that stage. My father was looking at me.

He nodded and turned away.

"She's a reminder to me too of what this nation has gone through over the past seventeen years. We've seen our economy stagnate. Our jobs shrink. Our competitive edge become blunted. Looking at the challenging situation we're facing, it seems pretty clear that we've got two options. We can shrug our shoulders and fold under the pressure, acknowledging and even *accepting* that our time as the greatest nation in the world has passed us by—as my opponent's rhetoric suggests."

Here he paused, and the crowd erupted in scattered comments. A man two rows back from us shouted "No!" and I had to suppress a giggle.

"Or! We can work to make our country whole again, to find that light, find the upside, embrace and re-adopt that American ingenuity and strength that has *always* gotten us through tough times and *always* will!"

We couldn't give a standing ovation, because we were already on our feet, so all twenty thousand of us raised our hands above our heads while we clapped, and all around me, the sea of signs waved wildly from side to side. I couldn't stop grinning and, judging by a quick peek at the twins, neither could Gabe and Gracie.

"I believe that our younger generation has much to teach us," the senator went on, to another smattering of applause, and I found my cheeks flushing even hotter. He motioned to our section. "My children see this nation as one of bound-less opportunity. They see a nation that is fair. That is just and kind. A land of freedom and promise. I share that vision with my twins, Grace and Gabriel. And I share it with my daughter Kate, who has weathered incredible setbacks in her life, incredible turmoil, and sits here with us today, brave and optimistic. She's truly an inspiration."

A tear streaked down my cheek. Meg was squeezing my

shoulder and the camera was on me before I thought to swipe it away. I never knew he felt like that. He'd never told me. Until now, with the whole world watching. I was aglow, lit from within.

He raised his hand.

"But—" he said, and the crowd quieted. "But. This next generation also needs the temperance of their parents' guiding hands. The wisdom of those who have come before, who have the knowledge and the experience to recognize the dangers and the threats facing our nation, even when those threats wear friendly faces."

I felt the light inside me flickering.

"Our nation cannot achieve greatness if it continues to be burdened with a broken border and a system of immigration that has failed us as citizens."

I held my breath. He'd balled up his fist to strike the podium. And the crowd was going wild.

"My opponent favors reform. I favor good old-fashioned *buckling down*."

Everyone cheered for that. I wished, half hoped that it was just another empty sound bite. But the senator went on.

"Under my administration, we will protect those who are waiting in line to enter the United States legally, and in particular foreign-born residents with advanced degrees, who hope to start companies, create jobs, and drive innovation— those who will share in our vision for the future. But we will aggressively prosecute those who will not abide by our rules for entry, who—make no mistake—are criminals from the moment they set foot inside our nation. The flood. Must. Be stopped."

The camera was still on me. I fought to smile. Penny was watching. All of the Diazes were, I knew it. My eyes were swimming with tears, and I prayed that I looked "charmingly overcome," not heartbroken.

I was too busy keeping it together to listen to the rest of the speech. When it was over, Meg grabbed my hand and lifted it in the air as we turned to the rapturous crowd to wave.

In the wings, Elliott was happier than I'd ever seen him. "You nailed it, Mark!" He wrapped his arm around the senator's shoulders, and I was glad, for once, that my father was too distracted to notice me.

~ 24 ~

The moment we got back to the suite, the walls seemed to tilt in like a carnival funhouse.

"I'll be right back," I blurted, at Meg's quizzical expression. "Need a little air."

I rushed from the suite, past our posted security officer, and around the corner to the elevator. Ducking inside, I pushed the button for one floor down, trying to remember Nancy's room number. 806? 808?

I needed to see her. She was the one who'd suggested the senator change his speech, given the photo of me with my friends. She could tell me how the campaign's official position had come about in the first place. Did the senator really believe the things he'd said? Or was he just using the issue to get more votes? I wasn't sure which answer would be worse.

Behind the door of 801, I heard the muted squeal of a baby. It was probably Lou's room. The impulse to knock rose and fled in a heartbeat. This was his private time—I couldn't intrude. I continued down the corridor, and after a few seconds of anxious indecision, rapped on 808.

Cal opened the door. He had a glass of red wine in his hand. His striped tie was loose and his hair mussed.

"Oh, I—s-sorry," I stammered. "I'm looking for Nancy's . . ."

Then I saw her, over Cal's shoulder, lounging on the bed and pouring wine from a nearly empty bottle into her own glass. She was dressed, thank God, except for her shoes, which were lying on top of each other in the middle of the carpet, but the scene was so odd, so intimate, that I backed away.

"I'm so sorry." I spun around and rushed away as fast as my feet could go without running.

"Kate!" Cal called. "Wait!"

The elevator wasn't coming, no matter how many times I shoved the button, so I fled into the corner stairwell and started to climb. Half a flight up, my escape stalled out. I clutched the railing and sunk until I was sitting. I couldn't go back up to the Coopers' suite. Not yet.

My head throbbed from trying to process the last twenty-four hours. And there was no one I could talk to about it.

Nancy and Cal. She was married. Two children. I'd never met the kids, but I'd seen their pictures, and a photo of her husband too. He had a beard. He looked like a nice guy. Maybe it was harder to be faithful to photos. Maybe the rules were different on the campaign trail, looser. Nonexistent. *Nancy and Cal.*

The image of room 808 rushed in again—but this time it was the senator answering the door and my mother looking up from the bed. I held on to the banister so hard it hurt.

Did my mom love him? Did she think he loved her? Was she stupid and selfish enough to hope to steal him away from Meg? I didn't like this woman, the mother I was getting a clearer and clearer picture of, and right now, I didn't like Nancy much either.

A door below me clanged and there was no time to scramble away.

It was Cal. He collapsed against the railing with relief to see me sitting on the cement steps.

"You've got this all wrong, Kate," he said, and his voice echoed so loud throughout the stairwell that he flinched and started again in a whisper. "What you're thinking—"

"I'm not thinking anything," I whispered back.

His eyes widened, dubious.

I sighed. "And if I were to think anything, I wouldn't tell anyone."

I will silently judge you, but I won't rat on you.

"She's married," he said, and I nodded, thinking that that sounded an awful lot like confirmation. What was *wrong* with these people?

"And I'm . . ." He sat down next to me on the steps with a weary huff. ". . . gay."

"Don't worry, I won't—"

My mouth stopped working.

"Wait. What?"

This time, it was my outburst that echoed down several flights of stairs. Cal half rose in alarm.

"Sorry," I whispered, grinning like an idiot. "I'm just . . . surprised!"

"It's not common knowledge," he admitted. "But it's not exactly a secret either. Nancy knows, obviously. She's a good friend of mine. A mentor, really."

So that explained the coziness of the scene. Nancy wasn't betraying her husband, she was kicking back with someone safe, someone she'd known for years. I felt myself blushing and tried to nod soberly. Then the next realization hit.

"What about the senator?"

Cal looked at me quizzically. "Your dad? Yeah, of course he knows. I told him as soon as he hired me. I didn't want there to be any whisper of scandal attached to his campaign." He laughed ruefully and nudged me with his knee. "Little did we know . . ."

"How did he react when he found out?"

Cal shrugged. "He didn't react at all. Just said he appreciated my candor, and we haven't talked about it since, except in terms of policy." He raised his eyebrows. "He's in favor of gay marriage, you know. Equal rights for all Americans under the Constitution."

"But . . ." I couldn't think of a better way of putting it. "*He's a Republican.*"

Cal grinned. "Kate—your dad is a *true* Republican. He has the same vision of America that Nancy and I share, a world where all individuals are free to achieve their potential, unfettered by the shackles of an oppressive government."

His eyes were gleaming with such fervor that I couldn't suppress a smile, wondering if he was making mental notes for his next speech.

"All individuals, huh?" Then my smile fell away. "All Americans, you mean."

"Of course." He looked confused. "Your father cares about people. He listens to the voters, their hopes for themselves and their children, their goals for their country. You've seen it."

I had. At every campaign stop along the way. Cal was right—whatever the senator's beliefs, he *cared* about other people.

"I'm not saying President Lawrence doesn't have as much empathy," Cal went on. "But here's the difference, as I see it. Senator Cooper has *faith* in those people, in their futures. He doesn't want to tether them to a support system, *feed* them to a behemoth of a government that consumes and grows greedier the bigger it gets. He wants to *free* them, so they can *soar. That's* why I'm on this campaign."

I stared at him, my jaw slack. He cleared his throat with a lopsided smile.

"And with that said . . . !" He stood, offering me a hand up with a chuckle. "I'm not sleeping with Nancy Oneida."

"Please tell Nancy I'm so sorry."

He rolled his eyes, not unkindly. "She won't even remember. Nancy's brain lives eight hours ahead of everybody else's. She's predicting the morning show commentary right about now."

When Cal left me in the stairwell, I didn't go straight up. I sat there in the hollow silence trying to reconcile the wildly different images I had of my father. The great listener who never asked me questions. The champion of the American dream who was anti-immigration. The loving husband who cheated.

My mother wasn't the only one who didn't make sense.

The senator *was* a good listener, though. I remembered

one visit to a small-town diner, seeing him stop to take an old woman's hand as she talked about growing up poor in Mississippi. She was very worried that television was eroding American values. To me, she'd seemed kind, but heat-addled. But the senator listened attentively, ignoring all the staffers who were trying to keep him moving along, keep him on schedule. And that scenario repeated itself over and over everywhere we went, whether it was a kid talking about her school or a veteran describing his last tour. He listened because he wanted to know—and you could see it affect him. It was the fuel that kept him going, kept that smile bright and his wave cheery, kept his speeches fiery.

Like the one he'd given tonight.

Now, sitting in an empty stairwell, listening to the low hum of the building's pipes, I wondered how many people had told the senator that they were afraid that illegal immigrants were taking their jobs. That cartels were moving in and taking over their cities, that they suspected even their neighbors of running drugs, that illegals were hiding everywhere, corroding the fabric of their lives. That *they* were the problem, these people who refused to play by the rules, who were criminals just by virtue of being here, who didn't care about America and what it stood for, wouldn't even bother to learn our language or customs.

He'd probably heard a lot of that. I'd heard some myself on the road, but I'd blocked it out. I'd wanted to be a positive part of the campaign, and it wasn't all sunshine and light, but *I'd* needed to be. It was that simple.

When I called Penny that night, she didn't bring up the speech, but I could tell by the way she carefully avoided talking about it that she'd listened.

"We were really proud of you," she said. "We all cheered when you came on TV."

I pictured the Diazes gathered around their television, probably crammed onto their floral-print sofa or sitting on the floor in the living room, their cheers slowly dwindling as the senator's speech hit home.

Changing the subject seemed like the best option right about now.

"You still cool to stay over on Birthday Eve?" I asked, kicking my shoes off the edge of the bed. "Bring your bathing suit, Pen. After careful reflection, I've upped the pool rating from an eight to a nine-point-five."

"I don't know."

My smile dropped away. "You don't know? Haven't we been talking about this for the past week?"

"Listen, I . . ." Penny sighed. "Kate, I really don't want to make an issue out of this. I just don't think it would be a good idea."

I couldn't talk for a second, feeling myself simmer with embarrassment—and anger too. I knew the senator's speech was incendiary, but why was Penny taking it out on me, her best friend, who had lived across the continent from her for the past year and who would be leaving in a matter of days?

And who was she to act so judgmental? She didn't even know him.

"He's not a *monster*, Penny."

"Neither are we," she shot back.

"Of course not!" I clenched a pillow, my cell pinned between my shoulder and my ear. "It's just, he only knows one side of it. If he could hear what people really go through— what your mom and dad went through . . ."

And that's when the idea hit me—a prospect so risky that my heart started to pound just considering it. I had almost managed to shove it down, filing it away under Impossible, when Penny said:

"Listen. Maybe you could stop by during the day instead. Papi said he'd cook for you, but I told him you were probably meeting with like the Ambassador to China or—"

"I'd love to," I said, then added quickly, before she could rescind the invitation, "*We'd* love to."

Saturday, August 2
Happy Birthday to Me
94 DAYS UNTIL THE GENERAL ELECTION

It took some coordinating.

First there were the Diazes—explaining my plan to them over the phone with Penny as cheerleader, assuring them over and over that Meg and the senator would keep their confidence, that the Coopers were open-minded people who'd simply never heard a perspective like theirs before.

"And once you've met them, if it doesn't feel right," I offered, "don't say anything. We'll just have a nice lunch."

That was the strategy Mr. and Mrs. Diaz finally agreed to.

I knew that Meg had made a big point of clearing the day of my birthday since we'd be flying back on a red-eye late that night. The senator had had a brunch with a high-level donor scheduled, but he canceled, telling everyone who would listen that his daughter was turning seventeen, so he'd be doing whatever she wanted. He sounded so eager, like he was relishing the opportunity to sacrifice a few campaign stops to dote on me. It was flattering at first. But after the fourth time he said it—always with plenty of approving ears around to hear—I stopped reading much into it.

Except for one thing. He was up for whatever I wanted to do. He'd said it. And I had witnesses.

After breakfast cupcakes, the Coopers presented me with a pile of gifts—a leather-bound journal from Gabe with a sketch in the front cover as an inscription, a sweet silver necklace with a star pendant from Gracie, and the somewhat mysterious combo of a backpack, Harvard T-shirt, and e-reader from Meg and the senator. Grandma Evelyn had sent her own contribution directly to the hotel—a tin of homemade chocolate chip cookies, with a note instructing me not to let the campaign take them away.

"This came too," Meg said, handing me a flat, brightly wrapped parcel with frayed edges, as if somebody had already unwrapped and rewrapped it. "In the interest of full disclosure, James took a look to make sure it was safe."

I turned it over, suddenly wary. The terrifyingly scrawled note said: "*To Quinn, Who Is Now 17. From Your Secret Admirer (in South Carolina).*"

"Wow," I blurted and looked up, giggling, to see everyone staring at me. "It's . . . yeah. It's cool, I know who this is. He's just . . ." I held up the note. "This was a joke."

The whole time I was opening what turned out to be the new Kudzu Giants album in vinyl, Meg had her eyebrows raised, awaiting further explanation. But the senator swatted at her with a complicit grin.

"Let the girl have some secrets." He rustled my hair and peered down at the album. "Kudzu Giants, huh? You might have to share that with me."

"Yeah, right, Dad." Gracie snorted. "You only listen to old-person music."

He shrugged, defeated, and Gracie cracked up, sending

Gabe into his own giggle fit. They were still laughing when, after another round of thank-you's, I led everybody down to the parking level, where James was waiting with the car.

It wasn't until we'd pulled out of the hotel barricades that the senator asked where we were off to.

"It's a really good lunch spot. One of my favorites."

"Mexican food, right?" The senator grinned. "Is it authentic?"

"*Extremely.*" I trained my eyes at the horizon. *Conveys honesty. Confidence.*

In the rearview mirror, I could see James shaking his head at me ever so slightly, but his eyes were bright.

James was the only other person in this car who knew where we were going. I'd had to tell him—he'd asked me for a location so he could secure it in advance along with the other agents assigned to the campaign. When I told him it was a private residence and gave him the suspiciously familiar address, his eyebrows had risen higher and higher, his arms crossing in amused suspicion.

"And . . ." I'd added sheepishly. "You can't tell the senator. It's, um . . . it's a surprise."

"I thought you were the one who was supposed to be surprised," he commented dryly. "It's *your* birthday, isn't it?"

Still, he'd kept his word. The house was deemed secure, he'd posted extra guards on each street corner to ensure that the press didn't follow us, and he drove in silence, the only sign of collusion the wink he shot me over his shoulder when we got on the freeway, heading to East LA.

The senator stayed on the phone with Louis the whole ride, going over staffing issues, and Meg was finally reading that

Time issue with me and the twins on the cover, a faint smile playing on her lips. Gabe watched the sky out the window.

But Gracie knew something was up.

"Where are we going?" She scrunched her nose as we got off the freeway. "Everything's in *Spanish*."

The senator peeked out, his brow furrowing, and I shot him a smile. "Like I said—authentic!"

When we reached the house, the Diazes were already arrayed nervously on the front yard, a smaller scale replay of last week's gathering—minus, thankfully, any banners saying *Welcome Back, Happy Birthday,* or anything else. I couldn't help noticing that the neighbor's house had a new "Reelect Lawrence" sign beside their mailbox.

The senator got out of the car and stood staring at the Diazes' house in confusion. I watched his eyes sharpen in one blink as he realized where he'd seen this view before—in news coverage.

I linked my arm through his and held tight so my hand wouldn't tremble.

"This is my best friend Penny's house," I explained. "The Diazes invited us for lunch, and I didn't want you guys to leave LA without getting to try some of Mr. Diaz's amazing cooking. Seriously, it's better than any restaurant."

Penny called out a greeting from across the yard. Mr. Diaz stood in the driveway, holding little Eva's hand and waving for both of them. Eva's hair was neatly braided and tied, but I could see her fighting not to rip it out, squirming in her church dress. Enrico stood in a military stance, his hands behind his back and his posture very straight. Gus, the Diazes' fat chocolate Lab, was doing a hopping dance from behind a plastic dog-gate in the front doorway. And in front of him, Penny's mom lingered on the house's low porch, smoothing her dress with a maniacal grin.

She was terrified. We all were—even the Coopers, by the looks of them.

As Meg stepped out of the car, she turned to shoot me a Significant Look, conveying in one slow blink that she was not born yesterday. I wondered how much she'd sussed out already.

But by the time the twins were scrambling from their seats, the senator had already recovered. He strode confidently forward to greet Mr. Diaz, hand extended and eyes bright as if this were just another campaign stop.

Mr. Diaz shook the senator's offered one with both of his own. "It is such an honor to meet you, sir." He looked like he was having a stroke.

"The pleasure's mine . . ." The senator paused to listen for Mr. Diaz's name, just as he always did out on the trail.

"Carlos, sir."

"Please, call me Mark."

Mr. Diaz turned to his family, who took the cue and hesitantly crossed the lawn. "This is Penny, of course. Penelope Maria when she's in trouble."

Meg chuckled and moved to greet the group, giving my arm a sharp pinch as she passed. I hardly felt it. This was happening. And so far, this was working.

"My wife Inez, My son, Enrico, who is home only briefly— he returns to Camp Pendleton on Tuesday."

The senator turned to shake Enrico's hand, a question in his eyes.

"Third Battalion First Marines, sir," Enrico answered, and I could tell by his fidgety hands that he was fighting not to salute.

The senator laid a hand on his shoulder, moved. "Thank you for your service, son."

Mr. Diaz beamed. "And our little one here is Eva."

"I'm not *little!*" Penny's sister tugged angrily on her braid. "I'm *eight.*"

At that, Gracie and Gabe perked up and before I knew it, everyone was moving into the house, leaving Penny and me alone in the yard.

"He does seem nice," Penny whispered. Then her smile dropped, her eyes clouding. "Are you sure about this, Kate?"

I took her hand and squeezed. "You can trust him."

Lunch was amazing—and not just the chiles rellenos and chicken mole that Mr. Diaz had labored over for my birthday, knowing how I loved that chocolaty sauce. The conversation flowed so naturally that it felt as if the Coopers and the Diazes were old friends. The senator asked a million questions too, eager to get to know them better.

Penny held her breath next to me. I did the same every time the chitchat went down another level, from what spices Mr. Diaz used (cumin, cilantro), to how he learned to cook (his abuela), to Penny's own ineptitude in the kitchen, as discovered when we were "lab" partners in sixth-grade home ec and she accidentally set a roll of paper towels on fire.

From chatting about school, we got onto the subject of

jobs, and although Penny and I tensed in anticipation, the topic ended up being innocent enough. Mrs. Diaz cleaned houses and made some extra money tutoring high schoolers in Spanish. Mr. Diaz was a housepainter by trade and landscape painter by vocation. He'd sold a few pieces in a gallery up in Ojai and he was a regular in the local art fair circuit.

As he described his art, I remembered something from the last time I'd been inside this house, the day after Mom's funeral. Mr. Diaz had propped a half-finished oil painting on an easel by the window, where the golden afternoon light streamed through. The painting depicted a long, empty road. I remembered now the sensation of being pulled into it, of longing to run down that road, hoping for something I couldn't name at the end of it.

"Do you paint local scenes?" Meg was asking.

"I do," Mr. Diaz answered. "And also places that I remember, like the village in Mexico where I grew up."

We were swiftly approaching the point of no return. For one painful moment, I wished I could rewind time, take back the phone conversation I'd had with Mr. and Mrs. Diaz, urging them to share their story. This lunch was going so well. Everyone seemed to genuinely like one another. My mom had been friendly with the Diazes, but not close. What if a real rapport blossomed here?

But I knew I was being silly. They very literally came from two different places. And in any case, time raced on. I held on to the wooden seat of my chair.

The senator rested his elbows on the table, his hands clasped as he listened. "How long have you been in the US?"

He looked intrigued, not appalled. That had to be a good thing.

Penny linked her ankle with mine under the table. Outside, I could hear Eva and Gracie shouting, Gus barking, and Gabe laughing in response.

"Twenty-five years," Mrs. Diaz answered proudly. "In December it will be twenty-six."

"And what brought you here?" The senator asked it lightly, suspecting nothing.

Mr. Diaz couldn't hold his smile anymore. He stared down at his fork, as if examining a speck of food on it. He wanted to tell. I could see it. But it was no small thing to confess.

Enrico turned to me and I gave the world's smallest nod.

"Go on, Papi," he said.

I reached my hand flat across the table toward Mrs. Diaz. "You can trust them."

My eyes found Meg's, and finally the senator's, watching as the realization slowly unfurled. There was confusion. And then came clear, heavy shock. You could see it, flooding their expressions. But to my immense relief, neither of them wavered in politeness. Not for one instant.

"Please," the senator said. "This is your home. Whatever you share with us stays here."

The Diazes exhaled as one.

"My village was very poor," Mr. Diaz started, and Penny sat back, her eyes half closed as if this were a familiar bedtime story. "There was no work unless you worked for men . . ." He shook his head. "Dangerous men. Men I grew up fearing. And without work, there was no food. Sometimes we did not eat for a day. Or longer. It is something that's hard to explain here, where everything is right at your fingertips."

Mrs. Diaz put her hand over her husband's and picked up the story, her eyes dreamy with recollection.

"I grew up three houses away from his. And when we were sixteen, we went to a village an hour away and found a priest who would marry us. My parents didn't like this—they had wanted me to marry one of the richer men in town, even if they were drug men, terrible people." She raised her eyebrows. "Now that I'm a mother, I don't blame them as much. They only wanted me to have more than they did. I want the same for my children, but their lives are their lives. I would never try to control them like that. My parents made it difficult for me to stay, wouldn't allow me to see my husband."

"My cousin had crossed over," Mr. Diaz said plainly. "He knew a way and he felt for us. He paid for our crossing. It was very difficult, and terrifying, especially having Inez with me. I could have gone alone, found work, and sent her help. It would have been smarter, but she wouldn't leave me."

"I wouldn't leave him." She smiled.

A mosaic of emotions flickered across the senator's face as he listened to their story, but what I saw most clearly was compassion.

"Were . . ." he started, but his voice came out hoarse. "Were you afraid of being discovered?"

Mr. Diaz looked at his wife and she squeezed his hand, passing strength to him through one little gesture.

"We are always afraid. We love this country. We are proud to be here. But we know that this country is not proud of us." He leaned forward to meet the senator's eyes, something imploring in his expression. "If we could have followed the rules, waited fifteen years for a visa and come over legally, I swear to you that we would have. But that was not a possibility. Not for us."

Meg let her breath out very slowly. When I turned to look at her, she was swiping the corner of her eye.

Then Penny spoke up and it was my turn to get teary. "I was born here in LA. Enrico and Eva too, so we're Americans. I wish they could be too."

"We're proud of our children," Mrs. Diaz said simply.

The senator turned to me with an unreadable expression. "We are too."

We rode back to the hotel in silence, the twins still perplexed about the tense room they'd walked into after running around the yard with Eva and Gus.

Finally, I got the nerve to cut through the quiet. "I'm sorry for the surprise. They're just really important to me, so I wanted you to know them. Really know them."

The senator nodded, but his eyes were troubled. He was staring out the window, seeing my city for the first time, the little missions with neon crosses in the window, the food trucks, the hand-painted signs in Spanish, a woman bent over her baby in a stroller as she waited for the light to change.

"They're good people." He said it almost sadly.

"You won't say anything," I blurted. "I told them they could trust you—"

"Of course we won't say anything," Meg said. "But I'm

surprised that you opened them up to this, Kate. You're smarter than that. What if the press had followed us here?"

"But they didn't. So . . ." I swallowed hard. "I don't need to worry, do I?"

I watched the senator for an answer, and found it in his thoughtful silence, the slack honesty of his features as he continued to process all that he'd heard.

He didn't say another word about it until we were back in Maryland, groggy from the flight, all of us staggering to our bedrooms to nap ourselves back into clarity. As I was setting down my bag, the senator came in and leaned against the doorframe.

"You know, kiddo—that took courage, what you did. And faith too. Faith in me and Meg."

I stood waiting for the ax to fall, the dreaded *but*. Seeing my expression, the senator stepped forward and opened his arms. I closed my eyes, and there he was, holding me up, solid and strong.

"Just wanted you to know we're proud of you," he murmured into the top of my head. "And that's all we're gonna say about it."

Proud of me. He was proud of me. Under the swimming sensation of fatigue, it was hard to keep from spilling over into hysterics as he stepped away and gently closed the door.

Penny called that afternoon.

"Okay," she said. "I get it. He's amazing."

～ 26 ～

Tuesday, August 5
Courting the Youth Vote
91 DAYS UNTIL THE GENERAL ELECTION

Nancy had a surprise for me. She swore I was going to like it and took me to lunch to talk it over.

"You've been asked to do a PSA for Rock the Vote."

She sat back and slapped the table in excitement, making our utensils rattle against each other.

"MTV?" My grin rose and fell in a millisecond. "Why would they want *me?* I can't even vote yet."

"Because," Nancy admonished me. "You're the It Girl of politics right now. Young. Gorgeous. Why *wouldn't* they want you?"

"Gorgeous?" I rolled my eyes.

"*InStyle* thinks you're gorgeous." Her perfectly groomed eyebrows skyrocketed, then in one fluid motion, she pulled a magazine from her massive shoulder bag and tossed it at me. It was earmarked to the middle—a random photo of me walking down the sidewalk in DC with Gracie two steps behind.

"*Street Style: Kate Quinn Cooper,*" read the caption.

Apparently they liked my shoes. "This is crazy!"

"Told you so." Nancy sipped her iced tea, made a face, and pushed it away. "Anyway, Senator Cooper thinks it's a great idea."

263

"And Meg?" I wasn't so sure she'd go for it. Seeing her kids on the cover of *Time* was one thing—but coverage in *InStyle* and MTV didn't exactly meet her upstanding-young-lady criteria.

"I'm sure she'll be thrilled," Nancy said tightly. "But it'll be just you and me on this trip. New York City. Have you been? You'll love it."

On the taxi ride from the airport into MTV's midtown NYC studios, I waited for a break in Nancy's phone calls to try to finally clear the air about LA.

"Nancy," I started, and she glanced up in surprise. "I'm really sorry I jumped to conclusions when I saw you in Cal's room. I didn't realize—"

"That he was gay?" She squeezed my wrist so hard it stung. "No one does. And let's keep it that way."

I scooted closer to the window. "But Cal said it wasn't a secret."

"He doesn't care who knows. I do. For his sake. He's young and stupid. Talented as hell, but . . . I tell him time and time again, *you* control the message. Nobody else." She smiled. "Rumor is a runaway horse. You can't just ride it. If you want it to go where you've decided, you have to yank way back on those reins. Does that make sense?"

"Sure," I said, distracted by the image of Nancy as a cowgirl.

"Which reminds me," she said casually, flipping through her iPhone. "They might pull a fast one. If they start asking questions, anything that sounds like it might be an interview, call me over and I'll put a stop to it."

"Oh," I said, suddenly confused. "So I'm not supposed to say anything?"

"Just the pre-approved copy."

Pre-approved. By whom? I'd certainly never seen it. So much for controlling the message.

As a production assistant guided us through the soundstages, I covertly searched for celebrities that I could brag to Penny about spotting, a continuation of our long-running game from LA. Penny had taken the lead with Matt Damon at the Third Street Promenade right after my Kudzu Giants close encounter, so I was looking for revenge.

Finally, in the greenroom, a familiar face popped out at me. *Very* familiar.

"At last!" he cried, jumping up from the sofa. "My costar has arrived!"

"Andy!" I nearly leaped across the room to greet him before abruptly remembering and slamming to a halt. "We've met, right? At that senator's party?"

I cocked my head, praying he'd play along. Nobody knew that Andy and I talked on the phone at least twice a week. Everyone thought I was chatting with Penny or some mystery boy back in South Carolina—the same one who'd sent me a birthday present—and I put up with their winking hints about "somebody special" just so I wouldn't have to cut the connection.

"Right." Andy narrowed his eyes in mock confusion. "Kat, was it?"

I stifled a snort.

Nancy didn't seem to notice. She was deep in conversation with what I presumed was the commercial's director.

As Andy and I got "styled," we made it into a game.

"So what's your connection to politics?" I asked him in the makeup chair.

"I'm the youngest congressman in history."

"That's cool. Congratulations."

"You?"

"Supreme Court Justice. I'm surprised you didn't know that, Congressman."

"Huh. I had you pegged as Miss America."

"I was just going to say the same about you."

The director of the spot, a young woman with spiky black hair and a Sneetches star on the back of her neck, had watched us warily at first, but when she sat to give us the rundown, she seemed to relax. As far as she was concerned, we were from rival factions, so it was probably a relief to see us bantering. Nancy looked less than pleased by our rapport, though, so I scaled it back as the day went on.

Andy would not relent. I tried to ignore him. But it was hard not to feel giddy at his closeness, the sparks shooting off of him, his actual smiles, not just imagined ones over the phone, that little boomerang scar crinkling every time. I hadn't seen him for weeks and I was buzzing. Hopefully, I was hiding it.

"So . . . what?" he murmured into my ear as we walked to the set. "Am I your dirty little secret?"

I stifled a smile. "You're secret. Not dirty, per se."

"Not *yet*. Did you get my birthday present, by the way?"

"Yes. Love it. So sweet of you. I don't have a record player."

He scrunched up his forehead. "Really? What's wrong with you? Well, Christmas is coming up."

"In five months."

"If you're that impatient, you can always come listen to it at my house." Andy grinned. "You've got my address, right?"

I elbowed him and an anxious production assistant ran up the corridor to walk between us, chattering about how great it was to meet us both and didn't we just *love* the energy here?

The spot was so simple it bordered on asinine, something along the lines of: "Your future's up to *you*—rock the vote!"

The director kept asking me for a little more attitude, which I didn't really understand, until Nancy stepped over to whisper in her ear, and she smiled tightly and called it a wrap.

Just before we were ready to go, though, the director slipped back over to us and said, as if it were a complete lark, "While we have you guys here all glammed up, maybe we could do a quick interview?"

I glanced nervously at Nancy, but she didn't see me. She was on her cell, one hand against her head and her whole body stooped as if she were taking in some sort of disastrous news.

Andy looked at me. "Sorry, Liz, I think we're both a little tired. Maybe another time."

It wasn't until she walked grudgingly away that Andy took my elbow. "What was *that?*"

I blinked. "What?"

"Are they beating you?" His laugh rose and fell. "Seriously, though. That redhead's the boss, huh? You do what she says."

I flushed. "It's not that simple. I didn't want to do the interview and she was supposed to bail me out."

"But *I* bailed you out." Andy winked. "You're welcome."

Nancy strode over, lips pursed. "All set?"

Before our teams could gather us up and cart us away, Andy cordially shook my hand. "Guess I'll see you next week, then."

I blanked. Was this some sort of code? Was he asking me out again?

"Debates?" Andy's eyebrows rose. "First of three—St. Louis, ringing any bells?"

He smirked, obviously thinking that if we were debating, he'd be the victor.

"I knew what you meant." I twirled my ridiculously trussed hair. "I'm just surprised they're inviting you along. Aren't you something of a . . . loose cannon?"

"We can't all be political poster children, Kate," he bantered back, and even though I knew he meant nothing by it, that last barb kept stinging the whole way home.

Nancy was distracted by some other snafu that apparently happened when the senator was leaving his office in the Capitol Building. A Spanish-language cable network had stopped him to ask about his immigration policy, and rather than smiling and moving on, he'd spoken with the reporter.

"He's going to have to issue a clarification in some form," Nancy barked into her phone to everyone she could get to listen. Finally, when she'd exhausted her call list, I had the chance to ask what exactly the senator had said.

"He said it was a complex issue that involved families and human beings, so he doesn't take it lightly."

I waited. She didn't go on.

"That's it?"

"That's enough." She ran her hand through her hair and I saw a glint of gray among the red roots. "We're so close here and he *cannot* get wishy-washy on core issues."

That sound bite didn't sound wishy-washy to me. It sounded thoughtful, if anything. It sounded like he had taken his conversation with the Diazes to heart. But I kept my thoughts and my smile to myself.

Perhaps remembering her audience, Nancy drew herself up, becoming the Nancy I recognized, comfortingly poised. She rested her hand on my arm.

"You're right, of course. It's *no* big deal, just fine-tuning. But that's why they pay me the big bucks!"

Her voice was false, singsong-y, her expression strained if you looked close enough, and I was sitting pretty darn close to the woman. It was like watching Santa Claus take off his beard. I'd always found Nancy so charming, so natural in her confidence. But now, sitting in this car careening down the FDR, her demeanor—the warmth, the human touch—now seemed as forced as my father's politician mask.

The realization was enough to unsettle me, make me wonder if I could be accused of the same crime. Was I really such a nice girl? A solid kid? A strong one?

Or was Andy right? Was I just . . . *beaten*?

When I got back to the Coopers' house that night, Meg was replaying a message on the home phone while the senator stood a few feet away, staring at it with a look of utter befuddlement. Hearing a familiar voice, I stopped to eavesdrop.

"Mark. It's your mother." *Grandma Evelyn?* "Just wanted to let you know I'm coming to your event on Thursday in Vermont. The Community Farmers one. See you there." *Click.*

The senator squinted, shaking his head. "One more time." Evelyn's voice filled the room again.

"Mark. It's your mother."

Little did I know that this voicemail was nothing short of earth-shakingly unprecedented. For the very first time in her son's political career, the reclusive Evelyn Cooper was actually planning to attend one of his campaign events.

By Thursday morning, the campaign was in a full-blown tizzy. Gracie, Gabe, and I had been meant to sit today's events out, but everybody was now jumping at the rare opportunity to document a full Cooper family tableau. What was meant to be a small, convenient blip on the campaign schedule had with one phone call become the centerpiece of the week, broadcasted everywhere.

Unfortunately, Evelyn wasn't exactly playing along.

On the flight to Vermont, Nancy perched anxiously on an airplane seat across the aisle from the senator. "She's not returning any of our calls. We're trying to coordinate, but I'm not sure what to expect here."

Not having spoken to Grandma Evelyn since we'd visited her, I wasn't sure what to expect either. Would she still find the Goodwin line continuing strong in me? Or would she be disappointed once she saw me, the political poster child in her Ralph Lauren sundress, smiling and waving like an automaton?

As soon as we pulled up to the event, I could see how ridiculous all the hype was. Beside a large, ramshackle community farm, there was a wide field where close to a hundred people sat in folding chairs around a central microphone and two portable speakers. Not bad attendance for the New England Chapter of the Community Farmers of America. But surrounding the modest crowd was a mob of reporters, invited by the campaign to bear witness to the fact that the senator's mother did, in fact, exist.

One problem—she was nowhere to be found.

"Maybe she chickened out?" Meg murmured to her husband.

The senator shot her a rueful smile. "I gave up on trying to figure out my mom's motivations a long time ago."

He turned to me, Gabe, and Gracie, and his expression brightened, solidified. Campaign face. But was it just me, or could I make out a bit of hurt in it?

When we reached the field, he slung an arm around me while he waved to the crowd, and instead of looking for the first camera, I hugged him back, just a little extra squeeze to take away the sting of his disappointment. He patted my shoulder in silent reply, then strode away to the microphone to the sound of polite applause from the assembled farmers.

The senator started his speech by ad-libbing a different version of the intro he'd planned.

"I'm here today, not just as a political candidate, but also as the son of a New England community farmer. I'm sorry my mom couldn't join us, but I think she'd have appreciated the chance to see firsthand what people like you are able to do for your communities, and to hear about the ways I plan to help you in those efforts if I'm elected president."

After the senator's comments, it was time for Q and A. And the first person to stand up—four rows deep into the crowd, microphone in hand—was Grandma Evelyn. She was wearing a denim button-down with the sleeves rolled up and a straw hat so ridiculously wide that I couldn't believe we hadn't picked her out of the crowd the moment we got here.

"It's Grandma!" Gracie whispered, squirming in her seat.

Gabe squinted. "What's she *doing*?"

Meg sighed through her smile. "I have no idea."

Evelyn tapped the microphone. "For those who don't know, I'm Mark's mother and I've been a member of this chapter since 1986."

The bored press corps erupted into life. The senator fought to wipe shock from his face.

"What a surprise!" He laughed. "I'm glad you could—"

She cut him off, pulling a crumpled piece of paper from her jeans pocket. "I have a few questions. Firstly—how do you plan to support small farms as we fight against corporate giants with their genetically engineered seeds cross-pollinating and ruining our crops?"

The crowd murmured agreement. The senator drew a deep breath and answered, as if she were any concerned citizen in the crowd. I was impressed. A few probing questions later, Evelyn passed the microphone to a young, bearded man in the front row and the senator's shoulders drooped ever so slightly as he finally exhaled.

As soon as the event ended, Evelyn was swarmed by press.

"Come on," Meg groaned, pulling us to her mother-in-law's rescue.

We reached Evelyn just in time to make out, "I wanted to hear what he had to say about some issues that are important to me. I liked his answers and he's got my vote."

The cameramen laughed, the reporters thanked her, and behind me, Nancy giggled with relief.

Despite her confrontational campaign appearance, Grandma Evelyn was more than happy to join us for lunch. But as soon as we settled into the roomy corner booth at a local diner, it was my turn to be interrogated.

"You look skinny. They're not making you diet, are they?"

"No!" I laughed.

She glared at Meg, who rolled her eyes.

"What about *school?*" Evelyn went on. "Have they signed you up? What are you—eleventh grade? What about college?"

I tried to shrink into the plastic upholstery, but Evelyn wouldn't break eye contact. She was even better at staring contests than I was.

"She's a senior," the senator corrected. I turned to him, my breath stalled. "And don't worry, Mom. We've got it all in hand."

All in hand. Did that mean they'd enrolled me?

I opened my mouth to ask, but Evelyn's skeptical squint stopped me cold. Asking would mean admitting that I didn't know. If anybody would judge me for that, it was my grandmother. Better to find out later, I decided, and feign confidence now.

I beamed through the rest of the meal, eating an extra-large portion of curly fries and strawberry milkshake to prove to Evelyn that I was diet-free.

When we said our good-byes, Grandma Evelyn shoved a crumpled piece of paper into my hand and whispered, "I'm gonna check up on you. Stay strong," as if she were passing a secret message to a hostage.

On the plane, I stared at the paper, where above her prepared questions, she'd scrawled a phone number that I had to assume was her own. The senator sat with Elliott, Lou, and Nancy, laughing about the disaster they'd just managed to avert. I curled up in my seat, wishing he'd leave them, walk over here, sit down next to me, and tell me exactly what he'd meant by "all in hand."

A strong woman would have walked over herself, demanded an answer. But despite Grandma Evelyn's vote of confidence, I couldn't muster the courage.

∽ 27 ∽

Tuesday, August 12
St. Louis: Debate Day One
84 DAYS UNTIL THE GENERAL ELECTION

Meg whispered last-minute instructions to the twins as the university auditorium's lights pivoted and the producer at the front began a silent countdown.

"Sit nicely, no squirming, no yelling, just nice clapping, got it?"

They nodded and I sat on my hands to keep from picking nervously at my nails. A second later, the entire crowd fell into a charged silence.

"Good evening and welcome to the first of three presidential debates," announced the moderator, a venerable news anchor who looked remarkably calm considering he'd frantically downed three glasses of water before the cameras started rolling. "The subject tonight is the American economy. Please welcome to the stage President Mitchell Lawrence and Senator Mark Cooper."

Across the gallery, Andy Lawrence let out a whoop. Knowing the cameras were all focused on the stage, where the senator and president were locked in a manic handshake, I narrowed my eyes and mouthed the words *It's on.* In reply, he shot me a leering wink. I had to fight to stifle my church giggles. The First Lady was too busy Barbie-smiling for the cameras to notice, but when I felt Meg's eyes on me, I returned my attention to the stage. The debate had begun.

It was basically a game show. Podiums, timers, a host who asked questions. The object of the game was to rack up the most crowd-pleasing answers in the allotted time. There would be polls later to determine which debater America considered the winner. But from here, it looked an awful lot like the senator was wiping the floor with his opponent.

Not that President Lawrence hadn't come out swinging. With the very first question, he attacked the senator's economic credentials, citing the fact that unlike himself, Cooper had never run a business.

"Well, Mr. President," Senator Cooper rebutted, "I'll grant you that I haven't had the experience of managing the *lucrative* family business that you have." I didn't miss the dig there. Mitchell Lawrence grew up rich. Senator Cooper did not. "But it doesn't take an MBA from Harvard to see that the economic principles that your administration has relied on are *failing* this country."

From there, he unleashed a torrent of statistics, and with every question that followed, provided more specifics, more data, saying "Let's look at the record" so much that it became a catchphrase. Before long, the president was shuffling behind his podium, visibly uncomfortable.

Then the moderator cited a quote that the senator had given the *Wall Street Journal* a few months back.

"'The borders are an economic issue. People who enter the country illegally pollute the workforce, stealing jobs and services that hard-working Americans desperately need.'"

The moderator took off his glasses. "You received some push-back on the language you used in that statement. Do you stand by it?"

The senator smiled in recognition of the question, as if he'd prepped for it in advance. "I do stand by that statement, especially given today's high unemployment, which my opponent's administration has done little to combat . . ."

He went on to talk about maintaining the minimum wage, supporting small businesses through tax cuts. They were similar talking points to the ones he'd used for previous answers, but my mind remained stuck in a loop, repeating that harsh word—the one the moderator had quoted. "*Pollute.*"

The president hadn't forgotten it either.

"I agree with Senator Cooper that these are serious issues facing our nation. But to call these individuals a '*pollution*' shows, to me, a lack of basic compassion. And without that—from my seat, let me tell you—you cannot have any understanding of what real Americans go through on a day-to-day basis."

There was a smattering of applause from the audience. I fought to maintain my placid expression.

A cloud passed over the senator's face. "By using the word *pollute*, I was highlighting the *economic* impact of undocumented immigrants, not the individuals themselves. I want to be clear about that."

Beside me, Meg grabbed the bottom of her chair, her smile taking on a lacquered look. I sensed that something had shifted, but I didn't actually grasp what had happened until we left the debate and watched the frenzied sum-up on the news stations.

"*Has Cooper gone soft on immigration?*"

"*I don't know how you can say you're not talking about individuals, when the whole issue centers around individuals. I mean, it's just double-talk.*"

"*We might be seeing a change in policy here, and I can't help wondering how much of it has to do with that photo that surfaced of his daughter Kate . . .*"

Hearing that sound bite, I immediately eyed the hotel doorway as a potential escape route, but drat—Elliott was already striding through and slamming it shut behind him.

"They're calling it a draw," he said, and the senator looked pleased. "You really fumbled that immigration question. You know that."

The senator shrugged. "I answered honestly."

Elliott shook his head like he was trying to get a fly off of him. "Has your position changed on this?"

The senator considered. "My position is that I need to know more about the issue before I can form a policy about it."

"It's a little late for that, Mark. I don't know if anybody told you, but you're running for *president.*"

The senator leaned past Elliott to look at me. "What did you think, Kate?"

I grinned. "I thought you did great. It was fun to watch."

The senator smiled and settled onto the sofa, gratified, but Elliott's head pivoted to take me in, his eyes narrowing. It was the same way he'd looked at me that first day at headquarters.

He was recalculating me. And not in a good way.

I made it to the door, escaped into the empty hallway, and didn't look back until I got to my room.

Andy had been calling or texting every ten minutes. I wasn't going to risk answering, not with the entire campaign machine surrounding me, but the boy was nothing if not persistent. Finally, I resorted to turning my cell phone off. But just as I'd flipped out my bedside light and settled under the covers, the hotel room phone rang. I picked it up with a gasp.

"Sneak out with me," Andy said. "Let's go do . . . whatever it is people in St. Louis do."

I covered my face with a pillow, smothering temptation. "No. Go to sleep."

"Good idea. What's your room number?"

I hung up and pushed the DO NOT DISTURB button with a smile that I'm pretty sure stayed on my face until morning.

We watched the second debate from the comfort of the Coopers' living room. Meg said her nerves needed a rest from the beating they'd taken last time.

"Really?" I squinted at her. "You didn't look nervous at all."

She laughed. "I've had a decade to practice the cool, calm exterior. It's a fine art." She turned to me with her eyebrows raised. "Don't try this at home."

The team was on-site with the senator in Denver. I was glad they weren't here with us. No cameras either. I curled up on the family sofa between the sleepy twins, nestling happily into the cushions as the debate began.

Meg stared up at the screen as if watching the world's most important tennis match, her eyes darting back and forth between the men. When the senator got in a good dig about a gaffe the president had made in a visit to China, she let out a joyful hoot and we all laughed at her.

But our smiles dropped off when President Lawrence countered by mentioning that he'd paid a successful visit to Mexico in the last month to talk about some of the issues plaguing both nations.

"My opponent prefers to bury his head in the sand when it comes to foreign policy." The president smiled, smug. "It's helpful not to have all the information—it allows you to see issues in black and white. I can see how that could be tempting. But as president of this nation, I simply can't afford to think in those terms. Too many people's lives hang in the balance."

President Lawrence was in full command of himself this time. He came across as both folksy and stately. I wasn't sure how he pulled off that balance, but it was probably a combo that had helped him win the presidency four years ago—and it certainly wasn't hurting him tonight. Next to him, the senator seemed ordinary, like a nice guy who was out of his depth.

Until he countered.

"While you were in Mexico, sir, I was speaking with people a little closer to home about their lives and their struggles. I listened to a young Mexican-American girl telling me about her dreams of attending college, and of helping her parents, who had entered the country illegally, realize their dream of becoming legal citizens of this nation. So to call my thinking oversimplistic I call playing loose with the truth."

Meg's hand flew to her forehead. I couldn't move. *Did he just say what I thought he said?* For a moment, I hoped Penny was watching, that she knew that she'd been heard. And then reality struck, and with it, panic.

Had he just outed the Diazes? He'd promised not to betray their trust. If he kept their names anonymous, did that count?

My pulse kept pounding as the moderator interrupted.

"Are you telling us, Senator, that you have met with undocumented immigrants in person?"

"It's important to me to learn as much about these issues as I possibly can, especially one as crucial to our nation's future as this one."

When the question was later posed on how best to address the problem of illegal immigration, I knew what the senator's talking points would be. By now, I had them memorized, a grim roll call—immigrants should have to prove their legal status in order to enroll children in school or receive medical treatment . . . stricter crackdown on those who employed undocumented immigrants . . . tighter border control . . .

The president went first. When he had finished his meandering answer about continuing to provide a path to citizenship for those who'd been in the country for twenty years or more, the moderator turned to the senator. But instead of jumping into the sound bites I knew he had prepared, the senator froze. It was just for a moment, one strong blink as he considered his answer.

I held my breath, wondering if I was seeing in that pause what I'd hoped to see from the moment I joined this campaign—a moment of truth, of careful consideration. The senator's conscience at work.

No—*Mark Cooper's* conscience.

He looked at the audience.

"We need to examine the root causes that lead people to enter our country illegally," he said. "And provide better options for those individuals."

Now I really hoped Penny was watching.

You could hear the pundit on the news station we were watching mutter, "Wow," and a ticker appeared instantly.

"Cooper backtracks on immigration."

Meg pressed her hands to her cheeks, physically holding herself together. I wasn't sure whether her reaction stemmed from awe or horror, but as the debate concluded, she reached over and squeezed my hand. And when she finally turned to me, I saw my own pride mirrored in her eyes.

The pundits were not so kind. They resoundingly declared the debate won by President Lawrence.

After Meg tucked the twins into bed, she joined me downstairs to watch the press's reaction roll out.

"Cooper's unraveling," one analyst was saying. "He led the primaries with tough talk on immigration and now he's completely betraying his base. They voted for him with this mandate first and foremost in their minds."

"I don't get this!" I started pacing in frustration. "Why are they being so negative? Isn't it a *good* thing that he's learning more about the issue?"

"It's a policy shift," Meg explained. "Very shaky ground."

"But why would voters want someone who never changes his mind?"

"They see it as strength." Meg sighed. "Consistency."

"It's not." I tossed the remote control onto the sofa. "It's insanity. Or ignorance. One of those."

Meg's face froze mid-laugh as her cell rang. She stared at it, confused, but muted the news to take the call.

"Yes, Elliott?"

His voice was so loud that I could hear it through Meg's cheek. "Who is this family? The illegal immigrants—friends of *Kate's*? Mark flat refused to tell me."

She blanched. "I won't tell you either."

There came a blast of violent sputtering that made Meg recoil from the phone, and then the screen went blank. She shook her head with another heavy sigh.

"When this campaign is done," she said, closing her eyes in meditation, "I am not going to miss that man one bit."

My own phone rang several hours later.

"I get *all* dressed up and she doesn't even show."

"Are you calling to gloat?" I climbed into my window seat and cracked open the window, breathing in the humid smell of green lawns and old oaks.

"No," Andy said. "But condolences nonetheless. I thought your dad made some really good points, personally."

I sighed. "America doesn't agree."

"It's a lot easier to get people scared than to calm them down. In the next debate, the winner will be whoever says that zombies are attacking and he's the only one with a plan to fight back."

"I'll suggest that. Thanks for the tip."

After we hung up, I heard Meg downstairs on the phone again, probably with the senator. I couldn't hear words, but I could imagine them—pep-talk words, cheer-up words. The last debate wasn't until October. Plenty of time to regroup, right? This wasn't so damaging.

His numbers plummeted.

"Even Fox News is against him now," Penny moaned. She'd become a rapacious news watcher in the past few weeks. "They're acting like he's a lost cause."

"Because of the debates?" I asked. Hearing her silence, my heart sank. "They're blaming me, aren't they?"

She sighed. "It's like they've completely forgotten the last few months . . ."

Sneaking a look at a few news stations myself, I could see that she was right. Never mind the public's sympathy, the bump in the polls following that first press conference, my "charmingly nervous" appearance at the convention—I was to blame. Everybody seemed to agree on that.

Especially Elliott. He had reverted to the silent treatment whenever we were in the same room, but I felt his eyes on me whenever I looked away, sharp and resentful. Silent or not, the message was clear. He wasn't trying to spin me anymore. He was trying to make me go away.

I was removed from the week's campaign schedule. There was even a new appearance scheduled at a local Children's

Wellness Day event that Gracie and Gabe were now slotted to attend without me. Meg tried to intervene but Elliott canceled it rather than include me.

On the road that weekend, we were all supposed to make an "impromptu" stop at a popular highway farmer's market to say hello and shake hands, but after I waited for Gracie and Gabe to get off the Locomotive, Elliott physically stopped me from following, his arm extended.

"You're laying low," he said to the air above my head. I was too stunned to respond.

Gabe turned back in confusion. "Let her out! Mom? Elliott won't let Kate out!"

It was only when heads turned from Gabe's shouting that Elliott was forced to sheepishly walk away. And I joined the Coopers just as sheepishly, smiling and waving, questioning whether all these supporters were really detractors in disguise. Did they blame me too?

I wondered where Nancy was in all of this. She'd called me the It Girl of politics just a few weeks ago. If that were the case, why were they burying me?

Uncle Barry was wondering the same thing. He called a day earlier than the usual Thursday check-in, worried that he hadn't seen new TV footage of me for a while.

"I'm fine," I promised him, and he seemed to believe me. As he chatted on about the summer heat and plans to surprise Tess with a vacation for her birthday, I felt my mind drift, watched the walls of the kitchen and imagined them inching closer and closer together.

Gracie and Gabe at least had friends to go hang out with

here in DC. I told myself I was content to play online Scrabble with Penny and read, but the silence of the house grew louder the longer it lasted. More than once, while everyone else was out campaigning, I thought I heard the front door open or cars pull up, but when I rushed to the window to look, only the empty front drive stared back at me. After three days of this, I started gravitating to the backyard in the vain hope that one of the security guards might feel like striking up a conversation.

And after more than a week of it, despite the fact that Andy was texting me photos of fish from his campaign visit to Alaska, I found myself praying that another mysterious invitation would arrive.

It didn't. But something else did.

Something I never would have wished for.

28

Monday, August 25
The Day of the Storm
71 DAYS UNTIL THE GENERAL ELECTION

Meg shook me awake before dawn.

"What's the matter?" I sat up in a panic.

"Tornadoes," she whispered. "We have to go."

I clutched the bedsheet. "Tornadoes? Here?"

"No. In Kansas. We're flying out in an hour."

A text came in from Andy as we drove to the airfield. "See you in KS?"

So the Lawrences were headed there too. Of course they were. It was the presidential thing to do. But why bring the whole family, if not for the cameras? Both the president and the senator were using this as a political moment and it was so transparent that it seemed like a misstep to me.

No matter how uneasy I felt, I knew to keep my mouth shut. They'd made it abundantly clear that my opinions were unwelcome.

Everyone but Meg, anyway. She still asked me to read her speeches. It was something.

As our plane started its descent toward the small Kansas airfield where we'd be landing, all of those thoughts left my head, replaced by a stunned, echoing *nothing*.

You could see it from here. There were houses, normal,

intact, neatly arrayed houses—and next to them, colorful rubble, a streak of trash, trees leveled. You could make out the path that the tornado had traveled, smearing the map as it went. A downed water tower. A circle of fire trucks. As we got closer, my eyes caught on a streak of brick along the roadside that had once been an overpass, an overturned tractor-trailer. And past all that, what was once the outside of a town, now no more than a razed field littered with fallen walls.

"This is . . ." My words ran out. "I can't believe this."

Meg rested her hand on my shoulder as she peeked past me out the window. "Neither can I. But this is why we're here. To see and to help, however we can."

The senator met us at the airfield with no cameras in sight and clutched the twins to his chest, as though he'd spent the night terrified for their lives. I shot him a wave before he had the chance to feel bad about not hugging me too. He smiled over Gracie's head at me, and there was sadness in it. He'd seen the same devastation we had from the air.

I glanced away, burying the theories I'd formed on the way here. How had I gotten so cynical? The senator wanted his family with him today. That was all.

Meg walked with me and the twins to the town square where the Red Cross had set up a temporary command station, while the senator lingered a few blocks away talking to FEMA. We'd just set to work unpacking boxes of supplies when the press showed up and started filming. And a moment later, we all looked upward as the sky filled with the sound of chopper blades. Emblazoned on the wide flank of the descending helicopter was the presidential seal.

When the First Family made their way down the ravaged block to the Red Cross station on foot, surrounded by security officers, staffers, and members of the press, I found a way to peek from the tent, hoping to catch a glimpse of Andy.

I saw him all right, walking a few steps behind his parents, hands dug deep into his trouser pockets—but it wasn't quite the Andy I knew. His face was gray with horror, an expression that mirrored those of all the volunteers around us. Andy looked older, more serious than I'd ever seen him.

A cameraman walked backward in front of the family, documenting the president and his wife shaking hands with local people. I watched Andy glance warily at the news crew and duck out of frame, his eyes searching for a place to hide.

I put down a crate of water bottles and waved, and when he spotted me, a spark seemed to flare inside him. He shot me that familiar lopsided smile, glanced over his shoulder at his family, and jogged over to hide in the tent with me.

"You're helping." It was more a compliment than a question.

I shrugged weakly. "There's not much I can do. I wish we could start rebuilding, but they're still finding people in the rubble, if you can believe it, and you have to be certified to help with that."

"It's awful." He looked confused, like he'd never been confronted with something like this before. Maybe he hadn't. "You look like you know what you're doing."

"I've volunteered after wildfires in California. And this set-up is a little like my mom's food bank."

"It reminds you of her."

289

"Yeah," I admitted. "It's weird—I can almost imagine she's here. Like she's just past that building where I can't see her."

He half smiled. "What's she doing?"

"She's . . . handing out canned goods super-fast—like a windup toy." His eyebrows knotted, and I laughed. "That was how she worked!"

"Where are you staying?"

I blinked, startled by the subject change. "A motel, I think. I'm not sure which one."

"I'll find out. Tonight, maybe . . ." He shrugged. "Another stroll?"

I glanced at the First Couple. "Are you sure that's a good idea?"

"They'll be too distracted to notice," Andy said. His eyes were locked on mine, intense, unwavering.

I looked away. Meg was watching from the other side of the tent, her arms full of first aid kits, but her curiosity piqued by our conversation. I picked up the crate again, hoping she wouldn't see how familiar we were with each other.

"And if they do notice," Andy went on, resting his hand against mine. "We'll tell them the truth. That we met. And we like each other." He leaned in. "A lot."

Andy's mom was looking for him. Hadn't spotted us yet. He groaned and stood.

"We *will* meet up tonight. No outs."

Before I could contradict him, he was gone.

After the senator returned and convened with the Red Cross leaders for a few minutes, he took us to some of the houses that had already been cleared. I saw a woman walking through the remains of her home, picking up items to throw away or keep, her eyes empty like she was sleepwalking. Across what used to be the driveway, a man was staring at his own home in disbelief. It had barely been touched by the storm, except for a few shingles torn loose from his roof and a tree branch that had broken through a front window. Next door, his neighbor's house was a ragged shell.

"What's going to happen?" Gabe asked. "Where will they go?"

"There are shelters set up," I answered. "In the school gym, at the Y. Some people will stay at hotels until their homes are rebuilt."

"I wouldn't want to stay at a school gym," Gracie said, her nose scrunched. "We're staying at a hotel, right Dad?"

He smiled faintly, rustled her hair, then wandered off to help a woman lift a beam off of what used to be a child's bed. I watched them talking, too far to hear what they were saying. The woman started to cry and the senator let her crumple against him.

I looked around for a camera. There wasn't one, and I felt like a terrible person for even checking.

This was my father. Not the senator from Massachusetts, running for office every second of every day, but just Mark Cooper, a guy who was trying his best to understand and to help. As he strode ahead of us, I rushed to catch up. I wanted to say something. That I got it, that I wanted to be a part of this, that what was important to him was important to me too.

But I couldn't think how to say it, so we walked together in silence. As we reached the end of the road, he put an arm around me and squeezed, kissed my cheek without saying a word, then strode off to join the aides who were waiting for him with clipboards and cell phones ready.

When we got to the motel where we'd be staying, I realized my own phone had been stuck in a bag all day. I had one message—a call from Penny. I sat on the edge of the hotel bed and listened, eager for the familiar voice on the other end.

But what I heard chilled me.

"Kate?" Penny was crying. "I don't even know how to say this. I.C.E. came this morning. They've taken them, Mom and Papi, I don't know where. To jail, I think?"

My hand shook the phone against my ear as Penny gasped a breath.

"Enrico's back at Camp Pendleton, and they were going to put me and Eva in foster homes, but Mrs. Washington took us, at least for now. We're together, but . . . oh God, Kate, get your dad to help them. Please Kate, take it back."

The message cut off so suddenly it might as well have been the sound of a bullet. *Take it back,* she'd said.

Her parents are being deported. And she thinks my father did it.

I called her, my fingers shaking against the phone's buttons. It went straight to voicemail. I hung up before the beep, my mind too chaotic for my mouth to form words.

How could this have happened? It couldn't have been the senator. He'd never do such a thing. But had his comments in that second debate tipped someone off? Could I.C.E. have traced our steps back to my birthday lunch in LA? It didn't seem possible. The only people who knew were the Coopers and James, and I trusted him. I trusted all of them.

Could it have been coincidental? Given that the Diazes had lived in LA for twenty-five years without anyone bothering them, it didn't seem likely. It had to be linked to meeting the senator. Had the Lawrence campaign hunted them down? Oh my God. Had *Marta* tipped them off?

I shuddered, my stomach souring—but the thought didn't ring true. Whatever her faults, she was dedicated to that community. She'd never betray them.

Some reporter, then? It would be a huge scoop—after the Denver debate, all of America must have been wondering who that undocumented family was.

I ran from my room onto the motel platform, determined to find the senator, beg him to help however he could. But a man was blocking my way, leaning on the railing as he smoked a cigarette.

Elliott. He turned to look at me, and was I imagining it, or was there a glint of amusement in his eyes? More than amusement. Triumph.

Suspicion hit me like a blast of wind, and with it a memory—Elliott calling Meg from Denver, his question a roar: "*Who is this family?*"

I staggered, a new picture forming of the man in front of me. "What did you do?"

A thin stream of smoke crept toward me as he exhaled. "Can you be more specific?"

"The *Diazes.*" My fists balled up, my breath coming hot.

He grinned slowly. "So *that's* who they were."

"They're being deported." And now I couldn't stop. "But you knew that, didn't you?"

"Why would I know that?" Elliott dropped his cigarette and let it smolder on the asphalt of the parking lot below, waiting, like this was a game and it was my turn.

And right then, I knew it. He'd done this. It was written all over him—his smugness, his shifty eyes. He must have gotten his hands on the security rolls from my birthday, and in his fury over the senator's sinking numbers, decided to eliminate the source of the problem. He couldn't get rid of me. But he could get rid of my friends.

He sighed as if bored, tried to pass by, but I blocked his way, staring him down.

Elliott's eyes were dark pools. There was an unsettling nothingness behind them. Chilled, I blinked.

He chuckled. Started away.

And I started to shout.

"Look at you! You're disgusting!" The words felt like poison, stinging my mouth as they left my body. "You're not even *sorry,* are you? Not even a little. These are people's *lives,* Elliott, and you don't even care!"

Elliott turned, his brow furrowed in mock confusion. "Why should I be sorry? You shove your illegal immigrant friends into the public eye, and shockingly"—he clutched his hands to his heart—"the *authorities* find out and *handle* the situation. Blame me if you like. I don't give a shit. This is *all on you.*"

I couldn't move. I reeled like he'd punched me in the gut. Elliott smiled.

"And I think you know that."

"Is there a problem?"

Over Elliott's shoulder, I saw Andy perched on the top step of the motel stairway, watching Elliott, his head lowered like he was ready to charge. My momentary surprise presented enough of a break for Elliott to sweep past me, slam himself into his own room, and pull the cheap curtains closed.

Andy hurried over like I was about to collapse. And then my knees went all funny and I almost did, except I grabbed his arm and he grabbed my waist and I blinked up to see his face close to mine, his eyes concerned, but that familiar boomerang scar quirking as he smiled.

"What the fuck, Quinn?"

I pushed myself gently away, hands trembling. The next breath I took felt sharp, like inhaling water, and I realized numbly that I had started to sob.

"Whoa," Andy muttered. "Okay. Come with me."

We both glanced around the quiet parking lot, almost lovely in the dusky light, then he took my hand and led me downstairs, around the back of the motel and along a desolate residential street.

When we got to an empty dirt road, Andy hung a right, pulling me lightly by the tips of his fingers. We got to a section of intact fence lining a wide ocean of wheat stalks. Without asking permission, Andy gripped my waist and lifted me so that I was sitting, perched above him on a long wood beam.

"Now." He placed his hands to either side of me. "What happened?"

"Elliott." I shook my head, bile rising in my throat. "He's evil."

"I can see that." Andy laughed mirthlessly. "But what exactly did he *do*?"

I drew a deep breath and told him, starting with Penny, what she meant to me, how I'd introduced the Coopers to her family, about the bridge I was trying to build between their two points of view. The joy I'd taken in seeing the senator's position soften and evolve.

Andy drew closer as I told him more and more, my hands clasping the fence so tight, I felt the wood splintering into my palms. His arm crept warm around my back, one hand sprawled steady against me—it stopped my shaking, made my breath more even, made me able to talk at all.

But when I told him about Penny's voicemail, he recoiled like I was toxic. I might as well have been. Elliott was right about one thing. This was my fault.

"How could I be so *stupid*?" I jumped off the fence and paced away. "I should never have exposed them like this. Meg was right. Everybody's right! I'm an idiot."

"No." Andy's face was as grave as I'd ever seen it. He held me in place, one hand on each of my shoulders, his feet rooted to the ground, planting me with him. "You are not an idiot. You are a good person who doesn't deserve any of this bullshit."

"It's Elliott. He's poisoned everything. He's a . . ." My mouth moved, soundless, scrambling for a suitable word.

Andy squinted at me, a smile dawning. "Go on. You can say it."

I squinted. "What?"

He cocked his head. "You never curse, do you?"

"My mom used to tell me that words had power. You should save the harshest ones for times when you really need them."

"Kate?" He took my hands and squeezed. "This is one of those times."

A laugh bubbled out of me. "You're right!"

He nodded.

"Fuck," I said. It felt awkward, but satisfying, so I said it louder. "Fuck!"

I turned, half expecting to see a group of horrified Kansans standing there, but my only witnesses were swaying crops and a few unimpressed blackbirds. I liked this, screaming, kicking the dirt road, and hollering into the sky.

"This has been a *fucked-up year!*"

I laughed, gasping for breath, and remembering Andy, twirled back to him.

His face had grown serious. And it wasn't the sympathy and anger of a moment before that I saw in him now. His eyes were pained, like I'd stabbed him. But just as I started to ask what was wrong, he blinked and started away, holding one hand out behind him for me to grab.

"Come on."

I fell into step and took his hand, feeling my body calm. "Where are we going?"

"To fix this."

As we neared the town, its streets humming with generators, I realized we were still holding hands. I glanced around
for onlookers, but no one was in sight, just empty news vans,
parked cars, the afternoon's last golden light dancing against
their metal roofs.

"I've gotta go," Andy said, turning to me with a frown.
"But listen. Fuck this campaign. Do not let them tell you who
you are. You're not an idiot. You're amazing, Kate Quinn. I
see you." He nodded at my confused expression. "I saw you
right away. That stupid press conference, grabbing that
stupid microphone. The real you. You're better than all of
them. Jesus . . ." He let out a desperate laugh. "You're even
nice to *vending machines!*"

I blinked blearily. "What are you—?"

"You're . . ."

He stopped abruptly, his jaw tightening. Then his hand
rose up to graze my hair and stuck there, and one step more
and he was close enough to kiss me.

And just as I realized that—he *was* kissing me.

Not accidentally. Very, very deliberately.

It stopped me utterly, rooted me where I stood. His lips
were soft but insistent, warm and opening, and after a
moment of shock, I was just another stalk of wheat, lit by the
sun, gently swaying, until my arms remembered themselves
and rose up to twine around his neck. And then, there I was,
breathing in his salty sweet scent, feeling the warmth of his
neck, his hair soft under my fingers, his hands exploring my
back, and—

He broke away, smiling. Not that half smile, that patented

Andy Lawrence smirk, but a real smile, a look of almost glee in his eyes.

"I'm gonna *fix* this," he called as he jogged away, and I was too dazed to ask what exactly he meant.

Up in my room, my giddiness faded as I picked up the phone to try Penny again. Again, it went straight to voicemail. I told the machine that I was sorry, that I'd never meant for this to happen, that I would do whatever it took to fix it, thinking as I hung up that I had no idea whether this could be fixed, or whether I would only succeed in destroying the life of the one person I cared most about in the world.

I'm gonna fix *this,* Andy had said. If only we could.

29

I should have taken the senator aside that night.

But when he came to grab me for dinner, the twins were right behind him and I didn't want to get them upset, and then he told me we were headed to a dinner that the campaign was providing for the whole town. And once we were there, standing in the town square with all of these people so grateful for the food, the chance to talk to the senator and take a break from their grief, it felt like the wrong moment. This was their time. Their crisis. Mine would have to wait.

I told myself I'd talk to him as soon as we'd returned to the motel, but Meg took me and the twins back before the senator, and although I stayed up as long as I could, staring at the dirty ceiling, hoping to hear his voice coming up the motel stairs, sleep took me and kept me until morning.

And then Meg was rushing us out, downstairs, into the waiting car, where the senator was locked in conversation with Elliott. I had to sit on my hands to keep from tearing at Elliott with my nails, pulling his smug face away from my father's ear. As usual, he didn't deign to look at me. It was lucky for both of us. If he had, I might have launched myself at him.

I told myself I'd talk to the senator during our flight, but Elliott stayed by his side the whole time. I could feel the clocks ticking, my sleeping cell phone smoldering in my bag, the flames growing with every second I didn't extinguish them.

Just tell him, my mind screamed.

Once we're home, it answered.

Thank God, Elliott left us at the airport. But as we reached the Coopers' house and deposited our bags in the foyer, the senator changed his shirt and shoes and turned around to leave for headquarters.

Before he could get out the door, I stood in front of it, blocking the way. And then my mouth clamped shut.

He laughed uneasily. "Something on your mind?"

I swallowed hard. *Now or never.*

"The Diazes are being deported."

I watched and hated myself for watching his reaction, trying to see whether shock registered.

It did. The color left his face, but when he looked up again, to my dismay, he simply sighed.

"I was afraid of that."

"*Afraid* of that?" I stared at him in disbelief. "I don't—I don't understand. Why didn't you *stop* him?"

"Stop—?" He shook his head. "Stop who?"

"Elliott." I said it quickly, before I lost the nerve. "He's the one who did it."

"Kate." The senator frowned. "I don't know what you're thinking here, but Elliott had nothing to do with this."

"I know you trust him, but—"

301

"But what?" He raised his eyebrows, waiting.

And what could I say? I had no evidence. Just a hunch.

He looked at his watch. "Kate, I need to—"

"It doesn't matter who caused it. We have to fix it!"

"How?"

"Call someone. Get a pardon. I don't know, how do you fix these things? You're a senator, can't you—?"

"No, Kate, I can't," he said sharply. "And if I could, do you really think that would be a good idea in an election year? Think!"

I shrunk back, and at my reaction, he reached out a hand, then let it drop.

"If it got out that I helped illegal immigrants get immunity, I'd be done. I'd have broken a promise I made to millions of voters."

"And what about the promise you made to the Diazes? What about them?"

He stared right back at me, unflinching. "I kept that promise. I never named them. That's all I can do."

He started away, but I grabbed his hand. He peered down at it as if I were a bug that had landed on him. Swallowing back my tears, I forced my fingers to hold on.

"Please," I said. "*Dad*. Please."

The word was out there. He looked me in the eye.

"I'm asking you to help me."

He smiled, sadly, but I knew the man better now. I knew what was real and what was faked for effect. His cheeks didn't crinkle the way they did with a real smile. His eyes were blank, like a wall had come down behind them.

This was the mask. My heart sank.

"And I'm telling you *I can't.*"

My hand went numb. Let go.

And then he was gone.

"Kate?" Meg's voice was a raw whisper. She'd been watching from the hall. Her eyes were glistening.

I couldn't face her, couldn't bear to look at any other human being right now, so I ran straight to my room, collapsing into tears, the house tumbling around me, the door slamming shut and the covers rising up around my head to drown out the screaming horror of all I'd done and failed pathetically to do.

My phone woke me up. Penny's name flashed. I scrambled to answer.

"What's going on? Are you okay?"

But Penny was yelling over me. It took me a few seconds to realize what she was saying.

"You did it—you're amazing! They're going to become citizens, they won't have to hide anymore. I can't believe this is happening!"

She was crying, but laughing too. There were voices in the background. Music. They were celebrating.

I sat up in bed wondering whether I was dreaming this call.

"The last three days have been a nightmare, not knowing what was going to happen, but Brad told us—"

"Wait, slow down." I shook the cobwebs out of my head.

Penny laughed. "Sorry! I'm freaking out."

"What happened?" My feet hit the bedroom floor. "And who is Brad?"

"He's from the State Department." She paused, confused. "I thought your dad spoke to him. He said he was under orders to help us. He's super-nice, and he found us a lawyer and got them green cards, and oh my God, I'm freaking! Out!"

I heard cars pulling into the front drive, the front door careening open and agitated voices filling the hallways. Staffers. They'd breached Meg's safe zone. Something was happening.

This. This is what's happening, I realized, staring at my phone.

The senator had changed his mind. After he'd left me yesterday, he must have had a crisis of conscience. He'd helped them after all. This was *happening!*

I danced into fresh clothes and hurried downstairs with a dizzy mix of joy and worry—for the consequences, the damage to the senator's campaign. But more than anything, I was lit up with gratitude.

When I spotted my father among staffers in the TV room, I nearly leaped over the sofa to hug him. But his expression stopped me cold.

He looked like someone had died.

On TV, the president was speaking.

"I've found myself in a unique position in the last few days—that of undoing a grievous and heartbreaking wrong. On August second, Senator Mark Cooper and his family shared a meal with the Diaz family, friends of his daughter Kate. There, he learned that Carlos and Inez Diaz, the parents of three American children, had entered the country illegally twenty-five years before. You may recall his comments in the last debate about his encounter with them." The president paused. "I myself was moved by his remarks, I must admit. Which is why I was shocked and horrified when I learned that at the same time Senator Cooper was speaking so warmly of the Diazes, the Cooper campaign was taking steps to have the family deported, the children ripped out of their home, and the parents thrown into jail."

Meg crumpled, clutching the arm of the sofa. I froze in place, legs tingling empty, about to give way as the world disintegrated and re-formed around me.

The senator hadn't helped the Diazes.

It was never the senator at all.

"When my son, Andrew, came to me with these allegations, I authorized the State Department to investigate, and if true, to undo the actions of Immigration and Customs Enforcement in this case. I'm happy to report that the Diazes have been reunited with their children, and that today they are taking steps toward becoming full and legal citizens of this nation. I do not argue that illegal immigration is not a serious issue plaguing this country. But to see a politician play with lives like they were mere pawns in a political chess match shakes me to my core. The Diazes did not deserve this. America did not deserve this. I call on Senator Cooper to respond to these allegations, and I call on Congress to investigate the clear breach of ethics by my opponent's campaign. Thank you."

He left the room, reporters screaming, his press secretary taking his place at the podium to answer their questions.

"Lies!" Meg's voice was raw with horror. "How can he just stand there and *lie* like that?"

"He believes it."

A voice behind me made my legs tense, ready for flight. I turned to see Elliott staring lazily over my shoulder at the senator, his fingers grazing his chin.

"You heard the man. His son, Andrew, came to him with these allegations. Now, I wonder. Who could have put such a crazy idea into Andy Lawrence's head?"

When his eyes landed on me, everyone else's did too. Just as I was trying to get my tongue to move, I heard a clip-clop-clip and gasped. Nancy's bright fingernails were digging into my arm.

She was smiling. It was terrifying.

"You and I need to have a *talk.*"

Meg rose, but before she could speak, Nancy had already dragged me into the senator's study and shut the door.

She laid her tablet on the mahogany desk and stepped away like it was about to explode.

"Tell me." She pressed her lacquered fingertips to her mouth and spoke through them. "Just tell me what this is."

I stared down at the glowing screen with little recognition. It was just some blog, with some celebrity photo, two people who weren't supposed to be dating caught out together. Three shots, posted one on top of the other, a couple out at dusk, holding hands, embracing—and finally a closer shot in which our faces were plainly visible.

Andy. Me. Kissing.

Someone had been there, then, in Kansas. Snapping pictures. In one of the parked cars, maybe.

The screen grew crisp and the room blurry. I could hardly feel my body, hear the voices outside the room, anything but the sound of my own shallow breathing. This was what I'd been afraid of for so long. And now that it had happened, I felt . . . nothing.

What was it Dina Thomas had said, back on the campaign trail? *The truth always comes out in time.*

"What is this website?" I asked. My voice was feeble. "I've never heard of it. Maybe we can have these taken down."

Nancy looked at me with disgust. "Every major website has picked this up. I'm surprised it hasn't hit cable news yet. If it weren't for that press conference, it would be the top story."

"Oh." Another breath scraped through me.

"Oh," she repeated, mocking.

She stared at me so long that I had to look up, had to meet her eyes just to get her to stop, and when I did I wished I hadn't. She was smiling that gentle smile of hers, but there was something sharp and glittering behind it. Something vicious. It had always been there, hadn't it? How had I not seen it right away?

"How long has this been going on?"

I shook my head. "Nothing is going on. He kissed me because he felt sorry for me. We're friends, that's it."

"Were you 'friends' *before* you met Senator Cooper?"

"What?" What was she accusing me of? My blood started

to rush back into my body, my nerves firing with each pulse. "No, I . . . no."

"Did you tell him about the Diazes? That your father's campaign was responsible for having them deported?"

She had her arms crossed like a TV district attorney. I'm sure she meant to look intimidating, but it had the opposite effect. Who was *she* to put me on trial? And what exactly was I being accused of? Telling the truth? Helping my friend?

"Yes," I snapped. "Andy was the only one who would listen to me. And thank God I told him, or else nobody would have helped them!"

Nancy's eyes fell and I heard the creak of the study door behind me. The senator stood in the doorway, Meg behind him, both of their faces deadened with shock.

"It's hit the news, then?" Nancy asked briskly. "I'll get the team here, carve out an hour this afternoon to regroup."

The senator spoke so softly I could hardly hear him. "That won't be necessary, Nancy."

Nancy stood very straight and very still. No one moved. I wasn't sure what was happening.

And then, after what seemed like an eternity, she nodded. "You'll have my resignation by this afternoon."

She strode out past them, shoving her tablet back into her bag.

"What . . . ?" I held on to the desk. "Why is she resigning?" Neither of them answered.

"Because of me?"

The senator blinked wearily past me out the study window.

I turned to look at what had caught his attention. It was a sparrow, sitting on a tree branch. When it flew away, he turned and left the room.

By the time my head stopped spinning all I could see was Meg staring at me.

"Go to your room," she whispered, and I ran.

In the empty foyer, Nancy was blocking the way up, perched on the steps, rifling through her giant bag for her car keys with shaking hands. Her stiletto was slipping off her foot. She looked so lost all of a sudden. So unlike herself.

Nancy Oneida was her job. Without it, what would she become?

"You don't have to resign over this," I said.

"Yes, I do," she hissed, scrambling up and straightening her skirt. "It was a condition of our agreement."

I shook my head. "What was?"

"You." She let out a tinkling laugh. "A sixteen-year-old bumpkin from the barrio. What was I *thinking?*"

"What are you talking about?"

"I went to bat for you, Kate." She dabbed at the corner of her eye, her face growing serious. "I thought I saw myself in you, if you can believe it, someone who deserved a chance. But I didn't realize how immature you'd turn out to be. How *selfish*. I'll never make that mistake again." She sniffed, then let out another hysterical giggle. "Not that I'll ever get the chance again."

The word *selfish* hit me like a low punch, but it was something else she'd said that was still pulsing cold through my veins. "Went to bat? What are you—?"

Something in her green eyes told me I should never have asked. But it was too late.

"I was the one who told him to acknowledge you," she said, so sweetly it stung. "He and Elliott disagreed with me. Mark wanted to put our efforts into denying it, hushing it all up until after the election. He couldn't see the *angle* in it. I made a case. I said I'd stake my career on it."

She leaned in to whisper.

"You wouldn't be here if it weren't for me."

I felt her breath on my neck even after she stepped away.

It can't be true. She's lying. She's leaving the campaign, bitter, taking it out on the easiest target. Senator Cooper wants me here—because I'm his daughter. Because I belong to this family, not because some aide talked him into it.

Not because there was a closed-door conversation in my uncle's living room for the better part of two hours . . .

"No," I heard myself say.

"I thought you were a star, but I was wrong." She smiled and started away. "You're nothing."

"I don't want to be a star." My voice came out as less than a whisper. It was the voice of a ghost. The voice of nothing. "I don't want any of this."

She watched with grim satisfaction as I groped for the banister and let it guide me downward, as tears streamed hot down my cheeks and I gasped for air like I was drowning. Then she turned, flicked her mussed hair straight, and left the Coopers' house for the last time.

Nancy Oneida was a skilled communicator. She'd gotten exactly the reaction she wanted out of me.

～ 30 ～

When the light outside was dimming, Meg came to my room, sat on the edge of the bed, and said, "Explain this to me."

I'd spent all day deciding how I would explain, what I would be willing to apologize for, what I had to defend. I'd gone over it again and again as I sat peeking from my window to see the campaign staffers' cars trickling out the gate one by one, hearing Gabe outside my bedroom door ask if he could check on me, hearing Meg say a quiet no, watching James pull the car around to the front drive, blinking out blankly as the senator got in with Elliott Webb and drove away.

I'm not sorry for helping my friends, I recited as the car disappeared past the oaks lining the front lawn. *I'm sorry I lied about Andy. I'm sorry you're not the father I hoped you would be.*

With her glasses on for the evening, Meg looked even more professorial than usual, probably as deliberate a costume choice as her gardening clothes on the day I'd met her. She wasn't here for denials, for tears, for guilt—just a simple recital of facts. It worked. I felt my defensiveness dropping away.

I told her about meeting Andy at the Tauber retirement party in Pennsylvania, how he'd started calling me after that,

311

and how I'd started calling him back. I told her the truth about Jake Spinnaker's birthday party. Meg winced when she heard that we'd gone to a fundraiser for the president, and I felt shame flood my face before realizing that her reaction meant she was surprised. That was a good thing. It meant the press didn't know about it either.

I told Meg that Andy and I had started calling each other a few times a week. That I was always careful not to give away anything private about the campaign, but that it was nice to have someone to talk to about it, someone who understood.

Her squint relaxed when I said that.

"You had *us*." Then she shook her head. "But I know it's not the same."

Had. Past tense.

"And then Andy was there in Kansas," I went on, my throat tight. "He showed up right when I found out about the Diazes, what Elliott did . . ."

Meg took her glasses off, fingers pressed to her nose like she was squeezing away a migraine. "You told Andy that Elliott did this."

Everything seemed blurry now in recollection. "I don't remember what I said, exactly. I just kind of vented."

Meg let out a quiet groan. "Kate. Why on *earth* did you think Elliott Webb had anything to do with this?"

"He hates me. And he's anti-immigrant. And—and when I accused him, he didn't deny it. It was almost like he was happy that I was upset. So I thought he was . . ."

As the words dried up in my mouth, I suddenly felt very small and very foolish.

"Getting revenge?" She shook her head. "Let me tell you something. Elliott Webb is a political animal. He would never do anything to jeopardize his own career. And in this case, that means helping your father to win his election. So—"

I turned away, but she grabbed my hand.

"No, I want you to think about this, Kate. Why would Elliott do something that would draw negative attention to the campaign? If he'd learned about the Diazes, wouldn't it make more sense to hush them up, keep the story quiet, rather than inflaming the situation?"

"I don't know." I knew how sullen I sounded, but I really wasn't in the mood for a lesson in political strategy.

She sighed. "Anyway, the White House is already issuing a retraction."

I gasped. "How—?"

"News travels fast. The LAPD made a statement around noon saying the Diazes were picked up by a random traffic stop. Their brake light was out, and when the police officer asked for ID, neither of them could supply a driver's license."

"Is that the truth?"

Meg looked confused. "Of course it's the truth. What, do you think we're bribing police departments now? Kate." She cocked her head. "You're *smarter* than this."

I swallowed, hollow with disbelief. "So this was random. It had nothing to do with us."

"No. It didn't. Not that it'll matter. The accusation is out there and it will stay out there forever. That's the way these things work."

Because of me. Because I couldn't keep my mouth shut.

"Now," Meg said, her voice a shade sharper. "What about these photos?"

"I didn't expect him to kiss me," I said, my heart stuttering at the recollection. "I think Andy felt bad for me. I'd been crying, he was just trying to get me to stop."

Meg looked doubtful.

I tried to laugh but it wouldn't come out.

"We're not dating, whatever that website said." My attempt at a smile flickered and died. "But I guess it's like you said. The accusation is out there."

Meg motioned me over. I swung my legs around the edge of the bed so she could slide an arm around my shoulders. We sat there, my head bowed as we rocked gently back and forth. With every rock, I could feel Meg forgiving me.

"I'm sorry this happened," she finally said. And then, her voice icy: "I could *kill* that kid."

"Andy?" I leaned away, confused. "Why? This isn't his fault."

"Kate. Sweetheart." She blinked as if seeing me for the first time. "Andy Lawrence played you."

I could only stare at her. "He—what?"

"Maybe this is all a little fresh for you, but think about this objectively." She brushed my hair back from my face and peered at me. "*Andy* finds your number. *Andy* calls you. Andy won't let up until you've gone out with him. You keep the campaign private, so he *keeps* calling. Keeps asking questions. I don't know if he was instructed to do this or took it upon himself, but the fact is—he got close to you, learned something damaging, and brought it to his father. And you've seen the results."

My mouth wouldn't make a sound. I couldn't deny her accusation. But I couldn't believe it either. Andy was my friend. He did this to help me. What she was saying was . . .

Exactly what I'd suspected from the moment he first called me.

The more I'd gotten to know Andy, the more authentic he'd seemed. He felt like the one steady thing in my life, a reliable voice on the other end of the line who could cut through all the political nonsense swirling around me. He was my lifeline to reality. And Meg was telling me that he was a liar.

Andy played me. It didn't ring true. But I wasn't exactly in a position to trust my instincts, now was I? I'd been wrong to accuse Elliott. Wrong to trust Nancy. And if what she'd maliciously told me this morning was true, then all of my hopes about the senator were wrong as well.

"This isn't your fault," Meg said, standing up. "But I'm going to be honest here. It's bad."

"Whose idea was it to invite me for the summer?"

The words charged out of me the second Meg's hand touched the doorknob. She froze, trapped by the question. I stared back, unflinching. I had to know.

"I think Nancy suggested it first. Why?"

Her voice was casual, but I could see her nerves at work. She wasn't quite mustering the cool, calm exterior I'd grown so used to. She knew what I was really asking.

And yet I couldn't voice the question. Couldn't even think it. It was too stark, too cruel.

"Did *you* want me to come?" I asked instead, standing

315

from the bed to face Meg. "Did you want to meet me? Get to know me?"

"Back in June?" She let out an exasperated huff. "You want an honest answer here, Kate? No. I didn't want *any* of it to be happening at the time. But . . ."

She reached her hands out.

"I'm glad *now*."

"What about him?" I couldn't lift my hands to hers. I felt like stone, every part of me heavy. "Is *he* glad?

Her eyes were pained. She backed away.

"Give him time."

~31~

"It's not fair!"

I'd picked the wrong time to come downstairs. Gracie's screams of protest were loud enough to silence the crickets in the backyard and nearly sent me careening out of the living room myself.

But Meg had spotted me, and by her expression, she needed backup. The senator was in Idaho, so it had fallen to his wife to tell the twins that they'd be off the campaign schedule for the foreseeable future. To Gabe, this was fantastic news. To Gracie, it was the end of the world.

I entered the fray.

"It won't be so bad, Gracie," I tried. "We'll get to hang out just the three of us when Meg's away. No supervision. Woo-hoo?"

Gracie's glare only deepened.

"This is your fault. You messed up, so we're stuck here with nothing to do!"

Yep, I thought. *Pretty much.*

"Watch your tone," Meg cautioned, but an idea had struck Gracie, her big blue eyes widening with sudden hope.

"What if just me and Gabe come along, and Kate stays behind?"

"I'll stay behind," Gabe offered, and Gracie not too subtly kicked him. "Ow."

Meg closed her eyes. "Grace. This is not up for debate. You're starting school in less than three weeks and I want you focused."

We all knew that wasn't the real reason. Governor McReady was whooping it up across the country with Carolee in tow and her school year down in Texas had already begun. This wasn't about academics. It was about politely burying me. The campaign had deemed it too conspicuous to exclude only me from appearances, so the official story was that all three of us were spending much-needed time out of the spotlight.

That was not where Gracie Cooper wanted to be.

"I don't want to stay with her," she said, turning away in a sulk. "It's not fair. We're your real kids. We should get to go. She's just . . . a *bastard*."

I gasped, stung, not just by the word but by the way she'd looked at me when she said it, aiming it with intent to wound.

But before I could react, Meg had launched herself across the room, landing in a crouch, her white-knuckled hands locked around Gracie's collar.

"You do *not* use that word, do you understand me?"

Gracie's face went red. "I . . . yes? I don't even know what it means!"

Meg let go. "It's an outmoded term denoting lineage in a patriarchal . . ." She groaned, frustrated. "It's a word you are never to use. Apologize."

"I'm sorry I called you a bastard."

She said it so mournfully that I almost burst out laughing.

Later that night, after Meg had gone to sleep, Gabe and Gracie snuck into my room with a flashlight, and then froze in the doorway, surprised to see that I was still up reading.

They climbed onto the end of my bed, Gracie a few inches behind Gabe, as if she was worried I might lunge at her. Gabe absently clutched the flashlight to his chest, so it lit up his face campfire style. I almost expected them to launch into a ghost story. Instead, Gabe whispered, "What does *bastard* mean?"

Gracie's eyes remained locked on mine. She really didn't know.

"It means somebody who was born . . ." *How to put this.* "Outside of a marriage."

I hoped it was dim enough in the light from my bedside table that they couldn't see me blushing.

"So . . ." Gracie looked as uncomfortable as I'd ever seen her. "*Are* you one?"

I smiled. "Yeah, kinda. But like your mom said, nobody really uses that word anymore."

The twins looked at each other. They weren't done.

"Did Dad love your mom?" Gabe asked.

They waited, patient as statues, while I tried to recover from the sensation of having been stabbed by the question.

"I don't know," I whispered. "Why?"

They glanced at each other again. Gracie inched closer.

"Mom said that when two people love each other very much, the man puts his penis in—"

"Okay!"

319

I cut her off, my hand pressed to her mouth. A giggle bubbled out of her and Gabe started to grin, and I couldn't help laughing myself.

"I don't know anything," I admitted. "I'm as confused as you guys are."

I fell back onto my pillow and Gabe and Gracie crept up around me, flopping onto their backs in imitation.

"And I wish we could be out on the campaign trail," I said, nudging Gracie. "All of us. But them's the breaks."

"Them's the breaks," she repeated, with all the world-weariness an eight-year-old could muster.

I'd hoped that our late-night bonding session would be enough to crack the wall that had come up between me and my sister, but when Meg hit the road the next afternoon, Gracie protested by locking herself in the upstairs bathroom, refusing to come out to say good-bye.

Meg smiled ruefully and gave Gabe and me each a kiss on the forehead. "Be good. Lou will drop by later, but call me or the campaign phone if you need anything. Or ask security."

"Got it," I said, simultaneously shooing her away and fighting the impulse to drag her back into the house.

When her car disappeared, Gabe grabbed my hand.

"Mom's only gone for the weekend," he reminded me. "Gracie will come out before then."

He was right. In fact, Gracie came out one hour later, once the smell of stovetop popcorn curled its way under the bathroom door and Gabe and I turned the volume way up on the movie we'd just downloaded. I hid a smile as Gracie clomped her way to the very far end of the sofa and sat with her arms crossed, a scowl etched deep into her face. It took her five minutes to sneak a bite of popcorn when she thought we weren't looking. But halfway through the movie, I heard her laughing and saw with relief that she had her legs kicked up on the coffee table, today's anger forgotten for the moment.

She'll forgive me, I told myself. *And then she'll get mad at me for something else. This is just being a sister.*

And the senator will forgive me too. I just need to give him time.

That last thought evaporated as soon as it formed.

Louis came by around seven with some takeout dinner and groceries. He had his baby at home and a very patient wife, so I knew he couldn't stay long. But even if it was brief, I was happy to see him. It occurred to me now that Lou Mankowitz was the one person in the campaign that I'd never felt uncomfortable around. He was also the one member of the inner circle that I'd gotten to see the least. When we were on the road, he was manning the shop at headquarters. When we were home, he was on the road, getting the field staff ready for the senator's arrival. But for the next four days, his job was restocking our cereal and ice cream and making sure we hadn't torn the house down in Meg's absence.

And . . .

"Sorry, kiddo." He really did look sorry as he extended his hand and I relinquished my campaign-issued cell phone.

Meg had warned me in advance that they were taking the phone back. Apart from this week's house arrest, it would be my only punishment for what I'd set in motion.

"You can use the phone in the kitchen," Meg had offered wryly, and I knew I was in no position to object, given the trouble that all the clandestine cell phone calls of the past few months had caused. Still, I wasn't relishing having to talk to my friends in the center of household operations, within constant earshot of Meg and the twins.

I'd hurriedly texted the new number, first to Penny, Lily Hornsby as an afterthought, and then to Uncle Barry and Tess, in case they didn't have it. Not that they were likely to use it—Barry had skipped this week's check-in call, and hadn't tried to reach me at all since Kansas, even after the word *Kategate* had started scrolling across news tickers again, accompanied by that lurid shot of me and the president's son. Maybe he'd figured that the Coopers were managing my media circus of a life just fine. Or maybe he was mad at me too.

Then, with a last burst of rebellion, I texted the house phone number to Andy Lawrence, Mr. Lurid Shot himself, wondering whether he'd have the guts to call knowing that Meg or the senator could be on the other end of the line.

"FYI—my cell phone's been confiscated. Here's the land-line . . ."

I hoped that had sounded casual enough. Warm enough. I hoped he would call, using some phony accent or fake name, and that they wouldn't know. Or even that they would. That Meg would pick up and realize that Andy really did want to connect, even after getting information out of me. That he cared.

With Meg gone, I might have the chance to talk to him in private.

If he called. Every time I passed the kitchen, I stared at the phone, trying to summon a ring through sheer force of will.

It didn't work.

One benefit of being unsupervised was that we could now watch the news to our hearts' content. Gabe grumbled, but Gracie was obsessed, flipping compulsively between channels, hunting for any mention of Meg or the senator—or even better, footage. She missed her parents, really, but she was putting on a brave face, pretending she was getting "prepped" for the moment we were called back to the campaign trail. I snuck looks over her shoulder, but every time my name came up, I made her change the channel. Watching myself get picked apart by complete strangers on national television was not worth the stress headache.

I'd made it a game. Whoever could get to the remote first after hearing the word *Kate* was the winner. I knew Gracie was a born competitor, but even so, I was shocked by how well the tactic worked. She dove over sofas, ripped the remote out of Gabe's hand, and on one impressive occasion, ran all the way downstairs, sprinted along the corridor and vaulted over a side table to get to the remote before me, suffering only minor bruises in the process.

But despite my attempts at avoidance, all the snippets we heard lodged in my brain, rearranging to form a mosaic of the campaign's spin.

I was a victim of that cad Andy Lawrence. He was the one with a sordid history of bad behavior and pranks. My only crime was naïveté. The cable news commentators ate it up and spat it back out. They had polls going—they always had polls going—and more than anything, America felt sorry for me.

I didn't feel sorry for myself. Even so, I waited for that phone to ring.

When it finally did, late that first afternoon, it was Penny, asking how I was doing, whether I'd managed to talk to Andy yet. And then in the evening it was Meg, checking in from Baton Rouge. Then Penny again the next day, wanting advice on dodging paparazzi.

"They're like camped out on the end of our block. What do I do?"

"Just smile at them and keep walking," I offered, remembering Nancy's first piece of media training.

"And . . ." Her voice dropped. "The Lawrence campaign keeps dropping by. They want us to endorse the president."

"You should," I muttered.

"Kate!" She made a sound like she was punching me through the phone. "Shut up, you know we're not doing that. Mom and Papi love your dad, especially now. It's not like he did anything to hurt us."

"He didn't do anything to help either."

"Yeah, he did," she said. "That day at our house. He listened."

Meg got back on Tuesday, not a moment too soon. Gracie and Gabe were fighting over a pool float, Gracie having accidentally punctured the other one with a stick she was pretending was a sword. When I went into the house to hide from the sound of them yelling at each other, Meg was standing in the kitchen, the house phone cradled on her shoulder as she slowly set down her luggage.

She looked confused. A little upset. When she saw me walk in, her eyebrows rose.

"It's for you, Kate."

My cheeks flushed, my heart thumping. *Of course. Andy picks* now *to finally call.* I took the phone, suspecting I was going to be hearing about this as soon as I hung it back up. Meg stepped into the living room, just within earshot, pretending to straighten up Gabe and Gracie's pile of toys.

"Hello?" I tried to sound cheerful, casual, not terrified.

"So you're alive."

I blinked. This was *not* Andy. This voice was female, dry, crackling with age and barely restrained irritation.

"Evelyn?"

"Call me Grandma." She snorted. "Those other two do, no matter how many times I tell them not to."

"How are you?" I craned my neck around the corner, but Meg was studiously pretending not to listen.

"Don't you worry about me, this call's about you. I want to know why you're still in that house. Don't you have an uncle who can take you?"

Just as I was staggering from the sting of that comment, she kept going.

"Or you could come and live with me." She sniffed. "I'm an old loon, but it's not so bad here. There's a school, I assume. I see people your age when I go into town. I could introduce you to them. And I've got a shotgun to keep the reporters away."

"I . . ." *Wow.* I was utterly at a loss. "That's very kind—"

"You don't want to. That's fine. I'm just reminding you that if you want to escape from the terrarium, I still live in the same place. Show up anytime. I've got a room ready. And a fully stocked pantry."

I tingled from the generosity of the offer but wasn't even remotely tempted to accept, having spent maybe ninety minutes with her in my life—a fun ninety minutes, but still.

"Whatever your reasons are for staying under my son's roof, I don't want you to feel like you're stuck there for the *wrong* ones. You're planning to go to college."

It was not a question, but there was a pause, so I stammered an answer.

"I—yeah. Definitely. My top choice is Harvard, but I've got a list going . . ."

"That's where Mark went," she groaned. "Can't be helped. In any case, I'm going to pay for you to go."

She kept talking over my astonished attempt at a reply.

"I've got money put aside, and you need it sooner than the twins, so you're getting it, and that's all there is to it. Not another word out of you."

My mouth shut obediently.

"So if you stay with Mark and Margaret, it'll be because you choose to, not because you need to. But like I said—I've got a room for you too. You just remember that."

There was something about her directness that cut

through my befuddlement, made me squint at the phone as I asked, "You don't like him much, do you?"

"I love my son. I just wouldn't wish him on anybody." She laughed. "He's a politician. Has been since college. I'm not saying he doesn't have his moments, but . . ." She let out a musical sigh, a little wordless tune. "I'm looking forward to his retirement. It'll be good to see the real Mark again."

When I hung up and left the kitchen, my stomach was tight with nerves. I wasn't sure what to tell Meg. Would she resent me for taking a college fund that was meant for the twins? Or Evelyn for trying to get me to move out?

Meg was out by the pool, laughingly fending off wet hugs from her dripping children. I watched them and made a bargain with myself.

I'll tell Meg what Evelyn said—as soon as she tells me why she bought me the Farnwell Prep summer reading list.

And if she doesn't bring it up? Do I dare confront her with the biggest question of my life—"What next?"

Meg glanced up at the window and then away. I leaned my forehead against the glass. *She'll tell me. Any day now.*

Thursday, September 4
First Day of Classes Back in South Carolina
Eleven Days Until the First Day of Classes
at Farnwell Prep
61 DAYS UNTIL THE GENERAL ELECTION

32

The senator came back, not that it mattered.

Both Thursday and Friday, he left the house before dawn, returning only after midnight. Meg said that there was an important vote in the Senate, but there was something apologetic in the way she told me, so despite my curiosity, I didn't even ask what the vote was for. Around 1:00 A.M. Saturday morning, I was up reading when the car pulled in, its lights scanning my bedroom wall as they circled the front drive, and a few minutes later, I heard his voice and Meg's rumbling from the living room. I dimly considered coming downstairs in my pajamas to say hello, but couldn't muster the energy to put on a smile.

He doesn't want to see me, I thought, but the truth was worse. *He didn't want me in the first place.*

He left again a few hours later for an event in Florida, and Meg filled me in on recent campaign developments. The senator's approval numbers were creeping slowly upward. The president had suffered a backlash from the Diaz debacle, so even though he was still leading in the polls, it was closer than it had been. Cal had taken over for Nancy as Communications Chief, and as I'd guessed, he'd been wringing out the Andy scandal for every possible drop of sympathy.

Cal was Nancy's true protégé. It was working.

"These people donated to the campaign mentioning you by name," Meg explained, passing me a long list, a stack of recognition cards, and a pen.

I scanned the list, astonished by the length of it, and by the comments people had made.

"Keep your chin up, Kate," Roberta S. Johnson from Tennessee said. "I've been there too!"

Somehow I guessed she didn't mean that she was also the illegitimate child of a politician.

"The Lawrences are scum," wrote Morris Scheindlin of Jersey City. "Your father has my vote."

I wrote a scripted thank-you to each of the donors, adding a happy face before my signature for the people who had commented that they were worried about me. My hand started to cramp, but I kept going into the evening. I might not have agreed with every stance the senator was taking, or even most of them, but the fate of the country wasn't exactly at the forefront of my mind—not now, when my own future seemed to be drifting further into limbo every second. Sixty-one days to go. I'd write and smile and keep my mouth closed, just like Meg. I would give my family no excuse to shut me out.

At 9:00 P.M., Meg was already starting to yawn, hovering over her own pile of acknowledgments, and I was only three-quarters of the way through my list. The phone rang and Meg startled like a shot had gone off. We both laughed as she went to answer it, but my body started whirring as it always did, wondering if this time it would be Andy, ready with an explanation, an apology, a joke. Anything.

"It's for you," Meg said—neutrally. My pulse returned to its regularly scheduled rhythm.

"Hey, Kate! It's Lily Hornsby?"

"Oh my God! Hi! How are you? We haven't talked in forever!" I pressed my fingers to my mouth to stop spouting exclamations, but she laughed breathlessly, as though she were relieved, making me wonder if she'd been nervous to call.

"I'm really good," she said. "I got your text, so I wanted to catch up. Everybody's been watching you on TV. Seems like things have been . . . um, kind of crazy lately?"

I leaned against the counter, a wave of exhaustion hitting, as if my body was answering the question for me. Meg looked up from the table. I flashed a smile and she returned to her signing.

"It's been . . . interesting," I admitted. "But it's really nice to hear from you."

Lily filled me in on her summer. She'd been working at a posh beach club as a waitress, which was awkward because she knew some of the members' kids from school and they hadn't been able to resist giving her a hard time. She'd started dating Scott, the tall kid I remembered from physics. She'd been "just friends" with him for as long as I'd known her. I grinned, glad to see my early hunch proven right.

"And now school started like two days ago, and I'm already counting down to graduation. Is that awful?"

I felt a strange shock hearing that, like I was Rip Van Winkle finding out twenty years had passed. It was the end of the summer. Gracie and Gabe were days away from starting school. And as far as I knew, I was currently two days deep into the "absent" list at Palmetto High.

"So, are you coming back? A lot of people have been asking and I don't know what to tell them."

I glanced at Meg. She was setting down her glasses, rubbing her eyes, giving up for the night. "I might be. I don't know yet."

"Well, I hope you do. Or I'll come visit you at the White House. Or whatever."

As I forced a laugh, I realized that the idea was no longer so bizarre to me. Despite the recent drop-off in polling numbers, the election was close. The senator could win. We could all be moving there in a matter of months. They'd have to take me with them, I knew. After everything, it would raise too many eyebrows to send me back to my uncle's house. And wouldn't they want me to live with them, anyway? The senator might still hate me, but Meg would fight for me to stay, and Gracie and Gabe would miss me too much to let me go.

Not that any of them had actually told me this. We never talked about the future. It was as though we were expecting the world to end on November fourth. *This* world would end, of course—the road, the relentless schedule, the political machine that never stopped calculating. But what world would replace it?

I'd told Meg a month ago that I'd finished the books she bought for me. And still, not a word about starting school. I could have asked, cornered her, demanded to know what the plan was for the future, but the more I debated which moment to pick, the more stubbornly I delayed. Maybe it was pride, but it didn't feel right to ask. It was like inviting yourself over to someone's house for dinner. *They* had to ask *me*—that was how these things worked—and then it would be my choice to say yes or no. Right?

Or maybe I just didn't want to ask the question and hear that they did, in fact, have an answer. That I was going back to South Carolina. That they didn't want me after all.

Meg got a call from the senator out on the road. She put him on speakerphone so he could talk to everyone at once. I yelled a hello along with Gracie and Gabe and that seemed to suffice. He sounded upbeat. A famous retired general had thrown his support behind his candidacy, apparently a major coup for the campaign. Things were going better, bit by bit.

That week, the senator's three children were quietly placed back on the campaign schedule. I aired out my dresses, ready to put on my American Girl costume and once again step into the role of Katie Cooper—trusted member of the team. I knew not to read too much into it. Gracie and Gabe were starting school in five days, so I was sure the campaign was just eking out all the remaining family appearances they could. Meg intended for her kids to start on schedule, presidential campaign or no.

And yet, she still hadn't said a word to me. My stomach had been in knots for the past few days as I dared myself to face her, the same running dialogue in my head urging me forward and pulling me back.

This is my senior year. It's important. Critical. I needed to say it, but every time I tried, my hands started to tingle, my throat shrinking dry. *One more day,* I kept telling myself. *She'll say something today. And if not, I'll ask tomorrow.*

Meg had wrapped us in such a campaign cocoon since Kansas that it came as a shock to get back on the Locomotive and prepare to stand in front of a crowd. I felt awkward all over again, like I no longer knew the basics, from dressing myself to waving. Wednesday morning, the day of our event, there were no clothes set out for me. Nancy was gone and Libby had been reassigned, so I supposed I was on my own.

Which was *great.* I could certainly dress myself, especially given the months of couture training I'd just had.

After twenty minutes of deliberation, I put on the skirt and sweater set I'd worn for that first press conference back in June.

The Locomotive felt different from the last time I'd been on it. Apart from Nancy, the top-tier staffers were all in attendance, but it wasn't the same light, jocular environment I remembered. The mood was studious, almost gloomy. The staffers read or typed or stared out the window—even Cal, who I couldn't help but notice had avoided eye contact from the moment I'd gotten on the bus, like he was embarrassed on my behalf. Every time two of the staffers started to chat, Elliott would crane his head from the back office and they'd quickly shut up.

As we pulled up to the New Jersey park where the rally was being held, I spotted a group of people waving signs. They looked like they were cheering until you heard the sharp, repetitive rhythm, saw their faces, wide mouths shouting.

One of the signs read: VOTE COOPER, VOTE HATE. Another: DEPORT COOPER.

They were here to protest. Many in the angry crowd were Hispanic. This was about immigration. It was about the Diazes.

I turned my face away as we passed them, trying to forget that I was the one who drew them here.

We parked, and Lou boarded the bus—as soon as his face popped through the door, it felt like the clouds had parted and the sun was finally shining again. I watched the staffers get up from their seats to stretch with sudden smiles. Lou strolled down the bus, greeting each one, and it occurred to me that despite how little I'd seen him on the campaign trail, in one sense, he'd been with us all along. As he passed through the aisle, I could almost see him drawing lines from one staffer to the next, holding them together.

"Okay." The senator strode out from the back office, the sad lines of his face uncreasing as he put on his practiced smile. "Shall we?"

He averted his eyes when I stepped forward. It was a defensive maneuver. I knew that. If he looked at me, the smile would drop off—and he needed that smile to do his job. I stuck on my own fake smile and pretended I didn't notice, or even better, didn't care.

Lou caught my eye. He didn't miss anything, did he? But he shot me a goofy wink and I relaxed a little, like all the campaign aides around me.

"What is she wearing?" Elliott said.

I blinked, surprised. He was pointing at me.

Libby giggled nervously, smoothing her braided bun. "You reassigned me! I'm not helping with Kate anymore."

Meg motioned to the door. "The outfit's fine. Let's go."

Gabe and Gracie hesitated beside the senator, their eyes traveling between all of us like spectators at a sporting event, Gabe's with trepidation, Gracie's with some emotion I couldn't quite read.

"No." Elliott pointed at me again. "Change. Don't you have pants? Something without a skirt?"

"I—" My voice leaked out of me and died. Everyone was staring. "I only have jeans. You guys didn't buy me any pants."

"Oh, so it's *our* fault."

Before I could scream "YES!" Meg stepped between us, her face growing red. "She's *fine,* I said. Let's. Go."

Elliott laughed sharply. "Great, Meg. You're the expert here, clearly. America already thinks she's a slut and now we're parading her around in a miniskirt. That's—"

His words cut off with a crack and I was still so stunned by what he'd said that it took the shouting and mess of arms and bodies pulling Elliott and Louis apart for me to realize that the unthinkable had just happened.

Lou Mankowitz had punched Elliott Webb in the face.

Lou was unrecognizable. Veins were bulging from his neck, and his arms were flying. The staffers fell back, suddenly eager to escape. Except Elliott. Despite the huge height difference between the two men, Lou had him by the throat, and was forcing him into submission with so little effort that

I wondered numbly how many fights Lou had gotten into during his "young and stupid" days.

When Elliott's knees hit the ground, Lou drew a breath, pulling himself into a polite crouch. "Apologize to the young lady."

"Screw you, Mankowitz," Elliott spat. "What the fu—?"

Lou smacked him. "Apologize!"

Elliott's eyes met mine and for maybe the first time ever, he looked like a human being. A scared one.

"I apologize, Kate. That was out of line."

Lou shoved himself away from Elliott, stomped down the steps, and disappeared behind the bus. All the staffers ran to the right-side windows to watch him march off. Libby hesitantly offered Elliott a hand up, but he swatted her away. His cheek was already livid red and rising.

Just as I found my breath, the senator lifted his hand.

"Okay, people!" The staffers quieted down. "We've got an event to get to. Let's go say hello. It'll be quick—and when we get back, we'll have round two. This time Cal and Chuck?"

Cal guffawed and nearly everyone else joined in. Not Elliott. Not me. Not Meg or Gabe, who was staring helplessly at me like I was a baby bird that had dropped out of its nest.

They all started out of the bus, including Elliott, but I just stood there, clutching my "miniskirt," reeling, like I was the one who'd been struck.

As he reached the doorway, the senator looked over his shoulder at me. It hit me that this would be the first time we'd made eye contact in weeks—except it wasn't eye contact, was it? He was staring at my shoes.

"I think you should stay behind," he said, and the doors swished shut behind him.

I peered out. It was like watching a silent film, seeing the Coopers wave to the crowds, file along the walkway to the podium, cameras flashing. When they got to the steps, Gabe turned back, searching for me in the dark windows of the bus. And then Gracie looked back too, her frown so deep that I wondered whether she was about to cry.

I shut and locked the door to the back of the bus and changed back into my jeans in the darkness. Then, without turning on the light, I slumped into the senator's office chair, feeling the cool leather warming against my cheek.

Why didn't the senator defend me, instead of Lou?

Why didn't I defend myself?

The whys blurred into silence. I woke up when the bus started moving again. And I didn't come out until it stopped.

33

The phone downstairs was ringing and no one was picking it up. The sound cut through my guest room door more and more sharply with each ring, until it finally reached through the haze surrounding me and was all I could hear.

I got up from the bed and peeked into the hall. Gabe and Gracie were sitting on the floor of Gracie's room divvying up a box of school supplies that had arrived at the house when we got back from the campaign event. They didn't seem bothered by the sound of the phone, which had just started ringing again after a twenty-second respite.

Downstairs, the study door was shut, and behind it rose hushed, angry voices. The senator. Then Meg. Then Meg again. I couldn't hear what she was saying, but this was obviously a conversation no phone call could interrupt.

When I got to the kitchen, it started ringing again.

Maybe it's Andy, my brain recited.

Yeah right.

I pressed the phone numbly to my face. "Cooper residence."

"Kate? Oh thank God! Did you just get home? I've been calling all day—got tired of leaving voicemails!"

"Uncle Barry?"

In one rush, my stupor dropped away, and I felt my knees get so wobbly that I had to sit down on the cool tile of the kitchen floor, clutching the receiver to my cheek with both hands as if it were about to fly away.

"Hey now." I must have made a noise, because his voice got gravelly, like a cartoon grizzly bear. "What's this? What's going on over there? Do I need to come get you?"

Yes.

"No!" I swallowed hard and swiped my face. "Everything's fine. I just hadn't heard from you for . . . a long time! I thought maybe you forgot about me."

I laughed, but it came out like a sob.

"Sweetheart, we've been away—on the cruise and then in St. Croix! Tess's surprise trip for her birthday?"

Of course. Now I remembered, a dim recollection growing brighter, Barry talking excitedly all summer about the cruise tickets he'd bought, in between asking me how I was and if I needed anything. Maybe those phone calls weren't as perfunctory as I'd thought. Maybe I just hadn't been listening.

Relief washed through me.

"How was it? Are you super-tan?"

He ignored the question. "We get back here, and the news is saying you're missing! What's all this about?"

"Missing?" I glanced down at myself to confirm that I still existed.

"Every channel's got the same footage of some event today that had all the Coopers out there except for you."

I'm not a Cooper, Barry. I'm a Quinn. Like you.

"I'll tell you what," he went on. "I don't care what plans

they've got, I'm still your legal guardian, young lady, and I'm not sure I like what I'm seeing on TV."

Now he was really putting on the stern voice. It warmed me right down to my toes. My uncle, who'd never met a phone he didn't hate, had cared enough to spend all day calling the house, hoping to reach me. That was saying something.

The door to the study slammed open.

"Fine." Meg somehow managed to shout quietly. "I'm out of it. I'm done."

And the door shut again.

". . . So you tell me if you're ready to come back, and I'll clear your room out . . ."

"Barry, I've gotta go. I—"

Meg stalked from the hallway to the living room, angrily cleaning an invisible mess, chopping bundles of magazines against the coffee table so they made neat stacks.

"I'll call you back, I promise."

"I'm gonna keep the phone with me. I'm here for you, you know that, kiddo."

I hung up, crept into the living room, and drew a breath. My senior year had started without me. I needed to know what to tell Barry. What to do.

I felt my heart thudding as I approached Meg, approached the moment of truth. My brain scrambled for more excuses, more delays.

But Lou Mankowitz wasn't here to fight this battle for me. I was going to have to fight it myself.

"Meg? We need to talk."

"I know." She looked up at me, her eyes brimming. "You don't have to do this anymore if you don't want to. It was unfair to you from the very beginning."

My resolve faltered. "What?"

She blinked and I kept going.

"No, I—" I swallowed. "I need to know what's going to happen next. School started last week in South Carolina, but if I get back there soon, I can catch up."

Her face wavered with confusion.

My heart beat faster. "But if you want me to stay . . ."

"Of course we—!" She shook her head, looked down at the coffee table. "You need to talk to your father. He's got some things to tell you. But . . ." She let out an angry huff. "Now is not a good time."

Yeah, I thought. *Now is a terrible time. Two weeks ago would have been much better. Or two months . . .*

Meg's cheeks were wet. I touched her shoulder.

"What's going on?"

She stared past me at the study door, her eyes steely. "He fired him."

My pulse raced with hope. "Elliott?"

He deserved it. It was long overdue. He should never have been hired in the first place.

"No." Her eyes met mine and they were dim, like all the humor in them had finally been extinguished. "Lou. He fired Lou."

I thought for a moment that I was just standing there, paralyzed.

But it wasn't the living room around me—it was the hall-

341

way, and that was my hand on the study door, turning the handle and staggering into the room, slapped back into alertness by a blast from the air conditioner and by the senator, slowly swiveling in his office chair to take me in with obvious apprehension.

He leaned back, his face re-forming into that oh-so-familiar expression. Poised. Confident. I spoke before it could fully set in.

"How could you?"

He feigned bewilderment. His acting was getting worse by the minute. And I no longer had it in me to play along.

As I slammed the door shut behind me, he half stood from the desk in alarm.

"Why would you fire Louis? He was your best friend. Your college roommate."

His mouth moved but nothing was coming out.

I stepped closer. "And he *defended* me."

"He *assaulted* a *coworker*." The senator turned back to his computer and started typing. "This isn't your business, Kate."

My hands were shaking, my skin hot against the blast from the vent.

But shaky or not, my hands were bolder than the rest of me. They reached out and slammed the senator's laptop shut. He rolled back, eyebrows raised. One blink, and he managed an almost amused expression, but he still wouldn't look at me.

My eyes were brimming, the whole room flooding, only a few minutes left before the water grew too high for either of us to survive. I braced my hands against the desk, trying to regain control of myself.

"Elliott called me a slut, Dad." I'd expected the word *slut* to hurt, but it was the *Dad* that really cut me. It was a lie. A joke. "He called your daughter a slut. Me. Your kid. And you fired the one person—the *only* person in that whole bus who would defend me. *You* didn't do anything. You . . ." I gasped a breath. "You made a *joke* out of it! And then you acted like it was my fault, like I'd caused the whole thing. Like I'd done anything except just stand there!"

The senator didn't say anything. I could only see his profile, his jaw clenched and temple thumping. A noise came out of me, almost a wail, and he didn't turn. As I blinked, the room drained and my face stung, but I was still suffocating and he wasn't doing a thing to help me.

"I'm your child. Don't you care? You made me, you're part of me, and you don't even care." *Stop talking, please stop talking,* but it was too late to stop. "I have a life, you know, my own life. I'm *supposed* to, anyway. I'm supposed to be going into my senior year. I'm supposed to be studying, graduating, going to college, but you don't care at all. You don't even notice. I might as well not exist. You *wish* I didn't exist!"

"Kate." His face dropped and I thought for one beautiful moment that he was going to tell me I was wrong. That he loved me. That I was overreacting. "It's late." He sighed. Opened his computer and shrugged. "What do you want from me?"

My breath stilled. The tears dried in my eyes so quickly that the room looked crystalline—bright, hard, sharp. It was as though I was seeing the way the world really looked for the very first time.

I considered for what felt like a long moment. It was an important question.

And then I had my answer.

"I want you to look at me."

He stared at the wall. Then away, out the darkened window. And then, finally, he turned and his eyes reached mine and held there. I found myself counting, one . . . two . . . three . . . waiting for something, anything.

We had the same eyes. But his were cold. There was no one there.

"Anything else?"

"Nope." I nodded. "Nothing else."

I wiped my nose on my wrist as I quietly shut the study door behind me and started up the stairs. Meg was waiting for me halfway up, her hands pressed together to her lips like she'd been praying. Slowly, she rose, hope and worry flashing in an alternating current over her face.

"I know you're angry, Kate . . ."

I shook my head. "I'm fine."

"What you were asking about before." She held my arm, her fingers trembling. "We already enrolled you at Farnwell Prep! You're starting on Monday. Mark was supposed to tell you a long time ago—we agreed he'd tell you." She swallowed down her frustration and tried to keep smiling. "We've talked to your uncle Barry and everything's set. He's shipping your things up—"

"We can talk about it tomorrow." I slid past her, my arm dragging behind me along the banister as I climbed.

"Oh." Meg dropped a step. "Okay. You're right. Tomorrow. Everything will look fresher in the morning."

Before I reached the top of the steps, I reconsidered. I hurried back down, and Meg's arms were open, ready, and then she held me tight, smoothing my hair over and over. I closed my eyes, trying to soak up her warmth, the smell of her moisturizer, the sharp line of her glasses against my head.

"Good night, sweetheart," she said.

Later that night, after Meg and the senator had gone to bed, I stood in the hall peering in at the twins, first Gabe, smiling in his sleep and then Gracie, her blond hair sticky with sweat. She'd kicked the covers off the end of her bed, just like every night.

In the back corner of the guest room closet, I found the old blue duffel bag that I'd packed for a weekend back in June. Buried among hanging dresses were the jeans and three T-shirts I'd brought with me from South Carolina. I folded them and put them in the bag.

I slipped in the bird sketch that Gabe had drawn for me, along with the photo of the three of us from *Time* magazine that Meg had had framed. I packed the little star necklace that Gracie had given me and the journal from Gabe, but left the birthday gifts from Meg and the senator behind. I buried the Kudzu Giants record behind a shoebox in the far corner of the closet.

As I went to close the door, my fingers lingered on the cotton dress I'd worn the night of Jake Spinnaker's birthday party. I clutched it hard. Closed my eyes. My breath hurt when it came. *Let it go,* I thought. *Let* him *go.*

I left the dress and shut the door. Then I zipped up the bag and waited.

Just after 1:00 A.M., I silently left my room, glided down the stairs and out the front door, latching the little switch on the handle so it would lock behind me.

Out on the dark porch, I checked the side pocket of my bag for about the tenth time. I still had five twenties in there, the same amount Barry had given me before I left. That should be enough for a bus ticket and a prepaid phone. And if it wasn't, at least it would get me close enough for Barry to come pick me up. It would get me away.

Left out the gate, then turn right when I reach the main road. I knew the route from our many drives into DC. The depot was a few miles down, on the right. It was dark, but the streets would be lit. I hoped there was a sidewalk.

It doesn't matter. Just go.

I started on my way, slowly, stifling the crunch of my feet against the pavers of the front drive.

The moon was almost full, the oaks along the property line casting black shadows against the blue lawn, the wind sending a whisper through their leaves. I fell into such a sad reverie listening to it that I didn't notice the footsteps approaching from the darkness.

I gasped.

The figure was large, approaching at a terrifying speed. But as he got close enough for me to pick out his features, my whole body slumped with relief.

It was James. He exhaled hard, his hand relaxing from the gun on his hip.

"What are you doing out here?" He whispered it, thank goodness. He glanced at the house, then back to me with a suspicious squint. "You're not sneaking out to see the president's kid, are you?"

"No." I shouldered my bag. "I'm going home."

He wavered, confused. "This is your home."

"No, it's not." I inched closer. "My uncle is my legal guardian. I go to school in South Carolina and it started three days ago. I have to get down there."

"At one oh seven in the morning?" He crossed his arms.

"They won't let me go. The campaign. They'll make me stay and I don't want to. I mean—*legally,* they have to let me go. But I'm not sure that'll matter to them."

James let out a slow sigh. I could see his morality meter swishing back and forth.

"Just let me go," I murmured. "I don't belong here."

Holding my breath, I willed my legs to move, one step at a time, past him, toward the gate.

He grabbed my arm. I turned.

"You can't just walk out of here."

I lifted my chin, trying for defiance. "Why not?"

He glared at me. "Because there's a news van parked right outside the driveway waiting for something to happen. You sneaking out? That's something happening."

Blood rushed to my face. "Oh."

"Oh."

I remembered Nancy suddenly, standing in the study,

mocking me, turning against me. But James wasn't Nancy. He was watching me with concern, trying his best to hide a kind smile under the usual tough-guy demeanor.

"Well, I won't go that way then. I'll . . ."

I glanced at the dark garden running beside the house. The fence was only a little higher than the ones I'd scaled in South Carolina, breaking out of the press siege with Tim the Awful Aide that bleary morning in June. *I did it once, I can do it again.*

"You don't want to climb that," James muttered, reading my mind. "There's barbed wire on the other side. And we've got two guards on duty who I didn't train, and therefore can't vouch for. They see somebody on top of that fence, they've got orders to shoot."

This time we said it together. "Oh."

James grinned. I spun around.

"News van it is," I said, and started toward the gate.

Behind me, James groaned. "All right. Where are you going?"

"Greyhound station. There's a bus at two oh seven, so I really need to get—"

"I'm driving." He jangled his keys and motioned for me to follow him back down the drive to where the SUV was parked. "Probably gonna get reassigned to a desk job for this."

"Then don't!" I whispered, slamming to a halt. "It's not worth it."

"You're right." He crossed his arms. "So go upstairs and go back to bed."

I stared him down.

"Didn't think so. We're at an impasse."

As I fastened myself into the passenger seat next to him, James peered ruefully at me over one huge shoulder.

"You know I have to tell them."

I managed a nod.

He sniffed, started the ignition. "But I'll wait until I get back. That'll give you a head start if the bus is on time."

"Thank you."

After I bought my ticket, James drove away. I sat on one of the depot's plastic benches with my duffel bag on my lap and watched the parking lot, waiting for James to come careening back, this time with the senator in the backseat. He'd run out, rip the ticket from my hand, and wrap me in a hug.

He'd apologize, and I'd forgive him.

But the bus was on time. And I got on it.

～34～

I settled into a window seat in the back and watched the world blur, the streetlamps streaking, lonely comets to light our way. When we hit the freeway, it felt like we were flying, like a cord had been cut between us and the station. Between me and DC. Me and the Coopers. Me and Andy. I was free.

It was my choice all along. Meg was right. And I chose to go. I chose *something*.

All around me were strangers traveling south, some transferring with me when we stopped in Richmond a few hours later, others staying behind to wait for buses yet to come, still others greeting family members, husbands, wives before veering off and away, never to be seen again. The sun was up now, bleary behind a curtain of cloud cover.

We stopped in a town called Dillon around noon, and I had time to buy a truck stop burrito and a prepaid phone before hitting the road again.

Nobody looked twice at me. Why should they? I was wearing jeans, my hair in a ponytail, my face bare. And I was on a Greyhound bus, not the Locomotive. Anyone who saw me might think, *Hey, she looks like that politician's daughter,* but that would be it. I was just another traveler, on my own like everybody else, heading to a destination of my choosing.

I began to smile. And on the last long leg into Charleston, I finally allowed myself to sleep, lulled by the now-familiar feeling of the road rolling underneath me and the soft pat of rain against the bus windows.

By the time we pulled into the depot, the sun had come out, bright enough for me to see the parking lot through the misty window. A gleaming black SUV was idling along the loading zone. James stood outside, eyeing the bus with a frown. When we stopped, he ducked his head inside the car to speak to whoever was in the backseat.

I hopped off the bus and waited to pull my bag from the undercarriage, my heart thumping louder and louder.

He'd come. This was his apology, wasn't it? He didn't want me to go. He'd be mad, I was sure, but still—he was here to convince me to come home.

And what would I say?

My bag on my shoulder, I rounded the bus and walked over to greet James, too exhausted to do more than wave. But when the door to the backseat opened, I was suddenly alert as I'd ever be, waiting for my father's reaction.

Meg stepped out, clinging to the car door. Behind her, the backseat was empty.

The last, dingy vestiges of hope blew out of me. I felt curiously weightless, as if I were falling.

Meg's eyes were red-rimmed, her mouth pulled down at the corners. "Get in."

I shook my head.

"Just to talk. I promise."

Inside the car, she grabbed my hands with both of hers, her eyes shining. Maybe it was from lack of sleep, but I had the sense that we were sitting inside a lucid dream. I knew this wasn't real. And I was ready to wake up.

"He's a hard person to get to know," she said, making me think of Lou, how he'd defended the senator that day in HQ, said he was worth it. I wondered if he still felt that way.

Meg winced, knowing it was the wrong thing to say, not the way she'd meant to start.

"I want you to come home. And so do Gabe and Grace."

I raised my eyebrows. "Gracie too?"

"She won't stop crying. Practically clawed her way into the car with me."

That chastened me. "Oh God, I don't want them to be upset. You guys mean a lot to me. It's just really hard . . ." I sucked in a dry breath, struggling to finish the thought. "I can't live with someone who doesn't want me."

Meg grabbed my hand.

"You're wrong about that. This campaign—it's everything right now. It's important."

"To him."

"To *America*."

I blinked up at her, surprised by the seriousness in her expression, the lack of cynicism.

She rested one hand on my knee, steadying me, or maybe herself. "I wouldn't have agreed to any of this—leaving my job, putting the twins out on the road, dragging you into the limelight, if I didn't think your father was *absolutely* the right person to lead this country."

Her smile flickered, a glitch in an old movie.

I sighed, my head falling heavy against the hard, cold window. "I'm not sure, Meg. He gives a good speech. And he's a great listener. Everybody's right about that. But who is he going to be listening to in the White House? Elliott?"

My finger traced a line against the foggy glass. Meg didn't say anything.

"If I were voting in this election . . ." I shook my head. Then I turned to her. "And honestly, Meg? If you weren't married to him, I don't think you'd vote Cooper either."

She let out a little laugh. An admission.

And after a moment, she sighed. "He's a good man. That's what I know."

"But *I* don't know that. I don't know him. After three months, I don't know him at all. And . . . I'm not even sure I want to."

She nodded, her face drawn. My heart pounded from the audacity it took to confess that.

Out the front window, I saw a battered pickup truck pulling into the bus depot, my uncle's faded logo shining like a golden beacon on its dusty side.

"You always told me it was my choice," I said. Meg gripped my hand more tightly, but it didn't sway me. Not this time. "I don't want to do this anymore."

I hoped she knew I didn't mean her.

"Okay." A tear ran down her face, and she swiped it away. She nodded. "Okay. But listen. The press is going to be all over you once they find out where you are. We'll tell them you're up at your grandmother's house in Massachusetts."

She squinted out the windshield, her mind whirring.

"But then they'll all descend on *her*," I said, uneasy.

"She'll be fine," Meg replied, and at her grin I remembered Grandma Evelyn's shotgun and nearly laughed myself.

Meg smoothed my outfit like she was seeing me off for school.

"I'll call and check on you every day." At my expression, she dropped her hands. "Every week, then."

"You'll be busy," I said gently. "And I need some time."

She sunk. It killed me. "Okay."

My uncle had already taken my bag from James and loaded it into the pickup by the time I climbed in beside him. He gave me an awkward bear hug, and when I pulled back, I saw his eyes fixed on Meg's car as it glided out of the parking lot, heading back to the freeway.

"I'm fine," I said. "Let's go home."

~ 35 ~

Monday, September 15
My Delayed First Day of School
WHO CARES HOW MANY DAYS UNTIL THE
GENERAL ELECTION

"You don't know half the trouble you caused . . ."

Tess's hairdresser friend Hildy was a bit of a gossip. I sat on a chair in the bathtub upstairs as she cut my hair and filled me in on the drama that had hit James Island while I was away.

"It was that principal who leaked your school records to the press. She got canned, but they've 'launched an inquiry,' whatever that means." Hildy chuckled. She snipped again. I winced. "I'm surprised you didn't hear about it. Made the news and everything."

So that explained why Palmetto High School was suddenly being so accommodating—allowing me to enroll under an alias and swearing up and down that they'd do their part in keeping the press at bay. I could only hope it would work.

"Done," Hildy said.

I counted to five before I dared look in the mirror. And then I gasped. I looked like someone else. My hair was bobbed now, grazing my chin. With the afternoon glow streaming through the pink shower curtain, it looked lighter, redder, the color of sunset.

I looked just like Mom.

Clutching the sides of the sink, I steadied myself, fighting the feeling of longing that had just swept over me. When I looked up again, I saw my own face, and found myself pressing my fingers to the glass of the medicine cabinet, as if it would bring her image back.

Mom resemblance aside, this haircut was a smart decision. It wouldn't fool anybody who'd already met me, of course, but from a distance, no one would think I was the infamous Kate Quinn Cooper.

Mid-September in South Carolina was too hot for jeans. Before I left for school, I rifled through my tiny closet until I found the one sundress in my wardrobe, then nervously checked myself out in the bathroom mirror.

This time, it wasn't my mother I saw. The girl in the reflection was me. And I liked this me. Not me from a year ago, or from before my mom died, or from the campaign trail. This was who I was today, the first day of my senior year.

And today, I was a girl who wore skirts.

When I parked my Buick in one of the senior spaces in the school lot, I scanned the road for a news van, a camera, a group of people who weren't wearing backpacks, any sign that the press had figured out I wasn't living with a cantankerous old lady on an organic farm in rural Massachusetts. But so far, Meg's ruse seemed to be working. I just hoped that Evelyn hadn't shot anyone yet.

The school looked unfamiliar to me, like I'd maybe visited it once or twice, but definitely hadn't taken classes there for nine whole months. Had I somehow managed to sleepwalk through my entire junior year?

In the lobby, I felt heads pivot, heard wisps of conversation attach themselves to me. Adjusting my backpack, I turned to see a clutch of junior girls smiling nervously in my direction. One of them waved and they all looked away, giggling.

So much for the haircut.

"Kate!" Lily Hornsby tapped me on the shoulder. "Oh, whoops." She dropped her voice to a whisper. "Should I be saying 'Katie'?"

So she'd gotten the memo. I hugged her, grinning.

"I think Kate is probably safe."

"Is it weird to be back?" She held the door for me as I searched my schedule for my locker number. Before I could answer, her giant boyfriend Scott careened around the corner with two other friends and kissed the top of her head. She turned beet red.

"Nice to have you back, *Katie* . . ." Scott joked. "We're hitting the movies this Friday. You down?"

"Sure." I smiled. "Sounds good."

Everyone looked surprised.

When I got back to Barry's house, his truck was in the driveway, but the house was eerily quiet. It took me a long beat to realize why. The TV was off.

I found Barry pacing the kitchen, looking for something to do, Tess shooing him away in irritation.

"You're not watching the news," I said.

He shrugged. "Didn't feel like it tonight."

I raised my eyebrows, unconvinced. He and Tess were trying to protect me, I knew, creating their own version of

Meg's campaign-free zone. It was probably just what I needed, but as the night wore on, I couldn't help wondering. And then mulling. And then obsessing.

Where were the Coopers today? On the road or getting ready for school to start? How had they explained my absence? Did they miss me?

When I thought about them, I felt a physical ache deep in my chest, as if leaving them had actually damaged my heart. It was a different sensation than what I felt about Mom, sharper but less draining.

It was sharper than the Andy Lawrence pain too, but oh man, that one lingered. I knew from his silence that Meg was right—that he'd used and discarded me. But that realization wasn't enough to block him from my mind. He popped up ruthlessly, in dreams sometimes, but in waking life too— passing a barbecue stand, hearing Kudzu Giants on the radio. Even vending machines reminded me of him. And my school had a lot of vending machines.

After a few days back, Lily shyly opened her locker, revealing a brand-new magazine photo of a *Triplecross* actor. I raised my eyebrows.

"No more Andy Lawrence, huh?" I asked, trying to keep the pain out of my voice.

"I don't like the way he treated you," she said, her chin raised in indignation. I gave her a grateful nudge, but as we rounded the corner into the hallway, she couldn't resist leaning over to whisper, "Was he a good kisser?"

I had to admit he was. And then I had to dig my nails into my palm for all of first period just to stop thinking about that kiss, daydreaming about it as if it were something I wanted to happen in the future, rather than an actual, disastrous, humiliating memory that I was dying to put behind me.

Then came the phone call.

Three weeks into the school year, Scott organized a study session for our first big calculus test, and when more people signed up than could fit in his house, I offered to host. Tess was thrilled—she baked cookies and fussed around the living room until Barry dragged her away. At first it unnerved me to sit here with my classmates, thinking about the last big gathering in this room, the way every eye had been fixed on the suited man in the armchair. But the more bodies and cheerful voices that were filling the room tonight, the more that memory faded like an Etch A Sketch drawing being shaken away.

Lily was struggling to describe Rolle's Theorem when my aunt crept in again. This time, she tapped on my shoulder.

"Phone for you."

Thinking a straggler was calling in the hopes of joining our group, I hurried to the phone to give directions, and kept one eye on the living room in case their conversation got ahead of me.

"Quinn." The voice on the other end of the line let out a melodramatic groan. "You are one tough person to track down."

My body went from hot to cold in a blink.

Andy. He'd found me. He'd called.

A month too late.

I scowled into the flowery wallpaper. "And how did you get this number?"

"I don't know if I've mentioned that my dad is the president?"

Funny. "Why are you calling me?"

"Because I'm finally allowed to."

My pulse jumping, I kicked the door to the living room quietly shut. "Explain."

He laughed ruefully. "They were pretty pissed off back in Kansas, Quinn. In order to help your friend, I had to tell them that we'd been hanging out. And . . ." He cleared his throat. "That I had these *feelings* for you. My dad didn't take that so well. But he did help—in his own, special, completely politicized way. Which . . ." I could hear him swallowing, his next breath shaky. "Yeah. Which I'm really sorry about. I—I had no idea it was gonna go that way, and I should have. I've been at this long enough to not be a total idiot, but it does happen from time to time." He let out a nervous laugh. Then went quiet.

My head was spinning. "So this wasn't . . . some trick?"

"What?" He sounded legitimately confused. "Wait—have you been watching Fox News? Quinn, come on now."

"Then why didn't you call me?" My hand gripped the ancient kitchen phone so tight that the plastic started creaking. "It's been a long time, Andy."

30 days, 22 hours, to be exact. Not that I was counting.

"I've been grounded. No phone access. *Supervised* Internet time. Yeah, I know, but—it's the White House. No shortage of supervision. Anyway, school started and they decided my punishment was over. Especially since you'd dropped off the radar. I thought you were locked up like me in the Cooper compound or wherever, but your stepmom told me you'd left . . ."

"Meg?" I stood up straighter. "She gave you this number?"

"Yeah, after I explained the seriousness of the situation, she—well, she hung up on me. But then I called back. I think it was the twelfth call that really won her over. You know how persistent I can be when the situation calls for it."

"And this situation called for twelve phone calls?" I had to press the heel of my hand against the countertop, bracing against his riptide pull.

"Thirteen. Fourteen, including this one." He chuckled anxiously. "Ummmm, did you not hear me say I had feelings for you? Do I need to spell them out?"

Yes! I thought, but before I could say it, he cut me off.

"It's a neat trick you pulled there, Quinn. Everybody thinks you're up in Massachusetts being *handled*. But you broke out. I'm jealous."

"It helps to have an uncle who's got custody of you."

"I'm gonna look into that. Or I might just sneak out and turn up at your uncle's doorstep asking for asylum. Don't laugh, I'm seriously considering it."

"Say you're sorry again." I slid until I was sitting cross-legged on the linoleum, grinning like the fool I was, knowing already that this battle was lost, over, done.

Andy didn't miss a beat. "How many times?"

"Just once. For now."

"I'm really, really sorry—that I trusted my asshole father and that we had the shitty luck to kiss within range of a telephoto lens and that I didn't manage to sneak out and call you sooner. And I am also encouraged by the fact that you just said 'for now,' implying that I will have further opportunities to apologize. And to say that I miss you. A lot."

I skipped the rest of the study session. I was right there in the room with my classmates, idly turning pages of the textbook, lost in daydreams of Andy showing up incognito, knocking on my door in his Farnwell uniform with a duffel bag slung across one shoulder. Even though it was a ludicrous thought, an impossible one, it was a fun image to hold on to.

Of course, there was also still a chance he was lying—calling me tonight out of boredom or lingering habit or mischief. There were plenty of reasons not to trust Andy Lawrence. But it occurred to me suddenly that trust wasn't an object, not something that arrived on your doorstep, solid and absolute. It was a decision, a leap. And if it was up to me, then here was my choice—I believed Andy.

He hadn't betrayed me. He did have *feelings*. And just because they weren't likely to lead anywhere didn't mean that they didn't matter.

We picked up where we left off. Except every time Andy called and my aunt or uncle answered, he claimed to be a classmate named Benjamin.

"Anybody who uses the full name Benjamin has got to be an upstanding young gentleman," Andy told me. "He's probably an Eagle Scout. He's in the Junior PGA and tutors third graders on his lunch break."

Whether it was the name or the voice, Tess was charmed. She kept asking when I was going to invite Benjamin over for dinner, whether we were planning to go to the homecoming dance together. It was a fun game, a reminder of how we became friends. Still, the further it went, the more petty it felt—especially when Uncle Barry was the one to answer the phone.

"May I ask who's calling?" His face shifted between enthusiasm and puffed-up protectiveness with every blink. "Well, Benjamin, she's doing her homework, but I think she'll be glad to take a break for a few minutes. Kate?"

He always hung around for a few seconds after he handed me the phone, like he was yearning for me to confide in him. It didn't feel right to keep lying. But when I finally confessed who was really calling, his bright eyes narrowed.

"That kid seems like bad news to me. On Fox & Friends, they said—"

I grinned. "That's just the Cooper campaign, Barry. They tried to make him look bad so I'd look better. It's spin, that's all."

He wasn't easily persuaded.

So when the phone rang the next night, and I heard my uncle in hushed conversation behind the swinging kitchen door, I leaned against the wall to hear what he was saying.

"She's not ready to talk to you, sir." His voice was tense, an uneasy mix of defensiveness and deference. "Like I said before, I'm looking out for her best interests here. I'm sure you understand. She's doing great. I'll keep you posted."

He hung up and I ducked down the hallway—then took a step back, reeling as I realized who had been on the other side of that phone call.

Like I said before, Barry said. How many times had my uncle turned him away? Had the senator been calling since I got here?

The next day, I got up the nerve to turn on the TV. And not just the TV—the news. My aunt and uncle sat quietly next to me on the sofa, watching me instead of it. I tried to remain impassive, a calm observer, but soon found myself clutching the remote and flipping frantically between channels, catching every little bit I could, barely understanding the context.

The senator's numbers had dropped off a cliff. For the past few weeks, he'd been trailing the president by double digits, and tonight, every station was reporting more bad news.

"The resignation of Calvin Montgomery comes as another huge blow to the Cooper campaign," one pundit was saying, and then on another channel, a reporter chimed in with, ". . . weeks after Cooper fired his chief strategist, Elliott Webb, insiders tell us that the campaign is in near-complete disarray."

I turned the volume up, my jaw hanging open.

I shouldn't have been happy. This news spelled disaster for the senator's campaign. But it set my heart racing, sent me scooting to the edge of the sofa as if that would help me learn more.

They showed press footage of Elliott, surrounded by paparazzi as he entered a restaurant in DC. He looked uncomfortable. I felt a rush of sweet vengeance, until the reporter talked over the reel—describing the multi-million-dollar book deal that Elliott had just signed.

He was a political animal, Meg had said. Whatever species that was, I supposed it was the kind that always landed on its feet.

Despite the sour taste that that bit of news had left in

my mouth, I went to bed feeling lighter than I had since the night I left the Coopers' house, and woke the next day restless with hope.

Emboldened by the news-scanning session of the night before, Tess had a confession to make. As I was riffling through my World History textbook, she tiptoed into my uncle's office carrying a tome of her own—but hers had a thick cover decorated with sparkly American flags. She laid it shyly on the desk next to me.

"I hope you don't mind," she said. "I started this while you were gone."

My face was in the middle of all of the flags—judging by the makeup, a photo of me from some campaign visit somewhere. And when I turned the page, there was another shot, me at the press conference, speaking into the microphone, and alongside it, a press clipping from a Charleston newspaper.

"You made a scrapbook?" I stared at the book to hide my chagrin. "Tess, that's so . . . sweet!"

The next page held another photo of me, standing beside the senator outside of a white, wooden town hall, overlapping with a clipping from a *USA Today* profile. She'd put little hearts all around it.

"We were so proud," she said, then corrected herself. "*Are* so proud. I just thought you might want to take a look."

After she left, I tried to get back to my homework, but my eyes kept veering to the scrapbook. With a groan, I decided to flip through and get it over with. After all, it was pretty touching that Tess had put all this effort in.

It was fun too, I had to admit, seeing it all laid out in the order it happened. Me on the road. In DC, Nancy just inside the frame. With the whole family in the airfield in Massachusetts. The *Time* magazine cover story got four pages all to itself. My eyes lingered over the shot of me, Gabe, and Gracie, as if I could reach in and pull them out of it, wrap my hands around that moment and clutch it to me.

Somewhere near the middle of the scrapbook was a strange document—not a press clipping or a photo, but a printed-out e-mail, with pressed flowers for a border. I flipped back and angled the desk light to get a better look.

It was from the senator. He'd sent it to Barry in mid-July, updating my uncle on how I was doing. It was the last paragraph that really caught my attention.

I'll never be able to replace her mother. And I'll never be able to get back the seventeen years that we lost not knowing each other. I won't be able to rewind time and see her walk for the first time, or laugh, or ride a bike, or even call me "Dad." But I wanted you and Tess to know how grateful I am for the opportunity you've given me to get to know her now. You're her home and her base, and I respect that. But let me reassure you once more that she's in watchful hands, surrounded by a family that already loves her very much.

All my best,
Mark Cooper

That night, I followed a hunch to the TV room, where, as I'd suspected, Barry and Tess still had the Shawna Wells interview saved on the DVR.

With a trembling hand, I pressed PLAY.

❦ 36 ❦

Friday, October 31
Palmetto High School Halloween
Aka: Alert! Kate Cooper Lives in South Carolina! Day
4 DAYS UNTIL THE GENERAL ELECTION

Thank God I decided not to wear a costume to school, because the morning of October 31, half the reporters in South Carolina figured out where I'd been hiding for the past month.

When I pulled into the lot, I saw the mob of them lurking just off school property, following the letter of the law, but to cross from my car to campus meant passing right by them. I contemplated mussing my hair or keeping my sunglasses on despite the cloudy day, but sensing the jig was up, I lifted my chin, checked my teeth in the rearview, and stepped out of my dilapidated Buick with my spine straight and smile in place.

I got halfway through their receiving line before they even realized I was there. They must not have been expecting a bobbed haircut. Then the noise hit me like a sonic boom, my name, over and over, voices raised with questions. I waved cheerily, letting it blur, walking past with as upbeat an expression as I could muster.

Just across the school property line, Lily Hornsby stood shell-shocked, wearing a pair of fairy wings over an otherwise normal outfit.

I let my smile drop away. "They found me."

"This is what you deal with all the time?" She glanced over her shoulder, then covered her face with her hands. "Ohmigod. They're taking my picture too!"

She was bright red and shrinking. I couldn't help but laugh.

"Watch," I said, then turned and waved at the group of photographers. "If they come after you, just smile and wave and walk away. You get used to it, trust me."

Lily turned very slowly, her eyes still huge as saucers. Slowly, her hand lifted and her cheeks did too.

"Smile and wave," she repeated, after we were safely inside the air-locked walls of our school lobby. "Got it."

I talked to Penny later that night, after I'd gotten off trick-or-treat duty and claimed my spoils in leftover Snickers. There were a lot left over. No one had come to the door. No one could get through the wall of reporters surrounding the house.

As usual, Penny didn't mince words.

"*What* are you still *doing* there?"

I shrugged. "Where else should I be?"

"At your house. In *Maryland.*"

I popped another mini candy bar into my mouth. "I haven't been invited."

"You told me Meg invited you. She enrolled you at that snooty school."

"Farnwell. It's actually not that snooty."

"So why aren't you there?"

"My father hasn't asked me." I sighed. "You don't understand, Pen. You don't come from the mother of all broken homes." She was silent for so long that I hastily added, "Don't get me wrong, I'm *glad* you don't. You're lucky that you can't understand."

Penny was quiet for another moment before she said, "Do you remember Zach Burgis?"

"Of course," I answered, not sure where she was going with this. Zach was Penny's boyfriend for a year before turning out to be a complete jerk. She'd lost her virginity to him the summer before I left.

"The week after we broke up, Papi was looking for something in my room and . . . he found a pack of condoms." She drew in a breath, the memory still raw for her. "Papi wouldn't talk to me. Just stopped looking at me, like I was dead to him. Avoided me until dinner, and then he stared at his plate or talked to Eva the whole time, every single night. I tried to get through to him, but he was so cold, I couldn't do it."

I listened in shock. They'd seemed fine when I'd visited.

"The day your mom died," she went on, and my heart seized up. "We got the call and Papi—he walked straight into my room and hugged me so tight and so long that I started to get nervous. He was crying—for her, for your mom of course, and for you—but I feel like he was crying for us too. And we've slowly gotten back to normal since then." Penny's voice was thick. I could picture her clenching her fists to fight back tears, like when we were little. "My point is—it's tough no matter what. Fathers, daughters? It's just tough. It is. But . . ."

I knew what she was going to say, but I closed my eyes, needing to hear it.

"You'll never have the chance to work this stuff out unless you *give* yourself the chance."

I smiled, missing my best friend like never before. "Is that your two cents, Penny?"

Penny tried to groan but laughed instead. *"Shut up."*

I ran into my uncle in the hallway as he was heading for bed. "Hey Barry? Next time my dad calls? I'll speak to him."

Barry nodded gravely, but as he turned away, I saw the beginnings of a smile on his face.

That night, the senator didn't call. He didn't call the next day either. Or the day after that.

I watched the news and understood why. It was the weekend before the general election, and he was everywhere at once, making as many appearances as humanly possible to try to shore up votes for the big day.

He'd wait to call again until after the election. And I was okay with that.

Andy more than made up for the lack of parental phone contact. He was out on the road with the Reelect Lawrence machine and going more than a little buggy.

"I'm losing it here, Quinn. If I have to wave one more time, my arm is going to fall off. I'm telling you. Save me a spot for dinner. I'm hijacking the copter and coming down there."

As I drove home from school the Monday of election week, I laughed to myself, remembering the hopeless desperation in Andy's voice on the phone the night before—but when I turned onto our street and stared out the windshield in disbelief, the grin melted right off my face.

The whole street was cordoned off. There were police cars at either edge of the block keeping traffic away, and between them I saw no press vans whatsoever. I thought for a second that Tess had called the cops, trying to keep her day-care parents happy. But then I saw the Town Car parked in our driveway, and suited Secret Service agents pacing the sidewalk, talking into earpieces.

I smacked the dashboard with a holler. Somehow, against all odds, Andy Lawrence had made good on his promise—*and* brought his entire security detail with him.

And he was calling me right now, on my newly acquired, Barry-approved cell phone, probably to find out where I was. I clicked speakerphone.

"Andrew H. Lawrence, I salute you! You are *the* best prankster in the world."

"Why, thank you! Do I get a plaque?"

After a quick glance through the driver's-side window, the police moved the barricade to let me through. I turned into the driveway a little too sharply, the brakes screeching as I came to a giddy stop.

"You're in a good mood," Andy said. He sounded confused—he must not have seen my car pull up yet.

"You're never going to stop gloating about this, are you?" I danced to the front door and turned the knob.

But it wasn't Andy in the living room, rising from that

same armchair, his eyes wavering, fearful, hopeful, lost, just like that day back in June.

My phone was still making noise. "Okay, Quinn? I have a shocking admission to make . . ." Andy's voice seemed to fade. "I have no idea what you're talking about."

"Hey," I murmured. "I'm gonna have to call you back."

This time, the senator wasn't wearing a suit. He had on a polo shirt and a pair of khakis, an outfit he seemed much more comfortable in. As comfortable as he could be, given the circumstances.

"Hiya, kiddo," he said.

"I'm gonna give you a minute," Barry said, ducking out of the room so fast I only saw a blur of leg before the door swung shut behind him.

All I could get out was a soft "Hi."

The senator returned to the armchair and I sat opposite him on the stiff, faded love seat that Tess loved so well.

His mouth opened, then shut again. His brow furrowed. But just as I was beginning to dread that this conversation would be a repeat of all the other empty ones, his voice shot out of him, low and clear.

"I don't like the way we left things, Kate." He leaned forward, elbows on his knees. "I don't like the fact that we 'left things' at all."

My eyes sank to my feet. My pulse had just jumped, flooding me with a muddled mix of guilt and defiance, so I didn't quite trust myself to speak.

When I looked up again, his blue eyes were trained on

me, waiting for me to meet them. And I saw something stirring behind them. Something real. Despite the security surrounding us, my uncle and aunt probably pressing their ears against the wall in the neighboring room, I had the sense that this was the most private conversation I'd ever shared with my father.

Because this is my father, I realized. *It's not the candidate. It's the human being.*

"Elliott's off the campaign," he said.

"I know." My voice burst back to life. "I've been watching the news—"

"To be honest, Kate," he interrupted, "I think I'm off the campaign too."

I shifted on the love seat, confused. "But the election's tomorrow. You can't just give up."

"Oh, I'll show up. I'll give it all I've got. I owe a lot of people that much. But I think what I'm saying is—whatever happens, I'm going to be okay."

He reached out and took my hand.

"And *we'll* be okay too."

It felt comforting to hold on to him, but I pulled back, still uneasy. He winced, thought for a moment, and nodded as if in recognition.

"I've got a lot of apologizing to do. More than I can possibly fit into this conversation. But I want to start by saying that I know I took my focus off of what was most important. Not just you—Meg, Gracie, Gabe." He raised his eyebrows. "Evelyn too, I suppose."

I smiled faintly in reply.

"You know that," he went on. "You as good as called me on it. But what you don't know, Kate, is that I started doing it a long time ago."

He bit his lip, struggling with how to continue, and sensing that he needed to get it out in his own time, I put my hands to my knees and waited.

"I met your mom in the middle of my first campaign," he said, and the room seemed to swirl around us. "She was a poli-sci major. I don't know if she ever told you that, but at the time, she wanted to go into politics and she saw the campaign as a learning opportunity. And at the same time . . ." He glowed with the memory, but there was pain mixed with it. "She was the most idealistic person I'd ever met in my life. Now, don't get me wrong, I was a true believer. I was on a crusade from day one. But she made me look like an empty suit."

His smile faded. He glanced down at himself with an expression of disgust before going on.

"She was beautiful too, Kate. I'm not going to sugarcoat it. I was drawn to her and she was drawn to me. And we were away from home and . . . we slipped."

He shook his head at my expression, whatever it was—shock, fascination, fear.

"I need you to know this—I *never* stopped loving Meg. She was working long hours, teaching undergrads while getting her PhD, and she was not about to derail her career to follow me around on the local campaign trail. I respected her for it, frankly. And I missed her all the time. But . . ." He swallowed, a sheen of sweat appearing on his forehead. "I fell in love with your mother too. It was impossible not to."

I had to look away from him. I'd wanted to know and honestly longed to hear these very words, despite how much I cared for Meg. If we had to choose, we'd all choose to be born out of love, wouldn't we? But now, sitting here, it was a horror to hear it. It was too honest, even for me.

"This is not an excuse," he said. "And it would be a lie to say it was the whole story. The truth is, I took advantage of your mom. I was thirty. She was a child."

I glanced up at him, about to argue, but his eyebrows were raised.

"She was only a few years older than you are now, Kate."

"Okay," I admitted. "That is a little creepy."

He laughed. It died quickly.

"I was ashamed of it. Of her. I turned my back on her and she moved on and I never looked her up again. It was the right thing for my marriage, but now, of course . . ." He motioned to me and I nodded, understanding. "Whoever I was before that, I buried it. I told myself that that man was weak. That man slipped—didn't keep his word, and even worse, he'd betrayed his own goals and aspirations, what he'd worked so hard for. I told myself that from that point on, I would keep myself moving forward with a kind of tunnel vision, doing whatever it took—in order to *serve*. But you know?" He let out a low whistle. "I wasn't serving. I was just winning."

His voice was full of bitterness, his hands scraping against each other, picking themselves apart, a battle of nails and skin. I reached out and held them.

"You've done a lot of good for a lot of people," I said. "I've seen it. You care—you actually do—and that's not something a lot of people can say."

There was something so pained about the way he peered across our linked hands at me, like he was allowing himself to hope, to feel for the first time in a long time.

"I had trouble with you, Kate," he said, and I started to lean away, but he held on. "Not because of you. You were perfect. *Are* perfect. You're considerate, moral, brave. But you reminded me . . ." He couldn't finish.

I swallowed through a dry throat. "Of her."

"No." He blinked. "Of *me*. Who I used to be. Somebody who would stick up for his friends, even if it was risky. Somebody who put other people first. Somebody who . . ." He let out a helpless laugh. "Somebody who screwed up a lot."

I blushed, but a smile fought its way through. "*That* sounds a little like me."

"And a lot like me. I wasn't ready to look hard at myself, but I think I am now. And I want you to know that."

I considered for a moment. There was something else I needed to ask.

"In the interview with Shawna Wells . . ." I pressed my lips together, suddenly shy, confessing that I'd watched it. He nodded encouragement. "Meg said that, right before that first campaign, you were trying to have a child?"

I didn't finish the story, but remembered it vividly. In the interview, they'd said that they couldn't conceive. They believed the timing was wrong then because I was the child that was supposed to be born. It was one of many parts of that interview that I'd found myself replaying over and over again, partly to make sense of it all, and partly just to spend more time with the Coopers, even if it was only over a TV screen.

"That's all true." The senator's expression made it clear that he was answering the question I hadn't asked. "We've talked about that a lot. And, you know, I wish your mom were still here. It's not fair that she isn't. But Meg and I both feel that you were meant to be our daughter too. Even after having Grace and Gabriel—in a sense, we were always waiting for you. And then there you were. Now—" He drew in a breath. "It took us a few weeks to see it that way. We needed to get past the shock. When we first found out about you, neither of us was able to think clearly. Well. I wasn't, anyway."

I could tell from the intensity in his eyes that he was apologizing. Nancy was right, then. He'd wanted to hush me up. And he was ashamed of it now.

So maybe he'd panicked that day in June. Maybe it was too much for him to process, so he'd reverted to political strategy, until Nancy talked sense into him. Honestly, I myself had expected him to disavow me. I'd been shocked when he invited me to DC.

Now I knew. The senator's heart wasn't in the right place then. But so what? I could see it today, beating, right here in front of me.

My fingers were shaking, so I slid them under my knees. "In the interview, you also said that being a parent is a more important job than being president."

I hoped I didn't sound too reproachful. That wasn't how I felt. Not now.

"I meant that too," he said. "But—I *understand* it a lot better now. I hope I can find a way to apologize in the way you deserve. I hope you give me that chance."

"Well . . ." I raised my eyebrows. "I can think of a good place to start."

He saw the humor in my eyes and smiled. "I'm sorry, Kate."

Then he peered at me, sad and nervous, and so hopeful.

"You're right, you know," I finally said.

He cocked his head, confused. I drew a breath.

"Whatever happens? We're going to be okay."

He beamed, gave my hands another squeeze, and stood, offering me a hand up.

"I'm heading to the airport in twenty minutes. Everybody's waiting for you on the plane—Gabe, Gracie, Meg. Will you come with me?" He stuck his hands in his trouser pockets and rocked on his heels, a nervous dance. "I want you with us for election night, Kate. I need my family with me. My *whole* family."

My mind whirred with images of past election nights on the news. They tended to be swanky affairs, no matter the outcome, so I'd need something formal to wear. My heart started to beat faster just thinking about it.

"What should I pack?" I asked.

He smiled. "Everything."

Tuesday, November 4
Election Day

When I woke up in the Coopers'—no—*our* farmhouse in Massachusetts, it took me a few bleary seconds to realize where I was, how I'd gotten here, what day it was, and why, exactly Gracie was sitting cross-legged at the end of my bed.

"Good morning," she said, then launched herself over the mattress to tackle me in a power-hug.

I glanced over her shoulder to check on my hanging garment bag. The gown was intact.

She murmured hot into my shoulder, "You're still here."

I leaned away, peering into her worried eyes. "Of course I am."

Gracie's expression clouded and I felt guilt pulse through me. She was making sure I'd stayed the night. The last time we'd been under the same roof when she went to bed, I wasn't there in the morning. How could I have put her through that?

"I have bad dreams sometimes," she said, picking at a loose thread in my quilt. "Like, the same dream, a lot? That Daddy goes to work, and I'm watching him, and sometimes he's walking but sometimes he's driving, and then he disappears and none of us can find him. And we look and look, but . . ."

"That's kind of what happened with me, huh?"

She nodded. "I wasn't nice to you all the time, so I thought maybe you didn't want to be my sister anymore."

I felt my eyes stinging, and then Gracie, seeing me crying, started to tear up too. "No, Gracie." I grabbed her hands. "It was never about you. You're the best."

She looked dubious.

"Look." I dug into the neck of my pajamas and pulled out the little star necklace she'd given me for my birthday. Her eyes widened to see it. "I wore this almost every day while I was away. It reminded me of my sister. Kept me from feeling so lonely."

"But you're not going away anymore."

"No." I grabbed her pinkie in a promise. "I'm not."

We all got ready together, eating breakfast in private before the campaign machine started up for one last day. As Gracie ran from the kitchen to give the senator a fresh mug of coffee, I caught a glimpse of her face—the eagerness in it, the need. And like that, all of my sister's bizarre actions from the past few months suddenly made perfect sense. She was just like me—terrified of losing her family, of not knowing her place within it, of having it all slip away.

As we waited outside the polling place in Boston where the senator and Meg were casting their votes, I held Gracie's and Gabe's hands tightly. A cameraman swiveled toward us and I raised their arms high and led them in a cheer that the gathered crowd caught and amplified. The day was sunny and crisp, the sky a deep, autumn blue. I couldn't help but feel optimistic.

The campaign had taken out a few suites in a swanky Boston hotel. In a few hours' time, its ballroom would be full of supporters, ready to cheer the next President of the United States or to mourn together their candidate's loss. I tried not to think too hard about either scenario as I changed into my last official campaign dress. It was BCBG, deep green—my favorite—and just the right mix of conservative and flirty. Meg and I had gone to a local boutique after hours last night to pick it out together. She fussed over the dress for a proud moment before returning to Gabe's clip-on tie.

I snapped a quick selfie and texted it to Tess, who'd made me promise to send more photos for her to add to the last blank pages of my scrapbook. The senator had invited them up to Boston to join us for Election Night, but they'd exchanged a panicked, completely intimidated glance before politely declining.

"You enjoy some time to yourselves as a family," Barry had said. "We'll be rooting for you from here."

We had managed to talk them into coming up to DC for Thanksgiving, though. It was nice to have that to look forward to, no matter what happened tonight.

In the suite next door, I heard voices and the dull drone of the TV. As soon as Gracie was done admiring her freshly curled ringlets in the mirror, we headed over. Past the door, I saw a wall of strangers. No Nancy, no Elliott, no Cal. Not even Libby. But as I was glancing at the TV, where Texas had just popped up red on a large digital map, I felt a shy tap on my shoulder.

It was Tim the Sullen Aide—but somehow, he didn't look as grumpy as I remembered. He was wearing a lanyard bearing a new, higher-level campaign title and a twitchy smile that I had never before witnessed.

"It's so good to see you!" I said, a little surprised by how much I meant it. "I wasn't sure how many people I'd know tonight."

He shook his head with that trademark Tim scowl. "A bunch of people left with Cal. He had a 'job offer he couldn't refuse' from Nancy's new company. It couldn't wait until after the election? *Coward.*" He said it with such venom that I thought for a second he was going to spit on the carpet. "Anyway. *Some* of us know what loyalty means."

I followed his eyes across the room and was rewarded with the most beautiful sight in the world—a short, bald, middle-aged man cracking a joke while pointing at the TV screen. The senator was quipping back, laughing easily. I could tell by the notable absence of a cell phone in Lou's hand that he wasn't here in an official capacity. He must have come as a friend.

It was no wonder the room felt so light, so relaxed and upbeat, despite the fact that the United States map on TV was getting bluer by the minute.

As the evening became night, even Lou couldn't keep the mood from sinking. Meg sat next to the senator, rubbing his knee when wins came in—and when yet another loss was announced. The senator's face got tighter and tighter, the pain behind the practiced smile impossible to disguise.

Just yesterday, he'd said he would be fine either way, but I saw now that the truth was a lot more complicated than that. This was his dream. And it was evaporating.

Gabe was the first to catch on.

"He's not winning, is he?" When I replied that it was still early, he shot me a look that was way older than his years.

Once the reality became impossible to ignore, the suite emptied out, except for me, Meg, the twins, and Lou—the new inner circle. The senator sat on the sofa with the TV muted, making phone call after phone call to his most loyal supporters and Republican colleagues, thanking them for all the work they'd done in the past year. I couldn't believe how well he was holding it together. One deep breath between calls and he would dial again, his voice upbeat, full of genuine appreciation for each person on the other end of the line.

In the face of devastation, he was doing his job. Watching him now, I saw what all those cheering crowds saw in my father, and suspected sadly that he might have made a great president after all.

At around midnight, they called it. We nudged the twins awake, left the suite, and rode the elevator in silence. At floor ten, I reached out for the senator's hand. He held on until we got to the ground floor.

The hotel ballroom was packed with cheerfully dressed supporters. Music played, the bar served drinks, the stage was colorfully festooned, a huge COOPER FOR AMERICA banner covered the wall, but there was no celebration at this party. The air was thick with stunned disappointment. It was like being on a cruise ship that had just learned it was sinking.

Tim held us in the wings until the cue came through on his earpiece, then waved us on with a sympathetic sniff.

We stood behind the senator while he gave his concession speech, the McReadys lined up beside us. Carolee's mascara was running. She'd been crying. I liked her better for it.

The senator's speech was so simple, direct, and lovely, that I knew he'd written it himself. The audience cheered as loudly as they had at any of his early rallies. It was disorienting. When we left, waving at the crowd, Gracie looked around, confused and upset.

"He's not going to be president?"

"No, sweetie," I said, squeezing her hand.

Her forehead knotted as she fought to form the next logical question. "Is it going to be okay?"

We all looked to Meg for the answer. She was watching the ballroom, where people were hugging each other, wiping their cheeks, patting shoulders, and waving good-bye—and where her husband was shaking hands with well-wishers, saying thank you one last time. Meg's expression was raw with grief. But then she turned to us, taking us in as if evaluating us academically. And at last, she smiled.

"You kidding?" She rumpled Gracie's hair, but her eyes were on me—a promise. "It's gonna be great."

∽ EPILOGUE ∽

Friday, March 24
A Perfectly Ordinary Day
140 DAYS SINCE THE CAMPAIGN ENDED

"So you're telling me you don't want to meet the Prime Minister of England."

I laughed, shouldering my backpack. "Yes, Andy, I want to meet the Prime Minister of the *United Kingdom*—"

"See? This is why I need you."

"But I'm not sure it's—"

"It's not like you haven't been to the White House before."

"This is different." I shook my head. "That was your living room. This is a *state dinner*. It's a . . . big public thing."

"And?" He smiled, teasing.

"And . . . I don't think it's a good idea to stay out so late the night before a calculus test."

He opened the door for me and we emerged onto the gleaming front lawn of Farnwell Prep, its borders bright with the spring's first tentative blooms.

"Such a goody-goody." He slung his arm around me. "You know the rest of the year doesn't matter, right? You've already sent in your application. And you're Mark Cooper's kid. Legacy goldmine."

"You're one to talk."

"Well." He grinned. "I didn't say I was worried about *my* chances either."

"Yes." I turned to face him, spotting the limo rounding the long circular drive to the school, a small presidential seal emblazoned on its side. "I'll come to the dinner."

"Dress sharp." Andy squinted in mock-concern and I swatted him away, but he caught my wrist and pulled me in for a kiss. The bite of the wind vanished as I nestled into him, feeling one of his hands steady against my waist, the other tracing my arm. I could have stayed like that forever, but behind us, Jake Spinnaker led a group of onlookers in a round of wolf whistles and we broke apart, blushing.

Andy pointed at me. "See you Sunday, Quinn."

I drove home in my trusty old Buick with the windows down, euphoria dampened by the dread I felt at the prospect of bringing up Andy's invitation. Never mind that it came from Andy, still not exactly their top choice of boyfriend material for me, even after five months of on-the-record dating. This was an invitation to a state dinner. At the White House. Where we didn't live. I'd have to play this one very carefully.

When I pulled up at our actual, perfectly lovely house, Meg was standing in the doorway. I was surprised to see her—since she'd started at Georgetown, she'd been pretty much locked in her office making up for lost academic time. I hoped nothing was wrong.

Shutting off the car, I hurried to greet her. Her face was serious.

"Your father needs to talk to you."

My heart thudded. With his name on three pieces of legislation going to the Senate floor next week, he was meant to be pounding the pavement in DC today, drumming up as much support as possible. "What's happened?"

"I'm going to let him tell you."

He was waiting for me in the study. As I stepped into the room, he stood, his expression grave.

"What's up?" I glanced behind me, hearing Gracie and Gabe scurrying in behind me. Whatever had happened, the whole family was concerned about it. And he still hadn't said anything. I stomped my foot. "Tell me!"

His face melted into a smile and we all held our breath. This was not the old, TV-ready, Cooper for President grin. It was a much rarer thing these days—a crinkly smile that flickered, wavered, didn't quite beam. It fought to appear and never stayed as long as we hoped it would. But it was his real smile, the authentic face of Mark Cooper, who didn't know who he was anymore, or where he was going. My father— sad, disillusioned, finding his footing a little more every day.

I loved this smile. And it was still on his face when he pulled an envelope from behind him.

It said Harvard. It was thick.

"Open it!" He tossed it at me, his eyes gleaming with excitement. "I'm dying here!"

I tore open the top, trembling, and peeked at the cover letter before glancing up again with flushed cheeks. "I'm in."

The room erupted in cheers, but before my father could dance me all the way around the room, I moved away, arms crossed. This was too golden an opportunity to pass up.

"Now I just have to hear back from all the other schools, and I'll make my decision."

His face clouded like a puppy whose treat has been taken away. "What other schools? We're talking about *Harvard* here! My alma mater!"

"And I'll give it serious consideration."

I couldn't hold a straight face, and besides, Meg was already groaning.

"Mark, she's giving you a hard time . . ."

"I guess we're not grilling tonight in celebration, then," he said over her, and the twins let out shouts of protest. This was the warmest day of the year so far, and they were delirious with cabin fever.

"Light the grill," I announced. "I'm going to Harvard!"

Upstairs, I changed out of my school clothes and glanced around my room. The ballroom-gowned granddame had been taken down at my request, replaced by the painting that Mr. Diaz had sent me as a very belated birthday gift.

"He wanted to give it to you in LA," Penny had explained to me. "But that day got complicated."

The understatement of the year.

I gazed at it now, the long road disappearing into the horizon. In this room, it was placed so that sunlight reached it from the bay window, making it seem cheerier, more optimistic. I liked it better than ever.

On another wall, I'd framed a collection of sketches by my genius brother, Gabe, as well as a couple of photos from the campaign summer. And on my bedside table, I'd placed a photo of my mom.

This shot was taken only a few months before the accident. The light was dusty around her, another arid day at the food bank. Here it made her glow, that beatific look that saints had in religious paintings. But if you looked closer, you could see that her shirt was dirty, some errant stain from a spilled lunch that was captured and memorialized forever. It was perfect. It was exactly the mother I knew.

I wished she were staring back at me from inside the frame, that she could see the home I'd made here, the people I had all around me. I wished she knew that I was okay, happy even. That I'd found out, and that I didn't judge her or blame her, but loved her even more somehow. And that I missed her, too. That I'd never stop missing her.

Outside, the twins were yelling, and the smell of smoke told me that my dad had lit the grill.

I gave my mom one more smile and went downstairs to join my family.

❦ ACKNOWLEDGMENTS ❦

My name might be on the cover, but this book truly belongs to the friends, family, and colleagues whose generosity, perceptiveness and overall dazzling brilliance brought this story and its characters to life.

First, to my wonderful agent, Katelyn Detweiler, who honored me beyond words by choosing me as her very first client, then promptly blew me away with her editorial skills, daily kindnesses, and business know-how. I'm glad to have you as a coconspirator and career guide—you've made me a cheerful and extremely grateful author. Thanks to Jill Grinberg and Cheryl Pientka as well, for their unwavering enthusiasm, support, and astute notes, along with Samantha Brody, Lindsay Sugarman, and Ellie Jurchisin, whose input helped whip this story into shape.

To my exceptional editor, Jessica Garrison—it's been so fun and fulfilling to live in this book world with you, to talk about the characters as if they were real and draw them more fully onto the page. Your editorial expertise and insights into human behavior have improved both my writing and this book immeasurably. Thank you for believing in a debut author, for caring about this book as much as I do, and for being a friend through the whole process.

My enormous appreciation to the whole team at Dial and Penguin Books for Young Readers, especially Lauri Hornik, Liz Waniewski, Dana Chidiac, and Namrata Tripathi, for their invaluable feedback at various stages of the book's life; to Heather Alexander for her above-and-beyond support; to Regina Castillo, copy editor extraordinaire, master logician, and wrangler of unruly calendars; and to the talented Jason Henry and Lindsey Andrews for so perfectly capturing the spirit of the book in their book and jacket design.

Lots of love to Donna Gordon, Charlotte Jones, and Pamela Thorne, my three moms, earliest draft readers, and biggest cheerleaders. Affection and appreciation as well to Emily Derr, Lexi Beach, and Adrienne Harris for being my best supporters, inspirations, and friends for the past . . . hrrmverylongtime.

Thank you Susan Johnston and the Wednesday Ladies for fueling my momentum every week from that sunny bungalow in Santa Monica when I first started on this path to writing—and for introducing me to my husband, as well! That was an excellent bonus. Thanks also to the online WriteStuffExtreme crew for your guidance and encouragement from the earliest germ of an idea and scraps of chapters, especially Mary Baader Kaley and Mary Frame, who read my first solid draft and managed to bolster my confidence even as they provided wonderful notes for improvement.

I am grateful to the amazing debut groups that have generously welcomed me into their ranks: OneFour KidLit, The Fearless Fifteeners, and—especially—the incredible ladies of the Freshman Fifteen, who have provided me lively entertainment, free therapy and boundless encouragement throughout the publishing process. (Buy their books next. They are fantastic!)

Thanks and kisses to my boys, Oliver and Henry, the best distractions in the world, to my dog, Molly, for always looking interested when I read her passages out loud, and to my husband, Rob—thank you for taking this journey with me, from the moment we met and I declared myself a writer to the millions of little moments when you insisted I make good on that promise. I love you madly and I'm grateful beyond measure.

And lastly, a special thank-you to the wonderful Elise Rainville, who left this world much too young. Without her loving child-care and good company, this book would not have been possible. We will miss you forever.

TURN THE PAGE
FOR A SNEAK PEEK OF
THE INSIDE OF OUT!

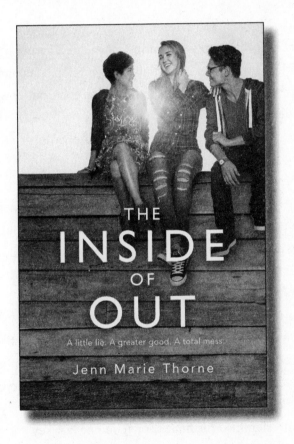

12

Friday at five, Adam was waiting for me in a corner booth at the otherwise empty Moonlight Coffee Shop, clacking away on his crippled laptop. The duct tape was gone, but now it had a binder clip stuck to the corner.

As I slid into the booth, Adam raised one finger and kept typing with the others.

"Sorry," he murmured, his keystrokes so forceful that the booth began to shake. He looked incongruously passionate, like a concert pianist playing a concerto only he could hear.

A waitress wearing frosted pink lipstick made her weary way across the restaurant, water pitcher and menu in hand. Her name tag said *Becky*.

"Nothing for me." I rested my chin on my hand, gesturing grandly to Adam as she filled my plastic cup. "I'm just here to be interviewed for an *article*."

The only reaction I got was an eye roll before she returned to her lonely post at the counter.

Adam slammed his finger down on one last key and pulled the computer lid shut. I was about to remark that he'd probably caused the screen damage himself with his *virtuoso* typing style, but then he grinned, and I found myself incapa-

ble of doing anything but grinning stupidly back. He had a
startling smile, sudden and breathless, like a little kid who's
been handed a bunny. His glasses slipped a little, and I had to
remind myself that it would be inappropriate to reach across
the table and slide them back into place.

"Okay, hi," he said.

"Hi yourself."

"You sure you don't want anything?"

"Nah." I hadn't brought a wallet.

"My treat."

I spun so fast the booth squeaked. "Actually, Becky, some
coconut cream pie and a ginger ale, thanks!"

The waitress sighed a yes.

"And I'll take some more . . . um . . . coffee." Adam stared
into his empty mug as if unsure of what he'd just consumed.

"Is this another school assignment?" I asked. "Am I the
follow-up to your award-winning cat boutique exposé?"

"Something like that."

Adam fussed with his phone, then slid it away. There was
a red dot flashing. Was he already recording? I smoothed my
skirt in readiness.

"My assignment this week was to report on a routine government meeting," he said, his pen tapping against the table
in a syncopated rhythm, making him sound like a beat poet.
"You had to come back with a story, no matter how boring
the context. When I drew 'School Board Meeting,' I wasn't
sure I was going to be able to stay awake long enough to find
anything worth writing about. But then . . . *you* showed up,
thank you."

I wasn't sure if that last bit was to me or to Becky, who was filling his mug, because his eyes were locked on mine. Hot-glued.

"You saved the day," he said, setting down the pen. "For me, anyway. I was sitting there mentally outlining a story on the death of high school wood shop, tying it into faltering American exceptionalism and the decline of the working class."

"Whoa."

"Yeah. But then you stood on a chair. And there was my story."

"Glad I could help." I would have kept staring at those eyes of his—rich brown framed in black—but my pie had arrived, and man it looked good.

"So. Daisy." Adam knocked back his coffee, then recoiled with a grimace. I handed him my water and he downed it in three sips. He shook his head, recovering. "Wow."

"The coffee's not good here."

"I'm realizing that."

"I was surprised you asked for more."

He sniffed his cup as if actually considering another sip. "Caffeine's more of a need than a want at this point. And . . ." He tilted the mug to display the branded logo: *Moonlight Coffee Shop*. "You'd think?"

I nodded in sympathy. "They should call it the Moonlight Mozzarella Stick Shop. Not that catchy, though."

"Ha!"

It took me a second to realize that that was Adam's laugh—a single "Ha," as if he were imitating the sound of someone laughing. This was a thing with him, then. I had to take another bite to keep from giggling.

"Are they good here?" he asked, head craned like he was dubious.

"Um . . . *incredible*. And I'm picky." I put down my fork and leaned closer. "I can always tell when a mozzarella stick is going to be a disappointment. There's something a little sad and soggy about it. Not quite golden enough. Not enough steam. Or *too* much, so the inside is runny and bubbling over and the outside is, like, null. These are always—*always*—perfect."

The diner was unnaturally silent when I finished my testimonial. I turned to see Becky watching me with wariness bordering on fear.

Adam looked unfazed.

"Okay!" he said, picking up his pen and click-click-clicking the end of it. "So you have strong feelings about mozzarella sticks."

"All fried foods, really." I needed to stop talking, or all of this was going to go in the article.

"What else can you tell me about yourself? Hopes, dreams, favorite band?"

He was probably kidding about that last one, but it was the easiest to answer. "Kudzu Giants."

His face dropped. "You like them?"

"Uh, yeah, who doesn't?"

"They're all right. I guess."

How had I gotten *that* question wrong?

"Hopes and dreams, then," Adam went on, pulling out a notepad. "Career goals? College plans?"

"Hannah and I are going to apply to a bunch of schools in major cities and pick one to go to together . . ."

Adam looked confused. "Hannah?"

"My best friend."

"Ah."

He'd started writing, so I added, "Hannah von Linden. Lowercase *v*. She came out a few weeks ago, actually. If you wanted to interview her too, I could set that up?"

His mouth twitched. "That's okay. You were saying?"

"Right. So we'll room together in LA or London or New York . . . maybe San Francisco, although I've heard it's weirdly cold there. And then, after graduation, I'll probably try out a bunch of different professions to see which one calls to me. Right now, I'm thinking I'll start with architecture."

Adam opened his mouth but no reply came out.

"As an intern," I clarified. "You need an advanced degree to actually design buildings, I assume. So I'll just learn the ropes at some firm and then maybe try out zoology? Or costume design. I'll have to see what I'm really passionate about."

"Makes . . . sense?" He cleared his throat. "Obviously gay rights is an issue you feel passionately about."

Adam's voice had abruptly deepened, like he'd prepared that segue in advance. Was this his Reporter Voice? Like Batman Growl?

"Yes," I answered, setting down my fork, and damn if my voice didn't just get deeper too. "But it's about more than gay rights. It's about the basics of how we treat each other. If you're telling a group of students that they don't have the same rights as all the other students, then you're creating an unlevel playing field, and *that's not what America is all about!*"

That was loud. Adam pretended not to notice.

"Was this something you decided to tackle on your own?"

"No, I'm speaking out on behalf of my school's LGBTQIA Alliance. We're pretty active—".

"How many members?" he interrupted.

"Six," I calculated. Then I added Hannah. "Seven." And Natalie, I supposed. *Blah.* "Eight."

He blinked, pen hovering.

"Eight," I repeated firmly. "And we've got a lot of supportive friends and family behind us." I didn't want it to sound like we were powerless. "Like hundreds. Of supporters."

"But the idea? To fight the rule . . . ?"

I smiled. "Yeah, that was me."

Scribble scribble. This was fun.

"Can you share any details about your plans for the alternative homecoming event?"

"As a matter of fact, I can!" I stole a bite of pie, a mini-celebration of what I was about to reveal. "We've found a local nonprofit that's eager to help. They've got a venue for us to use, free of cost." I leaned in to whisper. "It's hush-hush at this point. As you saw at that meeting, there are a lot of people in the community who would love to shut us down, so I really shouldn't talk specifics."

"Got it." Adam's eyes narrowed playfully. "So what's the name of the nonprofit?"

Mine narrowed back. "Nice try."

He laughed again, that single, sudden, "Ha!"

I giggled involuntarily, then took a bite of pie to stop.

What was going *on* with me? If this was the start of a crush, it needed to stop, posthaste. Whatever Adam's type was, it certainly wasn't an average-except-for-her-odd-hair high school junior of middling intelligence, no discernable talents, and questionable charm. I could see him going for a goth feminist-theory goddess. Or a world-weary singer in a smoky, run-down lounge. Or even a perky blond cheerleader— although he'd hate himself for it a little.

Adam flipped his notepad over and started filling another page. His fingers were ink-stained and restless. I pictured pressing my own hands against them so they would settle down.

Adam stopped scribbling and peered up at me. "I want to ask . . . and please forgive me if I'm prying."

My heart thudded for no particular reason. I nodded for him to ask.

"How long have you been out of the closet?"

Oh, right. That. "I'm straight."

"You're . . ." His eyebrows shot up. Then he sank against the banquette, scratching his cheek. "Okay."

"Is that bad?" I forced a smile.

He took his sweet time answering.

"Huh." He squinted at his notepad as if deciphering a code on it.

"If you want, you can put that I'm asexual." I peered around to see what he was writing, but he angled the page away from me. "It's part of the QUILTBAG spectrum?"

He blinked in confusion. "So you're really straight?"

"Last I checked."

"Do you have a boyfriend?"

"Um?"

"Not for the article. I'm just . . . yeah. Curious."

For somebody curious, he sure was avoiding eye contact.

"Why?" I leaned over the table, putting on a fake-sultry drawl. "You interested?"

He went beet red. Jeez, was it *that* embarrassing a prospect?

"Yeah, no, I, uh." He swiped his hand through his hair. "I was just wondering how he felt about all of this."

"My boyfriend doesn't feel anything."

Adam started to write that down, his shoulders sinking.

I squinted at him. "Because he doesn't exist."

He glanced up. "Right. Oh! No boyfriend, then."

Adam's lips parted like he was about to say something else. He didn't. A few seconds passed, and I realized if I didn't do something, we could be stuck in this freeze frame forever, so I glanced at my wrist as if there were a watch there.

"Is this enough for an article?" I grabbed my bag, pulled out a random receipt and scribbled on the back of it. "I actually have to run. But here's my email. And my number. If you need me, for whatever reason."

I felt instantly stupid for offering it. Should I have waited till he asked?

"Thanks." He rose when I did. "You off to a planning meeting?"

"No," I said. "Well, sort of. A football game. I need to . . . um . . . research homecoming conventions? I've managed to avoid going to any school sporting events my entire life, so, yeah."

"Research." His mouth teetered on the edge of a smile.

"Exactly."

For some reason, I didn't want to bring up QB. Probably because he was humiliating. Plus I'd just said I didn't have a boyfriend, which was *true*, but also complicated by the fact that I'd be an official Pirates wench-on-the-sidelines for the next three hours.

"High school football. Wow." Adam acted like I'd said I was going to see a Sumo match at my local dojo. "I've never been to one of those either."

"Really?" Call me hypocritical, but that struck me as weird. "You *did* graduate high school, right?"

"Yeah, but in New York. Brooklyn," he clarified, his chin rising on the word. "It was a magnet school. Not the most *sporty* environment."

The way he said "sporty" made me think of a Ralph Lauren catalog. He shuffled, put his hands in his pockets, and I realized he was waiting for something. An invitation?

"Do you . . . want to come?" As soon as I said it, I felt the diner tilt infinitesimally, like I'd upset the balance of the universe.

"I . . . uh . . ." He watched me and I thought for a few fraught seconds that he might say yes—but then his smile curdled into a smirk. "I'm kind of done with the whole high school thing at this point. But thanks."

My exterior remained placid while, inside, I shriveled into a raisin. *Wow* did I misread that situation.

He slid twenty bucks under his coffee mug, massively overpaying, and motioned for me to walk out ahead of him.

I stomped off under my own steam, not turning back lest he see my mortified face.

But as we stepped out onto the humid street, the palms above us whispering with the breeze, he cornered me for a handshake.

"Thank you, Daisy," he said, his glasses sinking in the heat. "That was a very entertaining interview."

My scowl melted despite my best efforts to keep it in place. Why were we still shaking hands?

"Glad I could oblige," I said.

"'Oblige,'" he echoed, drawing the word out like a song. He backed away with a grin, his fingers slipping from mine. "Such a great accent."

I don't have an accent, I thought, but by the time I caught my breath enough to retort, or to giggle, or to cry out "When will I see you again?" he'd already disappeared down the block.

13

As soon as I stepped onto school property, I felt the wrong-ness of this evening pulsing around me. It was Friday night. And I'd gone back to school. To watch a *football* game.

A little girl wearing a Pirates T-shirt bounced off me in her rush to join her equally fan-spangled family, and suddenly, I found myself pulled with the tide toward the ticket booth. On top of every other indignity, this was going to cost me four bucks.

The freckly sophomore manning the booth glanced up as I was trying to hand him my wadded cash.

"Daisy Beaumont-Smith?" he asked, staring at the blue ends of my hair.

"Yeah?" I shuffled, wondering if he was about to chuck his Gatorade at me, and if so, which way I should dodge.

"No charge for you."

He up-nodded knowingly. Knowing *what*, exactly? I gri-maced a smile, pocketed my cash, and continued past him, mentally reciting my new mantra: *"This is not a date, this is not a date, what am I doing here, this is not . . ."*

I climbed the stands to a comfortable distance from the field, and let people fill in around me. I wished Hannah were here. We could critique the stretching techniques of the opposing team's cheerleading squad, or share a "To Benefit the School Band" popcorn, or give each other a meaningful look and by silent assent get up and out of here.

But she was busy tonight. With someone else. Eating fried foods. Watching a movie. Probably one I wanted to see and would now have to rent by myself. Stretching out on her downstairs sofa, ignoring Mama Tan's comments about their food choices, giggling at some inside joke, building walls around themselves to keep pesky people like, oh, *me* out.

Swallowing bile, I texted her. *"You'll never believe where I am . . . cheering on the Palmetto Pirates! Woohoo?"*

It took her six minutes to reply with, *"Cool!"*

That wasn't much of a response. Not even an accurate one. Sitting here was the most uncool thing I'd done in recent memory. And Hannah of all people should have been the one to call me on that.

The crowd was pretty full by now. To my immediate left and right were two groups of rowdy freshmen who kept leaning over me to shout at each other. I almost offered to move, but that would have put me at the end of the row, where they might knock me off the bleachers with the force of their New To This School enthusiasm.

"Daisy!"

Sophie waved from the top row, where she was sitting with a bunch of her natural-fiber friends. They looked as out of place as I felt. I waved back, wondering if they came to every game or if Sophie was doing what I'd claimed to be doing, helping our cause by researching homecoming traditions.

That's what I had to assume Raina was up to when I spotted her two tiers down with a middle-aged gentleman in a Duke windbreaker. Her father! Raina did have parents! Come to think of it, now that I was in CIA mode, was that Jack with his family on the opposite side of the field? They looked surprisingly nice. And, way over yonder, yep—Sean Bentley, trying to politely extricate himself from a conversation with a cheerleader from the rival team.

I was just realizing that the only one missing from our club was Kyle, when I saw him clamber up the bleachers with his own family, all of them dressed in Pirates gear, his younger brother waving a school pennant.

They really were all football fans. They had authentic school spirit. Was it catching? If so, I was about to find out.

The field's speakers roared to life and everyone cheered, drowning out the mumbled announcement and generic sports music that followed. I stood with the crowd and watched our terrible football team race onto the field from the locker room.

As soon as he hit open air, QB turned to the stands. When he spotted me, his face lit up—a little. He jogged to join the team and kept scanning, his smile dropping a centimeter with every stride.

The game was what I'd expected. Lots of half standing, then sitting with a communal groan as the other team's pockets of fans went wild. We lost. We always lost, so I'd come prepared, knowing this would be more tragedy than comedy. The point wasn't the happy ending. It was the struggle.

QB looked so dejected after the game that I decided to tell him this on my way out. It sounded appropriately inspirational. But while I was tiptoeing down the bleachers in my interview skirt, QB got the first word in.

"Daisy! Let's hang out!"

"Now?"

"Yeah."

His teammates were trudging past, watching us with open curiosity.

QB had just lost the fourth straight game of the season. I couldn't embarrass him further.

"Okay, sure."

QB did a gleeful hop that made me laugh. "I'll meet you out front. Just a quick shower. I promise I'll smell better in a minute!"

Thirty minutes later, the crowds had all gone home and I was sitting on the curb of the school's front drive, watching lamplight pool on the dead border hedges and listening to the crickets start up their nightly party.

When they went silent, I knew he'd walked up. His blond hair was damp from the shower. And he'd kept his promise. Even with the nightly scent of low tide and mown grass thick in the air, I could smell QB from here, a mix of clean and sweat-salty that made me want to lean in.

I refrained.

"You wanna go to that diner on Walker?" he asked. "The one that's always empty?"

And so, for the second time in less than five hours, I found myself settling into the corner booth of the Moonlight with a guy who I was most definitely not dating. Becky was still on duty.

"What can I get . . . y'all . . . ?" Pouring our waters, she glanced up—at me, then at QB, then back at me with horrified admiration.